NEW

BEGINNINGS

CYBERSP@CE SERIES
BOOK THREE

JEFF W. HORTON

WCP

World Castle Publishing, LLC
Pensacola, Florida

Copyright © Jeff W. Horton 2014
Print ISBN: 9781629891927
eBook ISBN: 9781629891934
First Edition World Castle Publishing, LLC, December 19, 2014
http://www.worldcastlepublishing.com

Licensing Notes

Cover: Karen Fuller
Editor: Maxine Bringenberg

PROLOGUE

Salara Takar looked up from the illuminated instruments on the control panel in front of her and into the blackness of interstellar space, which appeared void at the moment of anything other than a beautiful, multicolored nebula, filled with blue in the center and surrounded by strands of orange, red, and green.

The black pupils at the center of her golden eyes tightened into small dots as she stared past the nebula and peered into the darkness beyond it. A few seconds later, she was able to make out two tiny specks of light in the distance, which according to the navigational computer was a binary star system, and the coordinates at which they would have to deviate from their present course in order for her plan to work. If her information was accurate, the binary star system would be at the peak of its stellar cycle, and the stellar flares of this particular star system were known to be particularly nasty. With luck the electromagnetic radiation given off by the flares would mask the course change so that by the time the ship's absence was detected back home, they would be long gone. She estimated she had only a few minutes before they reached the coordinates for the course change.

Takar glanced over at Captain Vale Kalise, the friendly, older pilot, a war veteran whom she knew had fought against the cleansing of the Great Purge. She liked Kalise and she respected him, despite their political differences. He had risked his life on more than one occasion in order to save hers, a debt she would forever be unable to repay.

"Captain, I need to check on a sensor for one of the fuel cells; would you mind taking over until I get back?"

Kalise, who had been preoccupied reading something on his data pad, raised his head and smiled. "Of course not, Salara. These ships are so automated these days that there's not much to do anyway. I've got a few reports to review here, but I'll keep an eye on things; go ahead and check on that sensor."

"Thank you, sir." Takar climbed out of the chair and hurriedly made her way toward the aft of the ship, glancing back to keep an eye on Kalise the entire way. The captain continued studying his data pad, which he began scrolling through, periodically glancing up to check on the instruments and the approaching binary stars before returning to his reports.

Takar stopped a third of the way into the ship and reached into a compartment that was directly underneath the access panel where the faulty sensor would be. She hesitated as she reached for the panel door, suddenly uncertain whether she could carry through with the plan. Salara glanced back at the cargo area, and in her mind's eye she pictured who, and what, lay beyond the door. That thought, accompanied with the blissful memories of times past, gave her the resolve necessary to follow through. She opened the compartment door, removed the hidden weapon tucked inside, and slipped it into a concealed pouch behind her back. Takar began walking slowly towards Kalise, who remained distracted, scanning through something on his data pad. Just as she raised the weapon and leveled it at her captain, however, something happened.

Perhaps he'd seen the movement when she raised the particle disrupter; perhaps it was some kind of precognition or his years of experience as a war veteran. For whatever reason Captain Kalise turned, and upon seeing the weapon in Salara's hand instinctively ducked out of his chair and onto the deck of the ship just as she pulled the trigger, which initiated a discharge from the disrupter. The blast struck the control panel in front of the captain's chair, causing the ship's engines to shut down unexpectedly. The lieutenant was thrown forward when the ship suddenly decelerated before emerging into regular space near a gold-colored planet orbiting the binary star she'd seen earlier. The sudden deceleration followed by a subsequent lurch forward threw Salara backward several meters, causing her to drop the particle disrupter and fall to the deck.

Takar anxiously searched for the weapon, which now lay several meters in front of her. She crawled towards the spot where it rested until Captain Kalise appeared from behind an instrument panel. He reached down to pick up the disrupter, but as soon as he wrapped his hand around it Takar grabbed his wrist. The captain and his co-pilot fought for control of the weapon with the stronger captain soon prevailing, but not before a single blast pierced the center of Salara's torso, mortally wounding her. Kalise knelt beside her, holding her head in his hand as he leaned over her.

"Why, Salara, why did you do it; why would you want to kill *me*? Please—I don't understand why you would do such a thing?"

Takar looked away for a moment before forcing herself to look him in the eye. "I'm sorry, my captain. You wouldn't...understand, I...." Lieutenant Salara Takar gasped one last time before heaving a heavy sigh as the spirit left her body.

Kalise continued leaning over her, trying to make sense of what had just happened, until alarms suddenly sounded.

"Warning; shielding is down and the transport is entering the atmosphere at a catastrophic angle of entry. The ship will disintegrate within thirty seconds unless action is taken immediately," the onboard computer warned.

Kalise ran towards his chair, holding to the bulkhead of the ship for balance before grabbing hold of the chair itself long enough for him to take a seat. The computer was correct; the ship was entering the atmosphere of a planet with the portside of the ship facing forward. The captain quickly activated the ship's shielding before grasping the steering control in a desperate effort to regain control of the ship.

The craft began shaking violently as the ship descended through a thick cloud layer. Once the ship finally began to slow somewhat, he looked up to find a valley filled with lush green vegetation rushing at him from all directions. Moments later the ship slammed into the ground and began plowing through a dense forest of trees, which further slowed the ship's momentum. The transport continued its forward motion, however, until it crashed into the side of a mountain. The powerful jolt caused Kalise to lurch forward, slamming his head against the edge of the control panel, followed immediately by the sickening sound of bones cracking and splintering. By the time the ship finally came to a complete stop, it lay imbedded more than halfway inside the mountain, buried without by dirt, rocks, and debris. Inside the ship, Vale Kalise still sat in his captain's chair, dead.

CHAPTER 1

"Life, for ever dying to be born afresh, for ever young and eager, will presently stand upon this earth as upon a footstool, and stretch out its realm amidst the stars."

H. G. Wells, The Outline of History, 1920.

"History; it is the only mirror before which we can clearly see tomorrow. It has been just over forty-five years now since my father, Dr. Nick Reynolds, and my mother, Dr. Kate Reynolds, revived an alien, sentient, living computer, an Entelli, that they referred to as Ignis. Existing in a dormant state since his ship crashed in Roswell, New Mexico in 1947, Ignis's reawakening was the direct result of a desperate effort by the United States government to find a way to combat the highly advanced Ares cyber warfare system, which had already caused the deaths of over a million Americans. The cyber warfare platform, an innovative and powerful system whose design was decades ahead of its time, had been commissioned by the former KGB agent Nikolai Chervanko, who threatened to use the weapon to bury the world in nuclear ash. My parents worked feverishly alongside my grandfather, Dr. Henry Summers, to reverse-engineer the alien technology they found onboard Ignis's crashed ship, which had been recovered by the United States government from Roswell. The spacecraft, which they named Prometheus, offered their last hope of finding a way to stop Chervanko before millions or even billions of lives were lost.

"Well, many of you know the story—about Chervanko's capture, and how Ignis and Prometheus gave us everything we needed to construct our own interstellar ship. This, of course, brings us to the event we have all gathered here today to celebrate, the 25th anniversary of humanity's first interstellar flight, *and* the formation of the Earth Space Alliance.

"It was twenty-five years ago today that I took Frontier, Earth's first interstellar ship, a craft modeled after Prometheus, on her maiden voyage to our nearest interstellar neighbor, Alpha Centauri. Who could have imagined back then the dramatic impact that single flight would have on humanity all these years later?

"Consider everything that has occurred as a result of that flight, and the work done to make it possible. Humanity hasn't had a real war in almost twenty years now. The Earth Space Alliance has been a phenomenal success, helping to peacefully disseminate the dark energy technology all over the planet, while also creating incredible economic opportunities in harvesting raw materials throughout our own solar system. The First Contact, which came about after an alien ship answered Frontier's distress call while I was stranded in Alpha Centauri, helped usher in lucrative trade with the many sentient species across the galaxy. Then comes perhaps the single most important benefit of all. Because of the Frontier program and the Earth Space Alliance, humanity has turned its collective energy away from war and strife and towards exploration of the universe, and the subsequent trade and interaction with other sentient species across the galaxy.

"The Alliance has already constructed a fleet of ships—enhanced versions of the ship I flew to Alpha Centauri—established trade agreements with over a dozen worlds, and funneled back to Earth some of the most incredible technologies imaginable. Our world is so preoccupied these days with discovering the universe that no one has time for war anymore. Finally, after millennia of conflict and war, humanity is finally at peace."

The audience at the FedEx Galactic Field in Landover, Maryland was filled to capacity, and once Hank finished his last statement, it seemed the entire audience rose as one before letting out such a resounding roar of applause, mixed with shouts, yells, and whistles, that Hank was certain it had been heard throughout the entire metro area. He joined in the celebration, however, knowing, as they did, that these accomplishments were something each of them had helped bring about, and they could all be proud of their achievements. After several minutes and with some encouragement from Hank, the crowd gradually quieted.

"I'm so very proud of everything we've accomplished at the Alliance; first under my father's leadership for two terms as President of the Earth Space Alliance, and then during *my* time here as president. I don't think I could be more thankful for the opportunity you have given me, nor could I have asked for a team of more dedicated, enthusiastic individuals than those I've worked with these last few years.

"With your permission, I would like to also take this opportunity to make an important announcement. Unlike my father, Dr. Nick Reynolds, who served two terms with the Alliance, I would like to announce that I will not be seeking a second term as president."

The announcement stunned everyone in attendance so much it seemed one might be able to hear the proverbial pin drop. "I have been asked by the League of Sentient Species to be Earth's ambassador there, and as important as my time with the Alliance has been, I feel I can contribute even more as your ambassador to the League. I haven't decided whether to accept this position, but I have decided that in either case I will step aside to let someone else take over the incredibly important responsibility for leading the Earth Space Alliance.

"Once again, congratulations to everyone for twenty-five amazing years leading Planet Earth out of its protective nest and out into the far and amazing reaches of the cosmos. Thank you." Hank turned, and without saying another word walked towards the exit before disappearing behind the closed door.

***

Hank drove his car to a pleasant-looking brick home in a rural neighborhood located outside of Ft. Meade, Maryland, where he set it down in a space along the curb designated for hover cars. He sat in the car for some time, staring at the house fondly, cherishing the precious memories that had flowed unbidden into his mind. He sighed and climbed out of the vehicle to begin the brief walk along the cobblestone path to the front door. He knocked at the door, and moments later he was greeted at the door by a sickly, aging Nick Reynolds.

"Hello, what can I…? Hank, my boy! It's been so long; how have you been, son?" Nick reached toward Hank, who immediately came close to embrace his father. "So I just saw the bombshell you dropped on everyone on television. How has everyone taken it?" his father asked. "Have you mentioned it to Jim yet?"

"No, I planned to drive by the general's place after leaving here, Dad. I haven't had time to call to let him know yet, so I thought I would swing by now that I do have some and just tell him in person. The alliance has twenty-five years under its belt now, Dad. I think it will be fine without me, otherwise I never would have made the decision to leave."

"Have a seat, son," Nick said, pointing to the sofa across from his easy chair. "Can I offer you something to drink, Hank?"

"Maybe just some water, Dad, if you don't mind."

"Of course not; give me just a minute." Hank watched as his father struggled to get out of the chair. He could see that his father's condition was worsening, and he grew fearful that his father might have less time than everyone thought. That thought must have caused him to grimace, because his father ceased trying to rise from his chair and turned to his son.

"I'm okay, Hank, really. You don't need to worry so much about me,

11

son…you have enough to worry about."

Hank jumped up out of his chair. "Here, Dad. Please…let me get it."

Nick smiled. "If you insist."

Hank walked into the kitchen and poured himself some water from the H2O station. One of the key benefits of the dark energy generators was that like hydrogen fuel cells, the waste byproduct was distilled water.

"You were right, you know."

Hank raised an eyebrow as he made his way back into the living room. "What do you mean?"

"Your speech, Hank—you were right. We *have* come a very long way in my lifetime; I scarcely can believe it myself sometimes when I wake up in the morning. The Alliance, the League, the trade and commerce, the peace; it's a wonderful world we live in at the moment, son."

"*'At the moment'*; what do you mean, Dad?"

Nick frowned. "Look, Hank, I don't mean to throw a damper on things. It's just that we live in an imperfect world, an imperfect universe; it's just a matter of time until…." Nick's voice trailed off as he looked out a window.

"Until something happens, Pop?"

Nick smiled. "Well yes, until something happens—I'm afraid it's simply the way of things, Hank. Oh, it could be far off in the future, or it might be today or tomorrow, but challenges that test us and push us have always been a part of life, and I suppose they always will. You have to learn to relish moments like these, boy, when life is good, when it seems as if the bad times are gone forever. Just don't ever expect them to last."

Hank nodded weakly in agreement. "I know, Dad, you're right. I've been trying to teach that to Nicole for a long time now."

Nick raised his head and looked Hank in the eyes. "So, tell me, how are Hailey and Nicole?"

"Well, as far as Hailey, you know how wives are, Dad. You can…." Hank stopped, realizing what he'd just said. "Dad, I'm sorry, I didn't mean to—"

"It's okay, Hank, don't worry about it. Look, I loved your mother very much and I always will. I've missed her these last two years, of course, missed her something terrible, but I also know that I'll see her again one day; soon, I expect."

Hank felt a lump rising in his throat, fearful that his father's words had been prophetic. "Come on, Dad, we both know you're far too ornery to die!" Hank said with a grin, masking his sorrow.

"Well, I am ornery…I've had to be. But I think I've done just about all that I can do to fight this thing, Hank. I even tried C-Vax last week—"

"C-Vax? But you're allergic to it, Dad; it could've killed you long before the cancer ever would have."

"I know, I know. The doctors tried to suppress the allergic reaction long enough for the C-Vax to do its job and eliminate all of the cancer."

"So what happened?"

"It failed. The allergic reaction was far too severe. The doctors even did a consult with several renowned oncologists, but they all agreed—nothing more can be done for me, son. They can continue giving me various other medications, some that will virtually eliminate the pain, which is wonderful; and they've given me others that have substantially retarded the cancer's progress, but eventually...."

Hank got up from the sofa, walked over to where Nick sat in his favorite chair, and embraced his father.

"I love you, Dad," Hank said.

"I know, son...I love you too." Father and son embraced for several moments, until Hank turned and walked back to the sofa. Nick smiled at his son, who managed a weak smile in return.

"So...," his father began again, noticeably trying to change the subject. "You never finished telling me about Hailey, and of course, my favorite grandchild, Nicole."

"Well, as you know, Hailey's been working on the Special Projects Team at the Alliance, testing and studying new alien technologies before deciding whether to submit them to the committee, who then evaluates her findings and recommendations and decides whether to give them the Alliance's stamp of approval for use on Earth."

"And what about Nikki?"

Hank shook his head in response. "She has got to be the most stubborn young woman on the planet, Dad. I've tried for several years now to get her to come to work for the Alliance, but she's refused."

"She's as strong-willed as her Grandmother Kate was, that's for sure," Nick said.

"Yeah, well, Nikki started this corporate think tank, which is great, and she's still doing that martial arts thing of hers."

"Well, I seem to remember a young man of my acquaintance who found his martial arts training valuable on at least a few occasions."

"Sure, I trained in some martial arts too, Dad. But for me it was a tool; for Nikki it's a way of life, an obsession even. Did you know that at one time, she was absolutely determined to enter the Alliance Defense Force?"

"You *have* been pressuring her to join the Alliance—"

"But not the military end! It's so frustrating, Dad. Nikki is crazy smart; I think she's far smarter than I ever was. I just don't want to see that go to waste."

"You may just have to let her find her own way, son. I know she's brilliant, but as you said, she's a woman now, and she's rather headstrong. Give it some time, Hank. I don't think God would ever have given her such a wonderful mind just to let it go to waste."

"I hope you're right, Dad."

"I am, Hank, just wait and see. But what about you; what do you plan to do about the ambassadorship to the League?"

Hank sighed and shrugged his shoulders. "I don't know; I guess I haven't decided yet."

"Really? Well you sure looked like a diplomat out on the campaign trail to me," he told Hank.

"I'm just not sure, Dad. I want to go, but I'm not really much of a politician."

"Then don't be one, son. I'm not a politician either, and I've never been one. When I led the Alliance, I always focused on how to get things done, rather than trying to win people's support. It seems to me this might be a golden opportunity for someone with a mind like yours, Hank. Think about the opportunity you'd have to learn about alien cultures and technology. I don't know, son, you might just find it's right up your alley."

Hank looked at his father with concern and a slight frown. "The League headquarters on Val is a long way from here, Dad, nearly a day's trip each way."

Nick raised his eyebrows and began nodding his head. "Ah, now I understand—you're worried about me?"

"No, Dad, of course not, it's just that—"

"You always were a horrible liar, Hank."

"Look, you said it yourself, Dad, you don't know how long—"

"No, I *don't* know how long I've got, son, but there'll be plenty of time for you to get here when it happens. It's cancer, not a heart-attack, remember?"

"I know, but I'd like to spend some time...."

Nick sat up in his chair and leaned in towards his son. "Hank...you know that I love you dearly, and that there's nothing I'd enjoy more than to spend time with you, Hailey, and Nikki. But you have your own lives to live. We can always keep in touch over quantum-links."

"It's not the same, Dad; what if you need something? What if you need to be taken to the hospital? You're all alone in this old house."

"Oh, now you're being ridiculous, Hank. I have a lot of fond memories of raising my family in this old house. Besides, I'm not an invalid."

Hank began shaking his head. "No, I think I'd better turn the ambassadorship down and stay here, Dad."

"What, and pass up an opportunity like that? Nonsense! Not because of me, you won't."

"No, Dad, seriously, I'm staying. I love you, and I'd never forgive myself if anything happened to you and I was halfway across the galaxy."

Nick let out a heavy sigh. "Well then, I suppose you could always invite me to come to stay with you and Hailey for a while…if it was okay with her, of course."

"Dad, that's a great idea! Do you mean it? Would you really do it?"

"Sure I would, at least for a while. After all, I think it would be quite something to live out my last days on an alien world."

"Okay, that seals it then. I'll let our current liaison to the League know right away. Thanks, Dad, you're awesome!"

"What about Hailey?" Nick asked, concerned.

"Oh, she's been after me to take that post for a long time, Dad, ever since they offered it; and you know how she *adores* you!"

Hank took his Quantum Link out of his pocket and made a quick call. Moments later, he'd conveyed the news to the League. He smiled, said thank you, and looking at his father, wondered how his life, like so many others, had changed so dramatically.

***

"Are you certain, I mean absolutely certain about this, Scott?"

The younger man seemed surprised to be questioned, even by someone as senior and respected as his boss. "Yes, sir, Dr. Goddard, I'm positive. Here, look at the data for yourself." Scott Miller handed Goddard his data pad, which still had the data and the graph on it. Goddard studied it for several minutes before pressing a button on his desk. A holographic image of his administrative assistant appeared over his desk. It was a rather pleasing image, at least Miller thought so.

"Judy, please cancel my appointments for the rest of the day; and find out where President Reynolds is at the moment, and how I can reach him."

"Yes, Dr. Goddard."

The older man sat down at his desk, manipulating controls on his virtual pad until an image of the solar system appeared over the left side of his desk, and a graph with a number of data points appeared over the right side of the desk. He hurriedly pressed a number of additional buttons until times appeared next to each of the data points.

"Extend data points out seven days," he instructed the A/I computer in his desk.

"The graph has been extended out exactly seven days from now, Dr. Goddard."

15

Goddard followed the data points and the adjusted image of the solar system. "No, no, no, no...!" Goddard pressed the button on his desk. "Judy, I need President Reynolds on the line immediately. Tell him this is a Priority 1 crisis, understand? Priority 1!"

"Yes, Dr. Goddard, I understand."

CHAPTER 2

Nicole Reynolds looked out of the corner office on the top floor of the office tower in which she worked, and reflected on her very significant achievements with a mixture of pride, disappointment, and boredom. Pride that at the age of twenty-five she was already the head of her own conservative think tank consortium, disappointment that it didn't seem as important as it once had, and boredom that it had now become less competitive for her, and not nearly as challenging as it once had been. She sighed at the realization that it was a downside to her inherited intellect, which she now suspected equaled her father's.

Nicole smiled. Her father had always been her role model, both brilliant and resourceful. But his genius had come at a price. He'd once recounted a time when he was still very young, when he'd been bullied and persecuted by the other children in his school because he was "different"; the story had inspired her. When he'd offered her the opportunity to join a martial arts class, hoping to enable her to avoid some of the suffering and humiliation he'd endured as a child, Nicole had jumped at the chance, determined that no one would ever bully or intimidate her the way her father had been. She had embraced her self-defense training and rejoiced at the confidence it gave her, diving into her training with a fire and passion unequaled by any other students in her training hall. Everything she did in class was with every bit of intensity and sweat she could muster; determined not to waste any time or effort, she made sure every drop of sweat counted.

As she'd grown older, Nicole had come to apply the same attitude she'd adopted in her martial arts training to nearly every other area of her life as well. In every class in every school she attended, for every doctorate she pursued, and later in all areas of her career, in everything she did she always gave one hundred percent effort, and she would do so again today.

"Athena, what time is my next appointment?" she asked the automated assistant, built into the intellicube sitting on her desk.

"Your next appointment is at two o'clock this afternoon, Miss Reynolds."

"And who is it with?"

"The appointment is with Frank Mallory, the director of major projects for Earth Space Alliance."

"You're kidding. Doesn't he know that my dad is on his way out now? Why do these Alliance people keep coming to see me?"

"I don't know, Miss Reynolds," answered the computer.

"Do we know what he wants to talk about?"

"No, Miss Reynolds. The appointment request only states that it is regarding a most urgent matter, which is why two other appointments were bumped."

"Great, now they're bumping my appointments. Okay, whatever. If the next appointment isn't until two, it means I have time to run an errand and grab some lunch. Schedule me as out of office on my calendar until two o'clock, Athena, I'm going out."

"Yes, Miss Reynolds."

Nicole left the office and proceeded to the elevator. Once she had specified the building and floor, the elevator commenced to moving down and forward to the correct building as Nicole considered what kind of gift her father might like best. He was leaving the Alliance and would soon be departing for his new position at the League of Sentient Species nearly fifteen light years from Earth, and she was determined to find him a suitable present at the specialty store nearby. It wasn't the best neighborhood anymore, but she knew she should be able to easily find something there for him; just one quick errand, then it was off to lunch.

Nicole was blasted with the blistering heat of summer the moment she opened the door. The mid-August sun hung directly overhead in a clear, cloudless sky, bearing down unmercifully on anyone who dared step out from under their protective roof to challenge it. She was thankful that at least the humidity was low, so the excessive heat was at least somewhat more tolerable than it would have been had the humidity been high, which it often was this time of year.

Nicole turned to her left and began walking down the hill toward the specialty store, located in an old building in a block of other, equally old buildings. She'd have to walk two blocks down the street before crossing the street to the building where the store was located. She allowed her mind to wonder carelessly, trying to ignore the intense heat and the sweat that now beaded on her forehead.

The store had just come into sight when she suddenly felt a sharp pull on her clothes from behind her, which jerked her backwards and off her feet for a moment.

18

"Okay baby, this doesn't have to be complicated, we just...oh my, what do we have here? My, you are a looker, aren't you?" She spun around to find two menacing-looking men—both with significant stubble on their faces, and each of them clearly older than her, probably in their mid to late thirties—standing in front of her. One of them, the man who'd jerked her back by her blouse, was wearing a t-shirt and held an ancient, semi-automatic firearm in his other hand, pointing it towards her abdomen. The other, dark-skinned man held an old but intimidating knife, which was banged-up but sharp. Nicole quickly sized up the two men, assessing they were probably drug addicts looking for some easy money, and possibly something else.

"What do you want?" she asked coolly, with no panic in her voice and only a tinge of fear.

"Well, we just want to take a little trip to the bank, where you'll make a withdrawal from your account on our behalf; after that, we'll see," the man with the firearm said with a vile grin, which told her things would soon end badly, either for her or for them.

"Okay, just please, don't hurt me!" she pleaded, feigning sudden fear. "Please, just let me find my car keys. I know...oh, I'm sorry!" she said, dropping the key and her purse on the ground in front of the man with the gun. Startled, the man reached down, still holding the weapon but with his finger slightly off the trigger. Nicole instantly recognized the oversight and leapt into action, allowing her training and her reflexes to take over. She took full advantage of the bent-over attacker's vulnerable position by striking the back of his neck near the base of his skull with a powerful, knife-hand strike before slamming her knee into the man's face, knocking him backwards and unconscious onto the sidewalk.

After seeing what she'd done to his friend, the second attacker, now angry and with a snarl on his face, lunged at her with his hand wrapped tightly around the handle of the knife. Judging by the knife thrust, she determined he was aiming for her abdomen, apparently expecting to succeed where his unprepared friend had failed. Nicole easily avoided the thug's stab, sidestepping to the left of his arm while simultaneously striking the man's arm at the wrist. There was a loud crack of breaking bone and the man screamed in pain, forcing him to open his hand and drop the knife. Nicole followed up the strike with a blow to the man's chin with the other hand, striking him with the heel of her palm. The man jerked upright and stood tall for a moment, wavering on the verge of unconsciousness. Unwilling to allow the man time to recover, Nicole stepped toward him by placing her left foot behind her right, raised her right knee into the air, and with an explosive sidekick thrust the heel of her right foot into the man's stomach just above the groin. The force of the powerful kick drove the man backwards four or five feet, where he collapsed in a heap.

With the attackers no longer posing a threat, she unconsciously began checking herself for injuries. A sharp pain drew her attention to her right side, where she found her blouse had been slashed by the second attacker's knife. She'd been careless by not turning sideways enough during the initial attack, thereby allowing the blade to get too close. Blood began to trickle from the site, and a quick examination revealed that it was only a minor laceration, easily remedied by a quick visit to a medical station close by. Nicole quickly reached into her purse and withdrew a handkerchief. She folded it several times before firmly pressing it at the injury to stem the bleeding.

"Athena?"

"Yes, Miss Reynolds?" the computer responded from her purse.

"Contact law enforcement, tell them who I am, that I was attacked by two men at this location, and that I am on my way to the medical facility on the corner of Main Street and Franklin. Tell the authorities I have a minor injury requiring treatment should they have questions. Tell them the two men who attacked me are either unconscious or dead."

"Yes, Miss Reynolds, I've already notified the authorities and I've sent them your message. Is there anything else I can do?"

"No, thank you," Nicole replied, without thinking.

"I'm merely an artificial construct, no expression of gratitude is necessary, Miss Reynolds."

"I know, Athena," she responded dryly.

***

It was just before two o'clock when Nicole arrived back in her office, her injury no longer painful or visible following the quick visit to the medical station. The medical treatment and the interview by the police had taken up the time she'd allocated for both lunch and the quick trip to the specialty store. She'd have to stop somewhere to pick up something for her father, as well as some food, since there'd been no time to do either during her lunch break.

Walking into her office, she soon realized she'd also neglected to pick up something else to wear for the meeting; she'd just have to cover the tear and blood stains the best she could.

"Miss Reynolds, your two o'clock appointment, Mr. Frank Malloy, the director of major projects for Earth Space Alliance, is here. Shall I instruct the receptionist to send him in?"

"Yes, Athena," Nicole replied. "Send him in." The door opened a few moments later and her receptionist appeared, with a big man standing beside her. He must have been around fifty years of age, around six-foot four, with short, neatly cropped salt-and-pepper hair.

"Miss Reynolds, this is Mr. Frank Malloy," the receptionist announced with a smile and a nod toward Malloy.

"Very good, thank you, Grace." The receptionist nodded toward Nicole and pulled the door closed again.

"Good afternoon, Mr. Malloy, I'm Nicole Reynolds," she informed him, extending her hand and shaking his. "Won't you please have a seat?"

"Yes, thank you." He was about to sit down when he noticed the cut blouse on her right side, with blood stains just below it.

"Dr. Reynolds, are you hurt?" he asked, pointing towards the bloodstain.

"I'm fine, Mr. Malloy, thank you. I was attacked by two men on the way to a nearby store two hours ago, but I've already had it taken care of. I'm fine now."

Malloy stared at her in disbelief. "You were attacked? Listen, we can meet later, perhaps sometime tomorrow; you must still be shaken up by all of this—"

Nicole shook her head. "No, I assure you that's not necessary; as I've said, Mr. Malloy, I'm fine. I was able to subdue my attackers without them ever getting off a single shot."

Malloy shook his head. "Boy, I'd heard stories about you, but to be honest I'd never believed them. Based on what I see before me now, I guess they must be true."

Nicole thought about pursuing a line of questioning about what people were saying about her, but she decided instead to let it go. She didn't really concern herself with what others thought about her anyway, and she was anxious to get home to change her clothes. Beyond that, however, Athena had indicated that the matter Malloy had come to discuss was important.

"I understand you had something rather urgent you wished to discuss with me, Mr. Malloy, so what can I do for you?"

"Dr. Reynolds, I understand that you hold a number of doctorates, including one in astrophysics, one in interplanetary relations, and the PhD in political science, which you acquired at the age of ten…is that right?"

"Yes, that's correct. Is that why you're here, Mr. Malloy, to discuss my many doctorates? I had no idea that was of such interest to the Alliance's Department of Major Projects."

Malloy offered a forced smile. "Yes, well, I was also told of your singular wit, Dr. Reynolds, and your aversion to small talk. Okay then, I will cut to the chase."

"Excellent."

"What I'm about to tell you is classified; only a few people anywhere

21

in the world know about this."

"I'm cleared at the highest levels."

"Of course. At 9:47 p.m. Eastern time two days ago, telescopes around the world detected a massive object moving through our solar system at an incredible velocity, a planetary body that had initially been hidden from our view here on Earth by the sun. This object, while considerably smaller than Pluto, is still a dwarf planet...a *rogue* dwarf planet. We had one of the Alliance ships check it out the same day it was spotted, and they confirmed both its size and its position."

"Heaven help us." Nicole felt her stomach tightening into a knot.

"While we don't yet have enough data to be certain, it appears this planetary body could be on a collision course for Earth. I'm sure I don't need to tell you, Dr. Reynolds, that if this dwarf planet *were* to strike Earth, it would mean the end of all life on our planet. There's nothing we can do to stop this, and despite everything our new Valhari friends have done for us by sharing so much of their technology, even they can't stop an entire planet. With the exception of our Mars colony, those we are able to evacuate from Earth, and the handful of human beings scattered across the galaxy, the human race could be without a home by this time the day after tomorrow."

CHAPTER 3

Nicole sat at the desk, stunned. As if frozen by shock, fear, and disbelief, her face was expressionless. A stranger had just walked into her office to tell her that the world was about to end.

"I...don't know what to say; this is so unbelievable. Is this some sort of prank? If it is, I don't find it the least bit amusing."

"It's no prank, Dr. Reynolds, I assure you."

"Then why are you telling *me*? You should be talking with my dad, or even my grandfather. I'm not involved with the Alliance except through my family. I run a think tank, Mr. Malloy. I guess I'm not sure I understand what I'm supposed to do here."

"According to our latest estimates, there is a sixty percent chance that the rogue planet will strike Earth. At this moment, the Alliance has your father and all Alliance representatives on shuttles to the Mars colony, along with their immediate family members and others considered crucial to the continuation of the Frontier program. In addition to Alliance members, the Alliance representatives are developing a list of individuals in numerical order for evacuations, which will continue until the planetoid has either passed us by or struck Earth."

"So I'm on my father's list, is that why you're here?"

"In part. I am also here to discuss a related topic with you. Once we are done talking, I will take you to the closest launch site for priority evacuation."

"Then why don't we get going and we can discuss this on the shuttle to Mars."

"I'm afraid that's not possible, Dr. Reynolds."

"Why not?" Nicole asked. It wasn't until she noticed the frown on his face that the answer dawned on her. "Oh—you're not on a list, are you Mr. Malloy?"

"I'm afraid not."

Awkward. "I'm so sorry, Mr. Malloy...I don't know what to say. Is there anything I can do to help?"

"Don't worry about it, Dr. Reynolds. Besides, remember that there is still a forty percent chance that the planetoid will miss our world altogether, which brings me to the other reason why I'm here."

"Okay then, please proceed," Nicole replied, having regained her composure and her manners, quite ashamed of how she'd been so surly with Malloy earlier.

"As I said, there is still a forty percent chance the rogue planetoid will miss us entirely, in which case the Alliance is determined that given the incredible technology now at our disposal, if we survive this event, we will never be caught this unprepared again."

"So you'd like me to help develop a plan for dealing with future planetary threats? I'd be happy to help, but it's really not my area of expertise."

"Well, no, we've actually got that one covered, Dr. Reynolds, thank you. There is another global program currently being developed as a result of this current crisis, however, that we *could* use your help with."

"What—?"

"As you know, when we made first contact with the Valhari, we were given a list of planets along with their coordinates, which were deemed to be suitable for human colonization. We'd like your help planning and recruiting a team, as well as a leader, to select and then colonize one of these worlds. This will help ensure that should another crisis ever arise that turns out to be an extinction level event like this one, the human race will survive. Assuming we make it past this current threat, the colonization effort will be given fast-track approval within the Alliance and all member governments."

"I'm flattered, Mr. Malloy, but why me?" Nicole asked, still puzzled. "I understand that my father is the sitting president of the Alliance, but surely there are more qualified people than me out there."

"We're not so sure there is anyone more qualified than you, Dr. Reynolds. Your extensive list of accomplishments is among the most impressive on the planet. The work you've done at your think tank here, such as helping that large mining outfit negotiate a major mining contract with the Anterans to mine on one of their moons, was genius. Helping the Alliance shape and then sell its policy on the development of new dark energy plants across the rest of the planet was very practical, and your improvement in the design of the quantum engines—well, let's just say that even the Valhari were impressed."

"Yes, well, there was a pressing trade issue with the Valhari at the time; the design just helped the Alliance strengthen their position in order to get product to them in time."

"Your solution was brilliant, Dr. Reynolds. What you've been able to

24

achieve in such a short time is quite extraordinary. Even beyond your own experience, your family's history with the Alliance and other sentient species is yet another compelling reason you were selected, Dr. Reynolds, but there are others. For example, the person who accepts this challenge will have to be someone with an exceptionally strong mind and incredible determination; I'm told that you possess a black belt in the Korean martial art of Taekwondo. Add in the fact that you hold PhDs in political science, anthropology, theoretical physics, and planetary sciences, and I think you can appreciate our interest in *you* for this position."

"Did my father…?"

"I can promise you that this *did not* come from him. In fact, when I first approached him about your possible involvement in this project, your father initially refused to even consider it, though eventually he acquiesced."

"What changed his mind?"

"The possible destruction of Earth and the end of the human race. When presented with the facts, your father soon came to believe as we do, that we need your help, and that you could be humanity's best hope for survival. So what do you say, Dr. Reynolds?"

***

Goddard looked over at Miller, who lay slumped over his desk, lightly snoring. He couldn't help but chuckle to himself, reflecting for a moment on his own days working at the Allen Telescope Array in California forty-five years earlier. He'd been there when the array had been hacked into by the Entelli named Ignis, the alien who'd initiated a distress call using the array. Fortunately for Ignis, that call had been intercepted by a Valhari transport ship that just happened to be traversing that particular quadrant of the galaxy. Goddard too had been a graduate student at the time, volunteering his time at the array, just as Miller was doing at the Alliance. Goddard thought about waking the student, but he decided it was best to let him sleep a little while longer. Very few would be able to sleep well once the rogue planet drew closer to Earth.

The aged scientist continued poring over the vast amount of data that now came in from a wide variety of sources. The majority of the data had been sent directly to his cube, along with Miller's, where it was sifted, sorted, and collated. He was looking at a holograph of the data, along with bar charts depicting the increase and decrease of the likelihood that the planetoid, now dubbed "Ronin" by the media, was going to impact Earth. Once he had the data presenting the way he wanted it to, he was ready to update the models with the latest data.

"Update models," he instructed the cube, after inserting it into its proper place inside his desk. The lines changed and new data points were added. Moments later, a slight grin began to emerge. He looked over to Miller, still sleeping soundly with his head on his desk.

"Scott....Scott, wake-up!" The exhausted graduate student groaned and raised his head slightly, before it plopped back on the desk and the snoring recommenced. This time Goddard wasn't going to let it pass; this was too important. He walked over to Miller's desk and began shaking his assistant slightly on the shoulder.

"Huh?" Miller sat up straight. "Oh, I'm so sorry Dr. Goddard; I must have dozed off for a second. I know there's no excuse for—"

Goddard smiled. "Don't worry about it, my boy. Come with me for a moment, I need you to see something!" Miller followed his mentor over to Goddard's desk. Goddard pressed a button and the display came back to life.

"Take a look at this data and tell me what you see," Goddard instructed. Goddard watched his assistant carefully study his data while sipping on a cup of coffee which, while not illegal in the United States yet, was about to be made so if the Congress had its say.

"So what do you think, Scott?" Miller looked at him with eyes so wide they looked like saucers.

"I think you'd better contact the president."

CHAPTER 4

"I can't believe we're doing this *now*, Captain; I mean, shouldn't we be blasting this 'Ronin' out of the sky, instead of taking off and heading in the other direction?" Jack Lincoln couldn't help but smile in response to the younger man's eagerness. The junior member of the team and the pilot of the second ship, Commander Luke Darren was, like most other young men his age, all guts and little patience. At only twenty-three, he was nearly ten years Lincoln's junior, but still one of the finest pilots in the Alliance; only Hank Reynolds had a more impressive record.

"We can't Luke; believe me when I say I wish we could. But this isn't just another two-mile wide asteroid threatening Earth, this is an entire *planet*, and it's almost here. There's nothing we can do to stop it, at least not this time. There's nothing we can do but hope, and pray, that the monstrosity misses Earth entirely."

"I just feel like we're abandoning everyone, sir. How can we leave Earth while everyone else dies? It feels like we're cowards and just saving ourselves from Armageddon."

Lincoln slammed his locker shut and turned to face the commander, casting a stern look towards the junior officer. "You stow that kind of talk this instant, Commander Darren, do you hear me? Neither of us knows what's going to happen...no one does. And we're *not* abandoning anyone, we're simply following orders."

"Sorry, Captain. It's just that our mission is for three days, and the collision is supposed to happen the day after tomorrow. What if we come home and it's—?"

"Gone?"

"Yes, sir," Darren answered softly, "what then?"

"Well, our orders are to scout out and evaluate the ten planets on the list; we collect the data, and we do our best to try to determine each planet's suitability for human life. If, when we return in three days, we are unable to return to any of the approved bases, we will fly to Mars Colony Alpha, and land there. If something has happened to Earth, senior Alliance personnel at the Mars colony will give us orders from there."

"What if the Mars colony is destroyed as well?"

"Look, Luke, I understand what you're feeling because I'm feeling it myself. You and I, however, don't have the luxury of seeking comfort and support in the arms of our loved ones as this thing approaches. Instead, we have to do something even harder; we have to leave them here in harm's way because that's our job, and because our being here when it strikes won't do anything to help save humanity from the next disaster. We carry a heavy weight on our shoulders, Commander, which is also a distinct privilege. You and I may be the key to finding a second home, and a second chance for humanity, out among the stars." He glanced over at Darren, who remained quite displeased about the entire state of affairs.

"Are you married, Captain?" The question jolted him, both because it was personal in nature, and because he'd not been expecting it. After taking a few moments to consider it, he decided it seemed appropriate for one member of the team to want to know more about the other; he decided to talk about it.

"No, not anymore...I'm divorced. My wife became disillusioned about the whole Alliance thing a few years into our marriage and decided she wasn't cut out to be the wife of an Alliance pilot. And you?"

"Yes sir, I am. We were married just under two years ago," he said with a smile before looking down for a moment. "We're expecting our first child; the doctor said it's a boy."

"Really? Congratulations!" Jack said, enthusiastically shaking the younger pilot's hand. Lincoln was genuinely happy for the junior officer until realization set in, and he began to understand the motivation for Darren's intense anxiety. He turned to look at his young friend, who still seemed quite downcast. "When's the baby due?"

"Two months, sir."

"I see," Lincoln replied. "I'm really happy for you, Commander," he said as he walked over to Darren and placed both hands on his shoulders. "Listen Luke, I'm sure that everything's going to be fine. I'll call in when the time comes just to be certain, and to set our minds at ease, okay?"

"Thank you sir," Darren answered, managing a weak smile.

"Good. Now I want you to stop all of that talk about everyone dying, Luke; it's depressing, and it's a distraction we can ill-afford. Besides, we have no way of knowing whether it will strike Earth or not; only the Lord God Himself knows what's going to happen in two days, and so far He's not telling. We can't spend what little time we've been allotted for this mission dwelling on what might happen; the Alliance wants a new colony in another star system established yesterday. We have to stray focused on the mission, Luke, and *only* the mission. The establishment of a new colony may be all that stands between the future of the human race—your son's future, Luke—and extinction…understand?"

"Yes, sir."

"Good. Let's finish suiting up and get to those ships then; I doubt they're going to fly themselves."

"Yes, Captain."

The two men left the locker room and made their way to the hangar where the two ships awaited them. The third generation, Frontier-class scout ships sat prepped and ready to go in the middle of a deserted hangar bay, a building designed to handle as many as fifty spacecraft—twenty-five scout ships and twenty-five transport ships. Jack looked them over with a smile that betrayed the pride he felt for being part of the Alliance, and the human race. The two scout ships were beautiful, a platinum-metallic color chosen for the third generation ships, which also included more space for a larger crew, if needed, an Entelli /navigational computer, teleport chambers, and pulse cannons, designed more for blasting asteroid debris than for battle.

"Wow, looks deserted in here without more ships," Darren remarked, looking around at the large hangar, nearly empty with all of the ships being used to ferry people to the Mars colony from Earth.

"It certainly does," his mentor agreed, looking around at the seemingly endless sea of concrete, which normally lay hidden from view beneath rows of the large Alliance ships. "The Alliance built a fleet of ships for a wide variety of reasons, not the least of which was dealing with catastrophes. I doubt that anyone had ever foreseen a threat quite like this one though. I mean, a rogue planet, speeding through the cosmos on a direct course for Earth; how could anyone have anticipated something like this?" His subordinate nodded in agreement as the two men approached their respective crafts; Lincoln walked toward the one on the left, while Darren made for the other.

"Okay, Captain, I guess I'll see you up there."

"Roger that, Commander. We're going to move quickly but thoroughly through the process of evaluating these planets and their suitability for human habitation. We have a lot to do in a relatively short amount of time, Luke, so let's get this done. Keep sharp and remain focused up there; since we're running with no crews, we're going to have to stay alert."

"Understood, Captain."

"Very good, then. I'll take the lead."

"Yes, sir."

Jack Lincoln approached the ship and upon touching it, triggered a doorway to open and a ramp to extend beside him. He walked up the ramp and entered the ship before gently touching the ship inside, which caused the ramp to retract and the doorway to close. He walked over to the pilot's chair, sat down, and strapped in for the flight. He shared his young friend's doubts about leaving at such a critical time, but he deferred to the decisions made by President Reynolds and the other Alliance leaders, many of whom he had come to trust over the last few years. Their mission had been given the highest priority by the Alliance upon recognition that for the first time, humanity faced the very real possibility of extinction. A collision with the runaway dwarf planet would destroy Earth; there would be no survivors. The Mars colony might survive, but such a violent destruction of its nearest neighbor posed a very serious threat to it as well. Jack somberly contemplated that it must be more than coincidence that for the first time, humanity had the means to escape a global cataclysm. It suddenly occurred to him that perhaps God had handed them the technology at just the right time to escape Earth's demise, and the thought that his home world might soon be destroyed caused a shiver to run down his spine.

Captain Jack Reynolds took in a deep breath and exhaled slowly to calm himself; he was an Alliance captain and he had a very important job to do...they both did. Lincoln reached over and picked up the cybernetic helmet, giving it a scrutinizing look. It had long since become routine, but having initially trained on a ship with a one hundred percent computerized navigation system, he was still adjusting somewhat to working with the Entelli. Without question things always went much smoother and more efficiently with an Entelli onboard, but it still creeped him out a little.

After taking another deep breath, he slowly raised the helmet and placed it on his head. The familiar surroundings of the ship's bridge suddenly vanished and he found himself instantly transported to the White Room, where he now stood before two black doors. On his left was a door labeled "Exit"; on his right, a door labeled "Enter." He opened the "Enter" door and walked inside. The door closed behind him and he found himself surrounded by darkness, until a replica of the bridge slowly materialized all around him moments later. He'd learned throughout the course of his Alliance training that after several millennia working with other sentient races, the Entelli found it usually made the pilot feel more at ease to project a replica of the bridge with which he could interact. As always, the Entelli appeared as a crewmember—in this case a human male, approximately thirty years of age in appearance. It wasn't anyone he'd ever met aside from this ship, but was rather a composite of millions or perhaps billions of human males the Entelli had browsed through in the Alliance database.

"Good morning, Captain Lincoln, how are you this morning?"

"I'm doing fine, thank you. How are you—I believe your name is Magellan?"

"Yes, sir, my name is indeed Magellan, and I'm doing wonderful, sir, thank you for asking. May I say what a privilege it is to be among the first group of Entelli to serve aboard a human ship?"

"Thanks, Magellan, but I assure you that the privilege is actually mine. Working with your people has proven to make interstellar flight much more practical and enjoyable for us. Perhaps, had my people understood just how beneficial it was to have an Entelli aboard our ships, we would have approached your people some time ago."

"Thank you, Captain Lincoln."

Jack furrowed his brow. "Mind if I ask you a question?"

"Of course not, Captain. We have a few minutes while I run some new calculations based on the flight plan I received just a few minutes ago."

"Good. I understand that when first assigned to a different ship, an Entelli will select a new name by which to be called by her captain and crew, which means that Magellan is not your true name."

"Yes sir, that's correct. Almost all sentient races with whom we interact are unable to pronounce our real names, so we often attempt to make it easier by choosing a name in the host species' language; sometimes it's a common name, sometimes it's a famous leader—"

"Or perhaps a world famous explorer?"

"Yes, sir," the avatar replied with a slight smile.

"*Very* appropriate, Magellan, given our mission," Jack said with a smile.

"Thank you, sir, I thought so as well."

Jack paused to look around the bridge of the ship, or the virtual representation of it rather. "Okay, Magellan, are we ready to take off?"

"I'm ready whenever you are, sir."

"Very good; please open a comlink with Mission Control."

"Comlink open, sir."

"Control, this is scout ship Alpha One, requesting clearance to depart."

"You're cleared to depart, Captain Lincoln. Happy hunting, and wish us luck, sir."

"I'll do one better, Control, I'll pray. God willing, Ronin will steer well clear of Earth."

"Roger that. Thanks Captain…Control out."

"Okay, Magellan, take us up slowly, and please open a comlink with Commander Darren's ship."

"Aye, Captain, comlink is open, sir."

The roof over the ships receded and the ship slowly rose from the hangar.

"Scout ship two, this is scout ship one, over."

An image of Luke Darren appeared above the control panel. "This is Scout Ship Two, go ahead, Captain."

"Okay, Commander," Lincoln began, pushing several soft buttons on his virtual control system. "So we'll meet up at the coordinates I'm now sending you, about halfway between Earth and the moon. From there we'll jump to the first planet."

"Copy that, Captain. See you at the rendezvous point, sir."

"See you there, Commander, over and out." The link dropped.

"Okay, Magellan, let's proceed to these coordinates."

"Yes, Captain." The ship lifted and moved forward before disappearing and reappearing less than thirty seconds later at the specified coordinates equidistant between Earth and the moon. Lincoln was soon joined by Darren.

"Okay, Commander, let's get this show on the road. The first stop is going to be Tau Ceti e, orbiting the star Tau Ceti. On paper, it doesn't look like the best candidate, but it's one of the closest. Now remember, Luke, we have only a few hours to spend at each planet, to collect the data and then move on to the next one. Mission Control will pass along the data we collect to the appropriate folks within the Alliance for them to evaluate. Then we'll re-visit the best three with someone from the Alliance leadership, who will then select the planet to colonize first.

"As for our first stop, we'll stay together until we get to the planet, at which point we'll separate; you'll start at the North Pole and I'll start at the South Pole. We'll then take an hour to survey our respective half of the planet's surface before meeting at a designated set of coordinates somewhere in the middle. At this point, I'll decide the best location for a base camp, and if it's safe, we'll disembark the ships and take a look around for ourselves, collect soil samples, etc., before moving on to the next rock. Understood?"

"Understood, Captain. I sat in the same mission briefing, sir, remember?"

"Indulge me, Commander. We're going to be extremely meticulous about this mission, Luke, remember that; there's far too much at stake here. The chosen planet could be a new home for the human race for thousands of years or more, regardless of what happens with that rogue planetoid. So yeah, I want to make sure you and I are on the same page every step of the way, understood?" Jack was a little sharper in tone and delivery than he really intended to be, but it was important that the younger, junior officer and he were both pulling in the same direction.

"Yes, sir, of course. Sorry, Captain."

"Forget about it. Are you ready to enter quantum space?"

"Yes, sir, we're ready."

"As are we. Okay then, let's get this show on the road. Prepare to enter quantum space in space in 3-2-1-now!"

***

The two ships slowed as they approached the next planet, a world slightly larger than Earth, orbiting a pair of binary stars. After already scouting the first seven on the list, they'd finally arrived at the eighth out of the ten planets identified by the Valhari as promising candidates for colonization by humanity, and it rated as high as ninety-nine percent on the Earth Similarity Index (ESI). As they approached the planet, they could see that it contained both vegetation and liquid water in abundance. Lincoln and Darren were exhausted after surveying the first seven planets and still had two more to go after this one, yet they remained optimistic, because on paper and so far up close, this planet looked to be the best candidate they'd seen yet for human colonization.

"Okay, Luke, you take the north again and I'll take the south. Scan everything and look for anything that could be a problem. I like the looks of this one so far, but we have to be as cautious and as thorough as possible. The atmosphere is mostly oxygen, helium, and nitrogen, in a mixture that we should be able to breathe okay, but when we rendezvous at the predetermined coordinates we wear our environmental suits out and keep our personal body shields turned on until we have clearance from medical that it's safe, understood? We don't want to inadvertently carry back any harmful biological agents."

"Understood, Captain."

"Let's plan to rendezvous in two hours, after which we'll take a closer look at a few of the major landmasses near the equator."

"Copy that, Captain Lincoln. Rendezvous back at the pre-arranged coordinates in two hours. See you then, sir." Darren's ship took off first heading toward the North Pole, where he would begin circling the planet beginning at the North Pole until he reached the equator, scanning and recording data and imagery that would be analyzed back at the Alliance headquarters over the coming weeks.

Jack took a deep breath, trying to keep a lid on his excitement. They wouldn't really know which planet was the best candidate until the medical scientists and techs at Alliance HQ had reviewed the data, but Jack had a feeling, a really good feeling, about this one that he'd not had with any of the others. Time was short, however, and there was a lot of work to be done.

"Okay, Magellan, let's get down to the South Pole and start our scans. I'm anxious to get down to the surface."

"Of course, Captain," came the response from Magellan's avatar. "Do I detect a bit of heightened expectation on this one, Captain Lincoln? It certainly does seem to be an ideal planet for human beings to colonize, just as the Valhari have said."

"Yes you do, and yes it does," Lincoln replied, answering both questions at once. "It's imperative we find another place to live soon, especially if—"

"No need to explain, Captain. I know it may seem woefully insufficient at the moment, but please try to keep in mind that there *is* a forty percent probability that this Ronin will miss Earth completely."

"How much time until it gets to Earth, Magellan?"

"Based on the information I've been provided, it should be there in approximately three hours and thirty-seven minutes, Captain."

"Thank you, Magellan. Are we nearing the south pole yet?"

"We've only just arrived, Captain."

"Excellent. Please commence scanning and recording. Let's get this done so we can get a good look at this one up close."

"Scanning and recording has begun, Captain."

Jack Lincoln swallowed hard. Soon he would know whether they'd found a new home for humanity; soon they would also know whether they still had an old one.

CHAPTER 5

"It's amazing, Captain," Darren said, looking around at the kaleidoscope of colors that surrounded them. Beautiful trees and lush grass lay over the floor of the rolling hills, valleys, and plains; a much finer grass than what was commonly found on Earth, and deep blue rather than green in appearance. The trees that dotted the landscape looked similar to the cypress trees found on Earth, but they had a dark red hue, much like the great redwoods in California. Every tree within their field of view also bore assorted fruit of all shapes, sizes, and colors; some were yellow like pears, some resembled what could pass for blue apples. Even many of the bushes bore fruit resembling grapes, figs, and blueberries. Streams of crystal clear water flowed through the middle of the active landscape.

There were also various types of animal life wandering the landscape, most beautiful in form and appearance, sporting a wide array of colors. The creatures seemed friendly enough though bashful, and always kept a great distance from the two men.

Jack glanced up at the sky as best as his helmet would allow. The Rayleigh scattering of the light from the binary stars on this world gave the sky a vibrant, beautiful golden color, unlike anything he'd ever seen before. In some ways it reminded him of Earth's sky on a bright clear day, only instead of a deep, vibrant blue it was a deep, crisp gold. When he tried to get a better look at the sky he found he was constrained by his suit, and for a brief moment, he even considered removing it.

"Better not do that, Jack. You know that medical has to clear the airborne pathogens; more than likely anyone living here will need to be inoculated." The senior officer was about to respond when Darren suddenly asked, "So are we ready to collect samples yet?" The transparent attempt at changing the subject was not lost on Lincoln.

"I know that, *Commander*," Lincoln replied, somewhat embarrassed to be chided, correctly so or not, by the junior officer. "The thought may have crossed my mind, but I wasn't actually going to take it off."

"Of course not, sir."

"These blasted suits, they're just so constraining! All right, you collect the soil sample and I'll collect the water sample."

"You've got it, Captain," Darren eagerly replied, seemingly thankful that a potentially unpleasant confrontation with his superior had been avoided.

Jack walked over to the large stream and knelt down close enough to be able to retrieve a sample. He was startled when he looked down into the water and found a large pair of deep blue eyes staring back at him. The aquatic creature resembled some sort of bizarre cross between a small, green monkey and a fish, with large eyes and a tail, but with fins and something resembling gills on the side of its neck. It stared at Jack for several moments, even after he'd finished collecting his sample, before suddenly turning and darting away downstream.

He stood back up and looked around as far as he could see in all directions. The twin suns were starting to set behind some distant mountain peaks, causing the golden sky to start to glow like the brilliant metal of the same name. Jack shook his head in wonder. The world was stunningly beautiful; pristine, unspoiled, and untouched by civilization. There was abundant water and plenty of oxygen already in the atmosphere, enough to very comfortably support a planet full of human life. Better yet, the temperature was comparable to that of Earth. The Valhari had been right...this world *was* perfect for human colonization. It was slightly larger than Earth and the gravity was proportionally greater than back home, but not so much as to be harmful or even all that noticeable, at least to most.

Jack stood gazing at the breathtaking landscape, trying to remember every detail. The two stars that made up the Meta-Stratus system, located in the constellation Taurus, had only recently been added to star charts. Without the Valhari's assistance, the Alliance would likely have never found this world, and he suddenly found himself doubly thankful for their help.

"So what do you think, Luke? It's perfect, isn't it, like a new Garden of Eden."

"'New Eden'...I like the sound of that, sir. It is quite magnificent, Captain, I must admit," Darren replied, before reaching down to collect a soil sample for the scientists back home to analyze. "Me? I'd like to own a lot just about where we're standing, close to a stream, with an incredible view and lots of room for a house. Yes, sir, this is the only planet we've visited that I can honestly say I'd like to call home...other than Earth, of course. It's definitely at the top of my list, sir."

"Mine too, Luke," Lincoln agreed.

"It would be a great place for someone who wanted to start over and build a new life," Darren suggested. "A brand new breed of pioneers, not so unlike those headed west back in the 1800s in the United States."

"You just may be right about that, Luke," Lincoln replied before looking through the samples they'd placed in the container. "Well it seems we've collected plenty of samples, along with the data and images of this planet, Commander," Lincoln offered as he sealed his soil sample and placed it in a small portable container along with the others. "Let's pack it up and head out."

"Do you think it will be a finalist?"

The captain took a look around at the lush grass, the beautiful golden sky, and the flowing hills. "I certainly hope so, Commander, because I wouldn't mind living here myself someday. Okay, pack it up and let's get moving. We still have two more planets to look at before heading back home. Once we're on route to our next stop, I'll call in to check and see if Earth is still there," Jack told the junior officer with a grimace. In the midst of their excitement they'd both momentarily forgotten about the grave, catastrophic threat back home.

"Sounds good. I'll be right behind you, sir. And Captain, please call me as soon as you know something...."

"I will, Commander, I promise."

"Thank you, sir."

The men boarded their respective crafts and the two alien ships soon began lifting from the planet, leaving its many inhabitants to puzzle over the meaning of the most unusual visitation. Soon, they were back in space heading to the jump point. Fifteen minutes later they were back in quantum space and en route to their next stop. Jack looked at the clock on the virtual console and decided it was time for them to contact the Alliance to learn Earth's fate, and after a quick call back home to Earth, Jack had the answer he was looking for.

"Magellan?"

"Yes, Captain?"

"Please contact Commander Darren."

"Yes, Captain." Magellan disappeared for a few moments before reappearing.

"He's on; go ahead, Captain."

"Thanks." The Entelli's avatar nodded politely before busying itself with other tasks.

"Commander Darren, you wanted me to let you know what I found out—about Earth?" Jack asked his co-pilot as the two traveled in quantum space on their way to a star system light years from Earth.

"Yes, sir, please—tell me what you found out. Is it still there?"

"Ronin did head toward Earth after passing Saturn, but en route it approached just near enough to Jupiter's massive gravity well that its trajectory was altered slightly."

"You mean…?"

"Yes, Luke, it missed Earth entirely, though it was a very close call."

"Yee-haw!" Darren yelled excitedly over the comlink.

"There were some earthquakes, tidal waves, and volcanic eruptions as Ronin passed by," Lincoln continued, "but our planet survived. The Alliance is now more determined than ever to do something quickly to ensure the human race's survival, should anything like it ever occur again."

"All right! Yes! Woo hoo! Thank you, Captain, thank you!"

"We'll have some time to visit with our families as soon as we get back, Luke, so I suggest you make it count. Once the Alliance techs have finished analyzing the data we've collected, the Alliance leadership will be making a decision on the top two or three candidates for colonization. Once they've made that decision, I expect they'll be wanting to send someone out immediately to select the planet to colonize."

"But why not colonize all of them, Jack?"

"The leadership discussed that possibility and it was decided that since colonization on such a massive scale would be such a colossal undertaking, we should do one first. Once we have one planetary colony under our belt, I expect the Alliance will explore colonizing more …perhaps all of the planets on the Valhari's list. Only time will tell."

"We're going to be famous, aren't we, Captain?"

Jack stared numbly back at the holographic image. It was a possibility he'd never even considered.

"I don't know, Luke, I suppose we will. It is a pretty amazing time to be alive, isn't it? A time when interstellar travel is such an ordinary event, and planetary colonization is a reality."

"Yes, sir, it certainly is."

"Well, now that we both can breathe a little easier, how about we finish what we came here for so we can get home? We're approaching the jump point for our next stop, Commander. Prepare to enter quantum space."

"Ready, Captain."

"Entering quantum space in 3-2-1…." Both ships disappeared from regular space as they entered quantum space on their way to the next planet.

***

The two ships had barely departed the Meta-Stratus binary star system when a third, much larger and intimidating alien ship suddenly appeared, emerging from quantum space just outside the same planet. The new ship looked very different and was of a completely different design. This ship was red, and more irregular in shape and form. Moments later, the strange ship landed on the planet's surface, only a few kilometers from the spot where Alliance ships had sat only minutes earlier.

CHAPTER 6

"We're entering the Venetian system now, Mr. Ambassador."

"Thank you," Hank replied to the pilot, still adjusting to the new title after serving for years as president of the Alliance. For a moment he felt a twinge of regret about giving up the post, but it soon passed. It *had* been a difficult decision, but he knew it to be the correct one. The presidency had, for the most part, become more political, and too constraining, for someone like him. Hank knew that he would be much happier among the stars, where he belonged, and his work as Earth's ambassador to the League of Sentient Species would become increasingly vital as humanity began leaving Earth to explore, work, and live throughout the rest of the galaxy.

Hank smiled in wonder as the ship drew closer and closer to the planet Val, the fourth planet from the star the Valhari called Venetia, and he found his mind starting to drift back in time. His mind was flooded with images and sounds from his childhood, and his slow march through adolescence as he grew into a man. His childhood had not been an easy one, facing bullies every day at the base school, jealous and resentful of him because of his highly advanced intellectual capacity. He'd grown up during the Transitory Period, the decades during which humanity began developing and testing the first interstellar ships capable of crossing vast distances of space in a very brief period of time. It was the transition between an old way of life and a new and very different one, a time during which humanity finally acknowledged that they were not alone in the universe.

Following his encounter with Ignis, a sentient computer from a crashed alien ship, Hank's father, Nick Reynolds, had unexpectedly found himself with a newfound talent, the ability to read and understand the alien technology aboard the crashed ship. This ability had enabled humanity to build its first interstellar spacecraft named Frontier, a ship a young and daring Hank Reynolds had flown to Sol's nearest neighbor, the Alpha Centauri system. It was, however, only the first of many interstellar test flights which would eventually enable humanity to leave its longtime nest, Earth, so that it could stretch its wings and fly amongst the stars. *What an exciting time to be alive!*

"Excuse me, Ambassador Reynolds?" The pilot jarred Hank back to the present.

"Yes?"

"I have an incoming transmission for you, sir."

"I'll take it, thank you." A holographic image appeared in front of him; a photonic representation of his longtime friend, the Valhari ambassador named Zing. A pale-skinned alien with large, black eyes, Zing had, decades earlier, been responsible for engineering Hank's advanced intellect.

"Dr. Reynolds, how are you? I trust you've had a comfortable journey?"

"I have indeed, Zing, thank you. I guess *I* get to play the ambassador this time too," he added with a smile.

"Indeed. I cannot convey how very surprised and pleased we were to learn that you would be the first ambassador from Earth since the Alliance voted to join the League. That you would surrender your position as President of the Earth Space Alliance in order to become Earth's representative to the League is a testament to your character. I, for one, could think of no finer representative for humanity than yourself, Hank Reynolds; welcome."

"Thank you, Zing. I must confess that I'm excited about the opportunity to interact with other members of the League, and I appreciate the opportunity to live on your home world."

"You are most welcome, Dr. Reynolds. I believe that you will find it to be a most enlightening, meaningful, and productive experience. I regret, however, that I will be unable to greet you at the spaceport upon your arrival due to a conflict in my schedule. With your permission, however, I have arranged for an associate of mine, Sortox Norwal, to meet you at the port before escorting you to your ambassador's quarters here in our capital city, Q'Tal."

"Of course, I look forward to meeting him. I must say, Zing, that when I first learned that the League rotates its headquarters between the League's member's planets of origin every ten standard years, and that it just happens to be on Val for another three standard years, I was thrilled. I've always wanted to visit your home world, after all of the wonderful things you've said about it."

"Thank you, Dr. Reynolds, I only hope that I did it justice in your eyes. For my part, I was extremely pleased to learn that Earth would finally be sending a representative to the League, and I was overjoyed when I learned that representative would be you. Earth's membership in the League will be such a positive step for your world; your people will learn so much more about the many opportunities that exist in the galaxy for trade and interactions of all sorts, amongst the many and varied civilizations spread out across this galaxy."

"Mr. Ambassador, I'm very curious about something. I understand that a standard year would be roughly equivalent to about one and a half of our solar years, and that it was defined long ago as the length of time it took for the founding member's planet of origin to orbit its star."

"That is correct," Zing answered.

"So how long has the League been in existence? We were only told that it was formed long ago."

"Long ago, yes that's correct; the League was formed approximately four-thousand standard years ago, although it was already a loose confederation of planets for at least a thousand standard years before that."

"That's well over seven-thousand Earth-years ago, Zing…thousands of years before our first pyramids were built!"

Zing nodded in agreement. "Yes, that is correct. The League has been instrumental in bringing together many of the sentient species spread out across our galaxy, where we have lived in peace for most of recorded history," Zing answered. "Now, if you will please pardon me, Dr. Reynolds, I'm afraid that I must cut the remainder of our conversation short."

"Of course, Zing, there will be plenty of time for us to catch up later."

"Excellent. Before we terminate this transmission, however, perhaps you would be kind enough to join me for dinner this evening? Once you've gotten settled in, of course."

"Certainly. I'd like that, Zing, thank you."

"Excellent. Oh, I nearly forgot to ask, is your wife with you? I'm quite certain my wife, Kirta, would very much enjoy meeting her."

"No, I'm afraid she's not with me yet. She had a few things to wrap up back on Earth, but she'll be joining me very soon."

"Wonderful news, Dr. Reynolds. Please tell her I look forward to seeing her again."

"I will. Say, I've been meaning to ask whether it might be possible to bring my father, Nick Reynolds, to stay here with me on Val for a while. He's been very sick and—well, I hate leaving him alone, and I thought bringing him here would really lift his spirits."

"Certainly, Dr. Reynolds, please bring him. As you know, in a very real sense your father is responsible for much of what has transpired these past fifty years or so. Had Nick Reynolds not left such a favorable impression on Ignis, the League might well have waited another hundred years or so before approaching humanity."

"Only if we hadn't destroyed ourselves by then," Hank replied sourly. Zing tilted his head slightly as a token gesture of agreement.

"Oh, there's one more thing," the Valhari added before terminating the link. "I have some rather fascinating news to share with you this evening when we have more time, something I believe you will find rather interesting."

"Sounds intriguing; I look forward to hearing about it at dinner."

"Excellent. I will see you this evening, Hank Reynolds. On behalf of the League and the Valhari, please allow me to once again welcome you to Val, my home world!"

***

The ship landed fifteen minutes later, carefully following the instructions for landing procedures given to the Alliance weeks before the scheduled flight. Hank found Sortox Norwal waiting for them at the base of the ramp.

"Welcome to Val, Ambassador Reynolds. My name is Sortox Norwal." Hank noticed the Valari wore a translation matrix around his neck, and that he'd heard the words as they'd entered his ears as sound, not his mind. "Unfortunately, President Zing was unable to greet you as planned, so he asked me to meet you instead."

"Thank you, Sortox Norwal, it is very good to be here," Hank replied, using the surname as well as the first name, the more formal manner used by the Valhari when addressing someone with whom they were not familiar. "I noticed that you're using a translation matrix instead of using telepathy; may I ask why?" Hank asked casually as they stood waiting just outside the ship, standing in the hangar next to the ramp.

"Yes, it is something we Valhari generally do, as a rule, as a courtesy to other species. Some races are far more sensitive than others when it comes to non-verbal communication."

"For the record, please feel free to use either when speaking with me, Sortox Norwal, since I understand your people feel much more comfortable with non-verbal communication."

"Thank you, Dr. Reynolds, I appreciate your thoughtfulness," Norwal replied, after turning off the translation matrix.

"Um, what should we do with my belongings?"

"Of yes, please forgive me. With your permission I will arrange to have your things brought to your new quarters."

"Yes, please. As soon as that's been done, the captain must leave to return to our home world. We have quite a few citizens who still need to be shuttled back to Earth from our Mars colony."

"Oh yes, of course. I'll see to it right away."

Norwal walked over to where several Valhari stood at a counter. One of them nodded to Norwal before pressing a button. Moments later another Valhari appeared with a cart, which floated less than a meter from the ground. Hank walked over to the captain, who stood waiting next to the ship.

"Captain Taggart, I believe I'm good to go. If you can please have someone help get everything off the ship, the Valhari will take it to my quarters."

"Of course, Mr. Ambassador. I'll be back in about a week, sooner if we get the evacuees back before then."

"Thank you very much, Captain, for everything. Listen, my wife and my father should be ready to join me about then; would you mind checking with the Alliance or with me before heading back, to see if she's ready? We might as well save you a trip if we can."

"Of course, Dr. Reynolds, please excuse me for a moment." Taggart turned and walked down a hallway before disappearing around a corner, while Hank looked around the strange, alien world. Nearly all of the buildings seemed to be made of some type of crystalline substance, which reflected light from the giant star which hung in the sky like a giant, life-giving orb, positioned a considerable distance from their world. Moments later Captain Taggart re-appeared, carrying two large suitcases.

"Here you are, sir. Do you have everything you need before I leave, sir? Are there any supplies from the ship you think you will need before I return?"

Hank smiled. "Thank you for your concern, Captain, but I'll be fine; I believe I have everything I need for now. I have friends here who will help me settle in, but thank you for asking."

Taggert just raised an eyebrow and nodded before Hank turned and began walking over to Norwal, who stood waiting.

"So, I have a lot of questions," Hank said to the Valhari as he followed him to a waiting transport.

"I'd be happy to answer any questions I can," his host answered, motioning for Hank to walk into the waiting transport. Hank complied and Norwal followed him in.

"The ambassador quarters in the League complex, please," he instructed the pilot.

"Yes, sir," came the pilot's reply.

"Interesting, I've never been in the presence of more than one Valhari at a time, except for the first contact ceremony back on Earth. I heard you instruct the pilot where to take us and I heard his reply, yet I heard it in my mind, not with my ears."

"You will learn the ways of the races who use non-verbal communication, Ambassador Reynolds. From what I have learned about your planet, human beings speak in different languages, do they not?"

"Yes."

"And when two or more people speak to one another in a foreign language in the presence of someone else who does not understand that language, that is considered rude, is it not? For the others to converse in another language, leaving the first person confused about what was said?"

"Yes, I suppose so."

"It is also considered rude among our people to communicate with one another using non-verbal communication in front of those of verbal races. We have two modes of projecting our non-verbal communication; there is a single-mode, where we speak to an individual, and there is a broadcast mode, where we speak to a group. This works since our communication range is localized."

"Interesting. Now, what about privacy? Is there a way to block off thoughts from non-verbal races?"

"Of course, you merely need to block off your thoughts...but why would you need to? Valhari do not force themselves into the minds of others; it is considered a horrific crime, and is something that has not happened since the dark times of our people!"

"I'm sorry, Sortox Norwal, I did not intend to offend you. I have much to learn and besides, I am a diplomat."

"Of course," his host answered, with a hint of a smile.

"What about communications, housing, food, and such?" The Valhari looked at him with a look that made Hank think of curiosity.

"Dr. Reynolds, we have been hosting races from other worlds for thousands of your years; I assure you we prepared for your arrival soon after you requested to join the League, when you were still president of the Earth Space Alliance. In your quarters you will find communication equipment for opening quantum communication channels with Earth or anywhere else. You will also have a selection of food that will be compatible with your physiology, including a wide selection of food from your planet."

"Again, please forgive my ignorance; as I said, I have a lot to learn."

CHAPTER 7

The restaurant was unlike anything Hank had even been in before. Sentient beings from all parts of the galaxy mingled there, discussing trade issues, political futures, and general gossip. He speculated that perhaps, in some ways, it was not so much unlike how the cafeteria in the United Nations building in New York had once been, with the obvious exceptions. One of the first things that struck Hank, after the incredible diversity in shape, size, and appearance of its patrons, was that a number of them were speaking the same language, though it was clear that they represented different worlds.

"You're staring, Dr. Reynolds."

Zing's comment startled Hank. "Huh? Oh, thanks, Zing. Sorry."

"It's perfectly understandable. I merely thought I should point it out to you before anyone noticed." Hank nodded. "It's not that often that the League brings in new members, but when it does, the staring seems to go with the territory."

"Yes, of course, thank you, Zing."

"You're quite welcome. As a member of the Guiding Council on the Emergence of Sentient Species, I've seen quite a few new ambassadors come into the league over the course of my considerably long life, and you're one of the most fascinating, Dr. Reynolds."

"Why do you say so, Zing?'

"Because your people are one of the most resilient races I have ever seen. Your life spans are incredibly short, relatively speaking, yet you take life in stride. Only twenty-five years ago your planet's technology was still rather primitive—though to be fair it was advancing exponentially—and the furthest your people had traveled was to your moon. Yet now here you are, traveling the stars as if born to it, taking interstellar space travel in stride as if you'd been doing it for a thousand years. You're sitting in a room filled with so many diverse races, unlike anything you've ever seen and so different from you as to certainly cause you panic, yet here you sit, behaving as if it's all routine."

"Except for the staring, or course."

"Of course."

"Say, Zing, I've noticed quite a few members speaking the same language to one another; what is it?"

"Loosely translated, it's 'The Common Galactic Language of the League,' though most simply refer to it as League Speak." Zing paused as if waiting for Hank.

"So, that was probably developed because of the technical problems posed by having so many ambassadors with translators in such close proximity?"

Zing nodded. "Yes, in part, but it also helps to bind us together as a single galactic community. League Speak was developed two-and-a-half millennia ago, and is now taught on most member home worlds as well."

"Hmmm, interesting. I'd like to learn it."

"You will my friend," Zing replied. "You will have access to the resources in your quarters, or you can attend classes taught here at the League headquarters."

"Great. I'll start looking the material over later tonight." Hank continued glancing around the room, trying not to stare at the others yet fascinated by what he saw. He also noticed that there were quite a few looks now coming his direction as well.

"We haven't had a new admittance into the League for some time now. A few of the other races were against Earth being admitted to the League, arguing that humanity was still too aggressive and primitive. But most of the races are very curious about humanity, and want to learn more about you."

"Like the Valhari did," Hank responded with a wry smile.

'Why yes, I suppose so. That's one reason I was hoping you would accept the invitation to join us after leaving the presidency, because I knew that if the other races measured humanity by what they see in you, your world would benefit enormously."

"How so?"

"You're extremely sharp, inquisitive, respectful, and thoughtful, all important qualities for a diplomat in the League. Through your interactions as an ambassador you may find that you will make a far greater impact here than you ever could have as president of the Alliance. Furthermore, you have a superior intellect, even among the gathering here today."

"I have you to thank for that, Zing." Hank thought he detected a slight upturn in Zing's expressionless face as he sat back in his chair.

"I'm not so sure about that, but I'll come to that in a moment. First, I have been meaning to ask you about the horrific circumstances around the close call your planet recently experienced with this 'Ronin.' Rogue planets like that one are extremely rare, nearly unheard of even among the oldest species out here. I'm just grateful that it missed Earth. I wish there had been something we could have done. Perhaps, given more notice—"

"Don't worry about it. There are ten billion people on Earth, Zing; what could you have done?"

"We would have done all we could. Please let us know immediately if anything like that ever happens again; we will certainly do what we can to help."

"I will, Zing, thank you."

"The Earth experienced volcanic eruptions, tectonic activity, tidal waves and the like when it passed by?"

"Yes, there were a few, but nothing serious; certainly nothing like what would have happened if…." Hank allowed his voice to trail off.

"I am thankful for your planet's good fortune, Hank Reynolds," Zing stated before taking a drink from the bright blue drink in his glass. "I understand that the Alliance has launched an initiative to investigate the list of planets we provided to it some time ago, worlds that could make suitable candidates for Earth's first planetary colony…outside of your own star system, that is."

"Yes, well, it's really Earth's *first* effort to colonize. You can't really count the Mars colony as a planetary colonization effort, at least not until the terra-forming has started, which is not scheduled to begin for another five standard years or so."

"Ah, 'standard year,' very good, Hank."

"Yeah, well, I'm trying. So, we've had ships scouting the planets on that list you gave us. So far several look promising. It seems Earth's brush with annihilation was enough to jolt people in my government awake to the danger. We're going to narrow it down to the most suitable planet on the list, and once we have a healthy, global colony up and running on it, we'll look at one or two more of the others on the list."

"Good, I'm very glad to hear that, Hank. After all, the galaxy is full of uninhabited planets, as well as infinite dangers. Establishing a colony in another star system was a wise choice. Had a global threat like this Ronin befallen your world only twenty-six years ago, your entire species could have been wiped out. It has happened before." Zing bowed his head for a moment before starting to eat. Hank did the same before doing likewise.

"Tell me something Zing, do the Valhari believe in God, or *a* god of some sort?"

"A deity?"

"Yes."

"Of course we do. Don't human beings?"

49

"Some do, others don't…it's up to the individual."

Zing looked up at Hank. "Ah, but what about *you*, Hank Reynolds? Do *you* believe in God?"

"Yes, I do."

"Good, then once we finish our meals, there's something I'd like to share with you."

The next fifteen minutes passed slowly for Hank. Three times now Zing had made reference to something he wanted to tell him, and three times he'd piqued Hank's curiosity. Eventually both of them had finished their meals, and Zing was ready to talk.

"So, do you recall what I told you about our visits to see you when you were still quite young; how we made some minor changes to your DNA? We were hoping to give you and your progeny some adaptations to help your people survive space travel as a species, such as an enhanced intellectual capacity and the ability for your body to repair itself much faster than a normal human?"

"Yes," Hank answered pensively.

"Did I tell you that we'd confirmed that you have exhibited both the enhanced intellect and the advanced healing ability?"

"I don't really recall, Zing, why?"

"I'll tell you why, Hank. A few months ago a technician looking through some of the data brought something to my attention."

"Okay, so where are you going with this, Zing?"

"Over the last twelve years we've had a number of humans volunteer to participate in a joint program, with the Alliance approval, with the objective of duplicating what we were able to accomplish with you. To our surprise, however, we found that the same modifications we'd made to your genes was wholly ineffective on theirs."

"What does that mean, Zing?"

"It means you were unique to begin with, Hank. Our procedure would have produced no result whatsoever with any other human being. Furthermore, somehow, for whatever reason, the change to your genes has enhanced your abilities far beyond our expectations, and given you the greatest intellect on your planet. Of course, you also have significant resistance to radiation and the ability for your body to repair itself. Something, or someone, Hank Reynolds, had already modified your genes so that you were born this way, but it wasn't *us*. It's as if you were meant to lead humanity to the stars."

CHAPTER 8

"Please allow me to congratulate you, Mr. President, on being elected the new President of the Earth Space Alliance." The president smiled back at Malloy, he couldn't resist it. He knew Malloy had supported Frank Miller, Clark's toughest competitor in the race leading up to the presidential election. But he also knew by reputation that Malloy was a good man to have on his team, a hard worker with an uncanny attention to details. Both were qualities that were indispensable for someone in his position.

"Thank you, Mr. Malloy."

"So how are you settling into the presidency, sir?"

"In all honesty my head's still spinning a bit, but I'm getting there. I'm just thankful that President Reynolds delayed his exit until after Ronin passed us by."

"Indeed, sir, that would have been a catastrophe of Biblical proportion."

"So, Mr. Malloy, I'm sure you're here to discuss something other than my first few months in office. What can I do for you?"

"Well sir, you know that since the near miss with the rogue planet there have been widespread calls for the Alliance to begin colonizing some of the worlds on the list the Valhari gave us."

"Yes, I'm aware of that. I'm also aware that the Alliance set the wheels in motion for that to happen before I was sworn in, and that two scout ships recently returned from surveying the ten planets on that list."

"Yes, sir, that's correct. My team's been reviewing the data from the expedition and we've already narrowed it down to three planets. I recently hired a highly qualified expert to assist with putting together a select team of scientists, which will go on an expedition to each of the three worlds to evaluate their suitability for human settlement.

"This expert will also select an individual to lead the colonization of the selected planet on behalf of humanity. She's developed a screening test that's been sent to a pool of over a million candidates worldwide, and

51

from that she has narrowed that pool down to twenty. There's one problem, however."

"Go on." Alliance President Joseph Clark was many things but he was no fool, and he could clearly see Malloy was driving towards something.

"With the exception of a beta copy of the test that she completed in order to evaluate the test's effectiveness, she excluded herself from the pool of candidates."

"So? That is not so unusual is it?"

"No sir, perhaps not; but I've seen the beta copy of the test that she completed. The scores are off the chart, sir."

"Are you trying to say that you believe *she* is the best candidate for the job?" Clark asked with some confusion.

"Yes, Mr. President, that's exactly what I'm saying."

"What makes you think that?"

"Mr. President, this test was given to some the best and brightest human beings on the planet. The list included Nobel laureates , chief scientists, and MIT professors, and nearly all of them have more letters after their name than the alphabet. These people are the Einsteins of our day, sir."

"Please get to the point, Mr. Malloy," Clark said, clearly growing increasingly impatient.

"My point is this, sir. This expert, who we tasked with putting together the team, scored at least twenty-five to thirty times higher in every area."

"Why is that so unusual, Mr. Malloy? After all, she designed the test, didn't she?"

"That's just it, sir. She'd never seen the exam until the day she took it. She'd merely given the designers an idea of what she was looking for, but that was all. She'd had no role in the questions themselves, so there's no way she could have known what they would be."

"Okay, I still don't understand what the problem is, Frank. It sounds like she's the best candidate, so just offer her the job."

"*That's* the problem, Mr. President; I *have* offered her the position, but she won't accept it. I've been asking her since before the test results came in."

This caught Clark's attention. He was beginning to suspect who the mystery woman was. "So who is this wonder woman, Mr. Malloy? Perhaps I could have a word with her to see if I can persuade her that it's in the best interest of the Alliance and humanity that she accept."

"That's what I was hoping for, Mr. President; that's why I came, to ask for your help. Her name is Nicole Reynolds, sir. She's President

Reynolds's daughter, and Dr. Nick Reynolds's granddaughter."

"I see. And you're certain she's the best candidate to lead the expedition to colonize this new world?"

"Yes, sir, absolutely. She is by far the most qualified, except possibly for your predecessor."

"He decided he could accomplish the most good for humanity by representing Earth at the League of Sentient Species, and I suspect he may have been right. We won't get him, but Nicole—maybe. Give me a day or two and I'll try someone who has considerably more influence over her than I do. Check back with me tomorrow, Mr. Malloy. I'll let you know what I was able to accomplish, if anything."

"Yes sir. Thank you, Mr. President," Malloy said, shaking Clark's hand before leaving the office.

Joe Clark sat back in his chair and sighed, wondering how his predecessor would react. He pressed the button in his desk.

"Yes, Mr. President?"

"Please contact Dr. Hank Reynolds, and let me know when you have him. He should be on the planet Val by now."

"Yes, Mr. President." A few minutes later the holographic image of his receptionist appeared. "I have Dr. Reynolds on the line, sir."

"Okay, thank you."

"You're welcome, sir."

The image of Hank Reynolds appeared. "Hi, Joe, how are you? Don't tell me you're tired of the job already! It's all yours; I'm happy where I'm at now," Hank said with a big grin.

"No, at least not yet, Hank, thanks. So how is the ambassadorship working out?"

"It's unbelievable, it really is. It's everything I hoped it would be, and more. So, what's on your mind? I suspect you didn't call me just to talk shop."

"It's about Nicole, Hank."

"About Nikki? Is she okay? What has she done?"

"Everything's fine, Hank, don't worry. Actually, I called because I have a favor to ask."

Hank's bewilderment was evident, even from light years away. "What favor? Something to do with Nikki?"

"Well, yes. I'm sure you recall that expedition you authorized before I took office, the one to evaluate the list of ten planets the Valhari provided some years ago?"

"Yes, of course," Hank answered.

"Well, we'd very much like her to lead the expedition to select and then colonize the new world before something like Ronin comes our way again. As you know, citizens are screaming for us to do something about it. Your daughter scored so high on the selection test that it's absolutely ridiculous. I may be wrong, but I expect you're probably the only one who might have matched or beaten it."

"Yes, okay, so what do you want me to do?" he asked. "Have you spoken with her about it? What does she say?"

"She's refused to do it."

"Look, I agree that something needs to be done, and I can see why Nikki would be a great candidate, but Nikki's a grown woman, Joe, and if she doesn't want to do it then I can't force her."

"I know, Hank, but would you at least talk with her about it? You better than anyone know how stubborn she is at times. We need the very best to lead this expedition, for the sake of the human race. Who knows what we might find out there? We need someone like her—someone like you—to lead this first team. Please, Hank, talk to her for me, will you, please?"

There was a long pause on the line, and for a moment Clark was worried the connection had been severed and the hologram before him just frozen.

"So what do you say, Hank?" he asked, just in case the line was still open.

"I'll talk with her, Joe, see what I can do. Nicole usually listens to me—"

***

"No, absolutely not! I keep telling you, Dad, I'm not interested. I agreed to help them find the right people, and if they asked nicely I might even help them select the right planet, but go there? Help them establish a new colony there? I don't think so."

"Nikki, listen to me. I learned the other day from Zing himself that whatever changed me, whatever changed us, it wasn't the Valhari who did it."

"What? Then who—?"

"I don't know, Providence, maybe? Don't worry about that now, Nikki; just believe, as I do, that we were given these extraordinary gifts *for a reason*. I know you never wanted any part of the Alliance for yourself, but why not help lead humanity on its first planetary colonization?"

"Dad, I—"

"Nikki, Earth was nearly destroyed a few months ago by a rogue planet. Who's to say something like that won't happen again, only Earth gets destroyed next time? Now, I'm not trying to push you into doing this baby, because it's dangerous, and we both know it. I know how smart you are, however, and how tough. I'm just asking that you consider it." Hank watched over the Q-Link as his daughter struggled over what to do.

"It's not the danger, Dad, you know that."

"Yeah, I know, Nikki. Of everyone in our family, you thrive on danger more than anyone."

"It's just the politics, the responsibility. I'm only twenty-five, Dad; what do I know about colonizing a planet?"

"I was younger than that when I took an untested spaceship to Alpha Centauri, and your grandfather wasn't much older when he faced down a master spy and saved the world from the horrors of nuclear war. Age has nothing to do with it, sweetheart; it's about who you are, and who you are going to become. You'd be the one selecting the new planet for colonization, baby, the one shaping the direction of a new civilization on that planet, and you'd be cultivating resources on an alien world."

"I'll think about it, Dad, okay?"

"That's all I was asking you to do, honey. The choice is entirely yours, of course."

"So who put you up to this, Malloy?"

"Actually, it was President Clark."

"President Clark? Hmm, I figured Malloy. They must be pretty serious about this." The expression on her face suddenly changed. "Where are you now anyway, Dad? Have you already left for the Valhari home world?"

"I'm already here Nikki, I arrived a few days ago."

"Really? Wow, so what's it like to be on an alien world, living among members of an alien race?"

"Probably not so different from living among people from another country, really. The language is different, the culture is different, and the people are different. Yet they are not so different from us really."

Nicole nodded politely at her father. "What do you think I should do, Dad?"

"Like I said, honey, the choice is entirely yours."

"Well, I suppose I could put one of my company's vice-presidents in charge of the think tank for a while, just until I see how it goes."

"I'm sure you'll make the right decision, sweetheart. Okay, Nikki, I'd better run. I have an important meeting coming up I really need to attend. I love you, sweetheart!"

"Dad?"

"Yeah, Nikki?"

"Please tell President Clark that I'll do it," Nicole answered, nearly biting her lip.

"Are you sure, baby? It could be extremely dangerous…I just don't know."

"Maybe it is time for me to try something a little more challenging, and building a new world would definitely be challenging."

CHAPTER 9

Jack Lincoln exited the elevator and walked along the top floor of the Alliance Headquarters, following his Alliance military escort along the hallway which effectively cut the top floor into two halves, with offices on either side. Along the way he passed a number of holostations, which depicted various images related to the Earth Space Alliance's brief but rich and vibrant history. While not overly luxurious, the building itself was at the same time both simple and elegant, a mixture of cutting edge technology and nature, including small trees, bushes, flowers, and skylights that dotted the hallways and open areas. Translucent walls along the outside of the building provided for a flawless view of the beautiful blue sky without, as well as the many transport ships that scurried about.

Soon, they arrived at a small, indoor natural area, complete with small acacia and giant strelitzia trees, which surrounded an elegant marble fountain with water trickling down a beautiful emerald waterfall. Above the fountain was a holographic projection of the first spacecraft to ever carry a human being to another star system, the ship named Frontier. It sat suspended above the fountain at the center of the large room, while a holographic narrator told the story of how Hank Reynolds had been stranded in the Alpha Centauri system in the damaged ship until the Valhari had come to his aid. Scattered throughout the natural area were small rows of comfortable-looking seats, which afforded the best views of the scenery while also maximizing the effect. Surrounding the natural area were several large offices with beautiful mahogany doors, each bearing the occupants' names with important sounding titles like Director of Interplanetary Affairs, and Secretary of Earth-Based Technology Programs.

His escort led Jack to a small row of seats in a waiting area at the edge of the fountain, near one of the corner offices, where he joined a man and a woman already there, each dressed in formal business attire. Lincoln felt underdressed in his khaki pants, blue dress shirt, and red tie. The woman sneered at him in contempt and Jack merely smiled back and nodded his head, thankful that he was a pilot, not a businessman.

By the time fifteen minutes had passed, the man and the woman had each been greeted and escorted away by their respective hosts, leaving Jack to wait even longer, alone. A flurry of people were continually coming and going all around him, as they had been since he'd first arrived at the waiting area, evidence of the growing amount of activity at the Alliance. He glanced at the time projected from the small cube he wore on his wrist and began tapping his foot. He'd been anxiously awaiting an opportunity to meet with the expedition leader, but now that the time had come, he found himself just wanting to get it over with. Darren had wanted to come with him, but Jack had insisted on going alone, hoping to get a better feel for who they would be working with before subjecting his younger friend to the intense scrutiny that was sure to come. He'd heard stories about his new boss, but he tried not put much stock in what other people said, preferring to make his own assessment. He was startled when a young woman spoke from just over his right shoulder.

"Captain Lincoln? Dr. Reynolds is ready to see you now," the assistant informed him.

"Thank you," Lincoln replied, with more of an edge to his voice than he'd intended. He'd been forced to wait over an hour and he was livid, but he doubted it was the assistant's fault.

The young woman escorted him to the double-doors that led into the corner office. With a gentle tap the doors swung open to reveal a rather large but Spartan office, with large windows that overlooked the Potomac River. Directly in front of him sat a large beech wood desk, where an attractive woman with dark hair and emerald green eyes sat. She was incredibly beautiful, and for a moment he began to worry there'd been a mix-up, because the creature before him bore no semblance to the distasteful, sour woman he'd been warned about. He stood staring at her while she glanced over some documents on her console, surprised at both her looks and her age. When she looked up at him what really surprised him, however, was the brilliant green fire that burned in her eyes. They were both alluring and frightening, like the eyes of a beautiful yet deadly jungle cat. She gestured for Jack to take a seat without saying anything; he smiled, nodded, and sat down in a one of the two chairs in front of her desk, his earlier annoyance with the delay now only a distant memory. It was only after five minutes of awkward silence had passed that she finally turned her attention away from her virtual console, and after touching a couple of buttons, three planets appeared above the desk.

"Captain Lincoln," she began coldly and professionally. "I'd like for you to take me, and a select team of experts, to each of these planets as soon as possible. I've been tasked with evaluating their suitability for human life, and selecting the one that will ultimately become Earth's first planetary colony. We must leave within a week."

"Commander Darren and I can be ready tomorrow morning if we need to, Dr. Reynolds."

"That won't be necessary, Captain. Just have the ship ready to go by this time next week; we should be finished with the preparations by then, and we should have the final list of team members identified and onboard as well."

"How many people are you planning to take with you?"

"There could be fifty people or more, along with the equipment they need to conduct their research. Can you accommodate us?"

Jack looked at her and smiled, trying to retain as much professionalism as possible. "Yes, ma'am, that should be no problem whatsoever."

"Good. Thank you, Captain, you can go."

"It's a date, then," he said, smiling at her again. His smile was met with an icy stare. He rose to leave but was stopped before he reached the door.

"Captain, you've been to these three worlds already. Tell me what you think of them."

Jack stopped and turned to face her. He noticed that her demeanor had softened slightly as he began to carefully survey the images.

"Well, Dr. Reynolds, as you know we scouted New Eden, and planets V-9, and V-10. We were mildly impressed with V-9 and V-10, and they certainly would support a human colony, but—"

"You were far more impressed with New Eden?"

"Yes, how did you know?" he asked her, slightly puzzled.

"You gave planet V-8 a name, 'New Eden,' while you referred to the others by their assigned designation."

"Oh, yeah, I guess that's right. Commander Darren was so taken by the planet that he said it reminded him of what the Garden of Eden might have looked like. I guess it kind of stuck."

"It's adequate I suppose, Captain."

"We found plenty of vegetation, alien fruit, wildlife, water—"

"I already know all of this, Captain Lincoln, it was in the data and you included it in your reports."

"Of course."

"So what I'd really like to know is this; which of these three planets would *you* want to live on, and why?" she asked, gesturing to the three images between them.

"New Eden, Dr. Reynolds, definitely. The air was easy to breathe, there seemed to be plenty of raw materials, and there was plenty of water and food. Furthermore, the planet was simply amazing, Dr. Reynolds. Yes, I would definitely be comfortable living there." At this Dr. Reynolds's face remained expressionless; Jack questioned whether it was that way because she worked so hard to make it appear that way, or whether it was the real her.

"Okay, that will be all then. Thank you for the information, Captain. I look forward to seeing it for myself next week."

Jack turned and reached for the door before stopping short. He felt a question welling up inside him and he tried his best to suppress it, but it was hopeless. As he stood there staring at her, admiring her form and the fire in her eyes, the question burst forth like a volcanic eruption.

"Oh, there's one more thing, a question I'd like to ask you."

Nicole looked up at him, looking slightly annoyed. "What is it, Captain? I have a lot of work to do here."

"Well, I realize we've only just met, and I wanted to tell you that I believe you are truly a beautiful, attractive woman, Dr. Reynolds. But if I may, I'd like to suggest you might make yourself a little happier if you tried lightening up a little."

Nicole's face grew flushed. "What are you talking about?" she asked sharply.

"You're still so young, and yet you seem so…bitter. I imagine you don't even have a boyfriend, because you keep everyone at such a distance. What happened to make you this way?"

"You certainly have a lot of nerve, pal, talking to me like that," she said, pushing away from her desk before standing and walking over to stand directly in front of him. "You should know that I don't tolerate people talking to me that way."

Jack threw up his hands. "Listen, I'm not trying to be mean or disrespectful in any way, Dr. Reynolds. In fact, I'm merely trying to point out what a beautiful woman you are," he said, edging slightly closer. "And I know for a fact that if you gave up some of that bitterness and that hyper-aggressive attitude of yours a little, you could probably have most any man on the planet that you wanted. You just need to lighten up a little."

"Listen to me, Don Juan, Dear Abby, or Sigmund Freud, if you weren't one of the best pilots in the world, if you didn't have more time logged in the Alliance ships, and if you hadn't already been to all three planets, I would probably toss you out on your ear, myself."

Jack grinned. "I'll bet you'd enjoy that too, wouldn't you?"

"Aagghh!" Nicole grabbed him by his wrist, spun him around, and pulled his wrist up his back while applying pressure until he howled in pain.

"Hey, listen, Dr. Reynolds, maybe once I've flown you around some, you and I can go out, have some dinner, and then maybe take in a movie?"

"Out—now!" she exclaimed, shoving him out the door.

"Hey, what about—?"

"Oohh!" Nicole slammed the door with enough force that a stack of papers blew off her assistant's desk.

Nicole walked over to her desk and sat back down, flustered and unsure how to process what had just happened. She should probably have him kicked off the project for what he'd said to her. Perhaps she'd select the other pilot, the one who'd gone with Lincoln on their scouting expedition, to take her to visit the three worlds. Even as she considered the option, however, she already knew she'd not remove Lincoln from his post as captain of the expedition, and she had no idea why—it wasn't as if she'd never fired anyone before.

Nicole shook her head and cleared her mind, forcing herself to turn her attention back to the task at hand. She still had a team to put together and she had less than a week to pull it off. She would need a botanist to study the plants, zoologists to study the animal life, archeologists, geologists, biologists, climatologists, and engineers. She'd already narrowed the search for each specialist down to a handful of highly-qualified people in each category, but now it was getting tough. She knew that she wouldn't be entirely satisfied with any choice she made, nor would she be entirely disappointed either. After another two hours of painstaking effort, she had her selections made and ranked in order by number. She would have her assistant go down the list and start calling the following morning. Soon, she would have her team assembled, a group of scientists and a dozen armed Alliance soldiers who would provide security and help with setting up and breaking down temporary habitats. A few more non-specialist slots remained to be filled, but she would have no difficulty selecting them.

One thing troubled her, however, as she packed everything up at the end of a very long day to head home. She'd taken much longer than she should have going through the lists, and it was all because of *him*. She'd been unable to get him out of her mind the rest of the day. He was incorrigible, insulting, and...charming? She flicked the light switch and walked out, uncertain about what it all meant.

CHAPTER 10

Professor Steven Sherman had been teaching archaeology at North Carolina State University for the past five years. A consummate archaeologist, he loved everything about his field, from the digging at the excavation sites to the piecing together of historical puzzles to teaching in the classroom; it was his world and it meant everything to him. The only other thing in his life more important to him during that time had been his wife, Edith, an attractive, unassuming woman of thirty, the same age as himself, who taught at the university's school of nursing.

It was just the two of them at home, except for Puckett, their dog, and Anthony and Cleopatra, the couple's two cats. It was not the way they had intended for their lives to turn out, of course. Like so many other young couples, they had once had dreams of a house full of children, of attending baseball games, and of enjoying family vacations at the beach. But those dreams had slowly faded away, giving place instead to an unexpected and unwelcomed emptiness in their lives.

The couple had tried for years to have children, but their determined effort ultimately proved fruitless. Once the tests had finally confirmed their suspicions, the topic of adoption had slowly crept into the occasional dinner conversation, before turning, over time, into a painful, annual ritual. Each year the topic of conversation would suddenly rear its head, an unexpected guest at breakfast, lunch, or dinner. Sometimes, while the pair sat relaxing together in the living room or just before bed, they would draw up a list of the pros and the cons of adopting, listing the many activities that they could do together with their children, before quietly going back to what they'd been doing, never returning to the topic again for another year or so.

Steven had long ago formed the opinion that the couple *should* try to adopt, because a family and a house full of children had always been the dream they shared, and because he knew how important it was to Edith. Following the years of disappointment, however, his wife had eventually succumbed to doubt, fearful of more heartbreak and uncertain if she could endure the grueling adoption process. Given how difficult adoptions had become, Edith also questioned whether they could afford the expense, and she doubted they would meet all of the government's extremely stringent criteria for adopting, which had nearly vanished as an institution.

Husband and wife had just finished another such conversation at the dinner table, with Steven once more trying to convince Edith they should at least try, that there was always a chance they might get lucky and an adoption would go through. As before, however, she would walk through the process with him, wanting so badly to push forward that she would edge ever closer towards making the call, before backing away at the last moment out of fear.

So the distraught couple had retired once more to the living room, where he picked up his data pad and began thumbing through one of his favorite non-fiction publications, Westmoreland's *Field Guide to the Archaeology of the Earth*. It was this same work that had inspired him to write his own, even more ambitious book, *Sherman's Field Guide to Extraterrestrial Archaeology: First Edition*. He'd written his book based on the volumes of research he'd acquired over the course of his years working at the Earth Space Alliance, including what he'd been able to glean from his many contacts there. And then, of course, there was also the vast amount of data collected from his many requests to the League of Sentient Species through the League's ambassador to the Alliance. Sherman had initially developed the book merely as an attempt to start a conversation and not to be a definitive work of science, but it had grown into something far greater along the way, the most comprehensive and exhaustive material on alien cultures and their histories to be found anywhere on the planet. The book was an overnight success, though not without its detractors.

The scientific community had been in an uproar over the information contained within the work, with cynics stoking a bonfire of controversy as to it's veracity. Frequently calling attention to the fact that Sherman had rarely left the country, much less Earth, the naysayers called the facts and conclusions detailed in the work as "junk science."

Steven decided to abandon his book and switched over to one of the larger newspapers, which included reviews of recent bestsellers. He'd only been scanning it for a few seconds when he came across something of keen interest.

"Unbelievable! Listen to this guy's review of my book, Edith," he exclaimed, nearly shouting to his wife, who was in the kitchen.

"'Professor Steven Sherman's recent work, *Sherman's Field Guide to Extraterrestrial Archaeology: First Edition*, would have been more aptly named, 'Sherman's Shoddy, Half-Baked, Pseudo-Scientific, Grossly

Flawed, and Unimaginative Comic Book.' The work is replete with supposition, guesswork, and third-party accounts of what past civilizations on alien worlds *might* have been like. Sherman's work includes no definitive evidence that these ancient, alien civilizations ever even existed, let alone that they even remotely resembled the way they are depicted in the book. With such maligning of the facts, perhaps Sherman is more suited to be a professor of literature, rather than archaeology.'" Sherman threw his data pad against a pillow on the sofa, where it bounced before settling, just as Edith walked back into the living room and sat down beside him.

"Come on, Steve, we both knew this was going to happen. It was a risk publishing a book like this having never been off-world, but think about it; you've published the first archaeological work on alien civilizations. That's amazing!"

Her husband frowned before starting to nod his head, and tried to smile. "Thanks, sweetheart. I guess I need to stop reading these stupid reviews, don't I?"

Edith nodded immediately. *"Before* you have a heart attack, if you please," she said with a smile, looking into his eyes before wrapping her arms around her husband's neck and pulling him close. The moment was interrupted, however, by an unexpected phone call. Steven took a sip of wine before reaching over to press a button on the device. An image of a beautiful young woman with blue eyes and blonde hair, which she wore in a long ponytail, appeared. She seemed to be in her mid-twenties, and was sharply dressed in business attire.

"Hello?"

"Good evening. Are you Steven Sherman...*Professor* Steven Sherman?"

"Yes I am. And you are?"

"My name is Rebecca Worthington, Professor Sherman. I work for Dr. Nicole Reynolds at the Earth Space Alliance. Dr. Reynolds will soon be leading a major expedition for the Alliance, an exciting and challenging mission, one which we thought you might be very interested in."

"Oh? Can you tell me more about it?"

"I'm afraid *I* can't, Professor. Dr. Reynolds can, however, and she'd like to invite you to her office to discuss this opportunity in person, assuming you're interested, of course. If you are, there's also some paperwork we'll need for you to sign, including some non-disclosure papers and such."

"When?"

"Tomorrow morning at 10:00 A.M. Can you make it?"

"Tomorrow morning? No, I can't, I have a class, I don't know how…"

"I understand, Professor. But I should warn you, however, that we have a very tight schedule to hold to. If you're interested in learning more and possibly being a part of it, you'll need to come in tomorrow morning to meet with Dr. Reynolds."

"Can you tell me anything about this expedition, where it's headed? Is it Egypt? Africa? China? Europe?"

"Let's just say that you'll find this expedition to be 'out of this world.'"

"Oh, I see. But, um…what about my wife?"

"I understand that she's a nurse?"

"Why yes, she is, but—"

"Excellent. Bring her with you tomorrow morning; I promise you, Professor Sherman, you will not be disappointed. I'm sending you the address and phone number. Take your time deciding, Professor. All we ask is that you call in by 7:00 A.M. tomorrow and leave a message with your decision. Please remember that coming in doesn't commit you to anything other than what's covered in the non-disclosure, and you're certainly not committed to participating in the expedition until you sign-on for it. Do you have any questions?"

Steven looked at his wife, who now sat across from him wearing a puzzled expression before shrugging her shoulders.

"No, I guess not."

"Very good then, Professor. Well, we look forward to seeing you tomorrow morning, should you decide to come in. Have a very pleasant evening."

"Thank you, you too."

The hologram disappeared and the couple sat staring at one another for several seconds, saying nothing.

"What was that all about, Steven?" Edith asked at length.

"I'm not sure, Eadie. I've heard rumors, but I really didn't believe it; I guess they're really going to do it."

"Do what, honey?"

"Unless I'm mistaken, I believe they're making plans for colonizing another planet, and we've just been invited to go!"

CHAPTER 11

The conference room was nearing capacity as people continued filing in for the pre-flight departure session Nicole had scheduled. She glanced around the room at the faces of the individual men and women present there, each of them highly qualified, and each one part of a couple or small family that had committed to living long-term on whichever planet was ultimately selected for colonization, pledging to make it their new home.

Time was growing short with their scheduled departure now only an hour away. Nicole waited another ten minutes before doing another headcount. The team's headcount had grown to forty-three people, with another hundred people in attendance, including the shuttle pilots and various key Alliance personnel associated with the program. Satisfied that everyone was present, she walked over to the podium to get things started. Behind her, at a table facing the attendees, sat Frank Malloy, the Director of Special Projects at the Earth Space Alliance, and Joseph Clark, President of the Earth Space Alliance.

"Okay everyone, we don't have much time now before departure, so we need to review the mission once more and afterwards, Alliance President Joseph Clark and Director of Special Projects Frank Malloy would like to say a few words.

"To begin with, I would like to restate our objective; this mission is to survey the three planets being considered for human colonization. Based on what we find on each world, we will determine which one is most suitable as a new home for humanity, and that world will be the first to be colonized. As you know, this effort has been given top priority by the Alliance following the recent near-collision with the rogue planet named Ronin. We will have twenty-one days, one week per planet, before returning to Earth, whereupon those who are still willing to go will work to finalize preparations for the colonization. Now, I don't want to paint too rosy a picture of this endeavor. Without question there will be challenges, hardships, and danger; we are going to encounter situations and predicaments no human being has ever had to face before. It will also be an incredible adventure filled with wonder, discovery, and awe. We'll be the first of humanity to live on an earthlike planet outside of the solar system, where we'll encounter all sorts of creatures that have never before been seen by human eyes; in short, the great privilege of building a new world. As you've all been told, in return for the enormous effort it will take to settle and build a civilization on this new world, you will each be rewarded with two sizeable plots of land to call your own, one near the initial settlement, the other located somewhere else on the planet. The Alliance may also authorize additional land grants, dependent on how events unfold. Shuttles will be flown between this new world and Earth on a regular, fixed schedule—at least every other week to begin with. Eventually, we anticipate shuttles to run at least once a day between the two worlds. This is an extraordinarily exciting time to be alive, and I'm very grateful to all of you for your willingness to be a part of it.

"Now, with that out of the way, please allow me to introduce the man who convinced me that *I* should be a part of this grand adventure, Director Frank Malloy." Nicole began clapping her hands and everyone else in the room soon followed. Frank Malloy shook Nicole's hand before taking her place at the podium.

"Thank you, Dr. Reynolds, for that introduction. To be truthful, I was afraid that she would not accept this position, given her enormous success with her own company. She was our first and really our only choice for this unique position of leadership. We haven't asked her yet, but it is certainly our hope that Dr. Reynolds will also accept the position as the first governor of this new world. After an initial term of four years there would be a general election and the inhabitants would be given the opportunity to select a new leader, though I seriously doubt any of you will want that to happen when the time comes. She has what is almost certainly the greatest intellect on our planet, and I can honestly say that it is my firm belief that there is no one on Earth who would make a finer leader for his new world...with the possible exception of President Clark, of course!" Malloy added with a smile, after casting a glance towards Clark.

"No, seriously, I too want to thank each and every one of you for being here today, helping to ensure the future continuity of the human race. There's not much time remaining now," he said, pointing to a countdown clock on the wall beside him, "so without further adieu, please permit me to introduce the head of the Earth Space Alliance, President Joseph Clark!" Once more the room burst into applause. President Clark shook hands with Nicole and Malloy before walking to the podium, motioning for everyone to quiet down.

"Dr. Reynolds and Director Malloy," Clark began, "words alone cannot convey the sense of pride, hope, and appreciation I have for you in your effort to carry humanity permanently out into the cosmos. Since the beginning of humanity itself, our fate has been tied directly to that of the planet on which we were created, Earth. Soon, thanks to the extraordinary efforts of everyone here, for the first time humanity will soon be spreading out into the vast, amazing universe in which we live. We now know that we are not alone, so we can expect to find plenty of company out there. In fact, Nicole Reynolds's father, Dr. Hank Reynolds, recently traveled to the Valahari's home world of Val, the current headquarters for the League of Sentient Species, where he serves as humanity's first ambassador. It truly is a remarkable, wonderful time to be alive."

Clark glanced over at the clock and started shaking his head. "You know how we politicians are," he said with a smile. "I could go on talking all day and all night, but then those of you going on this little expedition would miss your flight. I will end, therefore, by quoting a former president of the United States, Ronald Reagan. 'Mankind's journey into space, like every great voyage of discovery, will become part of our unending journey of liberation. In the limitless reaches of space, we will find liberation from tyranny, from scarcity, from ignorance and from war. We will find the means to protect this Earth and to nurture every human life, and to explore the universe.... This is our mission, this is our destiny.'

"With that, I wish you safe journey, great success, and may God bless you on this grand endeavor."

***

It had been seven hours since they left Earth, and despite the initial awe and wonder the expedition members had initially felt at traveling through deep space, Nicole noticed that it was wearing thin after so long. The trip was comfortable and the ships were spacious enough to allow them room to move about freely, but some of the passengers were already feeling slightly claustrophobic. Fortunately, the ships actually contained two levels, not unlike some of the larger airplanes from the late twentieth and early twenty-first centuries. The top deck included the bridge, main engineering, navigation, and a small recreational area, while the bottom deck included valuable cargo space, sleeping quarters, and general living space. Overall the ships were designed much like the original Prometheus ship, capable of carrying sufficient supplies and comfortable enough for extended, long duration flights when necessary.

After mingling with some the passengers for a while, Nicole decided to pay the ship's captain and his co-pilot, a younger man named Hal Blankenship, a visit on the flight deck to see how they were doing. She and Jack had both been disappointed when Luke Darren had turned down the opportunity to colonize another world, but with a new baby for Luke and his wife to think of, she could hardly blame him.

She found Jack in the pilot's chair, wearing the cyber interface helmet. Her father and grandfather had told her about the device, which linked the wearer with the ship's living navigational computer system, but seeing it firsthand gave her a sense of awe. With so much going on, it had never occurred to her to ask anyone how she would communicate with the crew while they were wearing the helmets.

"Um, Jack?"

"Hello, Dr. Reynolds. Is there something I can do for you, in regards to the trip I mean?" he added with a smile. "We can talk about dinner and a movie once we get back to Earth, unless you'd rather not wait, of course."

Nicole ignored his advances, more interested at the moment in how he was able to communicate with her. "How is it you are able to converse with me so easily? Aren't you interfaced with the Entelli now?" She looked at him and could see that he certainly didn't seem to be awake. "How can you see to fly with your eyes closed?"

"Oh, my eyes are open, in a virtual sense anyway. The Entelli create a virtual representation of everything going on in and around the ship. From my point of view you're standing here next to me. I suppose from your point of view, it must be a little strange, huh?"

"You could say that," she replied.

"Interesting. So what can I do for you, Doc?"

"I was wondering how much longer it will be until we reach V-10." She looking at him with a perplexed, troubled look. She found the unusual manner of communication troubling.

"We're just about there, Dr. Reynolds. I was going to make an announcement in just a few minutes. You might want to start getting the passengers suited up and ready to go. We have just under a week on V-10 before it's time to pack up and leave for V-9. I expect they're going to need all of the time they can find to get their experiments up and running before it's time to break them back down again. Any ideas how many sites you'll want to visit on V-10?"

"No, not really. We've identified a few sites that looked interesting, but we never made anything definite. What do you suggest?" she asked him with a sharp edge still in her voice, a lingering souvenir left over from their previous encounter. "After all, you *have* been there before."

"Well, the world looked much the same to me all over; light vegetation, sparse, scattered populations of indigenous animal life, and not much else. There's a spot near one of the planet's larger bodies of water we might want to take a look at, given the importance of a sufficient supply of water. Then there's a large valley nestled in the middle of a range of mountains on the other side of the planet. I'd think that sticking to one or both of those should be sufficient."

"Okay, fair enough. Let's set down in the valley first. Later, if we have time, we'll swing by the large body of water before heading to V-9."

"Whatever you say, Doc."

"Stop calling me that!"

"Whatever you say, Doc."

Nicole stormed off of the bridge, once again irritated with the arrogant and abrasive captain, and once again finding him both annoying and interesting at the same time.

Within a few minutes, Lincoln made the announcement that they were approaching the planet, and the passengers gathered in the main living area. Nicole walked over to a communications console and pressed a button.

"Yes?"

"Captain, we're all gathered in the main living area, and we were wondering whether you could give us all a view of the approaching planet."

"Certainly, ma'am. You and the others might want to have a seat, since it can be a little disorienting the first time."

"Of course."

A few seconds later the walls surrounding the living area slowly faded away, revealing the vast expanse of space on the other side. Where the front wall of the living area had once been they could now see a large planet, designated simply as V-10 by the Valhari, who had provided the Alliance the list of worlds suitable, in their view, for human habitation.

Within moments the ship entered the planet's atmosphere before plunging into a thick white layer of clouds that also had a slight silver tint to them. It emerged on the other side to reveal a planet that appeared to be, in some ways, much like Earth, with massive blue oceans, green vegetation, and brown land masses. There were also specs of white visible, which Nicole took be enormous, snow-capped mountains. Given the planet was considerably larger than Earth, Nicole knew the mountains, which at first appeared to be about the same size as on Earth, were in reality at least a hundred times larger than any mountains back home. There were also patches of red scattered across each of the various landmasses, a strange and inexplicable presence for which she could only speculate, concluding it could only be some type of plant life or algae.

The ship decelerated as it drew closer to the planet's surface and she spotted two mountains of such enormous size they had vegetation growing only around their bases. The top halves appeared to be only rock, with the tops capped off with snow and ice.

The time to disembark was fast approaching, and her thoughts soon turned to safety and the atmosphere on the planet. Based on data collected during the earlier scouting trip, it consisted mostly of inert, harmless gasses, which could be safely breathed in by human beings. These gases would act much like nitrogen in Earth's own atmosphere. V-10 also had twice the oxygen content of Earth, which scientists had long conjectured could enhance human life expectancy.

"Everyone please be seated, we're about to land," the captain announced over the ship's speakers.

Less than thirty seconds later the ship sat down in a valley located between the two massive mountain ranges Nicole had seen earlier. In the distance, she could see that her guess about the red vegetation was true. Red grasses and bushes covered the ground some distance from where they sat. Scanning as much of the landscape around the ship as possible before leaving the ship, Nicole turned 180 degrees to find a large body of water behind her, an enormous lake that she earnestly hoped they would find to be full of fresh-water. Her evaluation of the planet's surface was interrupted by the appearance of a holographic image of Captain Lincoln.

"Ladies and gentlemen, welcome to planet V-10. Instruments confirm that the air outside would technically be safe to breath, were it not for the certain presence of unknown alien pathogens and our bodies' lack of natural defenses against such pathogens. For the health and safety of everyone on this ship I must therefore insist that each of you wear your atmospheric regulators at all times while outside of the ship. In just a minute I'll be lowering the ramp for you to disembark, but first, I'd like to stress a few additional safety guidelines. Each of you will need to carry a pulse-rifle or a pulse-pistol as well as your personal shields, which you are required to carry on your person at all times. Stay in groups of three or more, with one person keeping watch at all times. I scouted this planet not too long ago, and while we didn't see any dangerous predators, that doesn't mean they're not here, understood? There's more of us here this time and we'll be making a lot more noise, so stay alert; it could save your life. I'd also like to encourage each and every one of you to remember the cause-of-death waivers you signed before coming on this trip. You were required to sign those waivers for one simple reason…you could die here; so let's try to avoid that and stay on alert, hmm? We have no idea what life forms are here, and it's my job to try to keep you alive. Any questions?" They stood together in silence until someone finally spoke up.

"How long will we be here, Captain?" Nicole turned to see Edith Sherman standing next to her husband.

"Well, we have less than a week at each planet, so figure on seventy-two hours in between setting up camp and then tearing it back down. We can stay an extra day, if needed, and simply make it up on another trip.

"Oh, one more thing, I'd like for each person's first time off the ship to be without any of your gear or instruments, and just long enough for you to get the lay of the land. Once we know it's safe, you can unload your instruments and begin your testing. Okay everyone, enjoy!"

Nicole quickly raised her hand. "Wait! Listen up everyone, I need all of you to stand in a line. I'll walk along the line, and when I come to you please count off. Once I'm finished you need to gather into ten groups; I'll join the smallest group to raise the number. Okay, let's do it."

Everyone quickly complied, clearly eager to take their first step onto an alien world. A few minutes later they were standing in their respective groups.

"Now before we disembark," Nicole announced as she joined the smallest team, "I'll say it one last time; please be sure to inspect each other's suits to ensure there are no tears, and that they remain airtight. I can't stress how important this is. Each of the three planets we'll be visiting this week have alien, microscopic organisms. While we could breathe this air, like the captain said our bodies will have no defense against the alien microbes; most if not all of us would die without the proper inoculations. We'll then decontaminate each time as we re-enter the ship, is that clear?"

"Why can't we simply go ahead and get the inoculations so we don't need the atmospheric regulators?" one of the junior scientists, a young man in his early twenties, asked.

"Because, Dr. Ransfordt, we felt it was unwise to fill your bodies full of vaccines for alien microbes unless it was absolutely necessary. Once we select a planet for colonization, you can rest assured that you and anyone else visiting the planet will receive the proper injections." Ransfordt nodded sheepishly, suddenly aware of how his over eagerness had led him to ask such a question.

"Okay then," Nicole said, looking back at Ransfordt. "If there are no further questions why don't we step outside for a few minutes to see what we can find, shall we?"

The hatch opened and the expedition members began filing out of the ship and onto the ramp, before leaving the ramp to take their first steps out onto a strange, new world. Nicole looked over the group as they made their way out of the ship, many of them with expressions of awe and wonder on their faces, with others registering the assorted expressions of anticipation, excitement, and fear. While most of them had taken Lincoln's warnings to heart, no one truly expected that one of their number would die here.

CHAPTER 12

"So what do you think so far, Dr. Reynolds?"

Jack Lincoln had come up behind her while she was scanning the horizon with the binoculars, with a cool wind from over the water of a nearby lake caressing her face. While it was somewhat cool despite the bright sun, the savannah-like landscape resembled something one might find in parts of Africa. Though she couldn't see it from where she stood, she had seen from the air that the nearby lake was enormous, nearly as large as one of Earth's oceans. She turned to face Jack before answering him. Under the light of the bright sun, she considered that he seemed considerably more handsome than she'd first thought.

"I suppose it's somewhat different from what I thought it would be, but I can see it being a potential site for a colony. We'll have to see what some of the test results look like. Based on the data you brought back for us, there's less usable land mass here than on the other two, but so far, we've seen no dangerous predators; in fact, we haven't seen any animal life at all now that I think about it. How odd," she added, now looking around, searching for any movement of life in the vicinity. Her search was interrupted when Susan Fitzgerald, a thirty-five year old woman and the zoologist on the expedition, walked over to her.

"Excuse me, Dr. Reynolds."

"Yes, Susan, what is it?"

"You asked us to let you know if we found anything unusual."

"Of course. What did you find?"

"Okay, so all indications are that this area is, or once was, home to an indigenous life form, something that is roughly akin to an antelope or a deer back on Earth. We found the remains of quite a few animals over by the edge of the lake just north of here."

"Okay, so where are the rest of the animals now?" Nicole asked, suddenly acutely aware of how significant the absence of animal life near such an abundant water supply was.

"Well, that's just it…according to Dr. Stoneway, the climatologist, this area is most likely in the middle of its dry season; there should be *plenty* of life here. This lake is an incredibly important fresh water source for any nearby life; in fact, it's the only source for a hundred kilometers. We ran some tests and it is mostly fresh water, so animals would have no reason to stray too far from it."

Nicole stopped to ponder the enigma. She knew her zoologist had uncovered something unusual, and significant. The real question was whether it was important enough for them to take valuable time away from other sites to investigate. She decided to leave it to the specialist.

"I noticed that as well, Susan; it's a bit eerie, isn't it? So what are you thinking? Is this something we should be concerned about, or is it something we could re-visit at a later date, once the decision's been made? We still have two more sites to visit on V-10 before moving on to V-9."

"Look, Nicole, I'm not going to beat around the bush on this one...the lack of animal life really worries me."

"Keep in mind it's an alien—"

"I understand that, but please keep in mind what you told me when you selected me for this expedition; I'm good at what I do. By the time I was contacted by your staff I had already spent a considerable amount of time over the last decade or so studying what data we had on non-sentient animal life forms on other planets in the galaxy. While there appears to be a considerable amount of diversity throughout the known universe just as there is back on Earth, there are also quite a few common, consistent traits we've found on nearly all of the worlds we've studied where life is found. One of the prerequisites for animal life, just as with sentient beings, is an abundant water supply; life nearly always tends to congregate around water supplies. We see this everywhere on Earth."

"I agree, what we have here certainly is disconcerting."

"When we examined the jaw structures and the teeth of the animals we found, we found that most, if not all of them, were herbivores. Based on the proximity of the remains to the water, the poor creatures were probably drinking at the edge when...something happened to them."

"Well, there you go, Susan. They were probably attacked by predators."

"Yes," Fitzgerald agreed, "that's pretty much where I've been heading with this. We found some teeth marks in a nearly all of the bones, though to be frank with you there wasn't much left to work with. It looked as if they'd been torn to pieces and nearly completely devoured. The only problem is that there are no signs of predators in the area, anywhere! We should see some kind of signs—droppings, tracks, something. I don't understand it."

"Maybe the predators simply left the area and then afterwards something, a storm maybe, covered their tracks," Nicole offered.

"I suppose that's *possible*," the zoologist replied weakly, clearly not buying into the dubious possibility. "But I don't know how—"

The conversation between the two women was unexpectedly interrupted by the sound of a woman's high-pitched shriek, followed by a man yelling.

"Run! Everyone—the lake, they're coming—we've got to get out of here, now!"

Nicole looked around to see where the screams were coming from before determining they were coming from the other side of a small hill directly in front of her. She ran to the edge of the hill for a better view and, looking down, saw one of the scientists racing toward them, with her husband no more than a hundred meters behind her. More screams erupted as everyone began running from the lake and toward the ship. In the distance she could see the reason why.

Something was emerging from the lake, bizarre-looking creatures with both fins and scales, legs and fur. The monsters were two to three times the size of a man, with large, powerful jaws and razor-sharp teeth. At the end of their webbed hands were long dangerous claws. To Nicole, the creatures looked like something out of a horror movie, or some kind of bizarre experiment in evolution, a creature perfectly at home in the water but with legs and hands that enabled them to move about on land. In the few seconds she took to assess the invaders, Nicole noticed they seemed to be crawling out of the water on their knees, leaping in a manner similar to frogs when they were in proximity to one of her team.

Suddenly it all made sense. The creatures had probably crept up stealthily on the herbivores as they stood on the shore of the lake lapping up water. The watery predators had almost certainly used their powerful legs to propel them out of the water and upon the unsuspecting animals standing on the banks, thereby leaving no tracks. With their potential prey too far away from the lake this time, however, the predators had been forced to abandon their more reliable stealth attack and their watery home. Nicole could see that as big and bulky as the attackers were, however, they could still move surprisingly fast on land; her team didn't have much time. While most of the expedition members had already made for the ship, some lingered, as if transfixed by the surreal but deadly situation.

"Hurry, everyone; run for the ship, now!" Team members were running towards the ship from all directions. Nicole pressed a button on her comwatch; an image of Lincoln appeared. "Captain, please, we need your help; bring weapons!" Lincoln, who'd been on the bridge studying some star maps, grabbed two pulse rifles, pulled his pulse pistol, and ran for the ramp. In the distance he could see people racing toward him as if running for their lives. Jack exited the ship and ran past them in the opposite direction; soon he was next to Nicole overlooking the beach.

"What's going on? What the...?" People were now running in all directions trying to escape the growing horde of beasts. "You've got pulse weapons, people; you'd better start using them, and I mean now!" Handing Nicole one of the rifles, Jack holstered his pistol, and after taking the other rifle in his arms they both began firing at the creatures. The mad rush by the alien predators toward the expedition members continued, undeterred by the colorful blasts of energy weapons striking the lake and shore all around them.

Then one of the animals closest to the team was struck by a plasma blast and killed, collapsing in a heap near the lake's edge. The line of creatures emerging up the bank suddenly stopped advancing, each of them now motionless, staring in surprise at the body of their fallen comrade on the shore. The deadly creatures kept their distance as the scientists continued scrambling away from the lake and toward the ship, watching as the last of the groups came running toward the ship from further down the shoreline.

The last member, Steven Sherman, ran for his life along with his wife toward Jack and Nicole, struggling to catch up to the others, pursued by several of the creatures that had not witnessed the fate of their fellow.

"Hurry, Steve! We've got to get out of here!" Nicole watched on in dread and terror as the couple raced toward them, and she could they would be unable to outrun the creatures, which seemed to be quite nimble on the ground despite being water-dwellers. When she saw that they were now only twenty-five meters away, Nicole started to breathe easier, even permitting herself a brief smile at Jack, who continued firing at the attackers pursuing the couple. Just as she turned back toward the pair, however, she noticed a quick movement out of the corner of her eye, like a flash of lightning. One of the beasts had leapt out of the water with blinding speed before locking its jaws and claws around Edith's leg. It had already drug her to the edge of the water before the first shot was fired, which missed, striking the water less than a meter from the creature's head. By the time the second blast was fired, the creature, and Edith, were gone. Two more blasts from Jack's pulse rifle found their mark, and two of the creatures in the group of pursuers dropped to the ground, dead. As before the pursuers stopped, repeating the scene from earlier.

Nicole watched on in despair with tears streaming down her face as Steve Sherman reached them. Upon seeing Nicole's face, however, he immediately turned around to where his wife should have been. The shock on his face when he couldn't find her struck Nicole like a slap across the face. It took a moment before the shock wore off enough for the awful truth to sink in for Steve Sherman.

"Edith—Edith!" he screamed, trying to race back toward the lake where the hungry hunters were waiting. Nicole recognized that the shock of seeing their own dead had finally worn off on the alien creatures when they began racing out to meet Sherman. Man and alien were no more than twenty-five meters apart when Jack and two other men snatched up Sherman and ran back toward the ship. Two men armed with rifles near where Jack had been sitting earlier fired plasma into the approaching horde, felling several more of them but failing to stop the rest this time. Seconds later Jack and the two men arrived back at the ramp and dragged the screaming man inside the ship, just in time to close the door before the first of the beasts slammed into the ship, followed in turn by many others. The creatures emitted eerie howls, which sounded more like whale songs than growls.

With everyone but Edith Sherman now on board, Jack jumped into his chair and took hold of the manual controls. The ship quickly responded and jerked up into the air. A number of the creatures could be seen falling off the ship while the remainder stood outside, howling upwards as the craft began moving towards the part of the lake where they'd last seen Edith. The ship sat hovering over the lake for almost an hour, with a number of the passengers and crew searching in vain for any sign of Edith. Nicole tightened her lips and noticed Jack doing the same, knowing as they searched that Edith Sherman was dead. Even if she'd somehow survived the vicious attack, she would have drowned long ago.

Nicole bit down on her lip, angry with herself for allowing one of the expedition members, someone *she* was responsible for, to die. The expedition leader shook her head as blood began trickling down from her lip. Nicole wiped her mouth and began making her way for the first aid kit. She took from it a pneumatic syringe and inserted a vial filled with sedative. She walked over to where Steve Sherman stood frozen in a state of shock, still restrained by two men. Nicole's heart grew ever heavier as Sherman babbled on, sometimes incoherently, about his wife and how she must still be alive. Sometimes he would scream, insisting that the captain let him go to find his wife, while at other times he would stand frozen, staring out a porthole at the surface of the water. With a quick and fluid movement Nicole inserted the syringe into his neck, injecting the chemicals directly into his carotid artery. Seconds later, Dr. Steven Sherman lay mercifully sleeping on a bed in the small infirmary, still restrained and with an Alliance guard posted to keep an eye on him should he awake. Satisfied Sherman would be out until sometime the following day, Nicole walked up to Captain Jack Lincoln.

"Take it up, Captain, we're done here." Jack turned toward her with a momentary flash of anger in his eyes. Nicole looked back at him calmly and impassively, conveying with her eyes what she felt in her heart, that she too felt as if they were abandoning Edith, while at the same time knowing with a certainty that she was dead. Nicole hoped that he would understand the heavy burden she now carried, that he would recognize in her eyes the look of a leader who would forever carry the painful weight of losing someone under their command. She decided he must have, because his eyes softened seconds later and he offered a kind smile.

"Yes ma'am, of course; there's nothing more for us here. Where to, Dr. Reynolds?"

"Just away from this cursed planet, Jack. Let's try V-9. This time, we're going to be a whole heck of a lot more cautious."

Edith Sherman was gone and there was nothing they could do. Nicole had no idea what she was going to say to Steve Sherman when he awoke. Two things she did know for certain, however, planet V-10 was off the list, and she was going to have a word with the Valhari.

CHAPTER 13

Nicole was impressed. Clark had been fully engaged throughout her lengthy presentation, and he'd asked more than a few probing questions about planet V-8, now commonly referred to as New Eden, as well as the others. They'd already discussed the death of Dr. Edith Sherman at length in private, soon after she arrived back on Earth, so it had been pointless to bring it up for discussion during the presentation, other than during the discussion about V-10 and the dangers associated with that particular world.

She'd had her doubts in the past about the new president of the Earth Space Alliance, especially since he was taking over for her father and grandfather, who'd each left behind some sizeable shoes to fill. But Joseph Clark was proving to be everything people had said he was prior to the election. He was a kind, friendly, and determined man, and she found him to be very personable in groups and one-on-one settings as well. He seemed to be a courageous man of character and conviction, willing to sacrifice his new position and perhaps life itself if necessary, in order to do the best he could in service to humanity. Nicole clicked off the holographic projector.

"And that's about all I have for you this morning, ladies and gentlemen."

President Clark was the first to speak up. "What about Planet V-9, Dr. Reynolds? It seems to me it was considerably larger than Earth, and it appears to have more land mass and natural resources."

Nicole looked down for a moment, remembering what her father had taught her growing up; *be patient with them, they're not like us...not yet.*

"Yes, Mr. President, that is true; V-9 is somewhat larger than Earth, it has greater land mass, and it has *some* additional natural resources. But one thing it doesn't have as much of is a very essential ingredient to all life, water. It therefore lacks the same quantity of oxygen-producing vegetation, and so it is, therefore, slightly more difficult to breathe. Now don't get me wrong, we could turn V-9 into a colony, as we could V-10, with varying degrees of intervention. In the case of V-9 we'd have to find a way to address the water issue, possibly finding and releasing water from the icecaps. In the case of V-10, we'd obviously have to learn more about and deal with the deadly creatures we encountered there before we could even consider colonizing it."

"I see. You seem quite taken with Planet V-8, Dr. Reynolds, the one you referred to as—'New Eden' was it?"

"Yes, New Eden, Mr. President," Captain Jack Lincoln offered with a smile, earning him a cool look from Nicole.

"I was quite taken with New Eden, Mr. President. It's a beautiful world, exquisite even. Lush vegetation, temperate climate, an abundance of water. It's amazing. You saw the images from the holorecorder, sir; surely you agree!"

Clark nodded. "No, you're quite right, Dr. Reynolds, it was indeed remarkably beautiful. What about predators like the ones you found on V-10?"

"There are predators and abundant wildlife, sir, but they certainly pose no threat to human beings. They scattered whenever we were near, and all of them seemed extremely docile as far as predators go. Remember too, Mr. President, that New Eden is also larger than Earth, with a proportionate amount of land and water, though not quite as large as V-9 or V-10."

Clark still wore a look on consternation on his face. "And there was nothing about this, 'New Eden' that concerned you then, Doctor?"

"Well, of course there are going to be plenty of challenges, sir. No human being's ever lived under a binary star, so we can't know with certainty what the long-term effects will be. But aside from the obvious obstacles…no, Mr. President, I can't think of anything that concerns me at the moment about New Eden. How about the rest of you?" she asked, looking around at the other expedition members who sat together off to the side of the room. All of them shook their heads.

President Clark then turned to Lincoln. "And what about *you*, Captain Lincoln. What did you make of the planet that many of us may well soon call home?" Nicole couldn't hold back the smirk when she saw Jack squirm in his chair.

"Oh, um—well—let me think about that for a moment, Mr. President." The captain said nothing for some time, so long in fact that Nicole began to wonder whether he was going to answer at all; what he finally said surprised her.

"Look, Mr. President, New Eden is one gorgeous planet, and I honestly can't think of one reason why we shouldn't begin plans for colonization right away. The atmosphere is clear, the landscape incredible, the climate mild, and resources abundant." He acted as if he might continue, but then stopped.

"But—?" Clark asked, seeing there was something else Lincoln was holding back.

"Well, sir, nothing in the universe comes without a downside; you know, the old Chinese Yin/Yang thing, opposites. New Eden probably should be the planet we select for colonization, but when the downside finally comes, who can tell what it will be?"

President Clark nodded in agreement. "My sentiments exactly, Captain. I suppose that every garden has its serpent, and no doubt we will find one on New Eden as well. Nevertheless, I can think of no reason why we should not proceed at this point, unless one of the expedition members has had a change of heart. What say you?" he asked, looking to the expedition team. "Does anyone wish to change their vote?" Every member of the expedition shook their heads, even Steve Sherman, who'd sat stone-faced during the entire proceeding. "Very well." Clark then turned to the others in the room. "Does anyone else in this room have a different opinion, based on the information presented here this morning? If so, please speak now or forever hold your peace." Silence fell over the assembly. After several moments of silence, Clark began nodding his head. "Very well then. Dr. Reynolds, would you be amenable to delivering your presentation once more to a combined gathering of the Alliance Senatorial Council and the Alliance Representative Committee? I can just about guarantee that if you show them what you've shown me this morning, you'll be heading back to New Eden in no time at all."

"Yes, of course, Mr. President!" she replied with a smile bathed in excitement.

***

"I'm so glad you came to see me off, Dad!" Nicole exclaimed, greeting her father at the door. She wrapped her arms around Hank before pulling him through the door and into the living room. "I thought you were tied up in trade discussions with the Valhari and the Anterans; what happened?"

"Simple; we reached an agreement much faster than I anticipated. I then hitched a ride on a Valhari ship that was coming to Earth anyway. Their ships are still faster than ours, but not for much longer," he added with a wink. "We're catching up quick."

"Dad, you've got to tell me all about Val…what's it like? What are the Valhari like…I mean *really*? I've always thought that they…." Nicole paused when Hank threw up his hand and smiled.

"Nicole! Hold on for a minute, sweetheart. I've got a surprise for you!" He walked back out the front door, returning with an older man

83

she'd not seen in a very long time.

"Grandpa!"

A broad smile appeared on Nick's face as Nicole ran over and embraced him. Nicole had forgotten how much she loved the family patriarch, and she'd not realized, until now, how much she'd missed him.

"Hello, Nikki. My, look at the young woman you've become! How are you, sweetheart?" Nick began coughing and he grimaced when it momentarily grew worse. The celebratory mood suddenly shifted as Nicole felt a chill in the air, as if a cold front had just blown in and swept away the warm, temperate weather.

"Grandpa, are you okay?" Of course they all knew the answer to her question, which remained verbally unanswered. "You shouldn't be traveling, Grandpa. Why didn't you stay on Val? The fleet leaves for New Eden tomorrow, so Dad will be heading back to Val anyway."

"I know, child," Nick said somberly, "but there are a couple of people I needed to visit, before I...well, you know." Tears began to form in her eyes, which she forced back. Nick Reynolds turned to his granddaughter with a pleading look in his eyes. "Nikki, honey," he began quietly, "won't you please come with us this time, with your father and me, to visit Mike and your grandmother? We were thinking we'd stop by there before dinner tonight, so we could—"

"No, Grandpa, I can't, but thanks for the offer; I really need to finish packing, and I don't know when I'll have time to catch another shuttle back. I promised President Clark that I'd help get the colony off to a good start, and who knows how long that could take?" She started busying herself picking up incidentals and surveying various rooms for items she might take with her; items that she might have missed when she'd finished packing two days earlier.

"Nikki, you haven't been to see him since—"

"No!" Nicole exclaimed, not quite yelling and not quite crying either, before leaving the room. She then walked into her bedroom where she sat down on the bed, staring down at the floor. A minute later her father knocked on the door.

"Nikki, may I come in?"

She paused for a few moments before finally assenting. "Sure, Dad, I guess."

Hank opened the door but stayed in the doorway. Nicole glanced up long enough to see a man who was struggling with what to say.

"Hey, are you okay, honey?"

Nicole looked up and managed a faint smile. "Yeah, I guess so."

Hank nodded his head a few times in response. "Okay, baby. Your grandfather and I will be back in an hour or two. We'll have plenty of time to catch up then, have some dinner and such; okay, sweetheart?"

"Yeah, sure Dad, sounds great," she said with a weak smile. She wanted to tell him that she *would* go with them to visit Mike; she wanted to tell everyone that she had so much more to say to him than they did, but she couldn't do it, not yet.

"Okay, honey, so I'll see you in a little while, okay?" She nodded, watching as he turned and closed the door.

She sat on the edge of the bed listening as the door closed behind the two men. She'd have to go with them one day, that much was certain. When that day finally came, when she did go to see Mike, she knew she'd have quite a bit to say and do, not the least of which would be to beg him for his forgiveness.

JEFF W. HORTON

86

CHAPTER 14

The ships emerged from quantum space one after the other, each some distance apart and a safe distance off to the side. Scientists had theorized that the staggered approach might be a safer way to move the mini-armada from Earth to New Eden. Having entered normal space, Nicole's ship took the lead, once again piloted by Jack Lincoln.

"So, Dr. Reynolds, what do we call you now...Dr. Reynolds, Governor Reynolds, President Reynolds?"

Nicole looked at Lincoln with such ferocity that she felt she might leap upon him. "What is your problem, Captain Lincoln? If you have some kind of a problem with me, I can easily find someone else to shuttle me and the others around. If you plan to stay here with us, however, I'm going to insist that you show me some respect. I am leading this effort, and I have hundreds of souls, soon thousands, to care for; and I don't have time to banter about with a despicable man like you!"

"Hey, hold on now, Doc, I think you've got me figured all wrong. I have nothing but respect for you. In fact I...." His voice trailed off, and he never finished the sentence. The question that lingered in Nicole's mind was why, considering how annoyed she was at the moment, she really wanted to know what he was going to say.

"Okay, Dr. Reynolds," the captain said in a much more professional manner, "it looks like we've arrived. Welcome back to New Eden, your new home!"

Within seconds they were entering the planet's atmosphere, this time to stay. The ships broke through the clouds and once again she laid eyes upon the world she would call home. The dazzling beauty of the golden sky, the red trees, the bluish grass, and the twin suns took her breath away.

"Captain," she began quite softly and tenderly, "please open up a channel with the other ships."

"Yes, Dr. Reynolds." Lincoln instructed Magellan to open a common channel between all ships. "Okay, the channel is open, Dr. Reynolds."

"Thank you." Nicole cleared her throat. "All ships, please hold your current positions for just a few moments. Ladies and gentlemen, fellow colonists, welcome to your new home…welcome to New Eden. Please take a moment to look out your respective ship and gaze upon the natural beauty of this world. As I'm sure you will all agree, the name they came up with when Captain Lincoln and Commander Darren first scouted this planet was most suitable. This planet, this strange new world, will be our home, and it will be our legacy for endless generations who follow. We haven't come to this world expecting a life of luxury and ease, we have come here to establish a new foothold for humanity; it is a tremendous obligation, and it is one I know you all share. I felt that this moment required something special. Now I understand that not everyone shares my belief in God, and that is certainly your prerogative; feel free to vote me out of office when we have our first election. But I'd like to share something that I felt appropriate for this moment.

"*'For the Lord your God is bringing you into a good land—a land with brooks, streams, and deep springs gushing out into the valleys and hills; a land with wheat and barley, vines and fig trees, pomegranates, olive oil and honey; a land where bread will not be scarce and you will lack nothing….'* May it be so with us, as we settle *this* new land, this planet, named New Eden. Captains, we will now descend to the planet's surface; please follow us down and land the ships in five rows of five ships. I'll see you all on the surface. Reynolds out."

"Nice speech, Dr. Reynolds," Jack told her. "A very nice speech for a very special occasion."

Nicole looked at him and managed a slight smile. "Yeah, you could say that again. A brand new world, with unknown dangers—"

"And many wonders," he reminded her.

"Yeah, I suppose you're right about that," she said without looking at him, staring out of the ship at the incredible splendor all around. Beautiful birds of blue, green, red, yellow, and white, more than a few with extra-long wingspans and some that were covered in a thin layer of fur or feathers, filled the sky around them. They fled before the intruders, some complaining loudly while sailing high above them in the sky.

Nicole watched them flying high above as the ship slowly descended before gently setting down in a grassy meadow. The landscape was captivating; Nicole made a mental note that she would have to be careful not to allow the allure of her surroundings to cause her to become oblivious to the danger surrounding them.

"The gravity here is slightly greater than Earth's. We shouldn't have any trouble adjusting at all, but the difference was just enough that the birds needed massive wingspans in order to sail the air currents." Nicole recognized the voice as belonging to Susan Fitzgerald, who now stood next to her, having approached unawares.

"Oh, hello, Susan."

"Hi, Dr. Reynolds. Say, Dr. Whitestone wanted me to let you know that she would like to be the first one to exit a ship; she, um, insisted upon it actually."

Nicole's eyes flashed with anger for a moment until she began nodding her head in understanding. "She wants to test the effectiveness of the vaccine herself before anyone else is exposed, is that it?"

"Yes; as I said, she insisted upon it."

Nicole grinned. "I have a feeling she's going to be a handful. Okay, where is she?"

"She's um, right there."

Nicole followed Fitzgerald's finger until she saw a middle-aged woman walking around outside the ship, with no atmospheric regulator, no suit, and no pulse weapon. She was exposing herself all right, more than she knew. In her mind's eye Nicole suddenly found herself back on V-10 during the predator attack, back to those horrible few seconds when Edith Sherman had—

"Dr. Reynolds, are you okay?"

Startled, Nicole turned to Susan Fitzgerald. "Yes, Susan, what is it?"

"It's Dr. Whitestone; it looks like she's waving for us to come out."

"Wait here, Susan." Nicole took two regulators with her and made for the ship's exit. She glanced back at Susan as she waved her hand over a control, causing a force field to appear behind and in front of her, part of the decontamination process, which allowed the system to purge any biological or chemical agents when entering or leaving the ship. A door then opened and a ramp appeared, which soon extended to the ground. She took a deep breath and waved her hand across another panel, which dropped the outside barrier, exposing her to the planet's atmosphere for the first time. She walked over to where Dr. Helen Whitestone stood waiting.

"It's absolutely wonderful, isn't it, Nicole? I told you that it was going to be fine when we were here last time."

Nicole exhaled as her oxygen depleted and she took her first breath of the alien air. She found herself immensely relieved to find she was able to breathe just fine. "I don't ever want to see you pull another stunt like this again, Helen, do we understand one another?"

The doctor wrinkled her forehead before nodding. "There's nothing to worry about, Nicole. The pathogens weren't all that dangerous anyway, but the vaccines I cooked up seem to have been more than enough to do the job. Every man, woman, and child aboard all of these ships have been fully vaccinated, or I would not have signed off on their coming.

Ambassador Zing was extraordinarily gracious in making their medical library available to me when I visited him and your father on Valhari. He even introduced me to a couple of their medical doctors, who shared some of their expertise. Based on what I learned, we should be safer here than on Earth."

"You went to Val?"

"Yes," she answered, momentarily stunned by Nicole's surprise. "Oh, I see why you're puzzled, my dear. Even before I was considered for this trip, I was asked by President Clark himself to look into vaccinations for our colonists; it seems he's come across some of my papers on avoiding interplanetary pandemics. I jumped on a shuttle to Val and the rest is history; your father arranged everything for me."

"My father? Hmm."

"He's a wonderful man, Nicole," she said with a smile.

"Yes, he is," Nicole replied. She then looked at everyone crowding against the transparent ship bulkheads, trying to see everything. She then looked at Whitestone, who nodded enthusiastically.

"Oh yes; as I said, it's quite safe. Everyone can leave the ships whenever you're ready."

Nicole nodded. She raised her right wrist closer to her mouth and tapped the small chip with a finger. "Okay, captains, please listen up. We're going to give everyone a chance to stretch their legs; afterwards, we'll begin unloading material to begin setting up camp.

"We'll begin by sending out the Alliance military onboard. I want them to set up a perimeter of about two-hundred square meters, after which you can begin debarking the ships, but no more than ten at a time and for no more than one hour at a time. Adults only at first; then, once we've determined the immediate area is safe, we'll allow children to disembark as well, but only one at a time and with a parent. Be sure to tell everyone that we'll be spending the night on the ships tonight, but if all goes well, we'll spend tomorrow night in our new camp. Also, remember to instruct the Entellis to have each ship continually scanning the area and remain on the lookout for danger. Finally, as we discussed, after the encounter we had on V-10, adult members, and I mean *every* adult member, will carry a pulse pistol with them today. I want people to stay in groups of five, with two in every five carrying a pulse rifle and acting as a lookout for the rest of the group the entire time. Am I clear? If any of the colonists selected to leave the ship can't abide by the conditions as I've laid them out, they will stay on the ship until I've given the all clear signal. Does anyone have any questions?" She paused and waited; after a sufficient amount of silence, she announced, "Okay, start sending them out."

90

CHAPTER 15

Nicole awoke to the sound of the alarm on her bed the following morning. She took a deep breath and muttered a few words of thanks. They'd had no problems and no encounters with unfriendly indigenous life, and the only medical emergencies had been a couple of minor scrapes suffered by some of the smaller children on a few of the red rocks they found scattered across the area. Accompanied by fearful parents, Dr. Whitestone had quickly allayed any fears about alien infection, calming everyone's fears by dabbing a little antiseptic on the abrasions before slapping on Band-Aids decorated with cartoon characters from a simpler era.

The planet rotated once every thirty hours, which meant that both days and nights were longer than on Earth, Once the two suns began to disappear behind the horizon, the captain of each ship made sure that they had everyone back on board at curfew; she'd ensured that everyone would have plenty of time for rest, even if some of them neglected to take advantage of the opportunity. She'd been able to get seven hours of sleep herself...not as much as she would have liked, but more than enough to get her through the day.

They'd unloaded some of the supplies the previous evening and had gotten off to a good start at setting up perimeter fencing around what would soon become the center portion of the compound. In a few additional hours they would have the fencing in place, after which they would erect a force-field around the entire compound as well as above it. While Nicole knew such measures might be extreme, she was determined that there would be no repeat of what had happened to poor Edith.

Nicole walked over to the dispenser station in her quarters, where she instructed the machine to pour a cup of cappuccino. A cup dropped down and liquid filled the cup. Conditions aboard the ship were a little cramped, but only because of the number of people aboard each ship, and because of the small compartments called P.O.D.S, Private Occupancy for Dressing & Sleep, which included a small shower/restroom for each person, with families getting a slightly larger space. Out of necessity it was somewhat Spartan, but Nicole was okay with it. She hoped that with any success, they'd be out of the ships within a day or two at the most.

She checked her watch before quickly finishing her cappuccino. Seconds later she undressed and stepped into the shower. The warm water on her face was very refreshing, caressing her skin as it rolled down her body, and she was surprisingly thankful for it. Perhaps it was the presence of something so familiar, in the midst of surroundings so strange and unfamiliar, that she found so comforting, or maybe it was the warmth of the water soothing her tired and tense muscles after a long trip the day before. While streams of water caressed her body, her mind drifted and doubts began to fill it. *Did we act too quickly? Should we have waited until teams had more thoroughly investigated the planet before landing with a fleet of ships? Is there going to be a repeat of V-10?* The questions troubled her and the possible answers doubly so. But there had been reasons for moving so speedily. No one knew when a calamity might befall Earth, no one knew when another race might claim New Eden, and perhaps most importantly, the rest of humanity needed a push; the throngs of people on Earth needed someone to take the risks, just as the early American pioneers had risked the savage, untamed west in an effort to make their way in the world. Nicole finished her shower wondering whether she and the other colonists were really so different from the early pioneers heading out west in wagon trains on their way to a better life.

Once dressed she immediately made her way to the ship's small dining area. In the lower part of the ship, it was both part of and adjacent to the main living area. There were only a few already there when she arrived, though more slowly began slowly trickling in while she ate a bowl of cereal. She finished eating, and after pouring another cup of coffee, she cleaned up the table where she'd been sitting and walked over to sit down on a sofa. She took out her data pad, placed it in verbal mode, and began quietly dictating to the computer's AI.

"Talking to yourself again, I see."

Nicole smiled slightly. "Are you stalking me, Captain Lincoln?" she asked without even looking up.

"If I said I was, would it help?"

"Not likely."

"Would you care for some company?" he asked her.

"Look, Captain, I've got a lot to do today. I really just need some time alone if you don't mind. I'm really sorry."

Jack threw his hands up apologetically. "No, no, that's all right, I understand perfectly. I know you have a lot to do, so you just go right ahead. I've already eaten so I just came down for a cup of coffee anyway."

92

He walked over to get a cup of coffee while Nicole sat there for a moment, just holding her data pad and looking after him. She didn't mean to offend Jack or hurt his feelings. She found him slightly annoying, but also charming and somewhat attractive. Besides, he might be helpful. She waited until he had his coffee and was starting back to the bridge.

"Uhm, Captain—I tell you what…if you have just a moment I would like to get your input on a few things; if you'd still care to join me, that is." Jack smiled and started to say something, but she gave him a look that quickly shut it down. "Can you spare a few minutes?"

"Sure." He came over and sat down across from her. "What's on your mind?"

"I'd like to make an announcement to all of the ships in about an hour. I need for the ESA military work crews to get to work on finishing the perimeter fencing and the encampment's force field before immediately getting to work on putting up the temporary housing units. According to the manufacturer and the tests we've run, we should be able to get one unit up and running every hour. Dark energy generators are onboard each ship to power each unit."

"Okay, I can do that."

"I would also like for you to announce that once the first shelter is up, hopefully by 1:00 P.M., I would like the leader of each functional group to meet me there to review their respective group's planned activities. Everyone's initial focus has to be on getting the camp set up and secure as quickly as possible. The next ships are due to arrive in three days with additional supplies, and I want to be ready."

"Okay, no problem. I'll make the announcements myself and I'll tell everyone that we'll let them know as soon as the camp's ready. Should I tell them that we'll follow the same routine as yesterday?"

"No. I want everyone who's not working on getting the camp set up to stay on board for now. They can start going out to run their experiments and collect their data once we've settled everyone into their respective shelters. Tell them that we'll probably start moving some of them into their temporary housing units later today; others may have to stay on the ships another night. We'll just have to see how it goes."

"Okay, done. Is there anything else?"

"Yes, there's one more thing. I need at least two members of the Alliance military to maintain a patrol around the perimeter of the encampment. We need to know a little more about the area, the topology, etc., and keep an eye out for surprises. Also," she began in a whisper, "I want to make sure we avoid what happened on V-10, so have them take scanners with them so they can scan the water as well."

"Understood." Lincoln rose to leave but turned back to face her for a moment, "Oh, by the way, *Governor* Reynolds, I thought I should share a little something with you before I get going. You sounded like a true leader just now...thinking ahead, thinking both tactically and strategically, doing what you think is best for everyone here instead of just yourself. I just wanted to let you know how impressed I am," he said with a warm smile before turning to leave.

Nicole smiled in return, his words echoing in her brain...*Governor Reynolds.*

***

The day wore on for the settlers, for that's what they were now, or pioneers...both terms applied to them in her assessment. Sitting at a desk inside one of the first completed structures on New Eden, Nicole looked over a status report on the camp's progress. The perimeter fence was completed, with the force field fencing surrounding it on the outside, and a large, reinforced gate was erected at the entrance of the camp. Twenty-five large habitation structures had been erected inside the fencing perimeter, twenty for housing, and five for other purposes including a laboratory, a small-scale medical facility, a dining hall, and two work areas. Each of the housing structures contained private quarters, living areas, kitchens, and bathrooms. Perhaps even more important to Nicole and to every other colonist was the luxurious space that the significant size of each facility afforded them, providing them considerably more room than many of them had anticipated, and adding to their increasing comfort level the longer they stayed on New Eden. Furthermore, with the housing units completed, each of the colonists would have time to settle into their temporary homes inside of the fencing before nightfall. It would take weeks, perhaps months, before the settlers would be free to set up their own long-term housing on their registered plots of land, but Nicole wasn't about to let that happen until the area had been thoroughly explored and the surrounding areas deemed safe.

Nicole finished signing a series of requisition forms and let out a heavy sigh. The workload had been intense and steady but she'd anticipated that before signing on. She'd just decided to break for lunch when the building she was in suddenly began shaking and rattling, causing her half-empty cup of coffee to tip over on the table and empty its contents on the table. Then she heard what sounded like a loud explosion outside, followed by a sound that had become more and more familiar...the sound of people yelling and screaming.

Nicole ran over to the door and looked outside. It appeared that whatever had happened had taken place outside of the compound, but the source of the explosions remained elusive. She searched the area with her eyes but saw nothing but men, women, and children frantically running around the compound, looking for their homes. It wasn't until she noticed several of the children pointing at something in the sky that her eyes shot upward, where she finally found the source of the disturbance. Hanging in the sky were three large and imposing ships, each one red and irregularly-shaped, almost like a crab—unlike any design she'd ever seen—each emitting a low roar. She ran out of the compound and to her ship, where she found Jack Lincoln sitting on the bridge.

"Captain, can you tell me anything about those ships?"

"I don't recognize the shape myself, Governor. Magellan, how about it, do you recognize the design?"

"Yes, I do, Captain, though I must admit to being somewhat astonished to see it. I haven't seen a ship like it for at least a hundred years."

"What is it, Magellan?"

"It's a Machrys ship, Captain," the Entelli answered. "They were actively recruited to join the League of Sentient Species on many occasions, but they've always rejected the opportunity. They keep to themselves, sir, always staying close; they have for a long time."

"What are they doing here?"

"I believe we're about to find out, Captain…we're being hailed."

"Put them through, Magellan," Nicole ordered.

"Yes, Governor Reynolds."

Following a moment's pause, a holographic image of their visitors appeared. The figure before them was quite alien, stranger than any she had ever seen. Like the ship, the creature was red, though a brighter red than the darker, more burgundy red of the ship. The hologram was that of a creature that stood atop four legs and sported two wiry arms. It had two large black eyes, with two antenna protruding from the back of its head. It was all she could do to stop from chuckling at the thought that in total, the closest thing Nicole could think of that it resembled was a cross between a praying mantis and an ant. A series of unintelligible clicks and knocks suddenly came from the hologram, with the creature's face taking on what appeared to be a somewhat angry countenance.

"Magellan?" Lincoln stared at the hologram, then the ships.

"The translators are coming online now, Captain."

"…we repeat, you are trespassing on Macryn territory in Macryn space. You must vacate this planet immediately. The shots fired were intended only to serve as a warning; next time we will not be so considerate. We will give you twenty revolutions of this planet to leave and take everyone and everything you brought with you. If you are still here at that time, you will be considered a threat and you will be dealt with accordingly."

"I am Governor Nicole Reynolds, leader of this colony and a representative of the Earth Space Alliance. We were told by representatives of the League of Sentient Species that this world was available for human colonization. We request time to confer with our ambassador at the league in order to resolve this—"

"The Machry have no dealings with the League. We repeat, you have violated Machry space. You must vacate this planet within twenty rotations, or you will be removed by force."

"Please," Nicole exclaimed, "We need more time to—"

The image terminated without further conversation. The ships rose slowly ever higher into the sky before suddenly accelerating at an impossible speed and disappearing into space. Nicole continued staring after the ships with a sinking feeling of dread that the Machry meant business.

"Magellan, what can you tell us about the Machrys?" Nicole asked, thankful that the ship's interface with the Entelli enabled her to speak directly to the alien, who doubled as one of the ship's computer systems.

"The Machry captain spoke the truth about their dealings with the League. They are a stubborn, ill-tempered race, full of bravado and blustering. If you're asking whether they mean to back up their threat, that is difficult to answer. They come from a hive-mentality, so they always speak in terms of 'we' and 'ours' instead of 'I' and 'mine' and are certainly capable of attacking, possessing both the technology and the temperament to do so. Since they have no formal relationship with the League, they are not beholden to abide by the League's laws."

"But I thought the Valhari and others in the League said this world was available for colonization, I don't understand!"

"As you know, Governor, my world is also a member of the League, and as a navigator I was aware that this world was on the list that the League presented to you. All I can say is that I have no explanation as to why the Machry would lay claim to this world, which is so far from their home world. Clearly they have done nothing to suggest that they have been preparing this world for colonization. The Machry have something of a reputation for trying to intimidate other races when it comes to something they really want, like a planet."

"You're saying that they have no intention of following through on their threat?"

"No, Governor, I'm merely suggesting that it is a possibility, and that their claim that this world is within Machry space is a highly dubious one at best."

"Now why would the Machry want this world so badly if it's so far from home for them?" asked Lincoln.

96

"That's a good question," Nicole replied. "I can tell you one thing, however; if the Machry have no basis for their claim, we're not going to simply roll over on this...there's far too much at stake." She paused and buried her head in her hands.

"Say, Governor, isn't your father the current E.S.A. Ambassador to the League; why not give him a call and ask him to look into it?" asked Jack.

Nicole looked up and smiled. "You know something, Captain? Sometimes—I'm really glad to have you around. Magellan, please contact the League on Val, I'd like to speak with my father, Ambassador Hank Reynolds." She then turned to Jack. "Let's wait until we know a little more about what's going on here, Captain, before we tell anyone else about this, shall we?"

He nodded. "Whatever you say, Governor Reynolds. I suggest we speak with headquarters about getting us some more Alliance troops and a little more weaponry here, just in case."

"I'm way ahead of you, Captain Lincoln, except I was thinking about *a lot more* weaponry."

CHAPTER 16

It had been a week since they'd first landed on New Eden, and Michael Billings was thankful when he finally found his team's name on the list for teams conducting research outside of the encampment. He'd been worried it might be as much as a month or more before his team would get to conduct their first real research, but there it was on his data pad. Perhaps the additional Alliance troops that had arrived two days earlier explained the timing, since research teams were still not permitted beyond the perimeters of the compound without an escort. It was, in his opinion, an overreaction, but after what had happened on Planet V-10, he understood the governor's abundance of caution. He smiled when he saw an old friend of his, Sal Goldstein, approaching from the direction of the dining hall.

"Hey, Mike old buddy, so you finally get to make it out today. I saw your name on the list this morning. Congratulations!"

"Thanks, Sal. So what's it like out there…as nice as it is inside the compound?"

"Are you kidding? It's incredible, Mike! You're gonna have a great time out in the woods, my friend, I didn't see a single species of—well, anything, that I recognized. The chlorophyll here is mostly blue and red, though there is an occasional green plant here or there. Oh, man, there's this one stream, in the middle of the woods just a hundred meters or so outside the fence. It's like crystal clear, and there are these beautiful jewels of all shapes and sizes…incredible!"

"What about the wildlife? That is your area of expertise, isn't it?" he asked Sal.

"Oh, don't get me started. There are so many life forms on this world with characteristics unlike life on Earth that we'll have to construct an entirely new biological classification! I've seen small deer-like creatures with wings, and I've seen birds with fur and tails…it's amazing. Now I know that as a botanist, it's your area of expertise and not mine, but I think you're going to find even more diversity in the plant kingdom than I did in the animal kingdom. Why, yesterday while I was resting on a large rock in the woods, I noticed a small plant about three-feet high growing at the base of a large tree. This plant looked a little like corn, except it had a blue stalk, with large red leaves and ears of green. I also saw a huge tree that must have been—"

"Stop!" Billings interrupted his friend and now stared hard at him with great intensity. "What did you say? Tell me again, Sal, describe it to me in detail, please."

"Okay, I said I saw an extremely wide and tall tree that—"

Billings shook his head. "No, before that!"

"Oh, what was I...? Oh yes, the funny-looking corn."

Billings nodded this time. "Yes, please, Sal, describe it to me, in detail."

His friend scratched his head. "Okay, let me think. Like I said, it resembled corn, since it had a stalk that was sort of a teal color, and there were seedlings that looked a lot like ears of corn, except they were green, and had large red leaves."

Mike Billings pulled out his data pad and began looking through images that appeared as holograms above it.

"Come on, come on, what was that called again? Aaarrgghh! Come on...casman...no, castor...no...castillan, that's it!" Billings pressed a button on his data pad and an image that approximated what Sal had described appeared.

"That's it! How did you know, Mike?"

"That's not important, Sal. Right now, I need you to tell me exactly where you found this plant."

***

When Dr. Michael Billings, the colony's chief botanist, walked into Nicole's office carrying some sort of a bizarre-looking alien plant, her first impulse was to throw him out of her office immediately. She had spoken with Billings on a number of occasions and he had always come across as a scientist who took his work quite seriously, so she knew that whatever his reason for the emergency meeting with her was, it must be serious, and the plant must somehow be an important part of that discussion.

"Governor Reynolds, my sincerest apology for interrupting your day like this, but I felt that a discovery I've made, with the help of a friend I should add, is important enough to warrant such an interruption."

"Dr. Billings, it's good to see you again; please take a seat." She gestured to one of the padded, high-backed chairs sitting across from the desk. The botanist held the plant in his lap instead of setting it on the floor, another indication to her that this discussion must somehow involve the plant. As if the Machry weren't enough for her to worry about, she now

100

feared that they might have some other crisis on their hands.

"So, Dr. Billings, what brings you to see me this afternoon?"

"This," he answered plainly, setting the odd yet beautiful plant on her desk.

"Doctor, I don't see...."

Billings raised both eyebrows. "You don't recognize it, Dr. Reynolds? Take a good close look. Surely you've been briefed on it!"

"But Dr. Billings, it's just a plant."

"Just a plant? No, Dr. Reynolds, it's not just a plant...it's a castilian plant! Castil is a drug that is derived from the castilian plant, which has been found on only a few worlds in the known universe. Castil, when consumed or injected into an organic body, can lead to extremely long life spans, making the recipient seemingly immortal. For human beings, it somehow alters the cell, dramatically enhancing the XPF gene in the human body, the gene that's responsible for DNA repair, leading to a healthier and much longer life."

"This? You're telling me that *this* is a castilian plant?" Nicole stared at the plant, both shocked and stunned by the news. "But it's so rare, I was told I'd never see one in person!"

"Normally that would be true, Governor, but in this case it is not. Remember that the castilian plant only grows in systems with binary stars, and even then, only in one out of 100,000 binary star systems. From what I've learned doing my research over the last decade, it seems all planets where castilian plants grow are either claimed or already settled by one of the major sentient races. As you know, the castilian plant is what enables so many of the sentient races to live so long, and it also plays a key role in their elimination of almost every disease. Those of us living here are going to make a lot of money, Governor. I just can't believe that none of the other races ever discovered its existence here."

"Yeah, it kind of makes one wonder, doesn't it? This is incredible news, Dr. Billings. Do you know how to process the plant in order to create the castil?"

"Well—that is—I'm not sure. I read an article somewhere that I should be able to track down. We should also be able to get the League of Sentient Species to send it to us, Governor, especially since your father is our ambassador there."

"Leave my father out of this, Dr. Billings. I'm sick and tired of everyone expecting me to ask my father for help at every turn!"

"Yes, of course, Governor," Billings replied sheepishly. "I meant no offense, I'm sorry."

Nicole let out a heavy sigh. "Oh, it's not your fault, Dr. Billings. I've been under a lot of stress. It is I who owe *you* an apology."

101

"Unnecessary, Governor Reynolds. So, given its value throughout the known universe, surely you can appreciate what it could mean for the colony; trade on a vast scale, jobs, growth, business, everything!"

"Yes, I *can* appreciate that, Dr. Billings." She tapped her hands on the desk for several moments while staring out of the window at the golden sky. "Did you see any more of these plants?"

"No, I didn't, but then again I was only looking for this one after my friend described it to me. I can guarantee you, however, that where there's one, there's more."

Nicole nodded. "Okay then, Doctor, I have a request. I'd like for you to go back out tomorrow to where you found this plant, along with five Alliance soldiers as an escort, to spend the day searching the area for more castilian plants. As you said, Dr. Billings, this is an extremely important find; humanity could now have its own source of castil. Will you go back out tomorrow to find more, and perhaps try to determine how much there is on this planet?"

Billings began nodding immediately. "Yes, of course, Governor, I'd be happy to."

Nicole smiled. "Good. Please come here tomorrow morning at 9:00 A.M. If you can provide me a list of any equipment and/or supplies you'd like to take with you, we'll have them waiting for you here if we can. Your escort will be waiting, and you should be able to get started soon afterward, okay?"

"Yes, of course. I'll also do some searching tonight to see if I can find anything about preparing castil."

"That sounds wonderful, Dr. Billings. That brings up another point I need to make before you leave."

"Yes?"

"We need to keep this quiet for a variety of reasons, Mike, none of which are nefarious, I assure you. We are only a fledgling colony here, and from what you've told me, we may be in the possession of one of the most valuable substances in the known universe. If word gets out, it could mean trouble. We have to keep this under wraps until we can get more Alliance troops here."

"The Machrys...is that why they were here earlier? Do they already know about the Castil?"

Nicole sat back in her chair and sighed heavily. "No one else here knows what I'm about to tell you, Mike, except for myself and two others, and now I guess—you. The Machrys claim that this planet is within their territory, but we are disputing that. We've discussed this with the League and they fully support our position."

"What? Are you saying that the Machrys might attack us at any moment, that there could be a war?"

Nicole stood up and walked around to the other side of the desk, where she sat down. For a moment, she found herself longing to be back in her executive office several light years away on Earth. "No, Dr. Billings, and there's no reason to think it will come to that. As I said, we've discussed this with the League of Sentient Races, and they have already been in contact with the Machrys Council, which assured the League that there will be no hostile actions taken and that they want to resolve the dispute amicably."

"Well, that's a relief then."

Nicole looked at him for a moment, her gaze suddenly fixating on him in a very serious way. "Listen, Dr. Billings, it is imperative that you say nothing to anyone about the castil plant and you must convey this to your friend as well, because doing so could inadvertently trigger an interplanetary war, one which we are ill-prepared for, at least at this time. The Machrys are not members of the League but they do respect the collective power it wields. If they learn about the castil, however, all bets are off, so secrecy at this point is paramount; even the troops who will be escorting you tomorrow will not know what you are looking for. When they ask you, tell them whatever you want—tell them that you're cataloguing alien plant species, searching for edible plants, whatever you like, just do not mention the castilian plants, am I clear?"

The intensity in her eyes must have alarmed the man, because he shrank back slightly.

"Yes, absolutely clear; I won't say a word about the castil, I promise."

"Good. If you break that promise, Dr. Billings, I will make it my mission in life to ensure that you regret that decision, am I clear?"

"Yes, Governor Reynolds, of course."

"Good. Okay, I'll see you first thing in the morning then?"

"Yes, first thing in the morning."

Billings stood, walked over to the door, and turned back for a moment as if to say something or ask a question. Nicole smiled slightly back at him as he opened the door and left the room. She grimaced slightly, regretting the tone she'd adopted with a colleague. She recognized that she'd had little choice, however, as everything she'd told him was true, though she had left out some tidbits of information. She pressed a button and the holographic image of her executive assistant appeared.

"Yes, Governor?"

"Please get the Alliance Headquarters on the phone, Horace, I need to speak with President Clark. Oh, and Horace?"

"Yes, Governor?"

"I also need you to contact my father's office on Val, and leave a message that I need him to contact me on a secure line as soon as possible, okay?"

"Of course, Dr. Reynolds."

Nicole sat back in her chair and took in a long, deep breath. They'd been there only a week and already she was embroiled in politics and a very dangerous situation with the Machrys. She also wondered what the view was was like from her office back on Earth.

CHAPTER 17

Steven Sherman looked around at the tall, rust-colored trees that surrounded him like great redwoods, which offered a stark contrast to the thin, blue grass. Though thankful to have his chance to finally leave the encampment to explore the surrounding landscape, he kept asking himself what he was doing on an alien world so far from home. It was this insane colonization effort that had cost him his beloved Edith after all, wasn't it?

Sherman shook his head in sadness. Yes, it had cost him his wife, but it had been something that they had each eagerly agreed to when offered the chance to participate. Dr. Reynolds had made the danger very clear to everyone, so he couldn't blame her for his tremendous grief. He'd resolved soon after Edith was taken from him that he would work tirelessly to make the colonization of another world a success. While he wasn't certain exactly what good an archaeologist would be on such an endeavor, it was at least reasonable to assume his knowledge of Earth's past could prove valuable, or that they might stumble across ruins of some ancient civilization that needed someone to research it. It was a moot point anyway, since he could always leave and return to Earth if he desired. They had already started running weekly shuttles to and from their home world to New Eden.

He stopped walking suddenly and began looking around in frustration.

"Is something wrong, Dr. Sherman?" one of the Alliance officers asked him.

"No…yes… it's just that I can't see anything from down here. I'm trying to find signs of other civilizations here, but I can't see more than forty or fifty feet in any direction. We need to try to find some higher ground."

"I'm sure Governor Reynolds would authorize the use of a ship if you'd like to get higher, Dr. Sherman." But the archaeologist either hadn't heard him or he was ignoring him, because he didn't respond to the suggestion.

"Wait a minute, what's that up ahead?" Sherman asked, pointing through several trees directly ahead of them.

"It looks like a large hill, or maybe a small mountain peak."

"How far would you say it is from here, a few kilometers?"

"Yeah, about that, sir. Why, you want to go there?"

"Sure, why not? We have time, don't we?"

The Alliance soldier looked at his watch. "Yes sir, we have just enough time to walk there and look around for a few minutes before walking back to the camp. We have to be back by dark though; as you know, Governor Reynolds has ordered everyone back inside the settlement by dark."

"Good enough. If we make it at least partially up the mountain or hill there, we should be able to get a better view of the surrounding landscape."

"Whatever you say, Doc. Okay men, let's get the man to that mountain."

Sherman was exhausted by the time they finally cleared the woods and entered an open meadow near the base of the tall mountain. Vaguely similar to mountains on Earth, it stood at the base of a range of mountains that extended in a semi-circle ahead and to the right of their position. He started looking around and noticed the two large moons in the afternoon sky, each considerably larger and closer than Earth's solitary moon.

"Would you like to take a break, Dr. Sherman?" the Alliance soldier asked him.

Sherman turned and looked at the man. "You know, I just realized that we've been walking together for hours and I don't even know your name."

"Lieutenant Tony Garcia, Dr. Sherman, at your service."

"Steve Sherman, It's nice to meet you, Lieutenant." Garcia nodded in response. "No, I'm fine, I just wanted to catch my breath for a moment and look around. I guess the heavier gravity here is catching up to me."

"It will take a little time but everyone should adapt just fine, eventually. You just take your time, sir, and we'll push on whenever you're ready."

Sherman managed a smile. "Actually, I'm good, Lieutenant. I'll rest once we get to the mountain. Once I've had a good look around we can note the coordinates of a few prospective sites, and head directly to them in the morning."

"Sounds like a good plan, sir. Okay, if you're sure you're ready then, we'll keep moving. We shouldn't have to climb very high for you to get a good look at the area. Once we get a few hundred meters up, you should be able to see over all but the tallest trees."

"Agreed," Sherman replied, before following Lieutenant Garcia towards the base of the mountain.

Now that they were clear of the woods and had an unobstructed view of the mountain, Sherman was struck at the somewhat unusual shape of the mountain's base. It was normal on one side, the right or southernmost side. The northern base, however, was extended slightly to the left, almost as if part of the mountain had broken off at some point in the distant past. He shook his head, dismissing the oddity, and began looking for a way to climb up the side of the alien mountain peak. Sherman started making his way along the mountain's unusual northern base when he came to a sudden stop.

"What's the matter, Doctor?"

Sherman just lifted his arm and pointed to the entrance of a large cave in front of them. It stood fifteen meters high and nearly as wide. It was an enticing invitation to a mystery he was loathe to ignore.

"Do we have a few minutes, Lieutenant? I'd really like to take some time to take a look inside." He could tell from the look on Garcia's face he was hesitant.

"I guess we have a few minutes, but is it safe? We're not really equipped for cave exploration."

"You carry lights in your packs, don't you?"

"Yes, but—"

"Great. If you can give me one, I just want to look around inside a little; we don't need to go in very far."

Garcia took a light out of his pack and handed it to Sherman, before turning to the four men accompanying them. "Smith, Martel, get your phase rifles ready, Tucker and Yu, we need some light inside this cavern; get out your lantern packs and toss a couple inside." The men obeyed orders and seconds later, they were walking into a brightly illuminated cavern.

Sherman looked around inside, looking for signs of anything unusual or out of place on the alien world. Just inside the entrance and no more than twenty-five meters to the left, something reflected some of the light, something…metallic? He immediately began walking towards it, so quickly that the others had trouble keeping up. By the time they reached his side, they all gazed in fascination at the source of the reflection.

"What the—?"

"Yeah," Sherman said with a smile. "I was kind of thinking the same thing. I don't know where it came from, but based on the way the mountain's grown up around it, I'd say that it's been here for a very long time."

The six men stood staring for several minutes, saying nothing, gazing

107

in wonder at the strange, alien spaceship that sat buried inside a mountain. The ship was a metallic blue in color, with half of it buried under rock and dirt. From what he was able to see, the ship had a triangular shape, and was much, much larger that the ships they'd come to New Eden on.

"This is incredible; have you ever seen a ship like this, Dr. Sherman?"

"No, I haven't. I must admit, before I took this job my wife and I...." He paused for a moment, fighting back the tears. There would be time later for more mourning. At the moment, his curiosity was getting the better of him. "...we used to look through the images of the various ships, mostly those belonging to the Valhari, along with ships from most of the worlds that make up the Alliance. It looks a little like a few I've seen, maybe, but no, this is something very different; and as I said, it looks old...I mean really old."

Sherman walked over to the ship, reached up, and touched its edge. Suddenly and quite unexpectedly there was a clicking sound and a portion of the ship receded, leaving a ramp which led inside. He was hit by a blast of very stale air. Tony Garcia walked over and placed his hand on Sherman's shoulder.

"Dr. Sherman, we should check in with Governor Reynolds about something this big."

The archaeologist turned to face him, staring blankly at him for a moment before shaking and then nodding his head. "Oh, yes, of course. Can I please borrow a light so I can look inside? It's hard to see anything more than a few meters inside."

The lieutenant handed a light to Sherman. "Here you are, Doctor. I'll call-in to Governor Reynolds, and I'll let you know what instructions she has for us."

Sherman nodded as Garcia walked a little closer to the two lantern packs.

"Yes? This is Reynolds."

"Governor, this is Lieutenant Garcia, Alliance Military."

"Yes, Lieutenant, I remember you, you're escorting Dr. Sherman...."

Sherman glanced over at Garcia, whose back was now turned to him, as were the others. He'd already worked his way closer to the ramp, and now saw his opportunity to act. He quietly stepped onto the ramp and began quickly walking into the ship. As soon as he reached the top of the ramp, he was nearly blinded when lights suddenly came on and the interior of the ship was now visible. He turned back just in time to see the ramp retract and the entrance to the ship close behind him.

Sherman smiled briefly before turning his attention back to investigating the interior of the ship. He was in a small, open area of the ship, with a hallway to both his left and to his right. He quickly worked to recall the direction the ship was pointed in, and after a moment's hesitation, he turned to his left and began walking down the hallway towards what he believed to be the front of the ship. He passed a number of rooms along the interior wall of the ship to his right, rooms he would investigate at a later time. The ship was even bigger on the inside than he'd believed it to be from the outside, because it took him several minutes to reach what appeared to be the bridge.

He was startled upon suddenly finding the bridge, for in what appeared to be the pilot's chair was a corpse, still somewhat preserved. It was incredible that the body was in the condition it was in, given how long he suspected the ship had stood there undisturbed. Perhaps there was something about the ship's atmosphere that had preserved the decaying tissue. He started chastising his rash action in boarding the ship, suddenly realizing that had the previous occupants not been oxygen-breathers, he would now be dead along with the long-term resident. He looked over the console for several moments before turning to leave the bridge. He nearly tripped over another corpse laying in the middle of the floor. The long hair led him to suspect this one had been a female of the species, though it was certainly not a definitive indication. It would have to do for now, however, as he was determined to make for the aft-end of the ship to see, perhaps, what the ship had been carrying. He walked down the long hallway, eventually reaching and then passing the small hallway through which he'd entered. He was delighted though surprised that the door remained closed, an indication perhaps, that Governor Reynolds had ordered the men to wait outside until she arrived. He hoped that was the case in order to give him more time to look around unencumbered.

It took him several minutes but he eventually reached a door, which appeared to lead to a cargo area, or the ship's hold. He walked closer to it and the door suddenly shot upward and disappeared. He looked inside for a moment before entering.

He was immediately struck by what he saw upon entering. Along both the left wall and the right wall of the ship's hold were what loosely resembled beds, which extended perpendicular to their respective walls. A semi-circular enclosure sat atop each table, covering it from end to end. Sherman walked over to the closest table and involuntarily jumped back momentarily at what he found. Inside the enclosure in which he was looking, which he immediately determined to be some sort of hibernation or suspended-animation chamber, was an incredibly beautiful humanoid alien with finely-toned lavender skin, perfect bone structure, and flowing white hair. This too had to be a female, and one he found to be immensely attractive.

Sherman hurried over to the chamber next to hers and found a male. He didn't recognize the species any more than he did the ship. He stood there for a moment, assessing what his next move should be, when suddenly, doing what it often did, fate intervened. While he stood next to one of the chambers, trying to decide whether to continue looking around or to check with his escort outside, the coverings of all the chambers in the large room suddenly began to recede, and the eyes of their occupants slowly began to open.

CHAPTER 18

Sherman stood there watching as the occupants of the strange alien craft slowly began to stir. Another quick glance around the room enabled him to estimate there were somewhere around fifty stasis pods, each occupied by one of the strange, exotic aliens. Now that several were awake, he could see they were golden-eyed, making them unusual yet strangely beautiful to look at. As they began stirring, the scientist in him wanted to linger, but his fear outweighed his scientific curiosity. Finding a ship full of live aliens was something he'd not anticipated. With more than a little sense of urgency he rushed out of the room and made for the ship's entrance.

He reached the open area and turned to face the outer hull of the ship, then waved his hand in front of the doorway; as he'd hoped the door opened and the ramp reappeared. He found Lieutenant Garcia and an angry Nicole Reynolds staring up at him as he walked down the ramp; the doors of the ship closed behind him.

"Dr. Sherman, what in the world did you think you were doing? You know that you're supposed to report finding anything unusual immediately, and I think this qualifies as unusual. Who knows what danger you might have put yourself in, or the rest of the colony for that matter?"

"I'm sorry, Governor, I really am, but there's something I need to—"

"I just don't understand why you couldn't call this in, Dr. Sherman. We have rules for a reason, and to go in unescorted? When we get back—"

"Governor!" His shout was enough to startle her.

"What is it, Dr. Sherman?"

"There's something I need to tell you. While I was in there—" Sherman was interrupted when the door suddenly opened and the ramp reappeared.

"Steve, did you—?"

Sherman shook his head. "No, Governor. That's what I was trying to tell you...there are people on that ship, and they're *alive*!" Sherman was familiar with Nicole and her reputation well enough that the sudden look of fear in her eyes surprised him. He turned around just as a figure appeared at the top of the ramp.

***

She estimated the alien was just over two meters tall, and similar to human beings in anatomical appearance, at least in form; from its musculature she assumed it was male. He had light, lavender-colored skin, long white hair, and golden eyes, and was dressed in something that resembled a gown or a robe.

"Zareen-kapla jara nosraki?"

Nicole had instinctively shifted her attention away from the alien for a moment, searching for answers, when her gaze suddenly fell on Garcia. She noticed the Alliance soldiers held plasma rifles pointed toward the ship, while the ship's occupants had similarly raised a number of unusual spears or swords with some sort of plasma energy crackling from them, which she was certain were some form of energy weapons.

"Lieutenant Garcia, lower your weapons!" she ordered.

The exasperated look on the soldier's face spoke volumes without ever speaking a word. "But, Governor Reynolds, we don't—"

"*Now*, Lieutenant!" she ordered.

Garcia tightened his lips in a grimace before ordering his men to lower their weapons. Nicole turned back to face the apparent leader of the alien occupants. He smiled at her before saying turning and saying something to his men, who immediately lowered their weapons as well. He then turned, smiled again, and nodded. Nicole turned back to Garcia.

"Lieutenant, do Alliance soldiers still carry field translators for situations like this?"

"Yes—well, I don't know about situations like this, Governor—"

"Lieutenant!"

"Yes, ma'am." He took off his backpack, removed a device with a strap attached to it, and handed it to her. "You need to push this—"

Nicole looked hard at him. "I know how universal translators operate, Lieutenant, thank you," she replied.

Garcia backed away and grinned tightly at her, not caring for the way she dressed him down in front of his men.

Nicole placed her head through the opening of the straps, which resulted in the translator hanging down from her neck. It was roughly octagonal in shape, with small indicator lights inside.

"Can you—understand me?"

"Zippit sorron kolnit z—who are you?"

"My name is Nicole Reynolds, and I am the governor of this colony."

"Ah, you have a translator device, excellent. We have similar devices in our ship as well, but alas, I had no idea I would need one so soon." His speech was smooth and his voice soft and sweet, unlike any she'd ever heard before. She was drawn to the stranger's golden eyes that sparkled and glittered in the light generated by the lantern packs.

"And you are?"

"Oh, please forgive me. I'm afraid that such an extended hypersleep has dulled my mind a bit, although the effects will soon depart. I am Jokar Motay, the captain of this ship and a leader among my people." He swept his gaze across the colonists gathered in front of the ship.

"Please pardon my asking, Captain, but of what race are you and your people? I'm afraid I've never met anyone quite like you before," she remarked.

He smiled again warmly at her. "We are of the Shataran People, from the planet Shatara in the Omnis star system. And you? I'm quite certain I've never encountered a species like yours before, I most certainly would have remembered," he said with another smile and a slight bow.

"We are human beings, from a planet called Earth in the Sol star system," she said matter-of-factly.

"Hmm, Earth; interesting." Motay looked around at the conditions of the cave and shook his head. "Please, I would be honored, Governor Reynolds, if you and your men would join us inside my humble ship. I'm sure it's not what you're accustomed to, but I believe you would be far more comfortable inside than you would standing in this damp, dark cave."

Nicole studied him for a moment. Despite his charming manners, she'd noticed that his men's eyes had never left her or those with her. But she knew this could also be an opportunity. She looked at the men with her and after a hard look, she was answered with several nodding heads.

"We'd be honored, Captain Motay."

Motay turned and began walking back into the ship. He stopped at one of the doors and waved his hand in front of it, causing the door to open. He and those with him entered a large room with a long table sitting in the middle, with cushioned benches on either side. Surrounding the long table was a series of tables with smaller bench seats. The room was also filled with armed Shatarans. Nicole looked over at Garcia and raised her eyebrows. He nodded and raised his eyebrows in turn, acknowledging her point; it was a good thing they'd lowered their weapons, because if there had been a firefight, they would have been far outnumbered and would clearly have been the worst for it. For the most part the Shatarans sat talking amongst themselves, though Nicole could tell that nearly every one of them was watching the visitors intensely, despite trying to appear to the contrary.

"Can I offer you some sort of refreshments? Our ship may be very old now, but rest assured that any refreshments the ship creates will be quite fresh. I'm not sure what humans like, of course, but I'm sure we have something here."

"Do you have any water?"

"Water? Two atoms of hydrogen, one atom of oxygen? Yes, of course." She noticed that Motay did not get it himself, but rather motioned to two of the Shatarans standing nearby, who immediately hurried to a station where, after pressing a button, water suddenly began pouring into several pouches, which were then set before them. Nicole hesitated, watching Motay just as he watched her. After a moment, he smiled before picking up one of the pouches and taking a long drink.

"Ah, refreshing is it not?" He paused and looked evenly into her eyes. "I like you, Governor; you're cautious when it comes to trust, you're wise in diplomacy, *and* you're curious. Were it not for the difference in your appearance I might think you were Shataran," he said with a grin.

Nicole then sipped at the water, and after finding it to be refreshing, took several long drinks before setting it back on the table. "I have many questions, Captain."

"As do I, Governor. But as you are guests upon my ship, please, you go first."

"How long have you been here, and how?"

"As to how long—I'm not sure your translation device will correctly convey measurements of time. We were quite surprised when we learned, just before you and I met, that we've been here for quite some time, nearly five-thousand standard years, which I believe would equate to just over four-thousand cycles around the binary stars in this system. As to why, I cannot answer, at least not yet. I know how long only because I checked our navigation system and noted the date in our star log. It seems there was an accident and the ship crash-landed on this planet. Our pilot and co-pilot are both dead, though it remains unclear how they died. Fortunately our ship deactivated non-critical systems and diverted power to the hypersleep chambers, or we would have died in our sleep long ago."

"Why didn't the chambers open upon the crash landing?" A flash of irritation appeared on the captain's face for the first time, though it was plain to Nicole that he tried to hide it.

"The system controlling the chambers seems to have been damaged during the crash. I'm not sure what happened to activate them."

"It was me, I did it," Sherman said, speaking to the Shataran captain for the first time. "I was the first to enter the ship. Of course I had no idea anyone was still alive on it. I was exploring the ship when I entered this

114

room and—"

"Ah, yes, that would have been what did it then!" exclaimed Motay. "The system was programmed to activate once someone entered the room from the outside. So to whom do I owe my eternal gratitude?"

"I'm Steve Sherman, Dr. Steve Sherman."

"A doctor? It's most certainly a pleasure to meet you, Doctor. I feel certain that you and our two medics onboard will find plenty to talk about—"

"No, no, not that kind of doctor, Captain; I hold a doctorate in the field of archaeology," Sherman explained.

"Archaeology, 'the study of ancient civilizations.' Hmmph. I suppose we're ancient enough to be studied, are we not, Dr. Sherman?"

Sherman smiled weakly.

Motay was quiet for a moment, as were the others, pausing for a few seconds to take in the solemnity of the occasion. The Shataran captain was the first to speak.

"Five-thousand years, that is a very long time. Everything that we knew...loved ones, friends, family...long-dead." The cheerfulness had faded from his face twice as fast as it had appeared, and the grave expression on his face darkened. "Everything we worked for, everything we fought for, gone." He turned his head in a moment of naked despair.

"It seems to me that despite your great loss, you have quite a bit to look forward to, Captain Motay. It's a new day, a new *age* for that matter."

Motay looked up at Nicole for a moment. "You're quite right of course, Governor. There will be much catching up for us to do, five-thousand years' worth to be exact. There is much to be done first, however. It seems we've awakened from our extended sleep only to find our ship buried in the side of this mountain, or whatever it is. It could take quite some time to get it repaired to the point that we can leave."

"At least the ship still has power," Nicole offered, "that's good, right?"

"Indeed,' he said before looking down, "there's still enough power to last quite a while."

Nicole turned to Sherman, Garcia, and the others. They all shook their heads just enough to signal they disapproved of what she was about to propose, but when she turned back to a seemingly despondent Motay, she knew what she had to do.

"Captain Motay, as a gesture of goodwill between our peoples, please allow me to extend the hospitality of our settlement to you and to your people, at least on a limited basis.It's not much, but perhaps it will offer you and your people the occasional distraction from your work here."

Motay looked up. "You are most gracious, Governor, but are you certain? Strange aliens in your settlement...would your people accept this?"

"Many of them are scientists, Captain Motay. I imagine they'll be far too curious to object," she said, wearing a smile of her own. *I'll make sure of it.*

CHAPTER 19

"You're telling me that their ship's been buried under a mountain for five-thousand standard years and they're still alive? You've got to be kidding me! Have you verified that, Governor Reynolds?"

"Yes, Mr. President...well, at least to the best of our ability. Their ship was constructed from material that even our Valhari instruments are having difficulty reading, but it certainly appears they're telling the truth."

"Where are they now?"

"They've been working diligently trying to repair the damage from the crash, and dig it out from under the mountain without it collapsing on them, of course. They're also working on repairs."

"I'm assuming that you've offered our assistance."

"Yes, sir. Their leader, Captain Jokar Motay, has been here to the settlement a number of times, inquiring about materials, etc. We've been helping with parts, materials, etc. as best we could. For the most part they stay to themselves."

"What planet did he say they were from again?"

"Shatara, Mr. President."

"Yes, Shatara. It seems like I've heard or seen that name somewhere, maybe in one of your father's reports. I would like to—" The holographic image of Clark suddenly distorted before disappearing altogether.

"Aarrgghh! That's the third time now. Captain Lincoln, isn't there anything we can do?"

"I'm a pilot, Governor Reynolds, not a communications expert. Even if I were, however, I'm not sure that there's anything we can do. It has to be interference from those coronal mass ejections that we've been keeping our eye on. They don't seem to be a direct threat to the planet itself, thank God, but they do seem to be wreaking havoc with communications."

"Bernice, can you get President Clark back on the line for me?"

"I'll keep trying, Governor."

"Thank you." She turned back to Jack Lincoln. "I know, I know. I understand that, Captain. If I had the time I believe I'd be able to figure out a way to get a signal through the flares, but with everything going on...."

Lincoln just nodded.

"Governor, I have President Clark back on the line."

"Thanks, Bernie."

"Nicole?"

"Yes, Mr. President, I'm here; I'm sorry about that, sir."

"More interference from the CMEs?"

"I'm afraid so; the flares seem to be getting worse."

"Okay, I guess we'd better keep this short then. Have there been any updates on the Machrys?"

"No, Mr. President, nothing since they first arrived."

"As I've said, Nicole, I was assured by the League's ambassador here on Earth that New Eden is well outside of Machrys space, though it is in roughly the same neighborhood. They've also just informed me, however, that the Machrys seem to have something in common with the Shatarans; they keep largely to themselves. Do you need more troops?"

"I think that would be wise, Mr. President."

"Worried about the Machrys?"

"Yes."

"Very well. All right, Governor Reynolds, please continue to keep me informed."

"Yes, sir. Reynolds out." The image disappeared once more.

She didn't mention her concerns about the Shatarans, though she sometimes thought perhaps she should. The truth was that despite how impressed she was with them, there was something about them, something just under the surface—a lingering doubt or question.

"Governor, there's another incoming message." Nicole did not miss the look of fear on her assistant's face. "Governor, it's the Machrys."

Nicole tightened her lip. "Okay Bernie, put them through."

"Humans of Earth. We are the Machrys. You have invaded Machrys space, and you are attempting to establish a colony within our sovereign territory, despite having been previously warned to vacate this planet, a warning that you've chosen to ignore. As it is not our way to wantonly destroy sentient life, we have, up to this point, refrained from taking corrective measures that might result in the injury or death of your people. We are therefore giving you one final opportunity to vacate this planet. If you do not comply, your settlement, and your people, *will* be destroyed. Leave now or perish, it is your choice. This is your final warning."

Nicole looked to Jack for a moment, then back to Bernice. "Bernie, I need Pierre over here as soon as possible."

"Yes, Governor."

Within five minutes there was a knock on the door. A man in an Alliance uniform, Military Commander Colonel Pierre Francoise, entered.

"Colonel Francoise, good morning."

"Good morning, Governor. What can I do for you?"

Nicole motioned to Bernice. "I need you to see something." She nodded at Bernice and replayed the transmission. When it finished, Francoise shook his head.

"I need your assessment, Colonel."

"May I be completely frank with you, Dr. Reynolds?"

"Of course, please do so," she answered before sitting down.

"I'm afraid that our situation is rather grim. We are in a very vulnerable position here, and we are not prepared to undertake something like this, Governor. We've already seen the size of their ships and a demonstration of their weapons technology, and it's clear that they are prepared to use those weapons if necessary.

"We have zero understanding of the enemy's military capabilities. We have no intelligence on the number of ships, the firepower they possess, their defensive capabilities, their troop numbers…in short we are completely unprepared to go to war with the Machrys. I'm not even certain we could repel them if this were Earth. We're like children with toy guns while the Machrys are packing the real thing.

"Before we even consider undertaking the defense of this settlement and this planet, we're going to need a lot more troops and a lot more equipment. We must also consider evacuating all civilians until the danger has passed."

"I need to contact President Clark about this," Nicole replied. "Anything else?"

The Frenchman rubbed his chin for several seconds. "I'm not going to sugarcoat this, Governor; I believe the safest course of action is to evacuate the colony and abandon the planet. We have a lot of civilians here and more coming every week. Now the Supreme Commander, General Cartwright, and President Clark may disagree with me, I don't know. From what little I do know about these Machrys, they have been traveling the galaxy since before the pyramids, and I believe it is safe to say that nowhere will our inexperience be more evident than in warfare."

"What do we need?" Nicole asked him candidly.

"We need anything the Alliance and the League can send us, including firepower, troops, lots of military intelligence, and equipment. We need ships; at least twenty armed with phase cannons, as many shield generators as we can get, a thousand troops armed to the teeth with pulse rifles, and at least anti-ship dark energy rail guns. Perhaps most importantly, Governor, we need all of this yesterday, since we have no

119

idea when the Machrys might launch such an attack. We might also ask Ambassador Reynolds to request military and diplomatic assistance from the League, perhaps they will help.

"Finally, it's my guess is that the Machrys are watching us at this very moment to see whether we are making moves to evacuate this planet. I recommend we generate some activity so that it appears we are preparing to leave; it could buy us some time."

Nicole let out a heavy sigh. "You're painting a rather grim picture, Colonel."

"I'm sorry, Governor. Believe me, it is not my intention to dishearten you in any way, I seek only to ensure that you are as informed as possible. We've never done this before; we've never been at war with an alien race. Who can know the outcome? I—"

A sound emanated from her communication system and Bernice's image appeared.

"Please pardon the interruption, Governor Reynolds, but there's someone here who would very much like to speak with you."

"I can't now, Bernie, I'm in a very important meeting, and I'm about to contact President Clark about our 'situation,' "Nicole replied, a little terse with her assistant.

"But Governor, that's why he's here."

"Who's here, Bernie?"

"Jokar Motay, the captain of the Shataran ship."

Nicole looked at Pierre Francoise before turning back to Bernice. "Okay, I'll speak with him, please send him in."

"Yes, ma'am."

Jokar Motay entered the room a few seconds later, bowing slightly to Nicole before kissing her hand.

"I understand this is a symbol of endearment to your people, Governor Reynolds."

"Indeed it is, Captain Motay," she replied, worried she was blushing.

"Please, there is no need to be so formal, at least not on my account. I would be pleased if you would call me Jokar."

"Fair enough, Jokar, then call me Nicole."

"As you wish, Nicole."

She stood, entranced for a moment, staring into his golden eyes until Jokar turned to face Pierre.

"Forgive me, Captain Jokar Motay, please allow me to introduce Military Commander Colonel Pierre Francoise."

"Ah, a military man. I'm very pleased to make your acquaintance."

"How is it that we can understand one another, Captain, without a translator?" asked Françoise.

120

Motay held up a finger, which he pointed toward a small, gold disk affixed to his left temple.

"We too have language translators, which allow us to converse with other sentient species. It intercepts incoming sounds in one language and translates the sound on the fly so we hear it in our own, and it interacts with the speech centers in our brains so that the words we think in our own language are actually generated by our vocal cords to create words in your language. You'll find that different sentient races handle universal translation slightly different. Honestly, after five-thousand years, I would have thought that there would be a common language among the races."

"I believe there is, Jokar, but we are new to the League of Sentient Species, so we have yet to learn it."

"I see," he responded, appearing somewhat surprised at that bit of information.

"So, what can I do for you, Jokar? Please have a seat, join us."

Their visitor walked around for a moment before taking a seat. "Actually, I believe the more appropriate question is what can *I* do for *you*? We intercepted a transmission earlier on my ship, a message sent to you by some old friends of ours, the Machrys."

"Oh, you saw that did you?" she asked him after a brief, nervous glance over at Colonel Francoise.

"Indeed. We are familiar with the Machrys, you see, and we thought we should offer assistance to our new friends and allies from Earth. We have experience with their weapons, stratagems, and their capabilities."

"But your knowledge is over five-thousand years old," Francoise pointed out.

"Ordinarily you'd be correct in your assessment of course, Colonel, but I believe that one thing you have yet to learn about the Machrys is that they are a stagnant race, and they are extremely predictable. My people had little difficulty defeating them in my day. Besides, the weapons on my ship, while they are somewhat dated I suppose, were at the time the most advanced and most powerful in the galaxy, far ahead of their time. If you prefer to deal with the Machrys on your own, of course, we will certainly respect your wishes and offer no interference—"

"No! We're not saying that at all, Jokar; are we, Colonel?" She stared hard at her military commander.

"No, of course not. Any assistance would be very welcome, Captain," he said cautiously. "We would be in your debt, sir."

Motay bowed his head slightly. "It would be our pleasure, Captain." Motay then turned to Nicole. "With your permission then, Nicole, I will take my leave so I can inform the others. We should move quickly, because I'm relatively certain you don't have much time before they attack in force." The Shataran rose to leave before turning back to Nicole. "Oh, there's one more thing; if you wish it, we could work with you on developing a planetary shield that would make this world all but impervious from attack. It would provide immeasurable safety to your people from anything like this ever happening again. I doubt we could do it before the Machrys attack, but perhaps afterward...."

"I believe I speak for the entire Alliance when I express my most sincere and deep appreciation for the offer of assistance from you and your people, Jokar; we are most grateful. I will convey to our president everything we've discussed."

"As I said, Nicole, it is my pleasure," he said with a smile, before disappearing out the door.

CHAPTER 20

Dao-ming Wu walked through the woods with her two Alliance babysitters following her closely. An attractive young woman with long, flowing black hair and fair skin from a small village just outside of Beijing, she had come along on the expedition so she could be part of history, one of the first human beings at the first human colony on another planet. She'd been selected, in part, because of her outstanding test scores and her exceptional work ethic. She also hoped that one day, after she'd married, her children and then later her grandchildren would talk of the day when Dao-ming, the first Wu to set foot on another world, did her part to establish humanity's foothold in the stars.

Dao-ming glanced over at her two escorts. She'd noticed when they'd first arrived to escort her on her expedition that the two soldiers were far apart in both appearance and age. The older man, Joe Hunter, had, according to some, been with the Alliance since its founding, and was one of the senior men now; some even said he would soon be the first to retire from the Alliance Military. His hair was gray, and he was easily old enough to be her father. The other man was about the same age as she, though not younger; she felt certain about that. He was handsome and, she learned, currently single, just as she was. They'd only been out on assignment together four or five times, but it had afforded them enough time together that she had learned a considerable bit about him.

He'd introduced himself as Daniel O'Toole from Great Britain…more specifically, he was from Ireland. He was Black Irish, with dark, wavy hair the color of a raven. Daniel had joined the Alliance soon after graduating with honors from university at the top of his class, before spending two years in combat school, where once again he'd excelled. His sharp mental acuity and his exceptional physical conditioning had earned him the opportunity to fly on several escort missions for the Alliance to the Mars Colony before serving there for two years. The young soldier had grown bored and restless always living inside, underground, or in one of the domed cities. As his commanding officer was aware of this, he'd offered Daniel's name up along with a glowing recommendation to Colonel Francoise, who at the time was chief of security for the Mars Colony.

As they left the safety of the protective compound behind them, Dao-ming was suddenly very grateful for the company of the two Alliance escorts, especially Danny's, and the protection they offered her from whatever unknown dangers that might exist on New Eden. Since their arrival, however, the colonists had encountered no indigenous life forms that represented a real threat to human beings, though it would be some time before they could know that to be a certainty.

The Machrys threat, however, hung over the entire colony like a cloud, deflating the excitement, wonder, and enthusiasm they'd experienced after first landing on New Eden. Following the governor's disclosure of the second warning message from the Machrys, many colonists had feared an imminent evacuation despite the offer of assistance from the Shatarans. Already rumors were circulating that the Shatarans had experience dealing with the Machrys, and that they'd volunteered to help fend off any Machrys attack should one arise. The message offered by President Clark was intended to assure everyone that steps were being taken to deal with the Machrys' threat. His directive that the civilians could either leave or stay had relieved the many fears and concerns that had arisen within the settlement, and while a few of the colonists had opted to catch a shuttle back to Earth until the threat had passed, most had elected to stay to see things through. Though it remained unstated, most of them believed that President Clark's confidence was the direct result of the Shatarans' offer to help, and their assurances that they would be able to turn back any Machrys threat.

Dao-ming had decided to stay, so Dr. Billings had assigned her the task of searching for the castilian plant. They'd already found quite a few, but the effort now was to find locations where the plant was found to be more plentiful, and remove one plant from each site in order for the medical personnel to begin evaluating its value to human beings, and for scientists to learn how to best process the vital compound from the plant.

They had been traveling on a path through the woods, on which she'd stayed for most of the search to that point. They had no sooner passed a large tree when off the path and behind some thorny bushes she spotted what appeared to be a number of healthy castilian plants grouped together some distance away. She turned to the two men who stood next to her.

"You can stay here, gentlemen, I will only be a minute. I need to collect one of those plants over there."

"Our orders are to stay close to you, ma'am," replied Hunter.

"Unless you plan to walk or crawl straight through those bushes with the inch long briars, I suggest you wait here; I'll never be out of your sight."

"Understood, ma'am. We'll just wait right here then."

Dao-ming smiled and nodded. "Good. I'll be right back."

The young botanist made her way through the winding bushes and briars until she reached the plants. Just as she'd thought, there were dozens of the plants grouped together in a large patch. It was the biggest patch seen yet, indisputable evidence that the castilian plants grew on New Eden in greater abundance than on any other world known to the League. Carefully she began digging around the base of the plant, patiently ensuring that she preserved the root system. She took out the container she'd brought along for transporting the plant, and placed plenty of the native soil inside the container. She then gently set the plant inside before filling the remainder of the container with dirt.

She was about to pick up the container with the plant to head back to the path when she heard the snapping of a stick nearby. Her head jerked up and she searched the area for movement. She was so startled upon seeing what stood no more than five meters from her that she staggered back against a thorn bush, letting out a scream as one of the thorns penetrated the back of her arm. So terrified was she that despite the intense pain, her eyes never left the creature, which appeared to be nearly as startled as she was.

The creature was dark greenish and purple in color and scaly, with a sharp, pointed beak, and stood upon its hind legs. It also had a long tail, pointed ears, and large black eyes. Despite what she interpreted to be at least some rudimentary level of intelligence, the fearsome appearance of the creature struck terror within her, and she screamed.

"Eeiiyyee!" She turned and ran in terror through the thorns and thistles, with considerably less care than she'd taken going in, and far less than her safety merited. By the time she met the Alliance guards on the other side of the thorn bushes, she was bleeding from several rather serious cuts on her arms, hands, legs, and her right cheek.

"What in the world happened to you, Dao-ming?" Danny asked, fretting and tearing his shirt into pieces to wrap around her wounds. "Look at you, you're a mess! We need to get you back to the settlement, now!"

"There is something in the woods, Danny, something...horrible. It's right th—" She pointed to the exact spot where she'd seen the creature, but after looking all around for any sign of it, soon gave up the effort.

"It gets kind of lonely out here, young lady, and we're all of us still adjusting to this strange world. Anyone could have—"

Dao-ming Wu's face grew hot and flushed.

"I did not imagine it, I saw it!" she screamed, partly in anger, partly in fear, and largely in pain. "Ohh...."

"She needs help, Joe. Look at these gashes, they look so deep." O'Toole's face was filled with concern for her.

The older warrior examined the wounds. "Yeah, she's losing a lot of blood, Danny."

Dao-ming looked back in the direction she'd come. As she worked closely with Billings, she was acquainted with the plant and what it could do, though she was unsure whether what she was about to try would help or even make things worse. But she knew if she did nothing, she'd die before they made it back to the settlement. She grabbed the younger man's wrist and tried pulling him closer.

"Over there, where I was working...there's a plant in a container. Please...bring it to me." She lay back, growing dizzy from the sudden loss of blood.

"No, Dao-ming, there's no time, we have to get you—"

"Please, do as I say, then we can go!" She wanted to explain to him, but she was too weak...so much, in fact, that she'd considered telling them that she wouldn't survive the walk back to the village.

The injured and weary botanist was relieved when, a very short time later, the young O'Toole returned with the plant in hand.

"Can both of you please take a quick look around to make sure it's safe?" she asked Danny.

"But you're bleeding badly, Dao-ming!"

"Please! I don't want to go anywhere until you've looked around."

The two men shook their heads and began walking around, occasionally looking back at her. Dao-ming quickly but carefully plucked three large leaves off the plant and began breaking the leaves until a sappy white substance oozed out, which she subsequently began rubbing on her wounds. Her eyes grew wide upon seeing the deep cuts suddenly start to heal from the inside out. After five minutes, none of the cuts were visible...only the blood remained. Moments later the two guards returned.

"It's safe, we didn't see a thing," O'Toole began, "I...look! The bleeding's stopped; how's that even possible? Your wounds, they were so deep, and now they're gone!" Hunter walked over for a closer look. "Look, Joe, they're gone!"

"I don't believe it," the older man said, shaking his head. "That's impossible."

Dao-ming smiled weakly. The castilian plan had helped heal her wounds, but she would need to ingest some of the plant if she were to make up for the loss of blood. She weighed the risk before deciding it was best to get back to the settlement to rest.

"Please, can you take me back to the settlement? I need to get to the infirmary."

"Of course. You just hang in there, okay? You're going to be fine, I promise." She looked into the young soldier's eyes, and finding strength there, she smiled again.

"Thank you." She wanted to tell them about the plant, about how its healing properties had healed her wounds, but at the last minute she stopped herself, her determination to keep her vow of silence aided by weakness and resignation brought on by her wounds. She would be fine with a few days rest, and that was enough for her. The two men placed her in a portable gurney included in their military backpacks. Ten minutes later they loaded her into the transport and were on their way back to the settlement.

It was a fifteen minute ride in the transport before they would reach the settlement. For the first time since her injury she laid back and allowed herself to relax. Weak and exhausted, her thoughts suddenly shot back to the moment when she stood staring at the terrifying creature in the woods; it was her last thought before everything faded into darkness.

CHAPTER 21

Explosions surrounded her and people screamed, but she stood, frozen, in the middle of town, watching as the Machrys ships destroyed everything she'd worked so hard to build. The ten Machrys ships hung motionless in the sky, reigning down terror from above. The ships opened fire with their main weapon, targeting the settlement. Buildings were disintegrated, people ran everywhere, screaming, bleeding, dying...Once again she was forced to stand idly by, frozen with fear, compelled to watch the dream she loved very much die a quick and painful death. Then she screamed.

Nicole sat up in bed and found herself waking from her nightmare in a cold sweat, thankful to find that it was only a dream. Suddenly, as if at a distance, she heard another thunderous boom; the sound caused her heart to stop as her whole body shook with fear. Then she heard the emergency warning alarm sound before her com system activated.

"Governor Reynolds, Governor Reynolds!"

"Bernie?"

"Yes, ma'am. The Machrys just started attacking the colony, Governor. They are demanding to speak with you immediately!"

Nicole slapped her cheek, walked over to the sink, and splashed some cold water on her face. "Okay, Bernie, I'll speak with them, but the second after you transfer the call, contact Jokar Motay and the other Shatarans and tell them we're under attack. He promised me that he'd be ready, so tell him if he's going to do anything, this is going to be the time. Please ask him to wait until I've finished speaking with the Machrys, and hold Jokar on the line until I've finished. Did you get all of that?"

"Yes, Governor."

Nicole took a deep breath. "Okay, put them through."

"Yes, ma'am; good luck, Governor."

A second later an image of the Machrys commander appeared on her holophone. "We are Admiral Skylok, commander of the Machrys Attack Fleet. You have been warned to abandon this settlement and leave

Machrys space yet you remain. Leave now and you may still be spared; stay, and you will be destroyed. We have ten ships above your settlement now and another ten orbiting the planet. Will you leave immediately or will you stay and perish? What is your decision?"

"Admiral Skylok, we do not desire any conflict with your people, we ask only that—"

"The time for discussion has passed. You have fifteen of your minutes before we level your settlement to the ground. If you plan to stay we suggest that you make peace with whatever deity you hold dear. There will be no further communications."

Nicole immediately touched a soft button on the virtual display. "Bernie?"

An image of her assistant suddenly appeared. "Governor, I cannot reach Jokar Motay. I spoke with one of his lieutenants and Captain Motay is supposed to contact us the moment he returns."

Nicole felt a cold chill run down her spine. For a moment she hesitated, and in her mind's eye she was transported back to a time many years ago. They had both been hiding when the strange man stepped into the bedroom carrying an old-style pulse pistol. She saw it happening again…her brother suddenly jerked away from her as she shook, crying, frozen in terror, watching as the man pointed the weapon at her little brother. She watched as her brother—

"Governor! What should I do?"

The scream from her assistant jarred Nicole back into the present. It would not happen again, not as long as she still breathed. "Get Jack Lincoln on the holophone, immediately. Then find Colonel Francoise and tell him I said to prepare for battle."

"Yes, Governor." Bernie disappeared for several seconds before reappearing. "I have Captain Lincoln."

"Thanks, Bernie."

Bernie nodded and her image vanished, replaced by Jack Lincoln's face. "Governor?"

"Jack, I need you to activate our evacuation plan immediately. Sound the alarm for all civilians to evacuate."

"But I thought the Shatarans—"

"We don't have much time, Captain! We have only ten minutes, so move!"

"Yes, ma'am."

Lincoln disappeared and Francoise appeared.

"Nicole, where are those Shataran friends of yours? They said they'd be here when we needed them, but where are they now?"

Nicole's countenance grew cold and hard. "What's the matter,

130

Colonel, losing your nerve?" she asked with a cold smile.

"No, of course not, it's just that—"

"Look, Pierre, we have no choice. Stand our ground or run like cowards the first time we're challenged by another race. We will fight, with or without the Shatarans, and if necessary, we'll die. Are the shield generators and phase cannons in place?"

"Yes, of course; we activated the moment we saw the Machrys ships."

"And the anti-ship dark energy rail guns?"

"In position and ready, as are the troops, and ten ships armed with phase cannons."

Nicole checked the time. "We have only a few minutes left before they start their attack. May God be with you, Colonel."

"May God be with us all, Governor." Francoise vanished.

Nicole stepped outside of the administration building where she lived and saw the huge Machrys ships positioned in the early morning sky only a few kilometers away. She could tell that the shield generators were both active, since the shield always glowed a deeper blue when there was more than one generator.

"Governor, you've got to get inside, now!" Jack Lincoln appeared in front of the building, took her by the arm, and began ushering her back into the building.

"Why aren't you evacuating the civilians?" she asked.

"Don't worry, Nicole, they're okay. I'd already started shuttling civilians out before you even called for me to; plus I recruited a dozen pilots to help. But for now, we need to get you inside, and maybe you can give a short and sweet bit of encouragement to all of the brave Alliance soldiers out there."

Nicole gave him another look, signaling how annoyed she was, again, but then she nodded; he was right. They had only minutes to spare, so she hurried to the holo-projector, selected broadcast, and switched it on.

"Alliance soldiers and citizens of New Eden. We are about to fight for our very survival, so as we go into battle, remember two things. First, the human race is depending on us to offer a chance for humanity to live on should anything ever happen to Earth. Second, we should all go into battle knowing that this is not the first time men and women have snatched victory from the jaws of death, and it will not be the last. As we fight for our lives and defend our new home, may God go with us; that is all."

No sooner had Nicole finished than the ships attacked. The ten ships began bombarding the settlement on New Eden with heavy weapons fire, pounding the shields, which grew fainter and fainter with each strike, buckling within the first two minutes of the assault. She knew Francoise had given the order to fire the anti-ship dark energy rail guns because particle beams struck the ships, which survived unscathed beneath their heavy shields. Several Alliance ships began firing their phase cannons, but the effect on the massive enemy ships was minimal. Nicole watched in horror as the shields protecting New Eden grew dimmer and dimmer under the heavy, continuous onslaught from the crimson energy pouring out of the Machrys ship.

She began to despair that all was lost, painfully aware that they were out-maneuvered and outgunned. Suddenly, a bright blue beam of energy exploded into the sky, originating from another location on the planet. The massive beam of energy struck the Machrys ships, tearing through five of them in nearly as many seconds, until what little remained of them turned into fireballs as they entered the atmosphere. The remaining five ships quickly turned and started for deep space before disappearing, along with the remaining ships orbiting the planet.

Cheers erupted all over the colony as the Machrys ships disappeared. Nicole looked at Jack with astonishment before leaping into his arms.

"Jack, we did it, I don't believe it! What in the world was that blue energy beam?"

"My guess, the Shatarans."

Nicole smiled at him.

"Yeah. I suppose that—"

Lincoln was interrupted when the holophone began beeping. Motay's image appeared above the projector a moment later.

"Jokar," Nicole began, "a powerful beam of energy just ripped through half of their ships in mere seconds. I don't suppose you or your people had anything to do with that?"

"Why Nicole, I'm hurt. Did you not believe me when I told you that I'd be there when you needed me? Yes, it took some time to get the weapon working and charged up after so long, hence the delay, but as you can tell it worked well."

"That was amazing, Jokar. I don't suppose you would be willing to share that technology with us, would you? It seems neither our shields nor our weapons were very effective against the Machrys. Had you not intervened when you did...."

"Of course, Nicole; we would be honored to share our particle beam technology with you. I suspect it will be some time before the Machrys try that again, but I suggest you consider accepting our offer to help in the construction of a planetary shield as well. I believe you will find our shields to be extremely effective against the Machrys, or just about any other race attempting to attack this planet."

"Thank you, Jokar, you have no idea how much I appreciate your willingness to assist us in defending the colony. As to accepting your help with a planetary shield, the answer is yes, absolutely yes, we'd be greatly in your debt. You know...," Nicole said with a smile, "Both my parents and my grandparents were scientists. I'd very much like to learn more about your particle beam technology and the planetary shields; perhaps we can even adapt them to our Dark Energy Quantum Generators; or better yet, maybe we can develop a new power source based on your designs."

"All that we have is at your disposal, Nicole."

"Thank you, really."

"You're welcome. I'll come over tomorrow morning and bring some designs and lists of the necessary materials."

Nicole looked down for a moment, as if lost in thought, or as if trying to decide something.

"Nicole, will that work for you?"

"Oh, yes, of course, Jokar, tomorrow morning sounds perfect; as you said, we don't know if or when the Machrys might return. My guess is that if they do come back, you can be certain we won't catch them by surprise a second time, they're be better equipped and better prepared."

"Indeed. Tell me something, Nicole," he began with a look if curiosity. "Are all humans as fierce, remarkably perceptive, and intelligent as you are? If so, I'm surprised it's taken humanity so long to make it to the stars."

"Thank you," she replied, without answering his question. "Listen, Jokar, I'm sure living within the small confines of your ship...well, I'm sure it must feel confining. How would you and your people feel about moving into the settlement with us? We've made a lot of progress and we hope it will soon become more of a city than a settlement as we continue to build. We can set up an additional building just for you and your people for a while, and perhaps later, you could choose housing on your own somewhere among us; what do you think?"

"That's a generous offer, and I thank you. Our intention is to finish digging our ship out of the mountainside and complete repairs to our ship, but perhaps we could, for a while at least and on a limited basis, live among your people. It might help facilitate the process of teaching you about our technology as well."

"Good, it's settled then. We can talk more in the morning when you arrive."

"I'm looking forward to it. Perhaps we could have lunch together tomorrow as well?"

"That sounds wonderful, Jokar, thank you."

"Until tomorrow then."

"Until tomorrow." Jokar's image vanished. Nicole's smile faded

133

when she turned to see a sour look on Jack's face. "What's the matter, Jack?"

He shook his head vigorously. "I don't know; something about Jokar and the other Shatarans just doesn't feel right. Don't you get the feeling that they're hiding something?"

Nicole smiled for a moment out of astonishment and exasperation. "They just saved your life, Jack, and my life, and the lives of everyone on this planet; show some gratitude!"

"I know, Nicole, I know. I can't put my finger on it, but there's something...."

"You're paranoid, and maybe...."

"What, a little jealous? Should I be?"

Nicole turned to Jack for a moment, with more astonishment on her face than perhaps she actually felt.

Jack grimaced. "Yeah, that's what I thought. I've got to go get the evacuees back to the settlement; I'll see you later."

Nicole watched as Jack left, wondering for some time whether he was right.

CHAPTER 22

Early the following morning Nicole finally made time to stop by to visit Dao-ming Wu in the medical center. She'd heard about what had happened from the two Alliance officers, but there were several aspects of the account that both intrigued and troubled the governor.

She walked into the infirmary and asked for Dr. Montrose, the chief of staff at the small hospital. Because of the unusual circumstances surrounding what had happened to Dao-Ming, she made it a point to check in with him first. She didn't have to wait very long, because less than five minutes later he came to where she stood waiting.

"Governor Reynolds, please pardon the wait. It's…well, it's a hospital so sometimes things come up."

"Relax, Dr. Montrose, I had something rather important to discuss with you so I wanted to meet with you personally, and privately, if we could. It won't take more than a few minutes, I assure you."

The doctor nodded before pointing to a small room less than twenty-five meters away. "Yes, of course; we can meet there; it's closer than my office."

"That will do nicely. Thank you, Doctor."

They walked in and Montrose closed the door behind them. "What's on your mind, Governor? What could warrant such a visit from you at this hour? Oh, by the way, unbelievable what happened yesterday; I'm assuming it was our Shataran allies who saved the day?"

Nicole smiled. "It's that obvious, is it?"

The doctor returned her smile. "Well, yes. I'm pretty sure the entire colony knows it." He smiled again before looking down; it was her cue.

"So, Dr. Montrose, I understand that you had an unusual patient arrive here late the day before yesterday, before all of the excitement."

"Hmm? Oh, yes, the Wu girl. Yes, very interesting patient, that one. I have her scheduled for a battery of tests later today. It seems she suffered some rather nasty gashes in her arms, legs, and her face, from some rather long and dangerous thorns. According to the two Alliance soldiers serving

135

as her escort, the wounds had bled profusely at one point before closing up and healing on their own accord, before she even arrived…incredible! I have no explanation at this point, I'm afraid."

"I believe I do, Doctor; that's one reason I'm here. I'm going to tell you something that only a handful of people know, and there's a very good reason for that. For now at least, I need your utmost discretion in this matter."

The doctor looked at her with a skeptical grimace before turning and looking out of a window and up at the two stars in the sky and the exotic, alien landscape. He turned to face her, nodding his head. "Governor, you can count on me; I'll keep this as quiet as I can."

"Anyone talking about this before we're ready will face expulsion from the colony, or worse."

"It's that serious?"

"Let's just say that if others learn what I'm about to tell you, we'll have more trouble on our hands than just the Machrys."

"I understand, Governor; you can count on me."

"Good." Nicole strolled across the room and gestured for Montrose to take a seat before doing the same. "A few weeks ago one of the scientists here discovered something that's apparently quite rare in the known universe, a castilian plant."

"Hmmm…castilian. It seems I may have heard of that but I can't place it."

Nicole offered a slight smile. "You may have heard others refer to it as castil, the processed version of the plant."

"Yes, castil, that was it, I—wait, castil, here, really?" Nicole nodded. "That's fantastic! I first read about it in a medical journal a year or so after the Valhari made first contact with Earth. That's wonderful news! Just think how much good we can do if someone's seriously sick or injured. Ah! It all makes sense now."

"I tell you what, Doctor; if you have someone come in that's seriously sick or injured, let me know and we'll talk; otherwise say nothing to anyone, or you risk the lives of everyone on this planet, okay?"

Montrose's face lit up. "Yes, of course, excellent, thank you! I can't wait to conduct my own research on the castil!" He looked up to find Nicole wearing a grave countenance. "Once you've given the all-clear of course." Nicole nodded. "Oh, and I'll cancel Dao-ming's tests immediately so we don't draw suspicion."

"No, no—don't do that. Just collect the results yourself and when you have everything, bring them to me so we can review them together, okay? I'd like to understand more about what the effects are on human beings before word gets out about the plants."

"Of course, whatever you say, Governor Reynolds. I appreciate your confiding in me about this, thank you."

"You're welcome." Nicole rose from the table. "So how is she doing anyway?"

"You can see for yourself if you'd like. All she really needed was some fluid and some rest while her body recovered from the blood loss. She was on the borderline of needing a transfusion, but as you'll see, she's doing much better now. In fact, I'm planning to discharge her once we finish all of the tests, probably sometime late tomorrow."

"Wonderful. Thank you for your assistance and for your cooperation, Doctor. If we can successfully keep a lid on this for now, I believe we're all going to be extremely pleased with what comes afterwards." Nicole stood, shook his hand, and turned to leave. "Oh, what room, Doctor?"

"Room 25."

Nicole nodded and left, confident the doctor would do as he'd promised. She soon found the room and knocked gently.

"Come in."

She gently opened the door. "Dao-ming? It's Nicole Reynolds; may I come in?"

"Yes, of course. How are you, Governor?"

"I'm fine, thanks, but I'm here to talk about you; it sounds like you had quite an ordeal all your own a couple of days ago."

"Yes, ma'am, I suppose you could say that. It was foolish of me to run through those long briars the way I did. I almost died."

"Indeed, and from what I understand, you nearly did. Your reason for such an act is one reason I'm here; as for the other I'm sure you already know."

"The castilian."

"Yes. I understand you're still with us only because you had the presence of mind to take a few leaves and rub them over your wounds."

"Yes. I knew I was already taking a chance rubbing it on the wounds so I was too scared to do anything more. I probably could have avoided a hospital stay had I ingested some of the plant."

"Yes, you surely would have, but not for the reason you might think. Had you ingested the plant you would surely be dead by now, since the plant is poison until it's been correctly processed."

"I didn't know—how could I have missed that?"

"Don't be too hard on yourself, Dao-ming; Dr. Billings had no idea either. Your little experience led him to run some tests on the plant you brought back and found it to be so." Nicole walked in until she stood by the girl's bedside. "Did you tell anyone about the castilian, Dao-ming? I must know if you did."

"I told no one, Governor Reynolds, as I promised. I must confess, however, that I came very close."

"I understand, and we would have dealt with it the best we could had you told them."

"Why are we keeping it a secret, Governor, if you don't mind my asking? Wouldn't it be good for everyone to know what we have, and to use it to heal the sick and injured, and to prolong life?"

"Yes, of course, but we're not ready yet, Dao-ming, we're not prepared. Being in possession of such a powerful and precious substance would bring scavengers, pirates, even other civilizations seeking it for themselves. Possession of a world where such a plant grows would mean great wealth and power, in addition to health and long life. The castilian plant grows only on planets orbiting binary stars, and on only one in every hundred-thousand such worlds. Among this select group of planets there are very few indeed where the castilian plant grows in such numbers. With such a rare and life-giving resource in our possession, we must be prepared, and strong enough, to protect ourselves from those who would destroy us just to get it."

"I see."

"Once we've established a civilization here and we're strong enough, we'll share this knowledge first with Earth, and then with the League. Until then, however, our best defense is keeping the castilian plant's presence on New Eden a closely-guarded secret. Can you help me do that?"

Dao-ming nodded. "Yes, Governor, of course. I will say nothing until you tell me, just as I agreed."

"Good. Now then, tell me what you saw that startled you so that you nearly killed yourself in your rush to get away from it."

The young botanist turned her head away from Nicole for a moment, whether to hide the fear on her face or for some other reason, Nicole could not say. When Dao-ming turned back to face Nicole, she had her answer; the young woman's expression said it all; it was as if she stood on the edge of a great cliff.

"The thing, the creature—whatever it was—was greenish and purple in color and had scales, a beak, and pointed ears. It looked vaguely like a reptile, but it stood on two legs like a man, and it had a tail like a lizard, and the most frightening, large black eyes…they were terrifying!"

Nicole considered stopping the girl before deciding that for the safety of the others at the colony, she should allow her to continue.

"Those eyes, it was as if they saw into my very soul. I was terrified; I've never been so scared in all my life! What was it, do you know?"

Nicole could see the woman had been frightened out of her wits, and decided she would tell the doctor as she left; perhaps she would need something to help her sleep for a few days. Without any prompting Dao-ming continued her recounting, having calmed herself a little.

"Oh, there's something else, Governor Reynolds. I can't be certain, but the purple I saw—I think it could have been some sort of clothing. It looked different in texture as well as color from the rest of it. Didn't the Valhari and the League say that this world was uninhabited?"

"Yes, they did, Dao-ming. Perhaps I'll look into this some more later this morning." The girl smiled. "By the way, I understand someone's been waiting to see you, but the doctor had not permitted visitors. Would you like for me to see if I can persuade Dr. Montrose to allow visitors?"

"Who...?"

"I believe his name is O'Toole; would you like to see him?" Nicole never regretted the offer, for at the mention of the young man's name Dao-ming's eyes lit up and a beautiful smile appeared, like the sun chasing away the clouds after a storm.

"Yes, please."

Nicole placed her hand on the girl's arm and smiled. "You bet; I'll see what I can do. Just get some rest, okay?"

"Yes, ma'am."

Nicole turned, walked out the door, and headed to a nearby nurses' station where she asked for Dr. Montrose. While she waited, she considered who she should talk with about the strange encounter in the woods. She decided to start with Pierre Francoise, followed by at least two others who very well might be able to shed some light on the matter.

CHAPTER 23

While she sat at her desk waiting for Jokar to arrive, Nicole found her thoughts drifting to how similar the Shatarans' anatomy was to human beings. Of course their eyes were gold in color, their skin lavender, and their hair white, but they were in many other respects similar. At the request of Dr. Montrose, Jokar instructed a few of his people to provide Montrose access to the Shataran medical database, and after reviewing some of it, the doctor had reviewed a few of his findings with her. Most of their internal organs were similar to humans, though there were several that, like the human appendix and tonsils, no longer served a vital function, and whose original purpose had been lost and forgotten over time.

Jokar himself had, in fact, made references to the selfsame similarities between their species on several occasions, while at the same time contrasting how different the Machrys were in comparison. While much remained unspoken by Jokar about the Machrys, it seemed evident that the Shatarans and the Machrys had a long and antagonistic history together; it was a subject that she hoped she could one day discuss with him in some detail.

She looked at the time and realized he would be there any moment. It suddenly occurred to her that her pulse had quickened and that she had become more fidgety as the meeting drew closer. The governor of New Eden realized that whether she liked it or not, she felt herself being drawn to Jokar. The Shatarans were an exquisitely beautiful race, and their temperament seemed so steady and their intellect beyond most human beings that she was taken with them as a whole. Jokar was without doubt a most charming and charismatic leader, and while the fact that he was alien troubled her as it seemed to be a barrier to a relationship, other such barriers had been broken down over the centuries; perhaps this one could be as well. The thought then came to her that he'd never mentioned whether he had a family or was even married.

"Governor, Captain Motay has arrived."

"Great, Bernie, please send him in." She stood up and walked over to the door just as Bernie escorted their guest into her office.

"Jokar, good morning and welcome back."

"Thank you for the invitation, Nicole."

Nicole gestured to a chair across from her desk.

"Please, make yourself comfortable."

"Thank you. I must admit that I am pleased to see you again so soon in person, and I look forward to a fruitful discussion. In fact, please allow me to get things started." He produced a clear crystal and handed it to Nicole.

"Thank you, but what is it?"

"It is a data crystal, which contains design specifications on the particle beam cannon we used to cut through the Machrys' ships. It also holds the design specifications for the global shield generator we discussed, and the materials we need in order to construct it. I understand that your computers are based on Valhari technology, so the crystal should interface with your computers."

"Excellent; thank you, Jokar. Could you make any of your engineers available to work with some of ours on the construction of the first weapon? Perhaps we could offer something in exchange?"

Motay smiled at her. "All I require of you is that you dine with me this evening."

"Okay," she replied, returning the smile. "It's a deal…I'd be happy to. I believe there may be something else we can offer you that will pique your interest."

"We have everything we need, Nicole, I don't think—"

"We have some castilian plant we can share with you, if you agree to show us how to process it."

"Castilian plant, here? Really?"

"Your people haven't seen it here?"

"Not around the ship, no, and we've been far too busy for exploration of the surrounding terrain. Castilian, here—incredible. Yes, thank you, Nicole. You must realize, however, that while we were sleeping the other sentient races must have developed a much better process for refining castil than what we used five-thousand years ago."

"Yes, I'm sure they have."

Motay studied her for several seconds. "Ah, I see. You are indeed a wise leader, Nicole Reynolds; these colonists are fortunate indeed to have you. Your colony, indeed your home world as well, would have some difficulty defending itself from some of the more barbaric of the sentient races out there."

"Our ambassador assures me that none of the league members would act in such a manner."

"Indeed, but unless things have changed—and I'm confident they have not—a number of sentient races have, like the Machrys, chosen not to join the League. Am I correct?" Nicole nodded. "And I'm confident that the Machrys still haven't joined the League, even after all these years."

"No, they haven't, though I understand that Shatara did, about the same time you crash landed here, from what I understand." Nicole was surprised by the smirk that appeared on Motay's face.

"Yes, it was being considered even in my time." Motay gestured to the crystal before focusing his stare on Nicole, but the change of subject, no matter how subtly handled, was not lost on Nicole. "The planetary shield and the particle-beam cannon will prove very useful to you in protecting this planet. In fact, possession of the castilian plant on this world will make you a wealthy and powerful civilization, Nicole. I congratulate you on your good fortune."

"Thank you." Something in his gaze troubled her, though not enough to cause her any alarm, and it soon disappeared regardless. She chalked it up to an overactive imagination or simply a lack of diplomatic skill on her part. "So, Jokar, the particle beam cannon, does it use dark energy?"

"I won't deceive you, Nicole; the particle beam cannon was a highly experimental weapon in my day, and only a few ships had them. There were some so powerful that they were called planet-killers. It is also very dangerous. The cannon derives energy by creating a micro-singularity inside of a reinforced force field. The power generated from the singularity is then directed through specially designed crystals, where it is focused into the powerful beam you saw when we fired upon the Machrys ship."

"The particle beam cannon may be dangerous, but so is having your planet attacked. What about the planetary shield you mentioned?"

"Yes. The planetary shields we built come in various designs. Some function by using shield generators, once again using micro-singularity power cells to generate the necessary power, deployed in orbit around the planet. Another design works by setting up ground-based shield generators in specific locations around the planet."

"How many are needed in space versus on the ground?"

"We've been able to create successful planetary shields around a planet this size with as few as twenty-five in orbit, and as few as seventy-five based on the ground."

"How long does it take to create these micro-singularity power cells?"

"Once we have the necessary materials, we can create perhaps one every five days. The process is slow and must be done carefully, for obvious reasons."

"So you don't inadvertently create a black hole that will swallow you and your entire planet with you?"

"Exactly."

Nicole mulled it over for some time.

""Well, like I said, at least with the micro-singularity power cells we have a chance of surviving an attack. We'll take a look at the list of materials on your list and get started on gathering them; hopefully we'll have everything we need to get started within one week."

"Excellent."

Nicole rose behind her desk. "Ready for lunch?"

"Indeed, I'm famished."

"Good. I admit to knowing little about Shataran cuisine, so hopefully the Alliance chefs will know more than I do. Maybe we'll get lucky."

"I'm sure it will be fine."

Nicole nodded as they walked out the door and began walking down the newly paved road on their way to the dining hall.

"Jokar, I'm curious about something. You haven't said anything about contacting your home world. If your interstellar communications are still down we'd be happy to relay a message for you."

Motay replied without missing a beat, as if prepared for the question. "Thank you for your offer, Governor Reynolds," he said, smiling. "No, we just wanted to wait until the ship was repaired and then surprise our people. It's been over five-thousand years, after all; we've waited this long, so we decided we can easily wait another few months."

Nicole considered his response before continuing. "Makes sense, just curious."

They arrived at the dining hall. The governor opened the door and Jokar walked inside, followed closely by Nicole. A few minutes later she and her lavender-skinned acquaintance were seated at a table in the executive dining room.

"Is everything okay, Jokar?"

"Yes, surprisingly it is. I've never eaten human food so I'm glad to have the opportunity to try some. Of course, I'm very grateful your chef took the time to prepare some Shataran dishes when he learned we would be here in your settlement from time to time."

"Yeah, me too," Nicole added with a laugh.

Soon, the two of them had finished their lunch.

"There's another matter I hoped to discuss with you, Jokar. It involves something one of our people saw the other day while gathering some castilian plants." Nicole reached into her desk and withdrew her data pad. A virtual panel appeared, and after pressing a few soft buttons, an image appeared above the device. "This is what she described to us; she did the best she could drawing this from memory. Have you ever seen anything like this before?"

Jokar Motay stared at the image, studying it for quite some time without saying a word. It was several minutes before he said anything.

"Jokar?"

"They are called the Hantari. They are vile, warlike beings, bent on galactic conquest, preying on weaker civilizations and anyone else who stands in their way. They once set out to exterminate an entire race back in my time, during what came to be known as The Great Purge. We thought we understood them, we thought we could trust them, but we were mistaken."

"What do you mean?" asked Nicole, now worried that the creatures were somewhere on New Eden.

"We took it upon ourselves to bring them into the galactic community before they were ready. We provided them with new, advanced technologies, and we gave them interplanetary flight. They proved to be much more aggressive than we'd been led to believe; after they were finally stopped and condemned during the Great Purge, a group of them broke away from the rest, convinced that they were destined to rule the galaxy with an iron hand." Motay paused and looked up at Nicole. "After that I do not know, for that is when we crashed here and fell asleep." Nicole simply nodded her head. "If they are here, on this world, then you and your people are in grave danger, Nicole. We will do what we can to protect you, but...."

"I understand."

"Perhaps we can attempt to help you find and detain—or if necessary destroy—these Hantari?"

"Yes, I believe your help in this matter also would be greatly appreciated."

"We're happy to help. Now then, shall we discuss plans for this evening?" She reached out to shake his hand as the meeting ended. Instead of shaking it, he took her hand and kissed it while looking into her eyes.

Nicole blushed.

CHAPTER 24

Hank had now been Earth's ambassador to the League of Sentient Species for six months and he was feeling it, exhausted after another long day of meetings. There had been a steep learning curve familiarizing himself with the many different races that made up the League, but he was finally learning how to pace himself and overall, he felt like he was starting to settle in nicely.

He'd learned a great deal about Val during his stay on the planet, and he'd come to learn that in many ways, the Valhari were much like human beings, though they were a much gentler species overall and extremely intelligent. They were, in many ways, what human beings had often hoped alien beings would be like, benign and magnanimous creatures.

Hank looked out of a window of his apartment, which overlooked a beautiful natural area that was the Valharan version of a park. In the center of the park sat a small lake, a vibrant deep blue, which resembled the deep blue oceans of Earth in color. Next to the lake stood a giant statue, which appeared to be made from a stone that resembled a composite of jade, emerald, and marble. The sculture had no face, and wore a long white robe with a hood. The sculpture, he was told, was a representation of one of the Valhari Ancients, whom they had called the Nameless One; the Valhari who had, thousands of years earlier, brought the Valhari together and set them on a path of tranquility and knowledge, and led them to develop a society and culture of peace and mutual respect. He had gently turned the Valhari back to worshipping the Most Ancient, who created the universe and all life.

Most of the Valhari, but not all, worshipped the Most Ancient. Hank had not yet learned enough about their religion to know whether this god was in any way like the Judeo/Christian God worshipped by billions on Earth, though he was beginning to suspect that it *could be* the same God. Many of the teachings were the same after all; a doctrine of peace, justice, compassion, and salvation from a sinful universe.

Hank looked up at the Valharan sky, gazing in wonder at the

amazing splendor all around him on Val. The Valhari people prized beauty; it was as important to them as the air they breathed. Zing had once told him that the Valhari strove for beauty, compassion, and understanding in nearly everything they did. Even the buildings themselves were works of art, sculptured out of precious gems and metals that glittered in the sun. It seemed that everything on the planet was a vibrant color of some sort. The clouds were white like those on Earth, but the sky was a light, pinkish, soft-orange in color, more like Mars than Earth. Glancing down at the park again his gaze fell on the long row of zithril trees. The most abundant vegetation on Val, the planet's native tree, the zithril tree, always grew with three trunks and six branches; if only one branch was damaged, the entire tree died. Each of the trees could produce as many as six different types of fruits on a single tree, with each branch often containing a different fruit. It was extremely nutritious and had once made up a significant portion of the Valhari diet. He had just picked up a bottle of the zithril juice and was starting to take his first sip when a holographic image of his assistant, Maria Montrosa, a human who'd come to Val to work with him, appeared on the holocom.

"Ambassador Reynolds, your daughter is on the line for you."

"Okay, thanks, Maria. Any more meetings today?"

"No, I believe your meeting with the Anteran ambassador was the last one scheduled for today."

"Okay, thanks Maria. Why don't you go on home? I'll finish up here; have a good night."

"Thank you, Mr. Ambassador. Have a wonderful evening yourself, sir."

Hank pressed a button on the holocom. The image of his daughter appeared on the desk in front of him.

"Nicole, honey, how are you doing? You were a little shook up the other day when we spoke following the Machrys attack. I—" Static and interference disrupted the image and the voice of his daughter so that he could recognize neither. A few moments later the interference cleared.

"Sorry, Dad. The flares…they're wreaking more and more havoc on our communications. Our planetary meteorologist tells us that within a couple of days we won't have any communications at all. We might even have trouble operating our ships until they calm down."

"How long are they supposed to last, honey?"

"No more than two or three months. Apparently we are approaching the height of the coronal stellar storm."

"Is New Eden in any danger?"

"No, we should be fine. We just may be without communications and transportation for a while. I have some good news, though."

"Great, let's hear it."

"The Shatarans are helping us build a particle beam weapon that we can use to defend New Eden from the Machrys, or other would-be invaders, as well as a planetary shield. The work has been going so well that we might have it done within a few weeks."

"That's fantastic news, Nicole. Have you had any more problems with the Machrys?"

"None."

"Interesting."

"Before we lose communications, Dad, I had something I was hoping you could look into for me."

"Sure, sweetheart, anything."

"Have you ever heard of the Hantari?"

"No, not that I can recall, anyway. Why?"

"One of our people apparently came across one in the woods. According to Jokar—"

"Who?"

"The leader of the Shatarans here."

"Oh."

"He says they're bad news. If they're here on New Eden, we could have a problem."

"I've encountered just about every intelligent species in the Milky Way here, Nicole, but I don't recall ever meeting or hearing of a Hantari. I'll check around though, see what I can find out."

"Thanks, Dad, I—" Once again the image became very distorted and her words unintelligible. It lasted longer this time, and Hank began to worry he'd lose her altogether. After several minutes the interruption finally faded slowly away.

"Dad?"

"Hey—Nicole, you're back."

"Yeah, but I doubt it'll be for long, so I'll make this quick. That weapon the Shatarans used to cut through the Machrys ships; guess where it derives its power."

"I don't know honey…dark energy?"

"No; micro-singularity power cells."

"What? Nicole, you can't have those on New Eden. You know how dangerous they can be; that's why they were banned throughout the galaxy."

"What choice do we have, Dad? The Machrys were about to destroy the colony; the Shataran weapon was the only thing that saved us!"

"I understand that, Nicole. What good did it do you, however, if one of those micro-singularity cells turns into a full-blown black hole, killing

149

you and destroying the planet? There's got to be a better way, Nikki."

"If there is, I don't know what it is at this point, Dad. *Our* shields and cannons were no match for the Machrys."

"Okay, I'll ask around about that as well. I imagine that once they understand the danger my daughter is in, and Earth's first colony, they might be more amenable to working with me on an arrangement for sharing a technology powerful enough to protect New Eden."

"Thanks, Dad. In the meantime, however, I have no choice other than to accept the Shatarans' offer to share their technology with us. Perhaps I can find a way to protect against a failure in one of the cells, which would greatly reduce the risk. It's worth…." Her image started wavering again. "…risk."

"I'm about to lose you again, Nikki."

"Okay, Dad. Let me know what you find out, okay?"

"You bet. Be careful now, I mean it. Take care of yourself, and your people."

"I will, Dad. Come and see me when you have a chance, okay?"

"Okay, sweetheart. I love you!"

"I love you too, Dad. Tell Mom that I love her too. Bye, Dad."

"Okay, Nikki, bye." Hank waved his hand and the virtual console appeared. Instead of the image of his assistant, Maria, he saw only "Offline."

"Oh, that's right," he muttered to himself, before walking across the room and out the door to his assistant's desk. He activated her console, and after a searching for thirty seconds, he came across Zing's contact information. Hank considered trying to contact Zing before deciding it could wait until morning. The Machrys, the Shatarans, and the Hantari, three races he knew next to nothing about. He knew only that the planet Shatara was a member of the league. After his last conversation with his daughter, he was now less concerned about the Machrys and was now focused on the micro-singularity technology the Shatarans used. What kind of civilization would play so recklessly with one of the most dangerous forces in the universe? There were a lot of questions and he needed answers soon. It wasn't just his daughter's life at risk, but the lives of all of the colonists, and perhaps Earth as well.

CHAPTER 25

Hank found an unexpected guest waiting for him outside his office door the following morning. He could barely contain his curiosity about what could have led Rojic Itanus, the Anteran ambassador to the League, to do such a thing; it was quite unlike an Anteran to surprise anyone. Whether the Anteran representative had been pressured to address an urgent issue of trade or politics, or something else, it must have been deemed too important to wait.

"Ambassador Itanus, it's good to see you again." The two bowed their heads slightly to one another, the generally accepted manner of greeting among League diplomats.

"And you as well, Ambassador Reynolds," Itanus replied, in the high-pitched vibration they used to produce sound.

"Please, come in, Ambassador," Hank offered after opening the door. Itanus smiled and nodded slightly before entering.

"Please forgive this unannounced visit, Dr. Reynolds," the Anteran began. "It's unacceptable and rude, and I apologize." His visitor was clearly unhappy with the break in formality, which Hank had learned was sacrosanct to the Anterans.

"That's quite all right, Ambassador. What can I do for you?"

"Well, it's actually more what I can do for *you* that's important, Ambassador Reynolds. I was contacted late yesterday, by our mutual acquaintance, President Zing."

Hank smiled, now possessing a more perfect understanding concerning the impetus for his guest's appearance. "I see."

"He informed me that you had inquired about a race of beings known as the Hantari."

"Yes, Professor Itanus, I did ask him about them," Hank replied, addressing Itanus by his civilian title. "My daughter, Nicole, is the governor of Earth's first colony, a planet we call New Eden. She said that another colonist had encountered a Hantari there."

This generated a response that was both unexpected and amusing.

The Anterans were creatures whose bodies were largely crystalline, and while normally they were a very faint light blue in color, they turned a faint reddish color when experiencing intense emotions. Hank frequently found their expressions of emotion to appear quite humorous, although he had developed enough self-control that he never allowed it to show.

"I find that statement quite remarkable, Dr. Reynolds; are you quite certain that your daughter said *Hantari*? Perhaps you misunderstood her."

Hank shook his head. "No, Professor, I'm quite certain. But I'm curious, why do you find it so remarkable?"

"Because, Dr. Reynolds, this is the first time anyone's reported seeing a Hantari for well over two thousand years. You see, the Hantari were one of the founding members of the League of Sentient species. Indeed, they were among the very first of all the sentient races in our galaxy to leave their home world and venture out into the cosmos."

"What happened to them?"

The Anteran cast a downward look for several seconds before looking back to Hank.

"No one really knows for sure. Some say that they grew so tired and weary of the war and the evil among the races that they left the galaxy altogether looking for something better, a more promising corner of the universe, if you will permit me to say. Others contend, however, that over many thousands of years they slowly lost their ability to procreate, and that despite their extremely long life-spans, they eventually died off as a race. Still others claim that the Hantari were attacked, destroyed by the very warring race they'd guided and nurtured. It is, I'm afraid, one of the many mysteries of the universe which is, despite our combined knowledge and technology, a question that we still have no answer to."

"So why did you come here this morning, Professor, to tell me this?"

"Well, yes and no. As I'm sure you are aware, President Zing is rather dogged at times in matters he deems of great importance, and as he is familiar with my scholarly background, it seems he felt I could be of service to you. I was a professor of interstellar archaeology on my home planet, having traveled extensively across this galaxy, researching the ancient past of the various races, and combing through archaeological evidence. I conducted some research on the Hantari while at the university, which is why I know so much about them. But there was another reason I agreed to come meet with you this morning, Ambassador Reynolds."

"And that is?" Hank asked, puzzled where the conversation was leading.

"If the Hantari really *are* still in this galaxy, if there are still some of them living amongst us, in hiding, and if what your colonist saw was

152

indeed a Hantari, then there must be some matter of grave importance that has drawn them back out into the open. The Hantari had, you see, become a very reclusive race, which is one reason no one is really certain what became of them. My point is this; your daughter could be in great danger, as could the rest of your colony, perhaps even your Earth."

The cold expression on the Anteran's face told Hank that the ambassador was deadly serious.

"I think she'll be just fine, Ambassador Itanus; they've already survived an attack at the hands of the Machrys. Of course, it didn't hurt that they had a lot of help."

"What do you mean?"

"They encountered yet another race there—in stasis for some time as I understand it...Shatarans. And from what I understand they really stepped up and saved the colony from the Machrys. They had some sort of powerful weapon that sliced through the Machrys ships, saving every colonist on the planet."

"Shatarans? Where is this 'New Eden' located, anyway?"

Hank gestured toward the door. "Please, Ambassador, let's step into my office."

The Anteran walked towards the door, which quickly opened to permit entrance. The two ambassadors walked in and took seats on either side of his desk.

Hank waved his hand, which generated a virtual system. He selected a few buttons and a star map suddenly appeared over his desk between him and the ambassador. After scrolling through a number of virtual star systems, the requested system appeared. Hank pointed to a planet orbiting two large stars.

"Here we are, New Eden."

"Hmmm," the Anteran muttered. "That is too close to Machrys space for Shatarans to be there. Surely they have broken the ancient treaty with the Machrys and the League if indeed they are on your colony."

"Well, in this case their ship seems to have crash landed there quite some ago, and they've only recently been awakened from stasis. In fact, when my daughter showed the Shataran leader a drawing of the creature seen in the woods, it was he who identified it as a Hantari."

"Yes, well, I suppose that makes sense then. You see, long ago, the Shatarans and the Hantari were very close. The Hantari, one of the oldest races in the galaxy, recognized the aggressive nature of the warlike Shataran people, but they also recognized a greatness in them, a capacity to accomplish tremendous and amazing achievements. In spite of the risk, they took it upon themselves to mentor the younger and less advanced Shatarans. Not wholly unlike what the Valhari have done with you, I suppose."

Hank looked up at his unusual guest, uncertain whether humanity had just been insulted, paid a compliment, or both. He was finding it difficult to interpret the meaning behind the words of some of the other races in the League, with the Anterans topping the list. But something also came to mind that concerned him.

"Wait a minute, Professor…are you saying that the Hantari were more advanced, and that *they* mentored the *Shatarans*? My daughter seems to be under the impression that it was the other way around."

"No, Hank Reynolds, I assure you that I'm quite certain. The historical record on both worlds, and on others, are irrefutable on this point."

"Interesting," Hank replied, puzzled as to what the discrepancy could mean.

"So," the Anteran ambassador continued, "the Hantari helped them achieve interstellar flight and helped them find and then inhabit alien worlds, taming the environment to meet their needs. During that period, it was quite common to find Shatarans and Hantari together. There was extensive trade between the two planets, and the cultures mingled freely between the two worlds. Eventually, the technological prowess of the Shatarans approached that of the Hantari, as the bond between the two worlds grew ever stronger. Their combined technological prowess was unlike anything ever seen in this galaxy, and the synergy they created sparked a technological revolution, with some of the greatest leaps in technology the galaxy has ever known achieved within only a few hundred years. According to some ancient records I found some years ago on Hantor, the abandoned Hantari home world, and in the archives on Shatara, the Shataran home world, this collaboration lasted a thousand years."

"So what happened?" Hank asked with a grin, enthralled with the tale.

The Anteran lowered his head in what to Hank resembled a sorrowful expression. "It is an unfortunate reality that all things in this universe eventually come to an end. With the great strides in science and technology, the two worlds soon surpassed all other races in terms of technological prowess and military power by an incredibly wide margin; that's when a disagreement broke out between some of the Shatarans and the Hantari. The Hantari wanted to share these technological advances with the other races, to the betterment of all species. Some of the Shatarans, however, had become drunk with power and a feeling of superiority; they had come to believe that the stronger, more advanced civilizations should do more than just mentor the lesser developed worlds,

154

they should rule them. The Hantari and the Shataran governments finally came to an agreement, with both insisting that the technology be shared, a turn of events that left the dissenters feeling quite bitter.

"Now this breakaway group of dissenters within the Shataran Federation was relatively small at first, but they were bold, and they were fearless. Over the course of only a few years, the Shataran dissenters rose to power within the Shataran government and soon ruled it. They quickly declared all Shataran technology off-limits to non-Shatarans, offering it only to civilizations willing to subject themselves to the will and governance of the Shataran Federation.

"As you might expect, the Hantari were very upset at this development. They spent years working to convince the Shatarans to reverse course, but their efforts were frustrated at every turn as the movement rapidly expanded within the Shataran Federation. The Hantari, disgusted at the turn of events that led to worlds trading their freedom and sovereignty for access to Shataran technology, finally decided to break-off relations with the Shatarans. After their break with the Shatarans, most records of what happened to the Hantari was lost during the time of the Great Purge; they—"

"Pardon me, Ambassador—what is this *Great Purge*?"

The Anteran now became quite sullen. "It is one of the darkest periods in our galaxy's long history, Hank Reynolds. After the Hantari faded from memory, the Shatarans' lust for power and glory grew ever more consuming until eventually, they and the worlds they controlled began selecting races they deemed 'unworthy' to continue. They began combing the galaxy for sentient beings, and if they were too inferior, too different, or if the Shatarans perceived they might one day pose a threat, they destroyed that world, Hank Reynolds, and every sentient being on the planet."

"But the Shatarans on New Eden saved the lives of every colonist on the planet," Hank protested, attempting to defend the race of beings that had saved his daughter's life.

"Oh yes, of course. So eventually, the genocide of sentient beings came to offend so many Shatarans that the movement began to wither before disappearing altogether. The Shatarans of today are nothing like their ancient forbears."

"So, they've finally become the noble people the Hantari wanted so much for them to be." Hank was stunned when he noticed another color shift to red, and what almost appeared to be a smile on the face of the Anteran ambassador.

"Indeed they have; the Hantari *would* be proud. Did any of this help you, Ambassador Reynolds?"

Hank nodded. "Absolutely. I can't thank you enough for sharing all of this with me."

"Then I am glad I came to your office this morning." Rojic Itanus rose to leave. "I should be going now, Dr. Reynolds, as I have taken up quite enough of your time."

"Nonsense, Ambassador Itanus, you have done me an invaluable service. If there is ever anything I can do to repay you, please let me know."

Itanus stopped and turned to Hank. "There is one thing you could do for me, Dr. Reynolds."

"Name it."

"Should you find that the Hantari are indeed on New Eden, I would very much like to ask one question of them."

"And what is that?"

"Where have they been?"

The Anteran then left Hank's office, leaving him alone to ponder a great many things; among them, what exactly was happening on New Eden?

CHAPTER 26

"After months of regular shipments of food and supplies from Earth, as well as a number of deliveries from several other League worlds, the coronal mass ejections from the twin suns have now intensified to the point that off-world communications are impossible, and the shipments of people and supplies is considered to be very hazardous. The colony will be on its own for at least a few months, until the storms on Meta and Stratus subside."

It was the first of many "State of the Colony" addresses she would be giving over the course of her term in office. Looking over the large gathering of men and women in attendance, she estimated at least ninety percent of the colony had turned out for the occasion.

"Fortunately," she continued, "the tremendous influx of supplies and people have allowed the colony to flourish. Due to the extraordinary efforts of our botanists, zoologists, and medical teams, we have now identified plants, fruits, vegetables, and even some of the animal life that are safe for us to eat. While the botanists have been conducting a number of experiments with select crops from Earth as well, and have had some success at growing them here under very controlled conditions, we have no intentions at this time of growing the same crops here that we grew on Earth. To the greatest extent possible we will eat food indigenous to New Eden, though on occasion we may grow food imported from Earth as well.

"The additional people and supplies have also enabled us to construct much larger and more permanent structures, including underground evacuation shelters that were built in the event of another attack from the Machrys, or anyone else. What has thrilled me the most, however, is the incredible progress we've made, with the Shatarans' help, on the construction of the particle beam cannons and the planetary shield. They are, in fact, something I'd like to discuss with you during this gathering."

Nicole looked around inside the auditorium at the odd assortment of people in attendance. She stood at a podium that sat between two tables on a stage, surrounded by key figures from around the colony. On her right sat Jokar and several other Shatarans, while on her left sat Jack Lincoln, Pierre Francoise, and an assortment of scientists and leaders in the colony. In the audience sat many of the colonists, as well as a reasonably-sized contingent of Shatarans, which Nicole had noticed seemed to unnerve both Lincoln and Francoise.

"I'm told by Dr. Williams, one of our lead engineers and the project manager for the particle beam cannons, that the first of the particle beam cannons is nearly ready to test. Dr. Yomatso, the project manager for the planetary shield, believes it too will soon be ready to test, hopefully within two weeks. These devices will enable us to protect ourselves in the event the Machrys, or any other race of beings, ever threaten our planet again. I would be remiss at this point, however, if I did not pause to offer my most sincere appreciation to the Shatarans. I would like to especially thank Jokar Motay, their leader, for not only using the particle beam cannon aboard their ship to stop the Machrys attack, but also for sharing that technology, along with the specifications for building a planetary shield. With these cannons and this shield we will, for the first time, be able to live at peace on this world without the constant fear of attack from the Machrys." Nicole turned and smiled at Motay. "Thank you, Captain Jokar Motay, for being such a friend to us in our desperate hour of need."

Motay stood and smiled at Nicole before offering a slight bow to her and those in the audience. She offered her hand, which he took and kissed before offering an unseen smile to Nicole. Applause exploded throughout the auditorium and continued for so long that Nicole was forced to signal for the crowd to take their seats once more. She was about to continue when someone in the audience offered up a question for her.

"Governor Reynolds, there's a rumor that the Shataran technology derives its incredible power from a black hole. Is that true, and if it is, doesn't that present an incredibly dangerous risk to the colony?"

"Yes," Nicole began, "the technology does use a micro-singularity as its power source, but it has a variety of safety measures built-in to guard against the power cell developing into a full-blown black hole. I've worked with their engineers to design an additional safety measure as well, one in which, should a micro-singularity cell be energized and containment fails, it will automatically generate a shield around itself which is powered by its own energy. The black hole would begin to consume itself before disappearing entirely.

"Listen, the energy output of these micro-singularity cells is far beyond anything we've ever seen. We'll continue working on finding an alternative power source for the shield and the cannons, but in the meantime, we'll use the micro-singularity cells. Believe me, I'm confident we've found a safe and effective way to protect ourselves, at least for the short term. To summarize, we expect that the cannons and the shield will be ready for testing within two weeks or less, and that once the shield is activated and the cannons online, we will all be able to breathe a little easier.

"If there are no further questions at this time, I would like to take a moment to thank each and every one of you for the tremendous work you've been doing to help get this colony, this vast, new world settled; our settlement here establishes humanity's first real foothold beyond Earth. Rest assured that we will not only survive here, we will thrive here as well.

"Lastly, an update on the stellar activity that's been affecting our communications with Earth; we expect it to be diminishing, allowing communications and shuttle traffic to be restored soon, once the storms on Meta and Stratus have ceased. Thank you all for coming, and may God bless New Eden."

The Gathering Hall, the only structure in the colony large enough to accommodate all of the colonists, was soon empty, with only those at the table and Nicole remaining.

"That was a fine speech, Nicole," Motay said with a smile as he walked over to her. She returned the smile and placed a hand on his shoulder.

"Thank you, Jokar. I meant every word, you know; we are very much in your debt."

"Then come to dinner with me this evening, so we can discuss other ways in which we might work together to help your people, and mine. What do you say?" Nicole, caught off guard by the invitation, said nothing. Motay waited patiently for a reply to his offer.

"Sure, yes, that sounds wonderful, Jokar, thank you."

Motay kissed her hand once more. "Wonderful. I'll stop by your quarters later, say around 7:00 PM?"

"Okay."

"Oh, there was one other thing—a request I'd like to make. I was hoping you might loan us one of your ships, just long enough that we could trade for the parts we need for the repairs we've been making to our own ship. There are several components we desperately need in order to get our ship operational again."

Nicole furrowed her brow. On the one hand she doubted President Clark would agree to it if she asked, but on the other she was responsible for the colony, and these were ships that now belonged to them.

"If it is going to cause you any problems whatsoever, Nicole, then please, do not fret about it. It will take considerably longer but we should be able to fabricate the components we need ourselves."

Nicole grimaced, recalling how Jokar and the others had saved the lives of everyone in the colony by firing on the Machrys ships.

"How long will you need it?" she asked.

"I would estimate it would be for no more than seven rotations of this planet."

"A week?"

"Yes."

"What about the Meta-Stratus flares?"

"We have already calculated what we believe to be a safe window for leaving the planet; it's dangerous, but at one time we had some of the best pilots in the galaxy. You can rest assured that my crew *and* your ship will be safe."

"Would you mind if I sent some of my people with you?"

"Certainly, if you insist, Governor, but I strongly advise against it. As I said, we believe we can safely take the ship through a narrow window between flares, but it will be extraordinarily hazardous. Furthermore, some of the places we plan to go to trade could be dangerous, and not receptive to an alien species they've never encountered. I would rather not be responsible for the safety of your men as well as my own."

Nicole nodded. "I understand, Jokar. Yes, of course. I will make arrangements for a ship to be made available to you and your men immediately."

"Thank you very much, Governor Reynolds." Motay bowed slightly, smiled, and turned to leave. Within a few minutes only Nicole and Jack remained.

"Nice speech, Nicole," Jack told her with a smile.

"Thank you."

"I have a request to ask of you as well, Nicole."

"Sure, of course, Jack. What can I do for you?" she asked, with concern in her voice.

"Be careful in your dealings with the Shatarans, Nicole. I don't trust them."

"What? You don't trust them, even after everything they've done for us?"

"All I'm trying to say is that you need to keep a closer eye on these Shatarans. They're extremely dangerous, we've already seen that. After all, think about it for a moment. We don't really know anything about them; we don't know whether their story is true about being in stasis so long, and we don't know what their intentions are, or if they're even serious about leaving once they're done making repairs to their ship."

Nicole threw up her hands in exasperation. Although she knew Lincoln was more suspicious than the other colonists when it came to the

160

Shatarans, she hadn't realized *how* deep his distrust ran. Why couldn't he be as open minded as the others, and realize that they were their friends?

"Look, Jack, you know that I've slowly come to respect you, and that I value your opinion highly, but I just don't understand what your problem is with the Shatarans."

"Yeah, I know," replied Lincoln, before muttering, "*That's* the problem."

"What? Just what exactly is that supposed to mean?"

Jack hesitated. "Never mind."

"Jack?" Nicole made it clear she wasn't overlooking the comment.

"Look, Nicole, I doubt there's anyone in the colony who hasn't seen the way you look at him."

"Who? What are you talking about?"

"Come on, Nicole—Jokar, that's who!"

The hint of anger in his voice surprised her. The captain had made his own interest in her no secret, but she now began to wonder whether his jealousy was affecting his judgment.

"I don't know what you're talking about, Jack, and I won't even dignify that last comment with a response; but I still don't understand why you're so suspicious of the Shatarans. What have they done to cause you such concern? Have you already forgotten how they saved our colony from a Machrys attack?"

"You've lost your objectivity, Nicole. I think you've allowed yourself to be swept away by this Jokar fellow. These Shatarans may well end up posing more of a threat to New Eden than the Machrys!"

"That's ridiculous, Jack; how could you even think such a thing? If they were going to do us harm, why save us from the Machrys, and why not act before now? It doesn't make any sense."

"Maybe I'm right, and maybe I'm wrong, but shouldn't you be just a little more suspicious yourself? Shouldn't you be looking at the Shatarans more objectively? Come on, Nicole, you're the smartest person I've ever met…you know things don't add up. Think about it. What's taking them so long to repair their ship? Why haven't they already contacted their home world, or the League? I think you need to be a little more objective in your dealings with them, don't you? After all, isn't your primary responsibility here the protection of the colony?"

"How dare you accuse me of putting my own interests ahead of the colony! Get out of here, Jack, now!"

"Nicole, listen, I didn't mean to suggest—"

"Get out!"

Jack said nothing else, other than pausing for a moment to look back at her apologetically. She watched him, filled with indignation as he sheepishly rose and left the room. She sat back down in her chair for several minutes, trying her best to convince herself that Jack was wrong, that she *was* still being objective, and that the colony was *not* in any danger. After a while she began to feel better about the situation, though a single, nagging thought troubled her for the rest of the day; *what if Jack's right?*

***

Twenty-five kilometers from where Nicole sat brooding, Michael Billings wandered among ancient ruins, in awe of the beauty of the ancient city. His assistant, Andrew Giuliani, stood near a wall, making notes of the various symbols and images that appeared there. The images were faded and worn down by time and by the elements. Billings soon joined him.

"Hmmm, that looks interesting," he said to his assistant.

"Yeah, they're old, very old—I was thinking maybe eight or nine-thousand years old."

"Yes, I'd say you're probably correct, Andy," Billings answered, straining his eyes slightly to make out what was left of the ancient lettering and faded images. "Very interesting find here—you say that you just came across this yesterday?"

"Yes, I came out in the same hover car yesterday with Dao-ming Wu. She was looking for more unidentified plant life and I was looking for—well, this!" Billings followed the lettering and the images along the long wall, which was still largely intact. "Who do you suppose built these ruins, Dr. Billings?"

"I don't know, Andy," he answered, still engrossed in the remarkable find. "It's probably from one of the League members, since whoever made these were already highly advanced at the time they were made. Perhaps if we take some holo-pics we can send them over to someone at Alliance or the League headquarters, to see if anyone can identify them."

Billings looked up and then down the long, tall wall. Evidently most if not all of the building's superstructure remained, though the weaker materials had long ago succumbed to the ravages of age and weather. He reached behind him without looking.

"Please hand me the holo-camera, Andy," he said, having determined the best angle and distance for capturing the text and images. He noticed some extravagant artwork, surrounded by a circle with strange symbols all along the outside. "I must get this recorded, it's remarkable. Come on Andy," he said, "I need that camera." He waited several seconds before succumbing to his impatience. "Come on, Andy, I need that *camera!*" Angry and frustrated, he turned to face his assistant. "Andy, I asked—" Andrew Giuliani was suddenly nowhere to be found. *How long has he*

162

been gone? "Andy—where are you? Come on, Andy, I need that camera!" He looked around the ruins before walking in increasingly large circles, assuming that Andrew had somehow not heard him.

After walking around for thirty minutes, he found himself back where he'd started, and with Andrew still missing. He began turning 360 degrees, searching the landscape for the man who was both his assistant and his friend. "Andy," he began, now worried for the young man, "where are you?"

CHAPTER 27

The proper landing sequence, along with the proper codes, had been buried deep within a database on one of the Alliance ship's onboard computers, exactly as he had been told. The pilot surveyed the red planet, taking note of the particularly massive city that was clearly visible from space, despite the fact that he was still some distance away. It was an impressive metropolis, built atop the Valles Marineris site, surrounded by a clear dome and the faint glow of a localized energy shield, and he marveled at it with a sense of both astonishment and awe. He was stunned that the inhabitants there had built anything so enormous on such a miserable, desolate planet as Mars. He found himself admiring them, as primitive and backward as they were, for having the courage to risk their lives so daringly by defying the raging storms, with nothing more protecting them than the flimsy material used for the dome and a pathetically weak force field; it was a wonder that the city hadn't already been destroyed.

As the ship neared the city, the pilot received a transmission.

"Greetings, and welcome to Mars Colony Alpha, the first colony on the red planet. Please hold your position outside the shield and state your business at the colony," the voice said matter-of-factly.

"Overnight business trip," the pilot answered in reply, staring at his companion.

"You're just here for tonight?"

"Yes, I leave tomorrow."

"Your ship's access code?"

"A76GT229-Alpha." The reply was answered by a silence that seemed to last an eternity. The pilot felt a bead of sweat form on his forehead before slowly trickling down his face.

"Access code acknowledged. Have a nice day, sir."

"Thank you." The force field opened in front of the ship, a gap no more than one hundred meters in diameter, but more than adequate to admit the considerably smaller ship.

The co-pilot took the controls as the pilot hurriedly put the contacts in his eyes, placed the appliance, and donned his cloak, along with the rest of the wardrobe he'd brought along for the trip, before checking to ensure his appearance would arouse no suspicion. He then picked up a dark case and set it by the door. The luggage was packed full of assorted items, which carried inside the successful outcome of the mission. His assignment, which was in itself only a small part of a much larger operation, could one day prove to be the determining factor to the effectiveness of that effort.

His co-pilot took the ship off autopilot as it neared the city, as the other walked over and waited for the door. Seconds later the ship landed and the man exited the ship onto the end of a long docking bay before making his way, along with the passengers and crews of other ships, toward a security screening area. A large, thick wall made of stone combined with a dense Valharan alloy stretched across the entire length of the docking bay and in from of the entrance to the city, with two small portals, each large enough to admit a single large man. As he drew closer the visitor noticed that at each of the portals stood a man in uniform, each man flanked with two other men armed with some sort of plasma rifles. The visitor recognized the insignia on each uniform as belonging to the Earth Space Alliance, a uniform he'd seen before. He felt a rush of panic, and the plan for the mission suddenly appeared tragically flawed to him. His mission now amounted to nothing more than wasted time on a wasted trip through countless star systems, only to arrive on a desolate planet in a desolate star system, which orbited an un-remarkable, averaged-sized star.

The visitor shook his head, trying to clear it and refocus on the mission. He neared the security check point, realizing that it was now the moment of truth. He was certain he would be recognized for what he truly was, after which he would be apprehended, detained, and most likely tortured by the authorities, before being executed. Regardless of what they did to him, however, he vowed that he would carry the secrecy of his mission, and more importantly the operation, with him to the grave, if necessary.

The man approached the back of a very long line with a large number of people already standing in front of him. At the front of the line, two Alliance soldiers questioned those nearest the entrance, while the travelers' luggage was laid upon a conveyor one piece at a time. The various bags and suitcases passed through a large scanner that clearly revealed the contents of each one. To his relief the procession of visitors moved along rapidly such that ten minutes later, there were only two others standing in front of him. The stranger felt satisfaction as he watched his bag pass through the scanner, revealing nothing but the aforementioned contents.

"Good evening, sir; can I see some identification please?" The visitor nodded before handing over his travel license, an impressive looking forgery that he and some others had created just the day before. "So, Mr. Helitel, is this your first time on Mars?" the uniformed man asked.

"Yes," the pilot answered with a smile. The guard looked at the paperwork and then at the man before waving him through.

"Enjoy your visit on the Mars Colony, sir."

The man didn't reply this time, but hurried to retrieve his bag as quickly as possible. Within twenty minutes the tall man had made it from his ship, through the line, and into the hotel, where he stood waiting at the front desk.

"Good evening, sir, and welcome to the Valles Marineris Hotel," said the hotel desk clerk. "Do you have a reservation?"

"No."

"That's okay, sir, we have a number of vacancies at the moment. May I have your name please?"

"Maruk Helitel."

"Can you spell that for me please?"

"M-a-r-u-k H-e-l-i-t-e-l."

"Very good, sir. Okay, you're all set, Mr. Helitel. You're in room 1197. Just take the elevator down to the eleventh floor, then take a right, and you'll find your room halfway down the hallway; I hope you enjoy your stay, sir."

Helitel bowed his head slightly at the clerk before turning and walking toward the elevator, taking a good look around the luxurious hotel as he did so. It didn't escape his notice that the hotel stood just inside the dome, which itself was surrounded by a weak force field.

He nodded his head once more to the clerk and entered the elevator, which he took to the eleventh floor before casually making his way to his room. Once inside, he walked over to the small sofa and sat down, resting his traveling case on the cushion next to him. The visitor then opened the case and began carefully removing the ten small containers that it contained, setting each of them down on the table in front of the sofa. Helitel picked up one of the closest containers and held it securely by the bottom before carefully touching three points on the decorated piece in a specific order, causing the top of the box to slide open. He reached inside it and withdrew a small, egg-shaped, multi-colored device that glowed quietly in his hand. The visitor pressed two small points on either side of the device, which caused it to start glowing multiple colors in a complex sequence. He repeating the same process until all ten devices sat in a row on the table in front of him, glowing in the same, complex sequence.

Next, he removed a small crystalline object in the shape of a diamond from his pocket, an innocent-looking trinket about the size of his thumb. He then pressed a recessed button on the top, causing a blue light to appear. Less than a second later, all ten devices sitting on the table began blinking together in unison with the small diamond in his hand, causing the man to smile with no small amount of satisfaction.

The man glanced over at the clock before standing and walking over to the bed. He sat down on the mattress, took a deep breath, and lay back, where he remained motionless for the next several hours, until finally the hour grew late.

Upon waking, he checked the time, stuck his head out the door, and looked around. Satisfied with what he saw, the man from the ship placed the egg-shaped devices back into the case, left the room, and began walking towards the elevator. Less than a minute later he was back at the surface level of the hotel. The elevator door soon opened to reveal the lobby area, which was vacant except for two young women who had just returned to the hotel and appeared to be heading toward the elevator and back to their rooms. He nodded in their direction as he passed them in the lobby, making his way toward the outer wall of the hotel nearest the dome, and in the opposite direction of the front desk. Walking parallel to the outer wall, he soon came to a small vent. Looking around once more to be certain he was alone and unobserved, even by holo-cameras, he opened the vent and quickly placed one of the egg-shaped devices inside. He casually turned, finding the hallway still vacant, and began making his way along the same wall toward the other end of the hotel. At the end of the hallway and close to a door leading out of the hotel and into the city, he found another vent, where he placed a second device. Content with its location as well, the man turned and walked toward the door before eventually walking out of the hotel altogether.

Outside of the hotel was the city, a large metropolis on the surface of a hostile world. There were roads, restaurants, office buildings, numerous buildings with apartments, houses, and even several parks with lush grass and trees. The man made his way through the city, staying mostly along the perimeter of the dome. Throughout the city, wherever he was able to find a convenient suitable location, he would leave one of the flashing devices, until finally he'd placed all but two of them at various locations along the edge of the dome in various, inconspicuous areas under some of the large buildings, where they would be extremely difficult to find. The strange man took the last two devices to the largest residence complex situated in the middle of the largest domed city on the planet. One of the eggs he placed in a darkened area behind the lattice, under a staircase at the back of the building. It was vitally important that the devices were extremely difficult to find, so he took great care to ensure that he was not seen, and that he'd done a sufficiently thorough job with concealment.

The last device he took to the center of the city, where the large park stood. While the park was surrounded by buildings, it was also far enough from any of them that it took him quite some time to reach the center where, looking straight overhead, he could see he was under the highest part of the dome. The visitor began seeking for and soon found a location far from the nearest path, a patch of ground that he knew would not be frequently traveled, and after digging a foot into the three feet of soil, he dropped the egg in. After covering the egg with dirt once more the man, satisfied with his work, began casually strolling back towards the hotel. He was tired, and would enjoy a good nights rest before leaving to get back to the others. It was difficult to imagine how the primitives lived as they did, and he considered for a moment that he might be doing them a favor.

Early the following morning the traveler checked out of the hotel and made his way toward the space port and the docking bay where his ship was docked. Soon, he would be back with his friends, his only family now, and he knew the beloved leader would be well-pleased with his work. He was nearly at the entrance to the hallway leading to where his ship was parked when he was startled by the sudden approach of a man in uniform. He glanced at the breast patch briefly and saw that the man was an Earth Space Alliance officer. He grew alarmed, causing his pulse to quicken and his heart to begin pounding. After all of the time and effort they'd spent planning and waiting, everything now rested on what happened next. His mind and his instincts struggled with one another. The impulses to fight or flee were warring within him, and were settled only by his contempt for the primitives.

"Good morning, sir. Can you please come with me?" the Alliance soldier asked, his face taught and his jaw tense. The man felt the hand of the Alliance officer tighten around his arm.

"Is something wrong, officer?" the man calmly asked the officer, who cast him a discerning look.

"Please just come with me, sir, *now*," he said again, more firmly this time. The officer was now pressing his hand on the man's back as well, urging him forward. Of course he could easily resist the soldier and escape, because his own strength far exceeded that of the officer, but he knew to do so would only draw more attention to himself and worsen the situation in the remote chance his activities had remained undetected. They walked briskly toward a large room just off the main hallway into the docking bay.

"I demand you tell me why you are detaining me, officer!" he said at last. "I have rights, and I have somewhere I must be today!" Following the

169

stranger's feigned outburst, the exasperated officer merely pointed behind him just as he heard a loud blast, followed by a series of pulse weapons firing. No less than twenty Alliance officers rapidly surrounded a mortally wounded man lying on the ground. One of the Alliance men stepped forward and took the weapon from the injured prisoner. The officer who'd escorted him toward the room stepped forward to speak with him.

"My apologies, sir," he said to the man. "As you can see, we had word that a dangerous criminal had boarded a ship and was headed here. It seems he arrived thirty minutes earlier than we were told he would. We were still setting up the perimeter when we got word he was already here. I apologize if I was a little too aggressive, but as you can see I did it for *your* protection."

The man smiled back at the Alliance officer. "Thank you, officer. It gives me such a warm feeling of security knowing that astute and diligent officers like yourself are keeping everyone here safe from such bad people."

"We're just doing our part, sir. Have a safe flight to your next destination."

"Have a wonderful day, officer," he remarked, wearing a big smile as he walked down the long hallway toward where his ship was docked. His mission had been successful, and he would be commended for a job well done. Soon, very soon, they would be executing the next phase of the plan and with a secure base of operations, they would soon pick up where they'd left off so long ago....

CHAPTER 28

Jack Lincoln walked into her office and collapsed into the navy blue sofa against the wall facing her desk. She could see by looking at him that he was exhausted, and her heart went out to him for all his effort and sacrifice.

"Any luck, Jack?" she asked him sheepishly.

"No." Lincoln sat back on the sofa and laid his head back over the back of the sofa until he was staring at the ceiling. "We've searched all day for that Giuliani boy, Nicole. We've searched on foot, we've searched by air, and we've even searched a good bit of the lake—nothing. It's as if he's vanished off of the face of the ear—New Eden. Whether alive or dead, we should have been able to find him."

Nicole looked at Jack with great sympathy on her face, while feeling more than just a little despair herself, since her news was even worse than his.

"Jack, I'm afraid I have some bad news. There are two others missing now as well. Two teenage boys were walking through some woods yesterday afternoon on their way to the other's house. It appears they never arrived. The parents of each teenager assumed their child was at the other's house until this morning, when one of the parents called the other's house to tell their son to come home."

Jack's face went pale. "What's going on here, Nicole? We've been scouring the woods all around the city looking for traces of Andrew Giuliani; now you're telling me two more are missing? This can't be a coincidence."

"I agree. Jack, are you certain you didn't see anything unsual out there while searching for Andrew?" She paused, before swallowing hard. "There had to be blood, or signs of a struggle, torn clothing—something!" The images of the ghastly attack on the other planet suddenly played in her mind, causing her stomach to tighten into a knot and a cold chill to run down her back. Her eyes started to water, and Jack walked to her desk and sat down on one of the sides nearest Nicole.

171

"Listen, Nicole, I know what you're thinking, but that was different. An attack like that *would* have left—evidence. I don't know what's happened to Giuliani and these two boys, but we'll find them."

"Thank's, Jack," Nicole replied, forcing a smile as she wiped he tears from her eyes. "This job—it's not exactly what I expected," she said glumly, looking up at him.

"I think you're doing a fantastic job, Nicole; I can't think of anyone who could do any better."

"Thanks," she replied, "and call me Nikki."

"Nikki?"

"Yeah, it's what my friends call me," she said, before staring nervously into his eyes with an impassioned smile.

"Okay, 'Nikki'," he replied with a smile of his own. Nicole looked away, trying hard to get a grip on her feelings. "So I understand that work has been progressing on the particle beam cannons and the planetary shield."

Nicole turned back to face him, thankful for his changing the subject.

"Yeah, it's been going very well," she answered. "The Shatarans have thrown themselves into the effort wholeheartedly. I've never seen anyone work as hard as they have. I keep trying to tell them that if we wait until the flares subside we can contact the Alliance again. The Alliance should be able to send us plenty of people and equipment to help with the effort, but the Shatarans don't want to wait."

"Why not?" asked Jack.

"Well, apparently Jokar says that based on his dealings with them, he believes the Machrys may well return once the flares subside, and in much greater numbers...." answered Nicole, raising her eyebrows.

"But—"

"That particle beam cannon they hit the Machrys with—I think it's much more likely that the Machrys will wait a while before attempting anything like that again. He insists, however, that we need to complete the construction and the installation of the cannons and the shield projectors *before* the flares subside, most likely by sometime the week after next. He could be right, but still...." She allowed her voice to trail off, betraying a hesitation that Jack quickly picked up on.

"Listen, Nikki, I'd like to get more involved with this little project, if it's okay with you?"

She eyed Jack suspiciously. "You still don't trust them, do you?"

"No I don't," he stated flatly, shaking his head resolutely. "I think they're up to something, Nikki, I just feel it in my gut. They're pushing really hard on this project, too hard if you ask me. It looks to me like they've got most of their own people working on this as well."

"Really?" the governor asked, surprised at his statement. "How do you know, Jack?"

"I did a flyby of the sites earlier when we finished today's search. There is a group of Shatarans at each site working with only one or two of our people to get the sites operational. It was the same way during the construction of the particle beam cannons and the planetary shield projectors. Not only are they pushing hard on getting this done, they were insistent upon thoroughly testing them as they went. Whatever else they may be up to, they want the cannons and the shield to work in a bad way, and I'd like to know why. You've got to allow me to be a part of this, Nikki, so I can keep an eye on them."

She looked at him for a moment, considering his request. She wanted Jack to be involved in the installation of the shield and the cannons because while she trusted Jokar, she knew Jack did not. He'd become a trusted advisor to her, and a friend, so it was important that he see the Shatarans the way she did...as an intelligent, advanced race of beings, as benevolent as they were beautiful to behold.

"I'd like to, Jack, I really would, but I can't. I need you to find out what's happening to our people. Besides, Colonel Francoise is working with Jokar's people on the cannons and the shield. I'm sure he'll keep an eye on them."

"Pierre? Give me a break," Jack scoffed. "He's so infatuated with their little toys that he can't see the forest for the trees. He saw what the PB cannons did to the Machrys ships and he's learning everything he can about them, along with the shield. He's like a kid in a candy store, Nikki. Why don't you put Luke on the S&R Team? If anyone can find Billing's assistant and those two kids it's him; the kid has a nose like a bloodhound."

"Jack, those kids need you."

"So does every other man, woman, and child on this planet, Nikki; every human being that is, to keep an eye on your Shataran friends."

Nicole grimaced. "No Jack, I want you heading up the search and rescue teams, that's an order."

Jack threw his hands up in the air. "Come on, Nikki, what gives? There are plenty of others more qualified than I am to lead those teams. A number of the Alliance soldiers here have led S&R teams before, I haven't. What's the real reason for having me look for those missing people?"

"The truth?"

"Yeah, the truth," Jack replied.

Nicole took a deep breath and sat back in her chair. "The truth is that the Shatarans have done nothing but good for us since we've been here—"

"Yeah, yeah, we've been through this before, Nikki, you can't—"

"No, *you* can't!" Nicole corrected him, her face now flush with anger. "I'm governor of this colony, not you, and I will do everything I can to protect it! Yes, we've been through this before; why do you insist on beating this thing to death? Jokar and the Shatarans protected us from the Machrys attacks, which would likely have killed everyone on the planet. They're also helping us build weapons that will ensure that such an attack will never come so close to ending what could be humanity's only chance at ensuring the continuity of our species should anything go wrong in our solar system. This colony is important to the human race, Jack, and I cannot jeopardize the safety of this colony by putting you in a position to irreparably damage our relationship with the Shatarans; do you understand me?"

This time Jack didn't answer right away, choosing instead to stare at her in anger before looking down and taking a deep breath. "Listen, I'm just—"

Lincoln was interrupted by a sound from the com-link. Nicole pressed a button and a hologram of her assistant appeared.

"Please pardon the interruption, Governor, there's a call from Colonel Francoise."

Nicole looked up at Captain Lincoln for a moment before turning her attention back to her assistant. "Thanks, Bernie; please put it through."

"Yes, Governor." The hologram disappeared and a few seconds later an image of Colonel Pierre Francoise appeared.

"Colonel Francoise, how is work progressing on the particle beam cannons and the planetary shield?"

"*C'est incroyable, Gouverneur!*" he replied in French, as he often did when he was excited.

"*Parler en anglais, s'il vous plait,*" Nicole replied, also in French.

"Pardon me, please. It is incredible, Governor Reynolds. Never have I seen anything as incredible as this! The Shatarans activated the planetary shield generators moments ago, each generator sending a steady stream of blue energy toward the sky. One of the Shataran engineers explained that beams of energy interact with the planet's magnetic field, spreading the energy wave evenly across a wide portion of the planet. With each of the shield generators strategically located across the planet, next to the particle beam cannons, the entire planet is now protected with this shield."

"Has the shield been tested yet?"

"That is one reason why I'm contacting you, Governor. The Shatarans fitted one of the Alliance ships with a particle beam cannon. They would like to send it up, along with a piece of an engine from an old transport."

174

"Hold on a minute, Pierre, who authorized installing a particle beam weapon in one of our ships?" Nicole judged by the pale complexion and the surprised look that no one had.

"I am sorry, Governor Reynolds, I should have cleared it with you first. Jokar suggested you would not object and I did not think so either—"

"Then you were both wrong, Colonel Francoise! From now on anything involving modifications to an Alliance ship requires my approval, understood?"

"Yes, of course," the colonel replied awkwardly.

"Good. Okay, now that we have that out of the way, what's the old engine for?"

"The Shatarans would like to use it as a target. The new shield will allow an energy weapon to fire from inside the shield, but not allow such a weapon to be fired through the shield at the planet. They would like to send the modified Alliance ship with the PB cannon out through the shield and have it fire toward a target on the ground, at a target of your choosing, Governor. Afterward, it would release the engine into orbit, before destroying it with a particle beam cannon."

Nicole looked at Jack, who simply shrugged his shoulders.

"Okay, Colonel, you have my permission to prepare for the tests as you described them. I'd like to see these tests myself when you're ready, so please ensure I have visibility to what's going on. If I need to travel to a particular site please let me know:"

"Of course, Governor, thank you. I'll contact you when they're ready."

The image then disappeared and Nicole and Jack were alone again.

"So how did it go the other night?" Lincoln asked unexpectedly.

"What are you talking about, Jack?"

"I understand you were on a date with Jokar," he replied dryly.

"A date? He's an alien, Jack! We just went to have some dinner together, that's all." She was being defensive, and she knew it, but she couldn't help it.

"Yeah, that's what a 'date' *is*, Nicole."

"Okay, whatever. So—it was enlightening; Jokar offered to share more of their technology with us, which, it seems, is substantially different from anything we've seen from members of the League. It also seems they've explored much of our galaxy, and they will provide us star maps, once they've been updated to reflect the relative positions of the stars today. Their medical science is also incredibly advanced, with much of it being based on the castilian plant."

"The castilian plant? They know about the castil?"

"Yes; they've used it for quite a while. Based on what he told me, I'd guess that the Shatarans were probably the ones who discovered what the plant can do and developed the process for creating castil."

"You didn't tell him we found it here on New Eden, did you?"

"Yes, but my guess is that one of his people would have discovered it at some point anyway."

"That's unfortunate, because if they didn't have an interest in this planet before, my guess is that they do now."

CHAPTER 29

Hank walked into the massive room and sat in his designated seat in the League Conference Hall, the auditorium where the representatives met to discuss the most weighty of matters facing the League. It was a large space, with all of the seating set in a semi-circle facing a stage and podium area. Translation devices were also available to each member, something all but a very few of the attendees would require.

It was the first emergency conference called since Hank had been representing Earth at the League, and it troubled him that he knew nothing about why it had been called. For some reason no one would talk about what the meeting was for; he'd attempted to find out by going through both official and unofficial channels, but no one seemed to know anything and if they did know, they weren't telling. To Hank's surprise even Zing would say nothing about it to Hank, except that he would find out what it was all about at the meeting. Based on the earnestness of his notification, whatever the issue was, it was clearly a very serious matter.

He watched as the auditorium slowly filled with diplomats from each of the member worlds, glancing up at the clock from time to time, waiting for the conference to begin. It was several minutes later when Zing, Hank's longtime friend and the ambassador from Val, appeared on the stage. Since Val was also the current host for the League, Zing, as one of the members of Val's ruling council, had recently rotated into the leadership role and was, therefore, the acting League president. He looked down and nodded at Hank as he approached the podium.

"Good morning, fellow members of the League of Sentient Species. I must apologize for the hasty manner in which this conference was convened, but I felt it necessary given the gravity of the threat we now face. It is most fortunate that it is such a rare event when a member of the League becomes entangled in something as horrific as war, and it is unfortunate that we now find ourselves at the crossroads of war and peace. I could go on, of course, but given the urgency of this matter, we must get right to it. Now then, to introduce the reason for our gathering, I introduce to you Ambassador Garuk H'Maadol, the representative of the planet Creshna-5, a League member world, who recently received a most unusual message. I give you, Ambassador H'Maadol."

H'Maadol strolled up onto the stage and approached the podium. The Creshnarian loosely resembled a dragonfly in appearance, though much larger and properly attired. It was, to date, the most alien of all of the sentient life-forms he'd encountered up-close; only one other species he'd seen pictures of came even close to the ambassador's unusual appearance.

Hank looked down at a League reference guide on his data pad, an encyclopedia of sorts that listed information and images for each League member, as well as a number of worlds with sentient beings who were not yet members of the League. He'd been provided the reference guide on his first day as ambassador, a tool he had soon found to be invaluable. He quickly ascertained that Creshna-5 was a world orbiting a star known on Earth as 55-Cancri in the constellation of Cancer. Hank discovered Cheshna-5 was reported to be a light-gravity world, which he determined was somewhat fitting for a world supporting winged Creshnarians. He looked back up as the diplomat from Creshna-5 began to speak.

"Good morning, my friends. I have been asked to come to you today to present some most-disturbing news to the League, in an effort to request the League's intervention in a situation that may well re-ignite one of our galaxy's most ancient conflicts. I was contacted a week ago by Chancellor Milaki Kax-Milkin, one of the most respected members of the Machrys Leadership Council.

"As most of you know, the planet Machrys is not currently a member of the League. They are, in fact, one of the very few of the ancient races that are not. Their reasons for not joining us are their own, and of course I believe we should respect their decision, though I still believe that could one day change. Since they are not League members and have no representation here, they came to my world, their most active trading partner, asking that we plead their cause to this most sagacious body.

"Five-thousand years ago, the planet Machrys was at war with the planet Shatara. It was a horrific conflict, one during which the Machrys suffered a complete and devastating defeat at the hands of the Shatarans. The end of the war was not the end of the conflict, however, as some of the more hawkish, charismatic members of the Shataran leadership persuaded the population of the Shataran home world that only by pursuing those Machrys responsible for attacking Shatara and therefore starting the war would they be able to ensure there was never another. So began an ongoing campaign soon came to be called The Great Purge. The Machrys were pursued halfway across the galaxy, where they were either destroyed or returned to what was left of Machrys, and confined in what the Shataran leaders termed, 'Reeducation Centers.'

"Over time, news of the atrocities, and the truth about the genocide committed during the Great Purge, made its way back to the citizens of Shatara. The vast majority of the Shataran people were so sickened by the carnage committed in their name and so disgusted with those responsible that they rose up and overthrew their own leadership, but not before nearly all of the Machrys who had escaped the destruction of their home world had been hunted and persecuted, nearly to extinction, across the galaxy."

The ambassador paused for several seconds, giving his audience an opportunity to digest everything he'd told them so far.

"Now, some of you may be wondering why I've given you this brief history lesson; well, I'm getting to that. Approximately thirty standard-days ago, the Machrys attacked an Earth colony, on the planet the humans call New Eden. Now the assertion by the Machrys Leadership Council that they were justified in attacking this colony since they consider it too close to Machrys space is a claim the League categorically rejects, and the Machrys know this. In the eyes of many of our members, the Machrys have, in fact, made themselves vulnerable to yet another interplanetary war. I'm quite certain Chancellor Milaki Kax-Milkin knows this unprovoked attack on a League world will not go unanswered; the League is certain to address this provocation with them in short order. The Machrys may not be a League member, but they do conduct a considerable amount of trading with member worlds and their world depends on that trade. In fact, their trade routes pass through League space; should the League elect to impose sanctions against them, the Machrys will end up paying a heavy price. Failing that, I'm told the League is prepared to intervene militarily should the Machrys attempt a second attack.

"But setting aside their attack on the colony for just a moment, what we must concern ourselves with now is with what happened *during* the attack that ultimately led to a Machrys withdrawal. The Machrys had correctly assessed that the humans would be unable to repel their attack, at least at that time. Indeed, the humans on New Eden were in great peril as they discovered that their weapons were little match for the shields on the Machrys battle cruisers, even as the colony's own shield quickly weakened to the point that it was about to fail.

"So the Machrys pressed their attack, with victory seemingly close at hand. Everything changed, however, when a blue beam of particle energy suddenly erupted from a point on the planet a short distance from the colony's main city, striking the Machrys fleet of attack ships and cutting through them as easily as one might slice through cloth with a laser. The Machrys officers aboard the battle cruisers had never experienced an attack by such a powerful weapon, but many of them had *seen* one. For the first time since the particle beam weapons were banned immediately following the Shatara-Machrys war, a Shataran weapon was successfully used to repel the attacking Machrys fleet. Had the Machrys attack ships not withdrawn immediately, they would doubtless have been decimated.

"This brings me to two very important conclusions. First, when the distinct blue particle beam energy first struck the Machrys ships, it was thought that the humans may have discovered the weapon on their planet and somehow unlocked the key to its operation. They soon learned, however, that there were Shatarans living on New Eden, their ancient enemy, and one of the oldest and most advanced sentient races in the galaxy, the same race that had, long ago, committed a most horrific act of genocide against the Machrys people.

"My second point is this...that crippling the Machrys fleet, though beneficial in the sense that it saved the lives of thousands of innocent human civilians, means that the Shatarans who fired this weapon have not only violated the treaty banning the use of the very weapon that drove the Machrys to the point of extinction, but that they have also violated Section 2, Article 1 of the treaty that ended the Shataran-Machrys War, one of the most important clauses in the entire treaty. This clause reads as follows: 'The High Council of the Shataran home world understands and agrees that all Shatarans are forever banned from coming within ten systems of Machrys space on pain of death.' This clause had been requested by the Machrys leaders in order to give their people some measure of assurance that the Great Purge was over. Indeed, the Shataran Government has honored this treaty for nearly five millennia, taking great care to ensure their people stayed far from this sector of space. The Shatarans on New Eden have, it seems, violated the two most important sections of this treaty, acts that we view as both disconcerting and unacceptable.

"This brings me to my third and final point. This attack on the Machrys ships, though supposedly initiated in an effort to save the human colonists from an unprovoked attack by the Machrys, constitutes an act of war. I believe the Machrys will eventually admit guilt in the attack on New Eden, before offering an apology and reparations to the colonists. What they will not do, however, is allow the Shatarans to finish what they started in the Great Purge. The Shatarans continue to possess a superior military, and the Machrys know this. Regardless, Milaki Kax-Milkin just informed me that they have already began mobilizing their military, ramped up their production of weaponry, and are building newer and more powerful ships in what they believe will be a second Machrys-Shataran war. They would rather die in battle this time than to be hunted like animals across the galaxy. Perhaps now, my friends, you can appreciate the gravity of our situation. Many would die on both sides, and there will be those from other worlds who die as collateral damage. It's also possible that this conflict could draw in other worlds as well, and this is something we must not allow to happen.

"While Ambassador Lotan, the representative from Shatara, is not here today, he assures me that this is most certainly *not* an act of war by the Shataran people against Machrys. He claims that his government knows nothing about what has occurred on New Eden, and that they are as determined as we are as to uncover the truth about what has occurred there. He has agreed to meet with a representative of the Machrys people here on Val within seven standard days to try to offer them an explanation for what has occurred, once his government has had a chance to look into this matter and hopefully come to a conclusion as to how this provocation happened.

"Ambassador Lotan has requested that a team from Shatara be allowed to visit New Eden and meet with Governor Reynolds, who just so happens to be the daughter of Earth's ambassador to the league, Dr. Hank Reynolds." Hank offered a slight smile and nodded.

"The Machrys have assured us that if the Earth colony agrees to permit this investigation to continue through to its conclusion, they will surrender their claim to the planet and as I suggested earlier, offer an apology and reparations. Make no mistake about it, however, this is a matter of grave importance to them. Not only does it suggest an act of war, but it has also forced the Machrys to relive the great carnage and suffering of their people so long ago, which to this day has not faded from their collective memory, and they seek justice and retribution for such an egregious violation of the treaty signed five-thousand years ago." Ambassador H'Maadol then turned to Hank. "Ambassador Reynolds, would your people consider allowing a Shataran delegation to visit your colony on New Eden to discuss this matter?"

"Mr. Ambassador," Hank began, aware of the perplexed and confused expression he must have on his face. "The Shatarans on New Eden fired their particle beam weapon at the Machrys in order to save the life of my daughter and the lives of everyone else on New Eden. We are indebted to them for the lives of every man, woman, and child there."

At this H'Maadol turned to face Zing, who then stood.

"Dr. Reynolds, my dear friend, without question we all condemn the Machrys attack on your colony. Indeed, there is some sense of irony that the Machrys attacked your people in a manner similar to how the Shatarans attacked their own world so savagely thousands of years earlier. Perhaps once this is all over, there is a lesson to be learned for all of us from this regrettable series of events.

"Please believe me when I say that everyone here is extremely grateful that your people survived the attack unharmed. The League *will* discuss the attack on New Eden with the Machrys leadership, and we will remind them that another such attack on a League member in the future constitutes an attack on the entire League, and that any such attack would be met with overwhelming force. That said, from what you have told me, my friend, the weapons and the shield now installed on New Eden will be far more than sufficient to repel any Machrys attack in the future.

"You must try to understand, however, that when the Machrys-Shataran war and the Great Purge finally ended, there were very few Machrys left anywhere in the galaxy; their entire race faced extinction. So now I must ask you again, Hank Reynolds; will Earth permit the Shataran delegation to visit New Eden so that they might determine who these Shatarans are, and what should be done with them?"

Hank paused to consider it before answering. "Ambassador H'Maadol, Chairman Zing, all League members in attendance, I will speak with our Alliance leaders and with Governor Reynolds, and I will recommend that such a visit be permitted, but there is one condition."

"Which is?" asked Zing.

"That a League contingent accompanies the Shataran delegation."

Zing looked to H'Maadol, who nodded.

"Such a condition is perfectly reasonable and acceptable, Dr. Reynolds, of course. Thank you for your decision, for I know your word carries great weight within the Alliance, and with the governor. Perhaps, if the Creator of all things is willing, you have just averted another ugly and perverse war.

"I would like to request that all member worlds help with our monitoring of the situation, and if you have relations with either world, do everything you can to help calm everyone involved. Meanwhile, we will begin assembling both delegations immediately. This meeting is therefore adjourned."

CHAPTER 30

It was still early out and the light from Meta and Stratus had only just begun peeking over the edge of the horizon when Nicole stepped outside of her home. She took in a deep breath, filling her lungs with New Eden's clean, fresh air. She had taken such early morning walks for years back on Earth, and now that she was able to relax somewhat, feeling safer with the planetary shield and the Shataran cannons in place, she had finally resumed her customary walks. *Just like back home,* she thought, before looking behind her at the two Alliance soldiers walking behind her; she allowed a thin, slight smile to creep over her face. *Well, almost.* At least they were giving her some room by trying to keep their distance, as much as they could without compromising her safety.

Her walk took her to the edge of the lake, which caused her to alter her course slightly until she was closer to the woods. She still avoided the water as much as possible, despite assurances from the many scientists who had carefully studied the lake and deemed it safe and void of creatures harmful to human beings. The disturbing encounter on planet V-10 had left its mark; she wondered whether the scar from that experience would ever heal.

Nicole looked up at the golden hue of the sky, which grew brighter as the twin stars rose higher and higher in the sky. The light from the two suns fell on her face, causing her to feel a glowing warmth inside her. She was stunned when she opened her eyes, only to see and then hear several blasts from the particle cannon.

"What—who authorized that?" Nicole asked in anger.

The two guards immediately closed the distance between themselves and Nicole, looking around in all directions as well as the sky for a possible attack. Nicole turned and hurried back towards the governor's building at a slow jog, taking her com link from a pocket in her coat. She fastened it around her wrist and pressed a button. A virtual console appeared and she pressed two digits. An image of Jokar Motay appeared in her comm.

"Good morning, Nicole; out for your morning walk I see," he remarked casually and calmly.

"Jokar, what happened? Have the Machrys launched another attack?"

The alien shook his head. "No, not an attack. Our sensors detected a Machrys scout ship just as it exited the planet's atmosphere. We fired at it but we missed; the scout ships are too small and too fast for the particle cannons to easily hit. The cannons are designed for the larger, much more powerful ships, like what attacked your planet last time."

"A ship? How could a Machrys ship have gotten past the shields, Jokar? I thought the shields would block any ship from entering the atmosphere."

"It does," Jokar confirmed.

"Then how—?"

"There's only one explanation, Governor Reynolds," he replied with a grin.

Nicole stared at him for a moment before replying. "The ship was here the whole time," she said, with some exasperation.

"Yes. It must have had some sort of phased shielding that prevented it from being visible or from showing up on our sensors."

"You mean it was cloaked."

"Excuse me?"

"Never mind," she replied with a grin. "It's something my father would say."

"I see," he replied dryly.

"So what do you suppose it was doing here the entire time since the shield went up?" she asked, furrowing her brow and tilting her head to one side, as she was prone to do when in deep thought.

"I can't answer that with any certainty," Jokar answered, "but perhaps if one of the blasts from the particle cannon had connected—"

"There are only two reasons I can think of that might explain its mission here; espionage and/or sabotage."

Jokar nodded. "Yes, I suppose you're right about that," he replied, before looking away for a moment. "I suppose we may never know for sure. I'm quite sorry we missed it, Nicole."

"It's okay, Jokar, thank you for trying. If your sensors hadn't detected it, we would never have known it was even here."

"Too true."

Nicole was about to ask him another question when her mind was distracted by the sound of a massive explosion from the edge of town. A plume of smoke rose to the sky until it was so tall it mingled with a bank of clouds.

"I've got to go, Jokar. There was just a massive explosion in town, it

184

looks like it might have been at the armory."

"The building where you store all of your weapons?"

"Yes, I'm afraid so."

"Oh my, how unfortunate. Please let us know if there is anything we can do."

Nicole gave him a nervous smile. "Sure, I will, thank you. Nicole out." She pressed the same button on her comm link and the image disappeared, along with the virtual panel. She cast a brief glance toward the closer of the two guards.

"I need a transport, immediately."

"Yes, ma'am," the guard replied, before hurrying off. Nicole pressed the button again and entered a different number. Francoise's image popped up.

"Yes, Madame Governor?"

"The armory, I need you—"

"I'm already on my way, ma'am. Jack was closest and he should be there by now. I imagine that explosion was heard on the other side of New Eden."

"Yeah, I bet it was. Okay, Colonel, meet me over there. I'll be in a transport momentarily and on my way. I want to know what happened there and I mean now."

"Yes, ma'am."

"Do you think we're under attack, Governor Reynolds?"

She turned to see the look of fear in the guard's eyes, though he was clearly trying to hide it.

"I don't know, solider…er…what was your name again?'

"O'Toole, ma'am, Daniel O'Toole."

"Daniel, I believe it is safe to say that we've had an 'event,' but we have no way of knowing exactly what happened yet. I can tell you that I do not believe it to be an attack like the one we had before. We have the planetary shield up as well as the cannons, so we should be safe from any attack from space. The explosion was at the armory, so my guess is there was an accident of some sort, perhaps even sabotage." About the time she finished the first Alliance soldier re-joined them in a transport. Nicole and O'Toole climbed in, and the transport whisked away to the Armory.

***

"Yes, I have seen a device similar to this before. Its design is slightly different, of course, but it's very similar. They're called zaktines. They're an implosion device, designed to cause just the type of destruction we saw at the armory. It's quite a clever device, actually; the fact that it implodes rather than explodes means that it causes considerably more destruction. They're incredibly precise as well."

185

"So that explains why everything was completely obliterated."

"Yes, exactly."

Nicole couldn't explain it, but she found the hint of a smile on Jokar's face rather disturbing.

"It's one of the few innovations by the Machrys that I actually considered brilliant."

"But I thought you'd been asleep for five-thousand years, Jokar," said Lincoln. "How is it that they're still using the same weapons today that they used then?"

"They're a dull-minded race, Captain Lincoln, quick to execute but slow to plan. They have practically no innovation whatsoever; that's why I was so surprised when they started cranking these things out during the war." Motay took the device he'd been playing with in his hand and handed it to Lincoln. "They've made some modifications over the millennia, but like you humans say, 'if it's not broke, why fix it?'"

"So you're saying that a Machrys, most likely the one onboard that ship you fired on, was our saboteur?"

Motay smiled at her again. "Well, I'm not really trying to suggest anything, Nicole. Now that you mention it, however, yes—I'd say that the Machrys aboard that scout ship was almost certainly your culprit."

For the first time since Nicole first met him, she gave Motay a long, hard look.

"Of course, who else could it be?" she asked.

Motay offered no response.

"I suppose the loss of your armory and all of your weapons leaves your colony vulnerable. Fortunately, you have our planetary shield and our particle cannon in place now, so that will certainly help. And we are, of course, here to help in any way we can."

"Speaking of that, how are the repairs to your ship progressing? Was your man able to retrieve the parts you needed for your ship? Perhaps there is something we can do to help?"

"No, I don't think so, but I thank you, Governor. Regrettably, the men we sent were only able to procure some of the components we needed, but not the most critical ones. It is most unfortunate, but we will need to fabricate these parts ourselves; the good news is that we should be able to accomplish this task before too long."

"Really? How long will that take, Jokar?" she asked, slightly surprised by his answer. In the beginning she'd felt certain they would have been gone by now. Something always seemed to happen...a problem would arise, a repair wouldn't go as well as expected, or they would be missing parts. Each time the explanation for the delay in their departure seemed perfectly plausible. Had she been a normal human being, perhaps she would have taken their explanations at face value, but Nicole was no ordinary woman.

"Oh, perhaps twenty or thirty standard days I suppose, perhaps longer."

"And then?"

Motay looked up at her for the first time with a most curious expression. It was hard at first for her to read the faces of the Shatarans. Their golden eyes made it difficult to discern their true feelings. She'd been around them long enough now, however, to discern that the irises in their eyes tended to brighten or darken depending on their mood. Looking into Motay's eyes now and seeing the irises darken in response to her question, she began to question whether she had misjudged the Shatarans.

"Oh, it's hard to say. We've discussed going back to Shatara, but everyone we've ever known is now long dead. We've discussed spending some time exploring the galaxy first as well, trying to catch up on thousands of standard years' worth of history. First things first, however. The first thing we must do is to get our ship fully operational."

"As I said, Jokar, we're willing to do what we can to help you get home."

Motay paused to look into her eyes. He didn't do it very often, but when he did, she felt the most curious sensation sweep through her.

"Thank you, Nicole. You know, I've been meaning to tell you that I believe there is something remarkably different about you, something that sets you apart. You're not quite like the other human beings on this planet, are you? You have a remarkably brilliant and well-ordered mind, and you are exceptionally intelligent, even by Shataran standards. Why are you so different, I wonder?" he asked, with intense curiosity.

"I guess it runs in the family," she said with a wry laugh.

Motay didn't respond, but after studying her for some time, he walked over to her sofa and sat down.

"You know, Nicole, it's possible that there are more Machrys ships on this planet, each with phased shielding to hide it from our eyes. If you'd like, I'd be happy to move some of my men into the city, as a precaution. We would bring some of our more advanced weapons with us so we'd not be unarmed, of course. It's your decision, of course, Governor; I simply wanted to offer you the option."

Nicole sat in her chair and studied Motay. She wanted to accept the offer because it seemed logical, it seemed like the right thing to do. But she had concerns as well. She'd enjoyed the quiet dinners with Jokar, and she'd discovered him to have the sharpest, most brilliant mind of anyone she'd ever met…with the exception of her father, of course.

At length, however, she decided it would be prudent to decline the offer, at least until she could sort what was troubling her so much about Jokar and the Shatarans. Yet while it seemed that there would be no more Machrys getting through the planetary shield, there well could be Machrys ships elsewhere on the planet, ships that could have landed before the shield was erected, perhaps even during the Machrys attack. Either option presented a challenge.

"No thanks, Jokar," Jack replied, answering for Nicole. "We still have enough weapons to get the job done; we appreciate the offer though."

Nicole reached up to where he stood next to her and placed one of her hands on Jack's shoulder. "Wait, Jack."

"But, Nicole—"

She stopped him with her hand before turning back to face Motay. "Captain Motay, on behalf of the colony, we accept your gracious offer."

CHAPTER 31

It was late and already well past dinner. They'd been going back and forth all day, and he felt as if he were slugging through a dense and tangled jungle with nothing better than a butter knife. They were making progress to be sure, but it was slow, painfully slow.

Hank sat back in his chair and took a deep breath. Trade negotiations had been challenging, with the Anteran and Therbian ambassadors both wanting to haggle over the cost for the amestite ore used in the construction of the newer and more powerful shield generators and transporters. Hank had been surprised and extremely pleased to learn the value that many of the other worlds in the League placed on coal. It turned out that diamonds were in high demand among most of the League members, primarily because of their use in a wide variety of technologies involving light, such as computer systems and laser technologies. As diamonds were easily created by applying great pressure to coal, the resource was in high demand. It was clear that both worlds were plentiful in amestite, just as Earth possessed coal in great abundance, and their ambassadors were more than willing to trade, but only after long, drawn out negotiations were concluded.

He glanced at the clock on the wall and noted that the break was about over. He chuckled, surprised that he had already come to think of the alien timepiece as a clock. On the day following his arrival on Val, his escort had brought him to the office to show him where he would be working. While they were passing through the office, Hank had noticed the "clock" on the wall and had been somewhat shocked to see what he thought was a thermometer hanging on the wall in his office. Cognizant of the fact that he was on an alien planet, he'd asked Sortox Norwal, his Valhari escort, why the Valhari felt it necessary to keep a thermometer on the wall of his office. Just as with Zing decades earlier, Hank felt certain that his host was laughing, though like all Valhari, Norwal's face had remained expressionless. Hank had come to believed that either the Valhari were incapable of expressing emotion, or it was merely something they seldom did.

"It's not used for measuring ambient temperature, Hank Reynolds," his escort explained. "It is a device for tracking the passage of time. Do they not have such devices on your world?" While he couldn't tell at that moment, Hank had been certain he'd blushed out of embarrassment at the innocent yet ridiculous oversight.

"Oh, a clock, of course," Hank replied, trying to save a little face at least. "On my world they are round. We wear them on our arms, or we hang them on the wall, just as you do here."

"And you hang 'thermometers' inside your dwellings as well?" he asked.

Hank pondered whether the question was satirical or mere curiosity, but it was impossible to tell with a Valhari. *They'd make great poker players.*

"No...well, most people don't," Hank answered weakly. "So...," he began, desperate to change the subject and hoping his host would permit it. "How does this timepiece work?"

"Each of these markings denote a standard hour, of which there are thirty in a standard day on Val. This light marks the passage of time throughout the day. The day begins with the light at the top, and the light travels down, marking the passage of the day." Hank had laughed loudly at the explanation for the operation of something so simple. He'd reverse-engineered the quantum engine, yet he'd been unable to recognize and discern the operation of something so simple a child could have grasped it.

The door opened and his assistant appeared, bringing Hank's thoughts back to the present.

"They're ready to begin again, Mr. Ambassador."

"Thank you, Maria."

Hank walked out of his office and made his way toward the conference room where they'd gathered for the negotiations. He was close to a deal with both worlds, but it would take more effort to get them to take it. Each ambassador had expressed an interest in trading for Earth's vast reserve of coal, and each knew the insatiable appetite that the Alliance had for their amestite. Hank had asked them both to participate so there would only one round of negotiations, a decision he'd regretted after being in the same room with them for less than five minutes.

He sat down alone on one side of the table, while Ambassador Yaltiksit Lorrie, who represented the Anterans, and Ambassador Tix Hiloo, from the planet Therbia, sat on the other side. Hank had taken time during the break to try to divine a strategy that would short-circuit the marathon negotiations, and he'd hoped the stratagem he'd settled on would do the trick.

"Okay gentlemen, are we ready to resume?" A nod from each ambassador served as their affirmation. "Good. So, before the break, we came across a few sticking points, which seemed to be slowing down our progress. You each feel that our price is too high, and you both prefer to obtain a greater quantity of coal than what the Alliance is willing to trade at this time. Now, I'm a bit anxious to get home to my wife today and to have dinner with my family, so here's my proposal. As I stated at the outset of these negotiations, the Earth Space Alliance wants to trade with each of your worlds for amestite. However, since we seem to be at an impasse, I'm prepared to offer each of you the same amount of coal as before at the original asking price, and the same quantity of coal I was offering to the other, at only three-fourths of the price. This way Earth gets what we want, one of you will get what you want, and the other goes home empty handed. So, what do you think?"

Hank sat back in his chair and smiled. At first, there was only silence, as each diplomat considered the offer. Both Lorrie and Hiloo were each afraid the other would accept the offer and get everything while the other went home empty-handed.

"On behalf of the Anterans, I would like to accept your most gracious offer," Lorrie said quickly.

"No! On behalf of the Therbian people, *I* would like to accept!"

Hank suppressed the grin struggling desperately to erupt onto his face. A few seconds later the two ambassadors fell into a shouting match.

"Gentlemen, please, settle down; take it easy, we have enough for each of your worlds. Since it seems that each of you suddenly found the offer compelling, I suggest you accept the original offer the Alliance has made before I determine some random way to select the one to choose who receives the coal; remember, the Alliance gets what it wants either way. All I'm offering you is a chance for each of you to get what you want also."

Each diplomat looked first at Hank and then at each other, before turning back to Hank.

"It is true what they say about you, Ambassador Reynolds. Your intellect is exceeded only by your wisdom," said Lorrie, with a slight bow of respect.

"I concur," said Hiloo, before also bowing his head. "Therbia accepts your offer as well, following approval by our leadership."

"Excellent," Hank began. "I'll get the forms you'll need to get your leaders to sign onto your data pads, and I believe we have a deal. Please pardon me just one minute." Hank stepped out of the room and walked the short distance to his office. Maria sat at her desk, busying herself with work until Hank finished negotiations.

"It looks like we have a deal, Maria, we just need to have them sign the forms and we're done."

"Excellent, Dr. Reynolds, congratulations! I'll get the forms loaded into the data pads before they change their minds, sir."

Hank smiled. "I think that would be wise, Maria." Hank turned to walk back to the conference room. His assistant connected the data pads to her console before looking up with a start.

"Oh, Dr. Reynolds, I nearly forgot to tell you; Ambassador Itanus stopped by just a few minutes ago. He said he needed to talk with you. He didn't say what it was about, but it seemed urgent. I told him you should be free shortly, but after waiting for only a couple of minutes, he said he had to leave and that you could reach him in his office no matter what time negotiations concluded."

"Really? Ambassador Itanus?"

"Yes, sir."

"Hmm. Okay, thanks Maria," he said, with a look of consternation. "Hand over those data pads as soon as they're finished. I'll wrap this thing up and contact the ambassador. He wouldn't have contacted me like this unless it was important; I must know the reason for his visit."

"Of course, Mr. Ambassador. Oh, here." She handed him the data pads, forcing Hank to smile.

"Maria, I think I'm falling in love with you."

Maria smiled back at him with a feigned, flirtatious look. "Well, that's all well and good, Dr. Reynolds, but let's just keep that between you and me; and please, don't tell my husband!"

"Or my wife," he said with a chuckle as he walked to the conference room.

***

"Ambassador Itanus, thank you for coming so quickly."

The Anteran ambassador hurriedly entered, and at Hank's invitation sat down in the chair across from his desk.

"You are welcome, Dr. Reynolds; I only wish it were under better circumstances."

"Wha—?"

Itanus held up a hand. "In a moment, Dr. Reynolds. First, please allow me to congratulate you on your successful negotiations with our trade ambassador a short while ago. I passed him on the way here."

"Yeah, well, I guess he wasn't very happy with the arrangement. Sorry."

"Oh no, Dr. Reynolds, on the contrary, he was actually quite pleased with the arrangement, and very impressed with you, I might add. He told me he'd never met anyone quite like you before. He said that if the rest of

192

the human race is anything like you, the League made a very wise choice indeed in admitting Earth as a member."

"Yes, well, please thank him for me when you see him again. That was very kind of him."

Itanus nodded. "I will certainly do that. Now I must tell you the reason for my unexpected visit earlier, Dr. Reynolds. Do you recall our conversation some weeks back, when we discussed the Shatarans and the Hantari?"

"Yes." Hank was focusing all of his attention on his guest, and he felt slightly awkward for staring so at one of the few new friends he'd made while on Val, but he could tell the Anteran was somewhat shaken by whatever it was he'd come to discuss.

"Well, after we talked I decided to stop in at the Valhari Central Library the next time I passed by it. I happen to do just that two days after we discussed the situation on New Eden. Something about the description you gave of the Shatarans, the timeframe, and the Machrys seemed relevant. I kept trying to remember, but I couldn't recall what it was. It seemed important enough that I decided to do a little research. While there, I came across some information about a key figure of the Machrys-Shataran war, one of the Shataran leaders who'd demonstrated a murderous disdain for the Machrys, bordering on pathological. It was he who led the most ghastly of the cleansing expeditions to wipe out the Machrys, murdering men, women, and children without hesitation and without remorse. He made it no secret at the time that he wanted every single Machrys either dead and buried, or in a museum."

"Didn't anyone ever try to stop him?"

"Yes, many tried, even some of his own people, but they were murdered just as mercilessly as the Machrys. From what I was able to find, he was always surrounded by a number of true believers, men and women who'd sacrifice themselves without hesitation in order to protect him."

"So what ever happened to him?"

"Well, as you know, the Shataran citizens themselves eventually rose up to depose their leadership. The Shataran leader who led the Great Purge was eventually caught on the other side of the galaxy along with his followers, where they were tried and sentenced to life in prison. Most people assumed the leader had been shipped back to Shatara, where he'd served out the rest of his life in the penal colony on one of the Shataran moons."

"But that's not what happened to him, is it, Professor?"

"No, Dr. Reynolds, it is not. From the research I did it appears that the Shataran government took great care at the time to cover-up what happened next, only releasing it centuries later, and even then doing so very quietly."

"What happened to them?"

"They disappeared on the way back to Shatara, and they were never seen or heard from again. The last known communications with the ship placed it in the vicinity of a binary system, but I was unable to find anything else that explained what happened to them. It was supposed at the time that their ship had been destroyed in a crash, or that it had been captured or destroyed by the Machrys, or by pirates. Searches were made, of course, but that ship was never found—until recently."

"The leader who disappeared, what was his name?" Hank asked, feeling a cold chill run down his spine.

Ambassador Itanus dropped his head. "It turns out that the prisoner transport ship crashed on a planet orbiting the same binary star system mentioned in the report, where the ship was partially buried in the side of a mountain when it crashed. I guess a malfunction must have prevented the stasis pods from automatically opening. Perhaps their captors considered them so dangerous that they left the chambers on lockdown, which means the only way to open the chambers was for one or more transport officers to enter the room first, presumably armed and ready.

"When the ship was finally discovered, quite by accident as it turns out, someone inadvertently must have entered the detainment area and triggered the reactivation of the stasis system. As incredible as it seems, this fanatical and extremely dangerous Shataran leader is still alive today, which is why I am here."

"The Shataran's name, Ambassador; what is it?"

"His name is Captain Jokar Motay. I am very sorry to have to inform you that your daughter and everyone else on New Eden are in grave danger."

CHAPTER 32

"Good morning, Governor Reynolds, how are you today?" Motay walked in and as usual, kissed her hand when it was offered to him, and waited until Nicole sat down before he did.

"Jokar! Good morning to you; I wasn't expecting to see you here for a while."

"Ah, yes, but it is always a pleasure for me when I have time to stop in to visit with you, Nicole."

Nicole offered a slight smile in reply. "Well, I enjoy spending time with you as well, Jokar. So tell me, is there something on your mind?"

Motay smirked. "A no-nonsense woman, always directly to the point, Nicole. Very well, then, here it is. I wanted to run something by you, but I wanted your permission before I do anything."

"Okay, what's on your mind?"

"My men have done little since staying within the boundaries of your city. We still fear the Machrys threat is very real, so I wanted to suggest a couple of ways in which you might benefit more from having them a round."

"Okay, go ahead, I'll bite," she said with a smile. "What are you proposing?"

"As I said, we still fear the Machrys threat is very real; there could even be another Machrys fleet on their way here right now, at this very moment, and we'd never know it."

"Why, because they'd be using phased shielding?"

"Yes. They were reckless the first time, because they believed they had a clearly superior and overwhelming force, which they did; rest assured they will not be so careless again. When they come next time they will come better prepared, and they would almost certainly be using their most advanced phased shielding technology that could, I'm afraid, make it nearly impossible to spot them before they get here."

"Then what do we do, Jokar? Just wait for them to show up on our doorstep?' Nicole said with a growing sense of agitation. She was responsible for whatever happened at the colony, and it weighed heavily on her at times like these.

"I said *nearly* impossible, which is sometimes far different than impossible. If we can put a couple of our surveillance technicians in your communications room, they could monitor the receiving station for any unusual signals or transmission. The Machrys use various encoded signals to coordinate their fleet movements. My men know what to look for with the Machrys, and their assistance could give you more advance notice of a Machrys fleet heading here to New Eden."

Nicole rose from her chair and walked to a window while Jokar remained seated.

"I don't know, Jokar; do you suppose there really *is* a Machrys fleet on its way here?" she asked him with a mixture of fear, doubt, and concern.

"They've done it before, many times. They *will* be back, and much sooner than later."

Nicole sat back down to mull it over. "Okay, you can place two men in there, but I want you to keep me posted on their progress, okay?"

"Of course."

Nicole sat there, staring at the beautiful alien sitting before her, his golden eyes, so intriguing....

"At the risk of offending you, I must ask you this question, Jokar; why are you helping us so much? And please don't patronize me by telling me it's just because you care."

Jokar smiled. "We *do* care, Nicole. It's also true, however, that we also have some mutual self-interest. The Machrys surely realize by now that you had assistance fending them off last time. My guess at this point is that they will be more interested in striking at us than they will you. So you see, you might find yourself in the position of helping us."

Nicole let out a heavy sigh. "I should've read the fine print before accepting this position," she said dryly, then turning back to her data pad.

"There was one other suggestion I had."

Nicole looked up with some surprise.

"Yes?"

"I would feel much safer if you were to allow my men here to patrol the perimeter of the city on a daily basis. Our eyes are better equipped to detect a shielded Machrys, whether they are wearing personal phased shielding on foot or whether they are in a ship."

"You believe there are more of them on the planet?"

"While I cannot say with certainty, I do think it likely."

Nicole stood and walked to the window. "A number of our people have gone missing over the last month or so, just disappeared without a

196

trace. I don't suppose you would know anything about that, would you?"

Nicole saw what looked like a furrowed brow for a moment, as if the Shataran leader had a flash of concern on his face, but it soon vanished as spontaneously as it had appeared.

"Most likely taken by the Machrys, Nicole, perhaps to use as leverage against you and your people at some point."

"Or something else."

"Such as?"

"The Hantari. Remember I mentioned to you that one of our people had reported seeing something, and you suggested it looked like a Hantari."

"Ah, yes, quite right. Yes, it could be a Hantari, though I believe it more likely to be the Machrys. They seem to have a keen interest in this planet. You must know that it was quite a bold move for them to attack a League member, even if a very recent addition. There must be something they really want or need here."

"You're thinking it's the castilian plant they're after?"

"More than likely, yes. Either way you and the colony are still in great danger, Nicole."

'And you think these extra measures will help keep us safe now that the word is out about the castilian plant."

"Yes. It's your choice of course, Nicole; I just don't want anything to happen to your people, or to *you*."

He stared longingly into her eyes, causing her to forget any misgivings she'd had about him before. At that moment, she suddenly felt flush, and found herself wanting nothing else but to be with him. Her brain knew it didn't make any sense, but her heart was overpowering her mind.

"Yes, Jokar, of course; I appreciate your concern for my—for *our* welfare."

"Wonderful! We'll start our patrols this afternoon. So then, where can we pick up some of your pulse weapons?"

Nicole looked up and stared at him for a moment, confused. "Pulse weapons? But they're ineffective against the Machrys, we've already seen that. Besides, after what happened in the armory, we have only a few left. Wouldn't it be much better to use some of your weapons instead?"

"Oh no, I assure you that once you catch a Machrys outside of his ship, if you can find him, your pulse weapons will prove more than adequate. As to our weapons, I'm afraid that we have a number of the large cannons left, but almost no small arms whatsoever. I'm afraid that our ship was a transport for the cannons and the shield projectors that we used against the Machrys during the war. In regards to what happened to your weapons supply in the armory, I certainly understand if you cannot spare any pulse weapons. Who knows, perhaps your Alliance troops will get lucky, and spot one or two of the Machrys infiltrators, but then again—"

Nicole hesitated. She didn't like giving their only remaining weapons to anyone else, even the Shatarans. Part of her trusted Jokar completely, causing her to feel guilty about the other part, which still had a number of misgivings about Jokar and the others; something just felt off about the whole affair with the Shatarans. Regardless, she'd seen hard evidence of just how effective the Shatarans were at dealing with the Machrys threat, and it seemed clear that the colony still needed their help with that. She suddenly regretted not inviting Jack to the discussion, but she'd long-since passed that point. She looked up at Motay, who sat watching her intently. She was taking too long to give him an answer, when she knew there was only one logical conclusion she could come to.

"Okay, Jokar, I'm going to trust you and your men with the last of our pulse rifles, but please don't make me regret my decision?"

"Nicole, have I ever given you any reason to distrust me?" He offered her another smile, kissed her hand, and for a moment, she thought he might also kiss her; she was surprised to find herself hoping that he would. Instead, however, he started making his way towards the door. "Nicole, would you please ask Colonel Francoise to deliver the weapons to the site of the old armory? It is an ideal location for us to begin our patrols."

"Certainly, Jokar, whatever you think is best. Thank you for your help dealing with the Machrys. They would surely have killed all of us had you not intervened."

At this, Jokar offered a slight bow. "It remains our pleasure to help in any way we can, my dearest Nicole. We will await Colonel Francoise at the armory site." He bowed once more before leaving her office.

Nicole watched him leave before walking back to her desk. She wasn't looking forward to the conversation she was about to have, so she decided to go ahead and get it over with. She pressed a button on her comm system.

"Yes, Governor?"

"Bernie, please ask Captain Lincoln and Colonel Francoise to come to my office immediately."

"Yes, Governor."

Nicole rose from her desk and walked over to the window, troubled that the further she got from her conversation with Jokar, the worst the agreement to hand over the weapons seemed.

***

Her heart was pounding in her chest as more and more adrenaline poured into her bloodstream. She'd never experienced terror like it before, which only added fuel to her desperation. Sliding the cover to the attic access slightly, she was able to look down into the room, where she desperately searched for Michael. She continued looking for him through the narrow slit of the opening, but the top of the closet blocked her view. She yearned to cry out to him, to make sure he was okay, but she was too scared.

She gasped when she saw a strange man with a gloved hand holding a firearm pass by the doorway. She tried unsuccessfully to get a look at the man's face, but she was unable to see it. She continued watching as the man, dressed in blue jeans and a flannel shirt and wearing a light jacket, walked around the room. She finally got a look at the man's face as he backed away and slowly bent down with his head close to the floor. The man had dark hair with a touch of gray, and had to be about the same age as her father. Looking at the man and seeing what appeared to be a kind face, she began to question who he was and why he was there.

She felt an icy chill pass through her as the man peered under the bed, and she suddenly heard the whimpering of a five-year old little boy.

"Hey there, little fella," the man said as he looked under the bed. "Listen, everything's going to be okay. Here, look what I have for you."

The girl's heart stopped, however, when she caught a single, quick sweeping movement of the man's other arm and—

Nicole awoke in a cold sweat, her heart beating every bit as hard as the girl from her dream. So vivid had the dream been that she sat up in bed for several minutes, until her mind cleared and she was awake enough to confirm that it wasn't really happening.

She'd only been awake for a few moments when her comm link sounded an alarm. Nicole jumped out of bed and picked it up off the table; as she was dressed in her night clothes, she answered the call in audio-only.

"Reynolds."

"I'm sorry to disturb you at this hour, Governor, but it's important."

Nicole could hear the nervousness in the Alliance soldier's voice. She looked and saw his name displayed as Lieutenant Foster.

"That's quite all right, Lieutenant Foster; in fact, you did me a favor. Tell me what's happening."

"We heard weapons fire around the perimeter of the city, just outside the new education building."

"Do you have any idea what the Shataran patrol may have been firing at?"

"No, ma'am. Captain Lincoln told me to contact you, and then he went to investigate. He thought you'd want to be notified."

"He was right about that. Okay, Lieutenant, thank you for letting me know."

Nicole quickly dressed and hurried to the door. An Alliance guard met her outside her door.

"Ma'am?"

"Take me to the perimeter of the city just outside where they built the new education building."

"But Governor, someone reported there was weapons fire there just a few minutes ago."

"Now, Commander Takata."

"Yes, ma'am."

Nicole climbed into the transport and was soon joined by the Alliance officer. Seconds later the transport was floating several feet off the ground and racing toward the outskirts of the city, and trouble.

CHAPTER 33

It was still dark out when the transport pulled up to the edge of the city, where Nicole found Jokar speaking with six Shatarans, each armed with a pulse rifle. She also noticed something that troubled her greatly; some other type of weapon was also attached to each belt, which she assumed to be of Shataran design. Had Jokar lied to her? She thought about asking him about it before deciding it could wait.

"What's going on here? I was told there was weapons fire. Is everyone okay?" she asked, concerned for Shatarans as well as her own Alliance soldiers.

"Yes, Governor, I believe so," Motay answered. "I only arrived here a few moments ago myself, but from what they've old me, it seems they spotted several Machrys just outside the perimeter of the city, probing the city's defenses no doubt. Once the Machrys saw they'd been spotted, they opened fire on my patrol. My men returned fire but regrettably, it was too dark and they got away."

"Were they wearing phased shielding?"

"Yes, and it's a good thing my men are patrolling this area now. It's so dark out here now that the Machrys scouts nearly went undiscovered by my people; your people would have missed them entirely. Our world is farther from our star than yours is, so less light makes it to my world."

"Yes, I guess it is a good thing. Can the Machrys get through the city's shielding?"

Motay smiled in reply. "Oh yes, definitely. It may take them a few nights to find a way through, but they will, trust me."

"Has your communications teams picked up any enemy chatter?"

"Yes, there has been some Machrys traffic, but no mention of another invasion force, at least not yet. But they *must* be on their way here for so much activity. I strongly recommend that you require your people to stay inside after dark from now on; it's the safest course of action. You might also want to restrict people to their quarters for a while, Governor, at least until we can determine what the Machrys are up to."

"I don't know—"

"What will happen when the Machrys get into the city? Who knows what carnage they might cause? I also suggest you permit me to move more of my men into the city, at least until we are certain the threat has been addressed."

"I don't think—"

"Please, Governor, I must insist. How can we keep the city safe if the city is overrun with Machrys? Once your Alliance is able to send more men with better weapons, our job will be done. In the meantime, we're already here, so why not let us help?"

"I'll think about it." She looked around the area. "It all seems quiet. Do they have everything under control for now?"

"Oh yes, very much so; you can sleep soundly, Governor Reynolds. The Machrys will not threaten you tonight, I promise you."

"Okay then, I'm heading back to bed."

"Good night, Governor."

"Good night." Nicole began walking towards the transporter before stopping. "Oh, I was told that Captain Lincoln was heading this way in response to the weapons fire. Have you seen him?"

"No, I haven't. Should any of my men see him, I will instruct them to tell him that you were here, that you're retiring for the evening, and that he should come by your office in the morning; is that sufficient?"

"Wonderful. Goodnight everyone, and thank you!"

Several of the Shatarans grinned at one another, until one of the more senior ones walked by and glared at them. The look alone proved to be more than sufficient as the other two immediately became stoic.

***

Nicole awoke the next morning to the sound of someone at her door, alternating between using the doorbell and pounding on the door. Nicole sat up with a start, and after sitting on the side of her bed long enough for her head to clear slightly, she stood up, put on a robe, and walked to the door. She found herself getting angrier as she neared the door, irritated at the rudeness of the person. She was startled to find Francoise standing in front of her doorway, frantic.

"Colonel Francoise, what are you doing banging on my door this morning?"

"I'm sorry, Governor, but I had to; please, may I come in?"

The way he continually looked behind him and from side to side greatly concerned her. She ushered him inside and closed the door. "What's the matter, Pierre, you look like you've seen a ghost!"

"There was nothing we could do, Governor Reynolds, nothing! It must have been *them* that destroyed the armory...now we have nothing!"

"What? Are the Machrys invading?"

Francoise stared at her for a moment with a wild look in his eyes. "What? No, not the Machrys, the Shatarans! They poured into the city overnight, each one of them armed with some sort of Shataran weapons *and* our pulse rifles. They must have been planning this, Dr, Reynolds, ever since we revived them."

"The Shatarans? No, Pierre, that's not possible; they saved us from the Machrys."

"They've seized control of the city, blocking all exits in or out. They've been gathering Alliance soldiers throughout the night and locking them up in the main conference hall."

"The Shatarans?" she asked, directed more to herself than to Francoise.

"Frankly, I don't understand why they didn't come to get you first."

Nicole smiled. "If I know Jokar Motay, it's likely he doesn't even consider me a threat. Maybe that's one thing we can use to our advantage. I'm sure he'll turn up here very soon, Colonel. When he does, maybe I can find out what he's really up to. He's nothing if not methodical, and you can be sure he has an agenda far beyond just taking over the colony." Nicole put her hands on her head and began pacing. "What about Jack, has he shown up yet?"

"I'm afraid not, Governor. It's not like him to disappear like this, I'm beginning to think the Shatarans saw him as a threat early on. He's never trusted them, and he's also an exceptional pilot, after all."

"You may be right, Pierre; he and Jokar often butted heads. Okay, so what do we know?" Nicole asked rhetorically. "They've clearly been planning this for some time, for what reason we have yet to learn. They have a weapon that was powerful enough to thwart the Machrys fleet of attack ships, and they've set up a planetary shield, which we thought was to protect us from the Machrys. I suppose it's safe to assume it was actually a means to protect them from the Alliance and the League. And beside each shield generator, they also erected a particle beam cannon like the one that took out the Machrys ships. It's safe to assume that they now have almost all of our weapons, along with their own, which they successfully kept hidden from us until last night."

"And don't forget about the communications, Governor; how can we even call for help if they control all communications with the outside world?"

"What about the communications equipment on the ships?"

"No, it is not possible. The ships will be heavily guarded. Our chances of getting to one are next to nothing. Besides, what good would it do? As long as the shields prevent anything from entering the atmosphere, the Alliance and the League are powerless to help now."

"Then we must find a way to disable the shields."

"But the Machrys—"

"Who do you think we should be more worried about, Pierre, the Machrys or the Shatarans?"

"Good point, Governor. One enemy at a time."

"Enemy? Not us, Colonel Francoise, I assure you." The voice came from outside the door, which opened to reveal Motay and three other Shatarans. "Shataran hearing; it's also somewhat better than human beings," Motay said with a smile.

"Yeah, the same way Shatarans can detect a shielded Machrys whereas human beings cannot, I suppose," Nicole answered with dripping sarcasm.

"Well, I may have exaggerated the truth about that somewhat. The truth is, I believe, our vision is not as good as yours, since our planet is actually closer to our star instead of farther away. Sorry about that."

"You exaggerated about a great many things, Jokar," Nicole said with a sneer. "What do you think you're doing? Give me back control of this colony, and then take your men and leave New Eden, and I mean now!"

"Oh, what fire! It's always been one of the traits I admired in you, Nicole."

"You've effectively taken control of our colony, Jokar, I know that. What I don't understand is why; I mean, it's not like we have a vast civilization here for you to conquer."

"Conquer? My dear Nicole, how you misunderstand us!"

"Then why have you taken over the colony, and why haven't you been telling us the truth? Why have you been taking our people?"

"Okay then, straight to the point, as usual. First, we haven't taken over control of the colony, at least not permanently; we only need it for a time. You see, after your people were kind enough to wake us from our sleep, we realized your colony would serve as an excellent base of operation for us until we could reestablish ourselves. We have much to catch up on after five-thousand years, after all."

"Then why not just leave, find another world, return to Shatara? Why are you so determined to stay here?"

"It's a long story, my dear; are you sure you wish to hear it?"

"Yes."

"Very well then, please sit down. It *is* important to me that you understand, Nicole, because I understand how special you are. You are intelligent and wise enough to understand what I am about to tell you, What must seem to you to be a very long time ago, but to us was only a few years ago, our people lived in relative peace with the other sentient species spread out across the galaxy. We traveled the universe, exploring and settling new worlds. Then one day one of our colonies was attacked, must like yours was, by the Machrys. They are nothing like us, Nicole; they are more like insects than they are a sentient species. They are also extremely territorial, viewing even the slightest provocation as an act of war. They attacked several of our colonies, which happened to be located in relatively close proximity to the same sector of space as their own. Our people thought they were safe and well outside of Machrys space, so they were totally unprepared when the attack began. Our people were slaughtered, Nicole, as waves and waves of Machrys ships rained death and destruction down on innocent Shatarans, including women and children, whose only crime was to seek a better life for themselves and their families by settling on a new colony. They came to these new worlds, where they faced hardships and struggles as they forged new civilizations out of the wilderness; in the end, however, they found only death.

"So with the obliteration of many of our colonies by the Machrys, our pacifistic leaders were soon replaced by ones with stronger views in regards to dealing with the Machrys threat. These new leaders came to power with the promise of addressing the Machrys threat to our people head-on; they assured us that they would not pay mere lip-service to these creatures in an effort to pacify or placate them, but rather they said that they would crush them militarily, and ensure the Machrys never slaughtered another Shataran anywhere in the known universe.

"We quickly learned all we needed to know about their technology and how it worked. We studied their stratagems and their methods. The Shataran people, who had long been free of conflict, applied themselves with tremendous energy and intensity to the art of warfare, and to victory over the Machrys.

"This is where I entered the picture. I was one of the first fleet commanders to go up against the Machrys fleet. My parents and my siblings had been on Telor, one of the first colonies destroyed by the Machrys. My intense hatred for the Machrys soon made me one of the most daring and accomplished commanders in the fleet. My men and I led the effort to push the Machrys fleet back towards the Machrys home world one system at a time. We suffered great losses early on, as we were totally unprepared for such a prolonged campaign of war. My people are extremely nimble however, and we learned quickly. We developed technologies that had never been seen before, powerful new ships, the particle beam cannons, the planetary shields. By the end of the second year of the war, we were on the offensive and we began to slowly decimate the vast military machine that had taken them centuries to build up. Within ten standard years, we had driven them all the way back to their home world. The fighting was ferocious there, but within a standard month, we broke the back of their military, and after another month of bombarding their defensive systems, the first Shatarans set foot on Machrys, officially ending the war. We imprisoned the Machrys leader and executed those we could find who had either ordered or participated in the atrocities before or during the war, especially those who took part in massacring the Shataran colonists.

"By this time, however, many of the very same Machrys war criminals who had instigated or taken part in the attack on our colonists had already abandoned Machrys and had made their way to one of the many Machrys colonies or outposts scattered across the galaxy. Furthermore, each Machrys colony had their own military leadership and military presence and were therefore a threat. Once we were certain we had a secure footing on Machrys, my men and I led the effort to decimate what remained of the Machrys fleet. We did everything we could to honor our promise to ensure the Machrys would never attack another Shataran colony, ever. We pursued their leaders to wherever they had fled, and we eliminated any military opposition we found there. Upon finding the criminals, we would arrest them, try them for high crimes against sentient life, and execute them. We were judge, juror, and executioner for many of the vile Machrys. When they fled from us, we pursued them across the known universe when needed, until we found the last one, on a frozen world many systems away from Machrys. Next we searched for those Machrys who had actively supported the attacks on the Shataran colonies, and we dealt harshly with them.

"Unfortunately, back on Shatara, some of our people had come to believe that we had exceeded our mandate to stop the Machrys, and some even began to accuse us of committing acts of genocide against *them*. I couldn't believe it! Support for our cause began to wither, despite the fact that some of the isolated Machrys military outposts worked to secretly rebuild their now decimated military machine. We all knew that once they were finished, they would bide their time, waiting to once again strike at Shataran colonies.

"My men and I believed in the cause, however, even after a new leadership structure was elected back on Shatara. Disregarding our orders to return to Shatara as war heroes, we continued the Great Purge, what some called our effort to deal such a devastating blow to the Machrys that they would never again dare attack us. Our disregard for the orders of our leadership soon turned the people of Shatara against us, however, forcing us to continue the Purge while on the run from our own military. We continued traveling from system to system searching for Machrys outposts, however, despite the risk of being caught, which we

206

unfortunately were less than a year after the election of the new leadership on Shatara.

"As was our custom then, we were tried and sentenced to the penal colony on one of the moons orbiting Shatara. We were on our way to the prison there when something must have happened, something that caused us to crash-land here on this planet, what you call New Eden."

"So the ship you were on is a prison ship."

"Yes. We were only political prisoners, however, victims of political change."

"But how can you say that? You slaughtered the Machrys to near extinction! I understand that you lost your family to an unprovoked attack by the Machrys, and that's horrible, but the annihilation of an entire race of beings goes far beyond justice. Can't you see that, Jokar?"

Motay sighed and lowered his head. "I suppose I didn't really expect you to understand what my own people did not, Nicole. I mainly told you all of this so that you would know the truth."

"So, what now?" Nicole asked, still fuming, though somewhat more sympathetic.

"We need time to determine what we want to do next...whether we return to Shatara or continue where we left off with the Machrys. I suspect it will be the latter."

"And what about my people? What do you expect us to do in the meantime? You must know the Alliance and more importantly, the League, will not allow this to go on. They will come and they will stop you."

Motay smiled. "Yes, they will come, eventually. But we control your communications, and the planetary shield, along with the particle beam cannons strategically deployed across the planet. Based on what I've learned since my awakening, these will work nearly as effectively against the League as they will on the Machrys. I believe it will take quite some time before they find a way to defeat our planetary shield, and by then we will likely be gone." Motay stood and turned to leave. "Your people are free to move about and conduct themselves just as before, only they must stay far away from the communications building, the ships, the cannons, and the shields. Anyone caught violating this ordinance will face incarceration, or worse, until we leave this world; which could be a while."

"What about our people you took? What's happened to them? Are they still alive?" Nicole asked as he made his way toward the door.

He came to a sudden stop and stared at her with a puzzled look. "I'm curious, Governor Reynolds. What people are you referring to?"

"Nearly two dozen of our people are missing; what have you done with them?"

"I'm afraid I know nothing about your missing people, Dr. Reynolds. We have taken a few today, but none before that. Perhaps you should send out people to search for them."

With that Jokar Motay left, leaving Nicole stunned by Motay's claim that he knew nothing about the missing colonists, and even more surprised at the fact that for some reason, she believed him.

CHAPTER 34

Nicole sat quietly in her living quarters, sipping on a glass of hot tea. She enjoyed it because it helped soothe and calm her. She had been going over her conversation with Motay a few days earlier, and racking her brain trying to determine what the Shatarans were up to. She knew he'd only given her part of the story, though she had determined that from his perspective at least, it was mostly true. Despite being over five-thousand years old, the Shatarans were still a surprisingly advanced race, forced to embrace a warrior culture after the brutal attacks by the Machrys. Finding a way to stop and overcome them was going to be a real challenge. She was running through various scenarios in her mind when she heard the doorbell. The face she saw after opening the door both shocked and thrilled her.

"Jack, you're alive!" She threw her arms around him and embraced him for quite some time. When she pulled away to talk to him, she could see that he was both stunned and pleased at the reception. "What happened to you, Jack, where have you been? Did you see the others that are missing?" She embraced him once more before ushering him into her living room, where they both sat down. "Can I offer you something to drink?"

"Maybe some water, and a coffee?"

"Sure, no problem, give me a moment." She returned a few minutes later, with both water and coffee in hand.

"Thank you."

She nodded in response. "Come on, Jack, tell me!"

"Well, it's a long story, Nicole. As you know, I heard the disturbance a few days ago and went to investigate. I was walking around just outside town, investigating, when there was suddenly a bright light, and I found myself transported to a beautiful room in a spectacular city. You'll never guess who greeted me there."

"The Hantari."

Jack jumped up out of his seat. "Now how could you possibly have known that? I figured that little bit of news would have knocked you off your feet, but there's just no surprising you, is there?"

Nicole smiled and looked away for several seconds before turning back to Lincoln. "I knew that someone had to be behind the disappearances, and after my conversation with Jokar several days ago, I knew it wasn't him or his people. That meant that it had to be either the Machrys or The Hantari. Jokar had lied about the Machrys being on New Eden, along with many other things, so it seemed logical that he'd lied about the Hantari as well. So what did they want with you and the others?"

"I was introduced to a Hantari named Hael-ta-Kelo, the leader of a group of Hantari, the last of their kind that still live in this galaxy. They were curious and wanted to learn more about us, about humanity, and about Earth. They also wanted to warn us that Jokar and his people should be considered extremely dangerous, and they wanted me to bring you a message."

"So why take only some of us; why not take all of the colonists?"

"I don't really know, Nikki. Their selection appears to have been largely opportunistic. They've taken our people to a place of safety within their city until this is all over with the Shatarans."

"What message?"

"What?"

"What message were they trying to get to me?"

"Oh, yeah, sorry. They have a way out of this that will minimize the loss of life, and see to it that the Shatarans are tried for their crimes."

"So they want to see Jokar and the others punished?"

"Seems so."

"Good, so do I," she said with a snarl. "I'm gonna see that Motay pays for everything he's done. He just shows up and he takes control of our security, our communications, and then our firearms, before turning us all into prisoners of war. I swear, Jack, if he harms one hair on anyone's head in this colony, I'll kill him myself. I'm sick and tired of running from people like him, and then watching them kill the ones I love! He'll wish he never woke up," she said, her face flush with intensity and anger.

Jack studied her for a moment. "Nikki, can I ask you a personal question, and if so, promise me you won't explode over it?"

Nicole considered it for a moment before answering. "Sure, Jack, go ahead, ask me anything."

"I've been wondering this since the day we first met. You're such a beautiful, attractive, and desirable woman, and you're so intelligent it's scary. Most of the time you exhibit a hot temper with such a vicious edge that most men run from you. *I* look at you and all I see is a ferocious tigress, determined to never let anyone get close enough to get to know her. Every once in a while, however, when you let your guard down, you come across like such a sweet, wonderful woman, one that any man would long to embrace. I just don't get it; what could have happened to turn what must have been a sweet little girl into someone so hard and bitter?"

Nicole felt anger surge up within her at his daring to ask such a personal question, yet she had promised him; and besides, she owed it to him. He'd shown her nothing but kindness and she'd been only cold and ugly in return.

"Look Jack, I normally don't discuss this with others, especially outside of my family; in fact, I've never discussed this with anyone *inside* of my family either. I—"

"Never mind, Nikki, it was stupid of me to bring it up. It's really none of my business, though—you know that I care for you, don't you, Nikki?"

She looked into his eyes and for the first time, she saw, really saw, that he did.

"My father was nearly killed by a man named Brian Durham before I was born."

"Sure, I read about it; the guy was a real lunatic. He stranded your father in Alpha Centauri and tried to kill your grandfather too. I believe he was eventually executed for the murder of General George Caprella, wasn't he?"

"Yes, he was eventually executed for it, but not before sitting on death row for nearly fifteen years, and for a man with as much wealth as he had, that's a lot of time to plan and execute your revenge."

"What do you mean?"

"When I was twelve years old, my brother Mike and I were home alone with a baby sitter; my mother and father were out attending an Alliance business function at the time.

My little brother and I were upstairs playing a hologame when we heard a loud noise downstairs…it sounded like a blast from a phase pistol, followed by the sound of something falling and glass breaking. I told my brother to find a place to hide just in case, while I climbed up into the attic through an access located in the closet of my room. While I was hiding in the attic, I looked down through a crack and saw a strange man enter the room." Nicole started tearing up and her voice began to crack. "The strange man was carrying a phase pistol; they were still very rare back then." Her tears were now flowing freely. "I watched as he leaned down to look under the bed where my brother was; I watched as he fired…." Nicole stopped talking and placed her head in her hands. Jack walked over to sit next to her, and wrapped his arm around her, saying nothing. "I watched him kill my little brother, Jack, and I didn't do anything! I just lay there in the attic, staring; I was frozen with fear, and I did nothing! I watched my brother die!"

"There was nothing you could have done, Nicole. You were still just a little girl; he would have killed you too," he said as softly and as reassuringly as he could.

"One of the neighbors must have seen the man breaking in or heard the phase pistol fire, because I heard a loud siren sound just before the man turned and fled the house. It turns out he was killed in a firefight with the police a few minutes later, but that gave me no comfort; my little brother was dead. You asked why I am the way I am? I was soft, Jack...I did nothing to save my little brother. I decided then and there that I would never be so soft like that again. It's made me tougher, I guess, and more callous I suppose; but that's the price I'm willing to pay, if it means never having to witness someone die on my account again."

Nicole stopped her recounting of the experience to look Lincoln in the eyes. He stared into her eyes with a look of understanding, and on his face was the trace of a smile. He said nothing else to her for quite some time; Nicole soon came to believe he was just giving her some space to vent. She'd not intended to display such raw emotion before him, though she had always felt like she could. He was a good man, a kind man, even if he was brash and difficult at times.

"Hey, are you okay, Nikki?" he asked softly, after holding her close for several minutes. Nicole pulled back a little and began wiping the tears that remained in her eyes. The emotional release had been cathartic, if embarrassing.

"I'm sorry about that, Jack. I certainly had no intention of unloading on you like that."

"Nonsense. I told you, Nicole, that I'm here for you, always, and I meant it. I am so sorry you had to witness something like that. I can't even imagine what it must have been like at such a vulnerable age."

Nicole just nodded. "Like I said, I never talk about it. So to answer your question, I suppose that experience has largely shaped who I am today. Are you sorry you asked now?" she asked with a thin, forced smile.

"Certainly not; I want to get to know everything about you, Nicole, the good and the bad, if you'll let me." She smiled at him for a moment before being overcome with an irresistible urge to kiss him. Moments later the two were locked in a long, passionate kiss. When they both came up for air, she was uneasy but had absolutely no regret whatsoever.

"Wow," was all Jack said, with a warm smile.

"I'm sorry, maybe I shouldn't have—" She stopped talking when Jack pulled her in close, and the two once more found themselves embracing. This time when they finished, she lay there with her head on his chest for several moments before breaking the silence.

"What was the message?" She sat back and looked at him, waiting for a response.

"What?"

"Listen, Jack, no matter what happens with this—with us, I'm governor here, and the colonists here are my responsibility. We can figure this out later, because right now, I want that son-of-a-gun off my planet."

"I could say I told you so—"

Nicole glared at him.

"Okay, I'm sorry. I won't go there again."

"What did the Hantari say?" she asked again.

"He said that we have a chance to stop the Shatarans, but it will take some careful planning and a lot of risk."

"Okay then, let's hear it."

CHAPTER 35

Jack Lincoln awoke to the sound of a scream. He jumped out of bed and out the front door, trying to determine where it had come from. An Alliance soldier who happened to be walking by came running to where Jack stood, also waiting to hear the scream again so he could determine the location it was coming from. Neither man was disappointed, because no more than a few seconds later, they heard it again. But this time the scream was joined by similar wails of pain from around the city. Jack and the soldier followed the closest set of screams to it's source, a home just down the street to the south of Jack's home. His knock on the door brought a man of Indian lineage, with a dark complexion, black hair, and a moustache; Jack could see that the man's face was full of anguish.

"What is it, what do you want? Can't you see how upset we are?"

"What's wrong, why are you and your wife so upset?" Jack asked the man.

"What happened here?" the Alliance soldier inquired, feeling almost ashamed for having disturbed them.

"You don't know?"

"Know what?" the soldier asked.

"Our children, they have taken them!"

"Who's taken them, sir, and why?"

"Those devils with the yellow eyes, that's who! Please, excuse me, I must go and see them at once!"

"How do you know the Shatarans took them?" Jack asked this time.

"Are you mad, Captain? Who else would have done such a thing? They must have broken into our home sometime early this morning and taken our young daughter, while we were still fast asleep. They left this note. Please, my wife and I must go, keep it."

The man handed Jack the paper as he and his wife pushed past the two men, closing the door behind them. Soon, they were well down the road, his wife continuing to wail as they walked briskly toward the Gathering Hall. The soldier looked over Lincoln's shoulder as he read the note, written in English.

Citizen of New Eden,

Do not be alarmed, your children are safe, and they are unharmed.

You may come to the Gathering Hall anytime today to discuss the timely return of your young ones. Again, there is no need for you to fear for them, your children are being well fed and well-cared for, and they will continue to be well taken care of for as long as we have your continued cooperation. Come to the Gathering Hall and we will explain what you must do in order to see your children again.

We strongly urge you to come to the Gathering Hall by no later than 6:00 P.M. today, or we will assume you are not coming, and that would be most unfortunate.

Thank you in advance for your cooperation,

Jokar Motay, Captain of the Shataran Protectorate

"I don't believe it!" the soldier yelled out in anger. "I've got two small children at home, have those bastards taken them as well? If they have, I'm going to go down there and I'm going to—"

"Easy soldier," Lincoln said to him. "Believe me, I know how hard it is, but we have to do everything we can to remain level-headed and smart; it's the only way we'll beat them. I don't think they'll do anything that stupid, at least not yet."

"What? Captain Lincoln, I've heard stories about you, about some of what you did during the last war, and about what you did on the world before this one, V-10, where the entire expedition was nearly wiped out by creatures coming out of the water. Are you now saying we should turn tail and run, to do nothing to save our children?"

"What's your name, son?"

"Adam White, sir, Sergeant Adam White."

"Listen, Sergeant...I don't have any children, but I don't like these guys any more than you do. If you want to get your children back, however, if you want your freedom back, you'll have to stay alive, because they're going to need you. If you go in there like this and do something stupid, you'll only get yourself killed, and what good are you to your children then?"

White hung his head low. "Then what am I supposed to do, sir?"

"Go to the Gathering Hall, find out what Motay and the Shatarans want, and if it's not something that's going to harm anyone else, do it. We'll find a way to deal with these animals, don't worry. I have a sneaky suspicion that we'll be rid of them soon enough, as long as we all keep our heads."

"Yes, sir. I need to go—"

"Of course, Sergeant, get going."

The young soldier ran off, presumably towards his own home, as Lincoln crossed the street and walked two blocks over to the Governor's Building.

Jack wasn't looking forward to giving Nicole the news, because he knew how she'd react. When he first heard the news he was worried for her safety, fearing the Shatarans might tire of her and kill her on the spot. As he thought more of it, however, he slowly came to realize that it had to happen, that Motay would be *expecting* Nicole to react violently to what he'd done. If she did nothing, the Shataran leader would surely grow suspicious and watch them much more closely than he might otherwise. Jack felt reasonably certain she'd come to no harm. She had no weapons, though he knew her to be rather accomplished in hand-to-hand combat against human men. She'd not be striking a human man, however, she'd be striking a Shataran man, and everything Jack had seen told him they were much stronger than human beings. He took a deep breath as he climbed the stairs leading into the building.

"I already heard, Jack, and I'm on my way to tell that—Shataran exactly what I think of him. Where does he get off thinking he can take our children?" She'd spotted him coming down the hallway as soon as she left her office.

"Nicole, please, I know you're upset and—"

Nicole stopped and stared at him with a look of surprise mixed with intense anger.

"What, Jack, and you're *not*?"

Lincoln shook his head. "Of course I'm angry, Nicole, but I don't want to see you get hurt...I want to see him get what he deserves. Come on, you know I can't stand the guy, I'd like nothing more than to see him gone, but we have to stick with the plan, it's the only way."

"Aarrgghh! If only I had a phase rifle in my hand right now, or even an old-fashioned shotgun, how I'd make that creature pay!"

"Yeah, and to think you went on a date with him," Jack said with a hint of a smile. The intensity of the look she gave him in response made him immediately regret the comment.

The two said little else, other than the short prayer Nicole heard Jack whispering as they drew close to the Gathering Hall. She couldn't make it all out, though she heard her name, or references to her, on several occasions.

"I didn't know you were a religious man, Jack," she remarked just before walking into the building.

"Oh, yes, I am, we've just never discussed it."

She paused for a moment before entering. "Then let me just say that your timing was excellent, thank you."

Jack nodded.

Nicole turned and entered resolutely into the Gathering Hall. The building was filled with scores of colonists, standing in a single line that snaked back and forth across the large room, waiting for their chance to talk with one of the Shatarans sitting at one of the dozen tables spread throughout the Gathering Hall. Shataran guards, armed with phase pistols as well as rifles of Shataran design, stood along the walls and throughout the middle of the Hall. At a glance she estimated there must be around forty armed Shatarans in the Hall, in addition to those at the tables. On a platform located at the other end of the large building she saw Jokar Motay, and immediately she made a beeline for him. Some of the other colonists who'd been waiting in line started to object, but upon recognizing who she was, and after seeing the fire in her eyes, they immediately backed away to let her pass. Within a couple of minutes she and Lincoln arrived at the platform, and immediately each felt a Shataran rifle sticking them in the back. Motay stood and walked to the edge of the platform, looking down at the defiant man and woman.

"Well, well, I was wondering how long it would be before I'd see you again. I should probably have both of you locked up as a precaution, but I do so enjoy our time together!"

"Jokar, you arrogant and ungrateful wretch, what have you done with our children?"

"*Your* children? I wasn't aware that you two had children together; how very interesting," he said with a smirk.

Nicole could see that he now felt secure, and that he clearly felt like gloating. "I know the Alliance doesn't concern you, but I'm certain that you fear your own people, not to mention the League; how are you going to explain your kidnapping young children and holding them prisoners?"

Motay glared at her for a moment, particularly when she'd mentioned the other Shatarans and the League, but he was a smooth operator and she knew it; within moments all fear or anger had faded from his face as if it had never existed in the first place.

"Nicole, Nicole, Nicole, when are you going to learn that I'm not some human barbarian imbecile that you can negotiate with? I'm a Shataran, a proud people who traveled the stars when your people still

218

lived in huts and caves!"

"Where are the *children*, Jokar?" she asked him, much louder this time.

"Oh, they're safe, Governor Reynolds, and they'll stay safe, as long as you and your people cooperate."

"Where are you keeping them, on your ship?" The look of surprise that registered on Motay's face told her all she needed to know. "You put them into stasis, didn't you, Jokar? I guess you thought it was the best way to keep them without causing you and your people a lot of trouble. Well, remember that your stasis chambers were built for Shatarans, not for human children. If anything happens to those children, I'll pursue you across the galaxy if I have to, but I'll never rest until I make you pay, do you hear me?" At this Motay's face went flat, and all emotion disappeared, replaced by a face resembling a chiseled statue. He walked down from the platform and stood towering over Nicole. Neither of the two said anything, and the contest was only ended when Motay tired of the little game and smacked her hard enough that it knocked her to the ground. Nicole looked up at Jack, who was poised to jump Motay, but she shook her head just enough for him to understand she was ordering him to stand down.

"Don't ever talk to me that way again, human trash," the Shataran leader snarled, before walking back up the platform stairs and to his chair. "I tried explaining our situation to you...I thought you might understand why we did what we did, but I see now that I wasted my time. We took your children only to ensure that the adults do our bidding while we're here," Motay said casually, as if discussing some local gossip. "We intend them no harm, I assure you," he said to her, loud enough that many in the Hall could hear. "At least as long as you do what we tell you to do." Motay then stood to address everyone.

"Listen to me, humans! My people and I plan on staying here only a short while. We have taken your children in order to ensure that you work for us while we're here. Once we have everything we need, we'll leave this world, never to return."

"What do you want us to do?" one of the men standing near the platform, a father by the looks of him, asked the Shataran.

"We know that the castilian plant grows here, in some abundance from what we've seen. My people and I just awoke from a five-thousand year sleep, and we have no means to start over somewhere else. We want you humans to gather a vast amount of the plant for us, and then process the plants into castil; don't worry, we will tell you how this is done. Once we have a sufficient quantity of this substance, you will need to mine a metal that we have also found here, and process that as well. We will use

219

this metal to complete repairs to our ship, and then we will leave you, and this world, in peace."

"That's all?" a woman called out.

"Yes, dear lady, that is all. With so many humans on this colony, you should be finished with these tasks in a very short time; before you know it we'll be gone and you can get on with your lives." A thousand conversations erupted at the same time, until Motay raised his hand. "All we need is for each of you to talk with one of my people at each table, give them your name and your children's names, and they will give you information you can upload to your data pads that will tell you all about the castilian plant, the corbisite metal, and how to process both. Thank you for your attention, and your cooperation."

Once he'd finished addressing the audience, he turned his attention back to Nicole and Jack. Nicole was the first to speak.

"That's it? We help you with the castil and the corbisite and you'll leave New Eden?"

"Of course, you have my word."

Nicole glared at him for several moments before turning and leaving the Gathering Hall. Once they had exited the building and were close to the Governor's Building, Jack felt it safe to speak.

"They're not going to leave after they get the castil and the corbisite, are they?"

Nicole stopped and looked him in the eyes. "No, Jack, they're not."

CHAPTER 36

"How much longer, Zing?"

The Valhari turned towards Hank. "We should arrive there any minute; you must be patient, my old friend."

Hank nodded. "I know, Zing, but as you are well aware, patience has never been one of my strong suits."

"How true," his friend replied. "But be mindful that the stellar flares in this system have been known for many cycles to wreak havoc on communications."

Hank looked up from the display for a moment to look into the Valhari ambassador's face. "That may be true, Zing, but even with the worst of the ejections, we were still able to establish some communication with New Eden, if however brief. No, if we've lost communications with them for this long, there's something wrong; it's as if they're simply refusing to answer."

"I remain firmly convinced that you are mistaken and that everything is fine on New Eden, Hank Reynolds, and that we will find that all is well once we arrive."

Hank shook his head. "If you really believe that, Zing, then why did you come?"

"Why, in the event that I am mistaken and you are correct, of course. I took the precaution of requesting that two battle cruisers accompany us on this journey, just in case."

"'Two battle cruisers? 'Just in case'?" Hank laughed, and this time, looking at the emotionless features of the Valhari, he was sure he recognized the hint of a smile.

The captain of the ship turned back to Zing.

"Mr. President, we are approaching the world the humans call New Eden."

"Thank you, Captain Starracus. Please ensure that shields for all three ships are at maximum capacity."

"Yes, sir," the officer replied before touching the console, causing the front bulkhead of the ship to fade away, revealing the golden planet, New Eden, seemingly motionless in the blackness of space, and bringing up images of the captains of the two escort ships. Hank turned back to his friend.

"'Shields at maximum?' You said you thought everything was *fine* on New Eden.'" He shook his head and grinned. Zing looked at him with his unblinking eyes for several moments before turning back to study the world before him.

"We've arrived, Mr. President," the captain remarked, just as the ships dropped out of inter-dimensional quantum space. The image displayed within the room shocked them. Beams of blue energy radiated upwards at various points on the planet's surface, forming a sphere of faint yet perceptible energy all around the planet.

"Why, Hank Reynolds, have you been holding out on me? I had no idea that your world already had planetary shields. Of course, we generally don't recommend this particular type of shield anymore, since they've proven to become extremely hazardous for the planet's population after so many years. I seem to recall that the League actually banned such planetary shields because of the danger many centuries ago."

"Um, Zing, we *don't* have any kind of planetary shields yet, though we have been in discussions with several races about the newer and safer models. I'm sure you recall that we have a lot of asteroids in our system."

"Yes, of course," came the reply. Zing worked quietly for several seconds, looking at various control panels as if he were cross-checking information.

"It appears we have another problem on our hands at the moment."

"What kind of problem?" Hank asked nervously.

A massive burst of blue energy suddenly erupted from the planet's surface, flashing in front of their ship.

"*That kind* of a problem," Zing replied while motioning to several of his men and pressing several soft buttons. A bell suddenly sounded.

"Captain, we're being hailed from the surface," the communications officer said.

"Very good; please open a communications channel," the Valhari replied. The image of a lavender creature with white hair and golden-colored eyes materialized before them, and Hank instantly recognized him to be a Shataran, a very specific Shataran, in fact. The Shataran leader held a scepter in his hand, which included a variety of beautiful, exquisite looking jewels, set in a beautiful gold and platinum scepter. Hank could easily discern that the craftsmanship was magnificent.

"Greetings, I am—"

"Yeah, we know who you are, Motay," Hank replied forcefully, interrupting the Shataran. "What are you doing on New Eden, and where is my daughter?"

"Ah, you must be the doting father I've heard so much about, Dr. Reynolds. It's an honor to finally meet you."

"Apologies, but am I to understand that you are Jokar Motay?"

Hank supposed Zing was trying to calm the already tense confrontation.

"Yes, I am," Motay answered, carefully evaluating the Valharan. "And who, or what, are you? I don't recall ever encountering one of your species before."

"I am Zing, acting President of the League of Sentient Species, and I am a Valhari. My home world is Val, located approximately one hundred parsecs from Shatara, and in the opposite direction from Machrys, from Shatara's point of view."

"It's a pleasure to make your acquaintance, Zing."

"What exactly was the meaning behind the blast of particle beam energy in our direction? As the current president, should I regard this to be an act of aggression against the League of Sentient Species?"

"No, no, of course not, Mr. President. We merely thought you were a Machrys ship, that's all."

"A *Machrys* ship, really? Where's my daughter, and what are you even doing on New Eden? This is a human, Earth colony, not a Shataran colony!"

"Why, she invited us to stay, Dr. Reynolds, I assure you. We defended your helpless, hapless colony against the hateful Machrys, after all, did we not?"

"I couldn't help but notice your scepter," Hank told Jokar. "Does that mean you're a king or an emperor now?"

"A king? Well, while I do like the sound of it, I must answer no, I'm no king—at least not yet. I'm merely a captain with a crew that is, well—quite loyal to me. Ah, but as for this relic, we acquired this from some of our Machrys 'friends' a very long time ago; a gift from the Machrys emperor after we first took their home world. We pried it from the stiff, dead hands of their emperor just after we terminated his life. From what I understand of it, this scepter has some sort of very profound religious significance to them, or at least it did in my time; it seemed their entire race revered it. They lost their will to fight once we killed their leader and took this relic."

"Lower the shields and permit us to enter, Jokar Motay."

Motay said nothing for a moment, then pressed a button on the virtual control panel. He seemed to be talking with someone out of sight for some time, before finally pressing a button to reactivate his voice.

"I'm afraid I cannot do that at the moment, President Zing, it is most regrettable. We erected this global shield for the colony in order to protect them from the Machrys, of course. Now, however, the control system seems to be malfunctioning." It was an obvious lie, and Motay was bold in pronouncing it. Zing pressed several buttons on their ship's control panel.

"From what I see on our scanners, your shield technology is quite impressive, if also extremely hazardous to use. My scans show that while nothing can enter from without, anything within the shield can pass through it to the outside. Please board a ship and come to visit us. Perhaps we can work together on what is needed to repair your shield generator." Zing turned to Hank, who nodded approvingly. Zing was going to flush out Motay one way or the other.

"That is unnecessary, President Zing. We—"

"But we insist, Mr. Motay," Hank said to him, frustrated at the delay.

This time Motay sat looking into the holo-projector with an expression of annoyance mixed with disdain. After staring at them for several moments, he threw his hands up in the air.

"Oh, well, we knew it wouldn't last for long anyway. I hate charades, don't you?" Motay reached to the counter and returned to face the camera holding two devices, each with its own handle and a single button on top. Motay held each one out in front of him so that they were easily visible in front of the camera.

"What are those supposed to be, Motay?" Hank asked gruffly.

'These are just insurance policies to ensure that the League and the Alliance leave us alone, of course. You see, Dr. Reynolds, two of my men paid a little visit to your other little colony, on that pathetic, lifeless little rock you call Mars. My team came back and reported to me what a miserable, desolate world it is; why anyone would live there intentionally is beyond me." Motay stood up before turning back to the camera.

"Get to the point," Hank growled.

"Well, leave it to you humans to build cities on such a barren world where millions of people live in an artificial atmosphere under such a fragile dome. While there, my man planted some rather powerful explosives inside the dome of that planet's largest city. If the explosives are detonated, I'm rather confident in saying that everyone living there will die." Motay smiled to drive home his deadly threat, before holding one of the detonators up in his left hand. "This is the detonator, of course, that will trigger the many explosives my operative planted on Mars. So you must be asking yourselves if that is the case, then what's this other one for?" He held an identical detonator up in his right hand. What Motay did next chilled Hank to the bone; the Shataran looked into the camera with an intense, hardened stare, and smiled. "I'll tell you what...instead of telling you the answer, I'll simply show you instead."

"No don't—!" It was all Hank was able to utter before the Shataran pressed the button on top of the second detonator, throwing it down on the desk in front of him afterwards.

"By all that's holy, Motay, I will make sure you pay for what you've just done!"

"Oh really, Dr. Reynolds, please; must you be so dramatic? I recommend that instead of blustering pointlessly at me, you contact your outpost on Mars."

Zing moved quickly, for a Valhari, and within seconds they had someone on the comlink with Mars.

"Commander Rodriguez." There was a look of terror on the man's face. That look, combined with the commander's distracted demeanor, as evidenced by repeatedly looking around at his console and over his shoulder, told Hank what he most wanted to know; something of consequence had just occurred on Mars. In the background a flurry of voices and activity could also be heard.

"Commander, I am Ambassador Zing of the planet Val, and acting President of the League of Sentient Species; with me is Dr. Hank Reynolds, Earth's ambassador to the League and former President of the Earth Space Alliance. We have a very important question we'd like to ask you; has there been any unusual activity there at your colony recently, say within the last few minutes?"

"Funny that you should ask, Mr. President," came the response. "There was just a massive explosion here a few minutes ago. How did you know?"

"How many dead?" Hank blurted out in exasperation, ignoring the man's question.

"No casualties, sir, at least to the best of my knowledge. The explosion was centered in the middle of the park here. It was rather scary, but the dome and the shield around us appear to be holding, at least for now."

"Understood. You should conduct a thorough search, Commander; we have reason to believe there are more, possibly many more, scattered around the city."

"Great."

"I know," Hank answered, with great empathy. "Don't worry, Commander Rodriguez, we're doing everything we can to keep you and the other citizens safe."

"Is there something you can tell me, sir, that will explain what just happened?"

"Yes, but I can't go into it now. Inform everyone in your chain of command about our discussion, and tell them I'll debrief them as soon as possible."

"Yes, sir. Thank you, Dr. Reynolds. I'll update the governor so he can update President Clark. Be safe, gentlemen."

"And you as well, Commander," Zing replied, before terminating the call.

"There, you see?" Motay offered. "No one dead—yet."

"I was told you were a monster, Motay, a mass murderer, but I guess I didn't know the half of it," Reynolds said with a scowl, wearing a tortured look filled with burning anger, hatred, and loathing on his face; contempt for the man who threatened his daughter's life, and the lives of millions of human beings.

"Mass murderer? No, Dr. Reynolds, I'm afraid history has not been kind to me and my comrades. I'm just a man of determination, and resolution. Now listen to me, Reynolds," he said, with a fierce snarl of his own, his golden eyes burning like fire. "You know *nothing* about me, or my friends who are here with me. We suffered beyond measure when those filthy Machrys attacked our colonies, killing millions of innocent, peaceful Shatarans. I lost my mother, my father, my wife, and my two children during one of the attacks; every living soul I cared about in the universe died at the hands of those mindless brutes. Yes, I vowed to hunt them down to the ends of the universe. When my government grew soft and weak, they turned against their own people by attempting to put an end to our efforts to rid the galaxy of the murderous Machrys. So pardon me if I seem cold to your supposed sensibilities, because what has been five-thousand years to you, has been only five months to me. Do you really think you would have done any different had the same thing happened to you?"

Ouch.

Hank sat back in his chair. Motay had made a good point, one that struck painfully home with him. Had it been Earth that the Machrys attacked, and had it been Nicole, Hailey, and the rest of his family who'd been so savagely murdered, would he have done any different? He wanted to believe that he would, that God would sustain him, but he knew deep down there was no way he could ever know for sure how it might have twisted him inside unless he'd been through it himself.

"Look, I can't pretend to know what it's been like for you and your men. Honestly, I don't know how I would have reacted had I been in your place, and I can understand that you might be driven to desperate measures to exact justice. What happened, however, happened five-thousand years ago, so your government might even be willing to drop any charges against you and your people, *if* you stop what you're doing. In my

226

opinion, what happens to you and your men is a matter for the Shataran government, the Machrys, and the League. I have no interest in judging you or passing sentence. All I'm concerned about at the moment is the safety of my daughter, the other colonists on New Eden, and those people at the Mars colony. My people had nothing to do with what happened to Shatara, Jokar Motay, so please disable the explosives, drop the shield, and leave New Eden. Go wherever you like, just leave my family and my people out of this; *we've* done nothing to you or your people."

Motay stood up and paced for several seconds, considering what Hank had said, before leaning into the camera.

"I appreciate your candor and *your* position, Dr. Reynolds, and in all honesty I do wish circumstances were different. Your daughter and your people have shown us nothing but kindness, and with the exception of fighting off the Machrys attack here, I'm afraid I've been something less than appreciative of their hospitality. I must confess that I, and those with me, find ourselves in a rather difficult and tenuous situation, I'm afraid. You see, we need to reestablish ourselves on another world, somewhere safe from prying eyes, so we can pick up where we left off so long ago. For such an undertaking, we will require substantial resources, so we can purchase the ships and build the army we will require."

"The colonists possess no wealth; they are mostly just scientists, or people looking for a fresh start."

"Yes, yes, I understand that, Dr. Reynolds. What your colonists *do* have, however, is an abundant quantity of castilian plants growing here; do you have any idea how rare that plant is?"

Hank cast a brief glance over at Zing. "I have some appreciation of its intrinsic value to the various races."

"'Intrinsic value?' Indeed, Dr. Reynolds, and much more. I have a strong suspicion that this plant is the very reason the Machrys attacked your colony in the first place. Some of their planetary scouts must have come across the castilian plants at some point, and decided it was worth taking the risk of attacking a League member. Had they been successful in destroying everyone in the colony, who would be alive to contradict whatever version of the truth the Machrys elected to put forth?" Motay reached off camera for a moment and came back in frame holding a leaf in his hand. "Only a few months' worth of harvest here would enable us to accumulate the vast wealth we need to finance our army, the wealth we will need to crush our hated enemy!"

"Take the plants and leave, Jokar Motay. There's no need for you to endanger the lives of any human beings in this endeavor. Simply collect the plants you want and leave," Zing told him, with an air of authority that had been absent earlier.

227

"Thank you, President Zing, that has been our only objective all along. Simply allow us to collect all of the castilian that we need, and we'll be on our way. We are working as fervently as possible to complete that very thing."

"And just how long do you expect that will take?" asked Hank. "You are holding my daughter and some twenty-five thousand colonists hostage down there, and we'd like to have access to them immediately."

"Well now, that might pose just a little bit of a problem, gentlemen. As I'm sure you are aware, Mr. Ambassador, the processing of castil requires many hours to harvest the plant, which must be done in such a manner that the leaves are not damaged, then the processing takes quite some effort. We've already enlisted quite a bit of help in this effort, which should help speed the process along. Just be patient, and we will depart in peace, I promise."

"Just how long are you talking about?" Hank asked, "And from whom did you enlist this 'help' you mentioned a moment ago?"

Motay paused for several seconds. "A number of the colonists volunteered to help us gather it, out of appreciation for saving them from the Machrys. Needless to say, they were extremely grateful for our assistance."

"As are we all, Captain Motay," Zing interrupted,. "However, I must agree with Ambassador Reynolds that you should drop the shields before this situation gets out of hand."

Hank looked at Motay for some time, studying him before speaking again.

"You've turned the colonists into slave labor for your cause, haven't you, Motay? How did you go about persuading them to cooperate, tell me. Did you kill some and torture others, or did you do both. Motay?"

The Shataran leader said nothing, choosing instead to stare at his adversaries in silence before finally speaking. "At the rate we are progressing, we anticipate it will take approximately two standard months before we have harvested and processed a sufficient quantity of castil. At that point, we will leave this planet. Once we are at a safe distance away, we will tell you how you can locate and destroy the explosive devices planted on your Mars colony. I must warn you, however, that any attempt to circumvent our shield or attack us while we are leaving here two months from now will surely result in the deaths of millions on that planet, and the deaths of those people will be on your hands, gentlemen. Until that time comes, you will keep your distance from the planet or risk being fired upon; Captain Jokar Motay out."

The signal terminated and Zing and Hank were left alone.

"Our people are not safe, Zing," Hank said, turning towards his old friend. "We have to do something before someone is killed. You know my people, and I know my daughter; they will not sit idly by as slaves to a five-thousand year old madman."

"I agree. We must inform the other League members about this situation. Perhaps the Shataran ambassador will be able to shed some light on options for ending this confrontation peacefully."

"And I will consult with President Clark and the Alliance; there are over twenty-five thousand people down there, Zing, and millions at the Mars colony." Hank knew the fear and concern he felt must be evident on his face, or his emotions were so powerful that Zing could sense them without even probing his mind.

"Nicole will be all right, my friend, I promise," Zing told him, placing one hand on his shoulder. "She has your intellect, Hank, and your wisdom. You must have faith in *her*, like I have faith in *you*."

Hank turned to him as almost any father would when his daughter's life was in danger.

"Really? How can you know that?" Hank felt a surge of emotion welling up inside at the thought of his daughter dying at the hands of Jokar Motay.

Zing leaned in slightly toward Hank. "Because she shares your spirit, your determination, your strength, and your faith; because she is *your* daughter."

"Yeah, that's what worries me, Zing; that's what worries me."

CHAPTER 37

Nicole looked up and watched as Jack touched the virtual console at her desk and made a selection, which caused a holographic image of the hallway outside of the door to appear above the console. Two Shataran guards stood outside, the innate discipline obvious to anyone who saw them. Each was armed with a plasma pistol and what the Shatarans called a particle disrupter. She and Jack had soon learned that was what the Shatarans called the strange weapons they'd seen them wearing. Jack waved his hand and the image disappeared.

"Are you sure you know what you're doing, Nicole? What happens if we get caught, or worse?" Nicole busied herself on the sofa, fiddling with the tool she'd removed from the drawer.

"They've taken away our children and our freedom, and they've turned us into their *slaves*, Jack. How can you be concerned about what happens if we get caught?"

"I'm not concerned for myself, Nikki, you know me better than that; I just don't want anything to happen to you. Everyone in this colony needs you...*I* need you."

Nicole stopped what she was doing and smiled at Jack. She thought it strange, as she stood looking at the man she was falling in love with, that it sometimes took such dire circumstances to bring people like the two of them together. She walked over and, standing in front of him, placed both hands on his face.

"I know that, Jack, and I need *you,* too. But if we don't get a message out to the Alliance or to the League, they'll never know how much danger we're in. Jokar is extremely intelligent and charismatic; who knows what he's been telling any ships approaching New Eden?"

"Yeah, I know how charismatic he is, all right."

Nicole smiled. "Still jealous?"

Jack grimaced. 'Maybe a little."

"Good. But don't worry, baby, that ship sailed a long time ago. For the first time in my life I know exactly what I want, and who I want it with." She leaned up and kissed Jack, pulling him in close to her until their bodies pressed against one another. She was surprised at how comfortable she felt in his arms, and she knew at that moment that she never wanted to leave them. Sometime later, the pair separated and the two smiled.

"And what do you want, Nikki?" he asked when they finished. She felt her cheeks blush before she answered.

"Wait until all of this is over and I'll tell you," she said tauntingly.

Jack raised an eyebrow. "Ah, being mysterious are we?" he replied.

"I suppose," she answered with a smile. "I'm a woman; I'm entitled, aren't I?"

Jack's eyes widened for a moment and Nicole's heart jumped.

"Yes, I suppose you are," he said in a hushed tone, walking forward and wrapping his arms around her. When he looked into her eyes it felt as if he were looking directly into her soul. At that moment, any lingering doubt that remained about Jack instantly vanished. All she wanted was to bare her soul to the man in front of her.

"I'll tell you what I want, Jack Lincoln," she said, still looking into his beautiful blue eyes.

"What's that?" he asked, edging closer and closer until she felt his breath on her skin.

"I...um...," she faltered. In her mind's eye she suddenly saw the faces of the colony's children as they played within the settlement, laughing, crying; suddenly, a surge of resolve welled up inside. She turned, walked over to a desk, and sat down.

"I want to get these guys, bad," she said, after bringing up a video feed from the camera outside. Jack grinned and walked behind her; placing his hands on her shoulders he began massaging them. Nikki suddenly realized her breathing was quick and shallow.

"I believe that, Nikki, but somehow I don't think that's what you were going to say."

She turned in her chair and looked up at him.

"I want to talk about it Jack, I do—but not now, later. Right now, we both need to turn our attention to finding a way out of this...crisis." She watched him for a reaction, and was relieved when he tightened his lips into a tense smile.

He took her hands and gently pulled her out of the chair.

"Nikki, I'm in no hurry for you to tell me whatever you want to tell me. I've waited my entire life for someone like you to come along, so there's no way I'm going to do anything to lose you now."

Nikki smiled and wrapped her arms around him. They embraced and kissed again, and Nicole felt a warmth pass through her unlike anything she'd ever felt before. She'd never allowed anyone to get close enough to her to form a serious relationship, and now she was scared. She'd denied herself the warmth and passion such a relationship could offer, focusing instead on her business and her career until the right man came along. Her heart sank upon the prospect that she might now lose the first man she'd truly ever fallen in love with. She pushed away from him. She was beginning to worry that if they didn't act soon, she might lose her nerve, and the entire colony and a lot of scared and frightened parents were out there, living in fear for the lives of their children. It, whatever it was, would have to wait until they were free of the Shatarans. She was finding being so close to Jack very distracting, and she needed to keep a clear head.

"What's the matter, Nikki?"

"Nothing, Jack. Come on, we've got to go." She looked up at him (he stood nearly six inches taller than her), and allowed the slightest hint of a smile to appear.

"Yeah, okay," he replied knowingly, as if reading her thoughts. "Let's break into our own communications building," he said with a smile. He was trying to lighten the moment a little and Nicole appreciated it. "It would be a lot easier if we had weapons, though," he added.

"We will, soon enough. Once we get to the Communications Building, I'd like for you to take out one of the guards inside and relieve him of his weapons; that will give us a fighting chance if there are more guards closer to the main communications room. Do you think you can you do that?"

Jack rubbed his chin. "To be honest, I'm not sure, Nicole. They appear to be a lot stronger than us physically, and while their anatomy may appear similar to our own, they *are* aliens." He paused for another moment and rubbed his chin. "Wait a minute, give me a moment." Jack walked out of the office and into an adjacent room he'd been using as an office. When he returned, he was carrying a knife. It had a large grip with holes for the fingers, with a small club or hammer on the handle.

"It's a survival knife. A crude weapon, I know, but helpful in some survival situations. They gave these to us when we were assigned to scout out the planets the Valhari told us about."

Nicole began shaking her head. "No Jack, I don't want this to escalate to violence, not if we can help it. They haven't killed or even injured any of us yet, at least no one we know of."

Jack smirked. "Oh all right, I'll just hit him with the butt end of the weapon," he said, holding up the clubbed end. "It won't kill him, but it should knock him unconscious—at least I hope it will."

"Well, unfortunately I guess there's only one way to find out," she replied.

"Do you have everything *you* need?" he asked her.

She rummaged through the pack she had prepared, and briefly held up a data pad.

"I think so. Here are the various frequencies and addresses we need to contact the Alliance and the League. All we need is for just one of the messages to get through and we're on our way."

Jack's face grew serious. "Don't get your hopes up now, Nikki. This could get a lot messier before it's all over, you know that..."

"Yeah, I know," she replied sullenly.

"Okay then, let's get going. Remember, you'll need to work quickly. We don't know how long it will take to reach someone with the Alliance; it could be less than a minute, it could take hours."

"Always the optimist, Jack," she said with a smile.

"Hey, I'm just saying."

The two walked down the back stairwell and into the basement. Nicole walked over to a wide bookshelf that stood against a side wall and began pulling on it.

"Nikki, what the—?" Jack stopped talking as he saw one side of the bookcase easily pull away from the wall, as if on wheels or some sort of track. "Okay, that's a little cloak-and-dagger, isn't it?"

"Hey, I'm the *governor* here, remember?"

"Yeah, I guess you are, ma'am," he said with a grin.

She slapped him on the arm. "Come on, handsome, let's get moving."

"Yes, Governor."

The two made their way through the underground tunnel, encased in a white, solidified, foam-like material developed for just such an application. The tunnel stretched on for as far as the eyes could see.

"These tunnels interconnect underneath most of the main buildings in the city. They were built by two teams with six people per team. Each of them with an Alliance security clearance high enough they can be trusted not to reveal the tunnels' existence to the Shatarans."

"Are all entrances to the tunnels hidden like this one?"

"Yes. Hopefully the Shatarans have not discovered them yet so we can slip by their patrols unnoticed. Based on what I've seen, I'm guessing there might be as many as three to four Shatarans in most buildings. There might be more where we're going, given the strategic importance of the communications room. The tunnel entrance to that building opens up just outside the door; that's where we'll encounter the Shatarans we'll have to deal with. Remember, as soon as we enter the room we have to render any guards unconscious and lock the main door. That should buy us the time we need to get a message off before the others break through, okay?"

"Okay, Nikki. Don't worry, by this time tomorrow those Shataran creeps will be out of here, and you and I can pick up where we left off."

"I like the sound of that," she said with a smile.

A minute later they arrived at the entrance to the Communications Building. A series of stairs led directly to a steel door with a biometric scanner next to it on the wall. Nicole looked at Jack.

"Ready?" she whispered. He nodded, holding tightly to his knife. "Here we go—"

Nicole placed her hand on the scanner, and the door jarred slightly as the lock silently released. She slowly cracked open the outside door and, peering inside, found only darkness.

"Come on."

The two crept inside, with Jack carefully pulling the door closed behind him to avoid making any noise. They approached the next door as quietly as they could, for both heard the sound of Shataran voices coming from inside.

"How much longer until we can get off of this rock, Ajiathar? I'm beginning to think *we're* the prisoners here, not these humans."

"Patience, brother," they heard Ajiathar reply. "Jokar has them working day and night harvesting and preparing the castil. He told the League ambassador that we'd be leaving in eight weeks; the truth is that at the current rate of harvesting, we'll be leaving in four. Of course, we'll leave some men behind to ensure the humans behave, but since we'll have their children with us, what will they do?"

"I will tell you what they will do, brother," the first Shataran replied. "They will continue harvesting the castilian plant for us, which we will continue to sell and use to finance our army. Once we are strong again, we will destroy the cursed Machrys once and for all."

"Well," said Ajiathar, "my shift is over now, so I relinquish control over to you. Peaceful night to you, Krothann."

"Peaceful rest to you, my brother."

Nicole and Jack heard the door open and close. She was grateful that they would have only one Shataran to deal with, and that he likely would be caught completely by surprise. Nicole then signaled for Jack to prepare and he raised his knife and nodded. She placed one hand on the door handle and held the other to start a count. "One, two, three!"

Nicole pushed the hidden door open to reveal a startled Shataran sitting in a chair in the middle of the room. They rushed in with Jack leading the way. The Shataran rose to flee the unexpected attack and attempted to retrieve his weapon, which lay on a table at the opposite end of the room. Jack closed the distance in seconds and whacked the Shataran on the back of the head with the butt end of the knife. She could see how

235

relieved he was when the big Shataran fell unconscious onto the floor.

Nicole, who by this time stood next to the door they had entered through, rushed over to the console now that the Shataran was down in order to send the communication out for help. Now more than ever, they had to make the Alliance and the League aware of what the Shatarans were up to. It was up to her and Jack to let them know that the Shatarans were planning on taking the colonists' children with them when they left, that they were leaving much earlier than expected, and that they would not be relinquishing control of New Eden anytime soon.

Just as Nicole took her first step toward the control panel, she was stunned when the door next to her suddenly flung open, with a Shataran standing in the doorway.

"Krothann, I forgot to tell you—what's going on here, what have you done?" He reached casually for Nicole, expecting her to be docile. Nicole moved swiftly and without thought as her years of martial arts training took over. The Shataran was much taller than Nicole, but he was close enough that Nicole was able to bend her right knee and push off the floor with enough force that when she extended her arm toward his head, the heel of her palm struck his jaw, nearly knocking him out with the single blow. She followed up the attack with a kick to the rear of the ankle of the disoriented Shataran's foot. The blow forced his legs to swing out from under him and caused him to land flat on his back, slamming his head onto the floor at the same time, rendering the Shataran unconscious. While Nicole confirmed that the two aliens now lying unconscious on the floor were both still breathing, Jack rushed over to close and lock the door as Nicole stood and rushed over to the control panel. She had just brought up the virtual display when the holo-projector abruptly activated, causing an image of Jokar Motay to appear. Nicole gasped when she saw it, and she felt a sick, sinking feeling in the pit of her stomach after Motay began clapping his hands.

"Well done, Nicole Reynolds...and you too, of course, Captain Lincoln," he said, looking and nodding toward Jack. There was a blast at the door and it fell flat onto the floor, with three armed Shatarans walking over it as they rushed into the room.

"As you might have surmised by now, Nicole, we actually discovered your underground tunnels soon after taking control of your fair city. I've been carefully watching you since the other day, and I only allowed you to roam freely because I was curious about what you might do next. Oh, and in case you were wondering, security on the shuttles was even tighter than it was here, so you were never close to succeeding in your plan. I'm sure you will understand, Nicole, that I must now place you both under arrest. You will both be closely guarded and, of course, you will not be allowed

236

any visitors."

"Under arrest? You can't place *us* under arrest, Jokar," Nicole shouted. "This is *our* world!"

Motay shook his head. "Actually, my dear, from the moment your people woke us, it became *our* world…you just didn't realize it until now. From now on you will do what we tell you, when we tell you, and how we tell you, or you, your people, and your children will all die."

CHAPTER 38

They sat together on the sofa in Nicole's apartment, where Motay had placed them both under house arrest. She lived in the tallest building in the city, with the only way in or out being through the front door. The Shatarans had placed a lock on the outside of that door, in effect turning the apartment into a jail cell. She was allowed to go out for supplies for herself and Jack once a week, but always with two Shataran guards, one male and one female. They'd lived in this manner for two weeks, and they were becoming increasingly nervous about the dire predicament they were now in. If the Shataran guard was right, they had only two weeks, perhaps less, before the bulk of the Shatarans left in their ship, taking the colony's children with them. The children, held in stasis aboard the Shataran ship, provided the leverage necessary to keep the colonists in line as slaves.

"Oh, Jack, what are we going to do? They must be close to finishing their castil processing, which means they'll be leaving New Eden with the children soon. Once that happens, we may never be free of them! The Alliance and the League, no one will dare engage them in battle out of fear of killing the children!"

Jack stroked the back of her head and neck. He'd been her only comfort during the entire ordeal, her only link to sanity during some of the most difficult moments of her life. In Jack's arms she felt better and safer, and surprisingly, given the circumstances, she even felt some measure of peace.

"I don't know, Nikki, but I don't think the Lord has brought us this far just to see us fail now."

Nicole looked at him and then towards the door.

"We could always try to overpower the guards," she offered, without acknowledging what he'd said.

"Yes, we could try. They've increased security though, Nikki, with two guards outside your apartment door and others throughout the building, not to mention the way they've secured our only way out."

"Not so easy this time, huh?" she asked sheepishly.

"No, I don't think so."

Nicole lay down in his lap and began to cry. "How will I ever be able to look those parents in the eye again, knowing that Jokar's taken their children halfway across the galaxy, that they may never see them again? It's my fault, Jack, all of it. If only I'd been less trusting of them, if only—"

"Stop it, Nikki," Jack told her, softly yet sternly. "You know as well as I do there was no way for anyone to know what the Shataran's were up to."

Nikki sat up and looked Jack in the eyes. "I've got to do something, Jack, *anything*. I'd rather die in the attempt to stop the Shatarans than to go on living with the guilt of letting them get away with this. I couldn't bear the thought of those children, in stasis—or worse, on some distant planet, so far from their families, and the looks on the faces of their parents and other family members."

"Okay then, let's do it," Jack said resolutely. "I'm sick of sitting around doing nothing anyway. First we'll break out of here, then we'll go after one of the shuttles. Once on a ship we'll be able to contact the Alliance, maybe even try to rescue the children."

"No Jack, this is my burden to bear, my guilt, not yours. I won't be responsible for your death as well."

"It's not your burden because it's not your fault. Besides, you're not doing this alone, Nikki, *that* you can count on. There's no way you're doing anything without me. I—"

Their conversation was interrupted by a brilliant flash of light in the apartment, which seemed to materialize from nowhere. They instinctively shielded their eyes from the bright light, which soon disappeared as spontaneously as it had appeared. When Nicole opened her eyes again, she felt a chill run through her as if the blood in her veins had suddenly turned to ice water, for she and Jack were no longer alone. In the middle of the room stood a creature, more alien than anything she'd ever seen, stranger even than the Machrys in appearance. Dressed in purple clothing that resembled silk, it's skin was dark green and scaly, it's mouth a sharp, pointed beak like a bird's, and it stood upon its hind legs. It also had a long tail, pointed ears, and large, penetrating black eyes. Nicole studied it for several seconds, and she had the strangest sensation that it was studying her as well. As she sat motionless on the sofa as if frozen, unable to move out of fear, it suddenly dawned on her that she knew what this creature was. Nicole glanced over at Jack and noticed the creature had done the same.

"Jack, this must be a Hantari; it matches Dao-ming's description of the creature she saw in the woods." Nicole walked over and picked up her translator and the earpiece, and handed Jack his. Once they had them on, she addressed the uninvited guest.

"My name is—"

"You are Dr. Nicole Reynolds, from the planet Earth," the creature replied. "You will not require your translation devices; you should find my English suitable for our purposes." Nicole stood shell-shocked. Not only was it intelligent, but it had already learned their language? Few species took the time or put in the effort required to learn another species' language. Some, like the Valhari, preferred telepathy, but even they had devices they used when telepathy wasn't the best option.

"How did you—?"

"Learn your language so quickly? I pulled it from the mind of one of your citizens when I scanned it, Dr. Reynolds. Please pardon the intrusion, but you must recognize that time is not your ally, and the danger you and the other colonists face is significant."

"Yes, I—er—we do." She glanced over at Jack, who seemed intensely uncomfortable. "Oh, this is—"

"Captain Jack Lincoln, Alliance pilot, yes. We met briefly a short time back. It's a pleasure to see you again, Captain," the Hantari said to him. Lincoln nodded weakly, never taking his eyes off the Hantari.

"Who are you?" asked Nicole, overcome with curiosity about the Hantari.

"I am Isoka Trillkanto, Third Prime of the Elder Council, of the Hantari Collective. I am one of the few of my brethren remaining on this world, or even in this galaxy for that matter." The Hantari turned back to Jack to address him. "As Jack Lincoln is aware, I am here as a friend, to help you." Nicole watched as Jack glanced down to a hand that still clenched the handle of the rather long, sharpened butcher knife.

"Oh, sorry," Jack replied, before setting it on a counter.

"We have been monitoring the situation here for quite some time," the Hantari continued, "and we grew concerned about how events have been unfolding. We are aware that the Shatarans have taken your children as hostages in their ship. We also know that they've planted explosives in one of the cities on the fourth planet of your home star system, on the planet you call Mars."

"Yes, that's correct," Nicole acknowledged.

"As I said, I'm here to help you. We know where their leader, Jokar Motay, keeps the remote trigger for the explosive devices they've placed on Mars. We will also help you gain access to a ship."

"Please don't mind my asking, but why are you helping us?"

The Hantari looked down at the floor for a moment. "The Shatarans are an advanced species, Dr. Reynolds, surpassing your own, at least for

241

the time being. Regrettably, we are somewhat responsible for your current predicament, and we seek to make amends."

Nicole furrowed her brows, utterly confused by the Hantari's stunning proclamations.

"I don't understand."

"We have been watching you ever since your arrival on this world, Dr. Reynolds. We know that you came here to colonize a new world for your people, and we know that one of your colonists accidentally reactivated the stasis chambers aboard the Shataran war vessel."

"Yes, but how does that make your people responsible for our current predicament?"

"Long ago, when the universe was still young, we Hantari were among the most advanced races in this galaxy. My people were one of the first of the space-faring races in the galaxy. I suppose we were much like you, Dr. Reynolds, curious and restless, wanting to explore the universe, which we did, and more. It was on one of our expeditions that we discovered a young race of beings called the Shatarans, a species that showed great promise. They were a bright, friendly species, peaceful and outgoing.

"In the Shatarans, we found a very promising race of beings, already on the verge of space travel themselves by the time we came across them. My people decided to take the Shatarans under their wing, seeing in them a great hope for the galaxy, and the universe. We took it upon ourselves to help this young race develop into one of the most advanced races in the galaxy, and we explored much of the galaxy together, mapping unexplored quadrants of space, identifying planets with races that would soon be capable of space travel, and spreading out across the many inhabitable worlds.

"Everything changed, however, when the Shataran home world was unexpectedly and brutally attacked by a newly emergent species called the Machrys, and millions of Shatarans died. We tried to reason with the Shatarans afterwards, but they would not listen. There were many like Jokar Motay during that time whose hearts were heavy, bitter, and filled with grief over the loss of their loved ones. Their grief soon turned into anger and hatred for the attackers, causing the Shatarans to yearn only for revenge."

"So your people helped the Shatarans, and now you feel some sort of responsibility for what they're doing now?"

"Not all Shatarans, only this particular group of Shatarans. Had we *not* interfered, and allowed Shatara to develop on its own, perhaps all of this could have been avoided. It was their advanced technology that drew the Machrys to Shatara in the first place. The Shataran civilization has grown and matured over the millennia since the Great Purge, developing into something that's far exceeded our expectation. Jokar Motay and his followers have, unfortunately, come out of the darkest period of their history.

"After our disastrous interference with the Shatarans, my people passed strict laws forbidding interfere with other races. In your case, however, we've decided to make an exception since, as I have stated, we are largely to blame for your current predicament. Our involvement in this must remain, however, minimal."

"Our people, the ones who disappeared—"

"As I'm sure you know by now, *we* took them. We wanted to learn more about your species, and we kept them to protect them from Motay and his followers. Please do not concern yourselves about your people, as I assure you that they have been provided comfortable quarters in our only remaining city on this world. When we came across Captain Lincoln, however, we decided to send *him* back to warn you."

"We tried to get a message out, Isoka, but they were way ahead of us," Jack informed the Hantari. "We were captured and imprisoned here."

"They will be done processing the castil soon," said Nicole, "and they will leave in their ship, taking our children with them. They will use them as leverage to ensure my people continue as their slaves, unless we do something to stop them!"

"We are aware of that, Dr. Reynolds; indeed, you must act quickly if you are to stop them. Now then, the remote detonator that Motay plans to use to detonate the explosive devices on Mars is kept in a locked cabinet in your old office, Dr. Reynolds. You must listen carefully, as I'm only allowed to assist you this one time, but from now on, no matter what happens, you *will* be on your own."

"We are most grateful for your intervention and your aid, Isoka Trillkanto. What do you recommend we do next?"

"That decision is, of course, yours, Governor Reynolds. I suggest, however, that you need to accomplish two immediate objectives. First, you need to find the remote detonator and save the lives of millions of human beings on the Mars Colony."

"And second?" asked Jack Lincoln.

"You must find and gain access to one of your ships, one that has an Entelli onboard. Once on the ship link with the Entelli; you can use it to interface with the Shatarans' centralized control system for the planetary shield, and shut it down. I must warn you, however, that should you destroy the detonator before you shut down the shield, many colonists will likely lose their lives as Motay, having lost his leverage over the Alliance and with League ships encircling the planet, will become desperate.

Conversely, if you shut down the shield before destroying the detonator, you will likely be condemning millions of human beings on Mars to death. To be successful, you must accomplish both objectives at the same time. It will be difficult, but it can be done."

"I'll take the detonator, Nicole, if that's all right with you."

"Okay, Jack, I'll shut down the shields." She turned back to the Hantari. "How will I be able to tell which ships have an Entelli onboard?"

"You will not be able to tell from outside the ship, Nicole Reynolds. I can transport you to the hangar bay at the same time I send Captain Lincoln to your office, but as I have stated, after that point there is nothing else I can do."

Nicole walked to the Hantari and reached for one of its hands. She took it in her own and held it with both of hers. "Thank you, Isoka Trillkanto, we are in your debt."

"Farewell, Nicole Reynolds. May the Great Creator prosper your way."

The Hantari waved his hand and another brilliant flash of light followed. When Nicole opened her eyes again, the Hantari was gone, but so was Jack, and the very room itself.

CHAPTER 39

Jack stood motionless, crouching slightly. To a casual observer he might have appeared to be a lifelike figure made of wax were it not for the eyes, which darted back and forth across the room. The teleportation had left him slightly disoriented and for a moment, he had no idea where he was. It took a few seconds to identify the small, not-so-secret passageway just outside of Nicole's office, which connected the governor's office to the other government buildings in the immediate vicinity. Slowly, it came back to him—the mission, the Shatarans; he had to find the remote detonator and destroy it. With the unexpected appearance of the Hantari, Jack had not given it much thought, but now it struck him like a slap in the face; how was he going to find the detonator? He had no idea where it was, what it looked like, or even how to destroy it without accidentally activating it.

He'd heard voices immediately upon materializing in the small hallway, and for a moment it seemed they were coming from either beside or behind him. He soon realized, however, that they were originating from just beyond the doorway; he could hear two, possibly three, distinct voices, though he could not tell for certain how many. The casual tone and the nature of the conversation suggested he'd escaped detection, so he relaxed a little and slowly turned his head, checking behind him just to be certain. Seeing nothing but an empty hallway, he edged closer to the door, hoping to learn all he could.

"But Jokar, what if they try to take the colony back after we leave? We need the revenue from the castil to finance the next Great Purge. Should the League take this planet, surely we will never have another opportunity to reclaim it, and the castilian plants are in greater abundance here than on any other world we've ever been to! There's enough here to fund our wiping out the Machrys a hundred times over!"

"Don't worry, brother, the League will not attack the Shatarans who stay behind to operate this colony in our absence, not with millions of lives at stake. Even if they do, I will leave instructions that our men are to detonate one bomb after another on Mars until the League ends its attack. The major races have grown weak over the millennia, Mentarek; they lack the determination and commitment necessary to stop us."

"You truly are a great leader, Jokar; all others pale in comparison."

"We will destroy the Machrys filth once and for all, my brother. We will recruit more Shatarans to our cause, and then we will build and fortify our army until it is unlike anything the universe has ever seen."

Jack heard someone stand up and start walking around.

"You saw what they did here...they attacked this world and they were going to slaughter these humans just as they did *our* people so long ago. They've not changed one bit over the millennia; they are the same cowards they were five-thousand years ago. Now that we're back, however, we'll make certain that no one is ever troubled by them again."

Jack then heard a drawer open, possibly a drawer in the filing cabinet behind Nicole's desk.

"Will you detonate one of them now, Captain?"

"I don't know, Mentarek; do you think I should? Perhaps it will give them greater pause should they think of trying to retake the planet." There was silence for several seconds, leading Jack to assume Mentarek was deliberating.

"I think not, sir; we don't want the League to think we're monsters, after all, do we?" There was a brief outburst of laughter, followed by the door slamming shut.

"Quite right, brother. All right then, what say we try to find some food that doesn't turn our stomachs, shall we?"

Moments later Jack heard the door close. He'd not heard more than two voices the entire time he'd been waiting outside the door. His heart sank for a moment as he considered whether the whole thing had been a ruse, and that Jokar had known he was in the hallway the entire time. The effort would have been in vain, and many colonists would either end up heartbroken over the loss of their children or dead.

After waiting several minutes and still hearing no activity inside, Jack finally readied himself and opened the door. It wasn't his own safety or even his own life he feared for, it was the countless millions of lives, both human and Machrys, that were at stake. Jack detested the Machrys for what they had tried to do at New Eden, and for what they *had* done to Shatara, but even they deserved a chance at life as a species, for without life, there could be no redemption.

Jack took a deep breath upon finding the room empty. He knew there would be at least two guards outside the door to the room, and from what he'd seen, their hearing was slightly superior to human beings. He wondered why Jokar had not stationed a guard outside the door to the tunnel, finally deciding that either there was a guard further down the tunnel, or that the Hantari had transported the guard out at the same time they had transported Jack in. Either way the coast was clear, and that was all that mattered.

He moved stealthily across the room, towards the filing cabinets he thought he'd heard opening while still in the hallway, where he felt certain Jokar kept the detonator. He opened the top drawer then the next, searching through stacks of ancient books, several data pads, and even a change of clothes. He went though the other three drawers in the file cabinet and still, no detonator. *Oh no, did he take it with him?*

Voices. They were still some distance away but they were getting louder and louder, which meant in all likelihood they were heading his way. He had maybe fifteen seconds before they would open the door, and it would all be over. He glanced around now in a fit of desperation, trying to locate a drawer that might hold the lives of so many within. The voices drew closer and Jack narrowed his focus. *Where is it?*

He'd decided to abandon the effort and head back to the tunnel when suddenly he saw it, a door underneath that was the same color as the underside of the desk. It was well camouflaged, and only someone searching for it as he had been would ever have noticed it. He quickly opened the drawer and once it was fully extended, he saw it. It was alien, and it looked every bit what a Shataran detonator would look like. Just as he reached for it the door opened and two Shataran guards walked in. Jack was relieved to see that at least Jokar wasn't among them. The two Shatarans stood there for a moment, frozen in shock, looking at the human that had somehow breached their defenses before staring in horror at the detonator he held in his hand. Jack knew at that moment that it wasn't just a detonator he held in his hand, but their lives as well. Each suspected that if something happened to the device, their leader would have them killed.

"Take it easy, human," one of them said. "You should be very careful with that detonator; if you drop it, millions of humans on your Mars Colony will die."

Jack was confident it was a lie, but it was a shrewd one. Perhaps Jokar wasn't the only snake in the pit. Jack examined the detonator for a moment before holding it up in the air, no longer worried about the detonator or himself. There was a trigger, with a guard protecting the trigger itself, all the way around. The detonator was also switched off, for none of the indicator lights he could see on the top were active.

"That's a good try," Jack said with wry grin, "but Mama didn't raise a fool for a son. This detonator has a guard around the trigger to prevent an accidental activation; besides, it's not even turned on. There's not even a remote chance of this thing going off even if I drop it." *There.* Just as he'd hoped one of the guards grimaced, a certain sign that he was right. Upon seeing that, he dropped the detonator on the floor, smashing it into pieces, before following up by crushing it with the bottom of his boot. At that moment he hoped more than anything that the Hantari were correct in saying that each detonator had its own unique signature, and that only that specific detonator could trigger an explosion on Mars from such a great distance. It was the greatest strength, and weakness, with that type of detonator.

Jack looked away from the shattered device and was just raising his head to smile at the Shatarans when he felt a blinding pain, and everything went black.

CHAPTER 40

The hangar bay was swarming with Shatarans; some were sentries making their rounds, while others were busy loading some of the Alliance ships with supplies. It was clear to Nicole that the Shatarans were much closer to leaving New Eden than previously thought. Only two of the Alliance ships had been left untouched, which was probably intended for the small contingent of Shatarans who would be left behind to manage the human slaves that would continue harvesting the castil for the Shatarans. The thing that really saddened Nicole the most was the fact that the Shatarans would only need to leave a few behind in order to maintain control; such was the disposition of the colonists. Their spirits were downcast and they had the look of having been beaten. She really couldn't blame them, however; their children were being held hostage by a very dangerous and cunning alien. Besides, everyone knew by now about the millions of people on Mars, many of them family members or friends of the colonists, whose lives might be snuffed out anytime by the simple pressing of a trigger.

Nicole looked around her and after several moments, decided she was about as safe where she was as she could be given the presence of so many Shatarans. She was hiding in a corner of the hangar, behind several large stacks of parts and supplies for doing repair work or maintenance on the Alliance ships. It was very unlikely that anyone would spot her where she was, so all she had to do now was wait.

She'd been there for fifteen minutes, watching them load one ship after the other, when she suddenly heard a sound, like a musical tone or a doorbell, echoing loudly throughout the hangar several times. Everyone inside the hangar then stopped whatever they were doing and slowly began filtering out the door. Glancing at the clock on the hangar wall, she took notice of the lateness of the hour, and concluded they were probably done working for the day. She could only hope they would not be back until morning, since even Shatarans, it seemed, were in need of rest.

After waiting for several minutes, Nicole carefully looked around again and found that all of the workers were gone, leaving only the guards who kept their appointed rounds. She watched them carefully and found that, much like their human counterparts, they tended to walk the same routes. She settled in, continuing to watch and study them for another thirty minutes, until she felt comfortable she had identified a definite pattern. There were only three Shatarans guarding the hangar, two of which remained inside, patrolling along the outer edge of the hangar, alternating between clockwise and counter-clockwise following every ten laps around the building. The third spent most of his time outside, presumably patrolling the exterior of the hangar.

Nicole took a deep breath and decided she was ready to move. She was nearest the two ships the Shatarans were leaving behind, so she would make a break for the ship closest to her position. In order to time it just right, she would wait until the third guard left to make his rounds outside, then wait until the two inside guards had completed their ten rounds. Just as they were preparing to shift directions, she would hurry to the closest ship and scurry inside. Unwilling to risk making any unnecessary noise she removed her shoes, placed them in her left hand, and watched as the third guard left the building. She began counting the rounds and ten minutes later, just as they were about to change directions, she made her move.

The hangar was rather large and there were a number of crates, containers, and loaders scattered throughout the hangar floor, helping to block their visibility, and giving her a chance, at least, of making it to the ship unseen. She paused behind one of the stacks and looked around. She'd lost sight of the guard closest to her and debated whether to run to the ship or to wait. Discretion got the better of her, however, causing her to wait. Her decision turned out to be a fortunate one because just seconds later, she heard the noise of shoes scuffling along the hangar floor off to her right. The Shataran guard, who could not have been more than five meters away, would have easily seen her abandoning her position behind a huge stack of crates as she ran to the ship.

She waited until the guard once more passed out of view before making her way to the ship. She held up her right hand and pressed the point on the top of ship just above the "E" that began the words "Earth Space Alliance." Her face twisted when, continuing to press the panel, it failed to open the hatch so she could enter the ship. She grew increasingly frustrated, painfully aware that at any moment the other guard would be upon her, and their hopes of lowering the planetary shield and saving the colonists would have failed. After spending over thirty seconds trying to gain access, she hurried over to her hiding spot just as the second guard made his approach.

While waiting for the guard to pass, she struggled to understand why she'd been unable to access the ship. Had the Shatarans altered the ship so that a human could no longer gain access to the ship's interior? The guard passed out of sight, but Nicole remained motionless, determined not to take a foolish chance again only to fail and get caught. She stood there, racking her brain, trying to remember if—then it came to her. In an effort to make it easier for everyone to gain access to the ships from the outside, they had lowered the panel to just underneath the midpoint of the ship. Nicole gently smacked herself on the head and readied herself for another try.

Soon after her epiphany, the guard passed her again and she prepared to run to the ship. She had just pushed off when she heard the outer doors of the hangar open, forcing her back to her hiding spot. She felt her stomach tighten when she saw four heavily armed Shatarans enter the building, led, she soon realized, by Jokar. The two guards walked up to their leader, arriving at almost the exact same moment.

"Greetings, Captain Motay," the first guard said.

"Greetings, brother; so, let's take a look at how work is progressing, shall we?" Nicole felt a chill run down her spine when she saw they were heading her way. Her hiding spot was only effective when hiding from someone approaching from the other direction. She would soon be discovered, and she'd be putting the lives of all twenty-five thousand colonists and perhaps millions of Mars colonists in grave jeopardy as well. Nicole was panicking; any moment they would be on top of her and there was nowhere to hide. Then it hit her; the two guards were now with Jokar. If they stayed with him, she would be able to make her way to a loader that sat behind the stack she'd been hiding behind. She made it to the loader and crouched down as low as possible, just as Jokar rounded the corner.

"Look at them," Jokar announced, gesturing to the ships sitting with their hatches still open, some of them with stacks of supplies and crates packed with containers full of processed castil visible from without. "Soon, very soon, we will be among the stars once more, brothers, for the first time in five-thousand years, and this time, with all of this castil, we'll be more powerful than ever. From what I have learned of our people since the Great Purge, we will find many new recruits on Shatara, many of them disillusioned with what has become of our once-great civilization."

"When will we leave, Captain?" one of the guards asked.

Motay looked at the guard for several seconds before answering. "Some will leave in two days, others will leave a few months from now. Don't worry, my brother, we will offer those who wish to leave an opportunity to do so, and those who'd rather stay we will offer great power and wealth, in order to ensure that the lifeblood of our new empire continues to flow!"

The guard nodded before smiling with enthusiasm.

Jokar turned to leave. "All right gentlemen, keep a close eye on our treasure, for we depart just after the sun rises in two days!"

A short time later the four Shatarans left and the doors closed behind them. Nicole made her way back to her hiding place and waited for the guards to return to their previous routine. It was over twenty minutes later before the third guard left again and she had her chance. This time she made it to the ship, placed her hand under on the panel on the underside of the ship, and the hatch instantly opened. She quickly walked inside and pressed the panel to close the hatch. She then quickly made her way to the bridge of the ship, where she pressed a button on the control panel, causing the virtual display to appear. After pressing a couple of soft buttons, the ship's outer skin became transparent in one direction; she could now see out, but they could not see in…at least that's how it was supposed to work.

She then waited until they made their next round, breaking out in a cold sweat as one of the guards made his next approach. Her heart raced and her breathing grew shallow. A cold chill passed through her when she noticed the guard seemed to be looking directly at her. Did something about the Shataran physiology enable him to see through the one-way configuration? Panic set in when it occurred to her that she might have pressed the wrong button, causing the skin of the ship to become fully transparent. The guard drew closer and Nicole, now convinced that the Shataran could see into the ship, and that he would notify Jokar at any minute, began formulating a plan of escape. She might not survive long, but she owed it to the other colonists and those on Mars to try. She stood staring in terror, then awe as the guard approached and then passed by the ship, continuing on his rounds with no evidence of any concern. Breathing a sigh of joyous relief, she waited until the guard had walked another hundred paces without alerting anyone before deciding she was safe, and that she'd made it inside undetected, and allowed herself to relax.

Nicole sat down in the captain's seat and took yet one more deep breath, forcing herself to settle down, wanting to have a clear head and a focused mind for what she would attempt to do next. After a couple of minutes had passed, she stood up and began walking around the bridge, looking for something. Her efforts were soon rewarded when she came to a small, helmet-looking device, resting in a small storage area near the navigation officer's station.

Memories came flooding back, times sitting at home in the living room, listening to her father tell stories about interfacing with an Entelli named Ignis, the same Entelli her grandfather and great-grandfather had interfaced with. Both of them had described their experiences using similar adjectives, words like fantastic, surreal, and unique, and they'd found Ignis to be very likeable. She'd never had the opportunity to interface with an Entelli, however, due in large part to her decision as a child not to follow in their footsteps working with the Earth Space Alliance, and interacting regularly with alien beings. She found it ironic that she now, in some ways, found herself going beyond what even they had experienced in her dealings with three alien races none of them had ever met, namely the Shatarans, the Machrys, and the Hantari. Furthermore, she now lived on an alien world, trying to defeat an alien enemy bent on genocide, risking her life in an effort to save the lives of millions of beings from two very different worlds. In that moment, she came to realize that, ironically, she had finally learned that she was indeed her father's daughter.

She sat back, took a deep breath, and placed the helmet on her head. In what seemed like an instant she found herself surrounded by bright, white light. She winced but soon realized that it was merely a reflex, since in reality there was no white light. Looking around she made out a floor that was only a little darker than the brilliant white that surrounded her. When she looked up, she was surprised to see a door in front of her, and another behind her. On the door in front of her was a sign with large, navy blue letters that read Enter. Behind her was a very similar door, with a sign that said Exit. *It's just as Grandpa described it.*

"Okay, Nicole, you've come this far, might as well keep going and see this through," she whispered to herself, before opening the door with the Enter sign above it, and walking into the fantastic world that lay beyond.

JEFF W. HORTON

CHAPTER 41

There was nearly as much dark inside the room as there had been light in the one before. The contrast was so overwhelming that it took a moment for her to make the adjustment. She was looking around, trying to make out anything, when she suddenly noticed what appeared to be some sort of room a short walk away. Had it been there earlier and she was just now seeing it, or had it just appeared? She shook her head and tried to focus. The room was open with no walls, but there was a large, comfortable-looking sofa, a recliner, and a chair placed around the room, with a large, oval rug on the floor in the middle. Several book cases stood next to where a wall should have been, and a warm lamp next to the sofa provided plenty of light. The entire scene left Nicole bewildered, and confused.

Clarity soon came walking towards her in the form of an old man. She stared at the face as he came closer, because it was a face she'd seen before, somewhere. The eyes of the man in front of her fixed on her and the expression was blank, before smiling warmly at her a moment later—then she remembered. The man in front of her closely resembled someone she'd never met, but had seen before. Her Grandmother Kate had shown pictures of *her* father, Henry, Nicole's great-grandfather, to Nicole when she was still little girl, and her grandmother had spoken of him often. Always Kate had used only the kindest, most heart-warming terms, words that were, on occasion, accompanied with tears of happiness.

"Nicole Reynolds," the Henry-figure in front of her announced, "it is a very great pleasure to make your acquaintance." The man extended his hand and she instinctively placed hers in his. His hand was as warm as his smile, and when they'd finished shaking hands he gestured for her to sit. She sat on the sofa and he sat down next to her.

"You look just like my great-grandfather, Henry Summers. How did you know—you pulled it from my mind, didn't you?"

"I could have Nicole, but no. Actually I met your great-grandfather just before he died. He was truly a wonderful, remarkable man."

"Yes, so I've been told," Nicole replied, finding that she was now smiling back at the man who seemed so—real. Suddenly, she realized what he'd just said. "You met him? You're kidding!"

"No, I am not," he said with the same, grandfatherly smile. Nicole gasped.

"That's incredible! There's only one way you could have met him...you must be Ignis!" Henry-Ignis just smiled and nodded. "Oh, I'm so glad it's really you, how fantastic! I was so worried. Of all the Entelli I could have stumbled into, what are the odds it would have been you?"

"I'd say about one in ten," he said with a smile.

"What do you mean?"

"There are only ten Alliance ships with Entelli onboard currently on this planet."

"That's not what I meant, Ignis," she said wryly.

"I know. Perhaps it's even more remarkable than you already believe, Nicole Reynolds. There's always been a sense of something special about your family's destiny, as if someone were leading you to this very moment. As I once told your grandfather, Nick Reynolds, many of us believe there is a Creator, the ultimate being, unlike any other in the universe. On your world you refer to him as God, the Lord, the Judeo-Christian God in your holy book, the Bible. We have similar names for our deity; many of us even believe it to be one and the same being. As I believe people of faith have proclaimed on your world for many centuries, Nicole Reynolds, the Lord works in mysterious ways. I have no doubt that our meeting was no accident, just as my meetings with your grandfather and your great-grandfather were no accidents either. But I sense you are here for something far more urgent and serious than idle conversation, Nicole Reynolds. Tell me please, what troubles you?"

"Can't you read my mind?" she asked, somewhat confused. He smiled again and laughed politely.

"We can, and we do, to some extent anyway. That's how I was able to identify who you were, and so appear as your great-grandfather, Henry. But reaching into another sentient being's mind, particularly if we have not been invited, makes us very uncomfortable, so we try to never probe too deep unless we've been invited; except for emergencies, of course."

"New Eden Colony has been invaded by a group of Shatarans, stranded here for thousands of years. They've been in stasis since just after the Shataran-Machrys war."

"Invaded by Shatarans? Are you certain of this, Nicole Reynolds?"

"Without a doubt. They've enslaved our people, and are holding our children in stasis to ensure the cooperation of the adults. They've also placed explosives on a planet next to our home world, a world we call

Mars, where millions of human beings live. The Shatarans have threatened to use a remote detonator to activate the explosives on Mars if the League tries to attack them. They intend to finish what they started during something called the Great Purge." She watched as Ignis's face darkened slightly.

"I see. I've been in a stasis of my own, of sorts, since the last flight, so I've been inactive for some time. I'm terribly sorry, and shocked, to learn that this has happened; the Shatarans are an advanced race; they've never done anything like this, at least not since the Great Purge."

"Well, they have now."

"Yes, of course. So, how can I help?"

"I'd like for you to try to access the Shatarans' planetary shield control system, to shut down the planetary shield the Shatarans set up, and get a message out to the Alliance and/or the League."

"And what made you think of seeking out one of my people, the Entelli?"

"Jokar, the leader of the rogue Shatarans, captured me, along with Captain Jack Lincoln, an Alliance pilot, and had confined both of us to my apartment. Jack and I were preparing to try a desperate, doomed escape attempt to stop what the Shatarans were doing, when we were paid an unexpected visit by a Hantari. He told us where the detonator could be found, and suggested an Entelli might be able to access the Shataran system and shut down their shield."

"Oh, how shrewd it was, too. Hmm, a Hantari…how clever, and *unexpected*. I had no idea there were any Hantari left in the galaxy, much less here on New Eden."

"Neither did we. Listen, Ignis, we need to move quickly. Once Jokar discovers the detonator has been destroyed, I fear he will destroy the colonists, before abandoning this planet."

"Nicole, I'm so sorry." Henry/Ignis frowned and furrowed his brow. She wasn't sure what felt creepier, the fact that he looked so much like the pictures she'd seen of Henry Summers, or that he was inside her mind.

"Jack's working to find and destroy the detonator. Can you access the Shataran computer that controls the planetary shield? Will you help us?"

"Will I help you? How can you ask such a question? Of course I'll help you!"

"The Hantari told us we must bring down the shield at the same time as the remote detonator was destroyed. I was delayed getting into the ship, so Jack's probably destroyed the detonator by now. "

"Then we must act quickly."

"Can you bring down the Shatarans' planetary shield?"

"Shatarans…who would have ever thought they were capable of

something like this? Well, let's see—yes, I believe I should. The Shatarans are an advanced race and to be forthcoming, I don't know that I could hack the system at their present level of technology. But—"

"The Shatarans *here* are still using technology that's over five-thousand years old," Nicole said, finishing for him.

"Correct. Okay, give me a moment, I'll be right back." Ignis disappeared and reappeared a few seconds later.

"What happened?"

"I was able to access the Shataran computer system controlling the planetary shields." He waved his hand and a massive screen appeared. Next, a large, black chair appeared as well, with several virtual buttons. A larger, green button next to a blue one had been placed in the middle. Ignis gestured for Nicole to sit in the chair.

"Simply press the green button to broadcast to the Alliance, and the press the blue button to disable the shield control system."

"Thank you, Ignis, really."

"You are very welcome, Nicole Reynolds. As I've known your family for many years, I consider myself privileged, and honored, to be of assistance now, and to help you and the colony. But the truth is that any of my Entelli brothers would have done the same thing. Earth is a League planet now, so we are both morally and legally obligated to assist in this matter, though I would gladly have done so regardless of Earth's status, given the chance. Yours is a remarkable people, Nicole Reynolds, and I'm so grateful that in your greatest hour of need of all Entelli, it was *I* you found here. Now then, are you ready?"

"As ready as I'll ever be. I wish I knew for certain whether Jack has destroyed the detonator."

"Wait just a moment, Nicole, perhaps I can try to find out. I should be able to access the security system, and the cameras." Nicole pulled her hand back from the button that would have lowered the shields. "Where did you say they were?"

"The Hantari told us that Jokar kept the detonator somewhere in my office; he didn't say exactly where." A holographic image began to materialize not far from where they were sitting, and she watched as her office was suddenly replicated in every detail visible to the holo-recorders installed throughout her office.

"There, Ignis, look!" She pointed over to where several pieces of an electronic device rested on top of her desk. On the floor, what they were able to make out of it anyway, were a number of smaller fragments from the same device.

"That's it, it has to be!" She rose and walked over, staring down at the image of the desk.

"It does look like a detonator, well—an antique detonator, of course. You believe Captain Lincoln is responsible for destroying it?"

She smiled before answering him. "I do; it must have been him. But where is he now, Ignis? See if you can find him, will you please?" Now she was worried for Jack, as well as for the rest of the colony.

"Of course." Three-dimensional images taken from various cameras throughout the colony flashed before her so quickly she could barely make anything out at all.

"Oh, no." That was all Ignis said, before the images suddenly faded away, save for the living room with the sofa, chairs, and lamps.

"What's wrong, Ignis, why did you stop scanning for him?"

"Because I, um, well I—"

"Ignis!"

"Because I found him, Nicole," he said plainly.

"You did? Then why did you turn it off? Oh no, he's not—?"

"*Dead*? No, Nicole, at least not yet."

"Show me, Ignis, please." Her great-grandfather's double shook his head.

"No, Nicole, I shouldn't."

"Show me!" she said again, more defiant this time.

Ignis shook his head and frowned before turning as if to watch as another room materialized; it was not her office this time however...rather, it was something quite different. A long table that loosely resembled an old-fashioned examination table like the one medical doctors had once used sat in the middle of the room. Jack lay stretched out on the table, his wrists and his ankles held fast by bands of energy. He was stripped down to his waist, and a number of cuts and abrasions covered his torso. She was struck at once with a blast of emotion, a mixture of profound concern and anger as she watched Jokar, who'd been walking around the table, extend a device towards Jack's torso. When it was nearly touching him, it released a crackle of energy into Jack's body, only for it to exit from another part of his body. His back arched high off the table and Nicole could see Jack was screaming in pain.

"Ignis, can we hear what they're saying?"

Ignis nodded.

"Where are they, Ignis?" Nicole asked.

"I believe they may be in the infirmary."

Nicole nodded, turning back to listen to Jokar.

"We call these 'pain sticks,' Captain Lincoln," Jokar was saying, before touching the stick to Lincoln's forehead. The energy flowed just under the skin and exited out the other side of his head. Jack screamed again. "They're aptly named, are they not?" Jokar bent over Jack, his eyes filled with hatred, and stared down at Jack. "Where *is* she?"

"I've already told you, I don't—know," Jack said, barely whispering it while grimacing in pain. "I didn't even tell her what I was going to do; she was still at the apartment when I left." Nicole smiled slightly. Jack had spoken the truth, at least in part.

"I tried to tell her," Jokar said with more compassion. "I tried to explain to her what we're trying to do here, what the Machrys did to *my* people, but she wouldn't listen. Those murderous beasts killed an untold number of Shatarans, peaceful Shatarans, who were doing nothing but minding their own business, Captain Lincoln! Did you know that in one city alone, over ten thousand Shataran children were murdered by those Machrys monsters? Please understand that we have no interest in making enemies of your people, Captain, but we are determined and we will do what we must; we've taken a vow, you see, a vow that we will destroy the Machrys, every last one of them, until they're all dead, or we are. Now tell me, I'm running out of time and patience, Jack Lincoln. Where is she?" Jokar walked over and leaned into Jack's face. "Come now, Captain, is she really worth all of this pain and suffering?"

She watched as Jack turned his head and spit blood out of his mouth. Watching him squirm and writhe in pain, knowing his suffering was, in part, because of her, tormented Nicole; she hung her head and began to cry.

"Leave—her—out of this, Motay. I—told you—she had nothing to do with it."

"Honestly, Captain Lincoln, you expect me to believe that you did this all on your own? I know her, Jack, she is cunning; there is more to this plan of hers than just destroying the detonator. My question is, what else is she up to? It must be something rather important, for her to leave *you* here to die! Nicole is as devious as she is fearless; she knows what I'll do to her this time when I find her. That detonator was my insurance against being taken by the League, or maybe even by your pathetic little 'Alliance.' I tell you what, you tell me what it is that she's up to, and I may even let you both live. Come on, Captain Jack, surely it's better than this!" Jokar then touched the pain stick to Jack's chest, causing his body to jump and buckle.

About that time a door was opened and Jokar walked over to speak with someone. After a minute or so, he turned back to Lincoln.

"I must leave for a short time, but don't worry, Mr. Lincoln, I'll be back soon enough."

Jokar Motay left the room and Lincoln was left alone for what felt like an eternity of painful waiting. He had nearly lost consciousness when he heard a noise from across the room. He lifted his head just off the table looking in the direction of the sound, expecting to see Motay returning with the instrument of barbaric torture in his hand. The door slowly opened, and a figure wearing a long, flowing, blue robe with a hood that covered the wearer's face entered the room, then walked directly to the examination table before stopping next to him. It was the last thing he saw before passing out.

CHAPTER 42

Hank Reynolds walked over to the bed where his father lay still asleep and sat down next to him. He picked up the data pad lying on the table next to the bed, an ancient novel written centuries earlier, a man with the vision to imagine a different kind of war between human beings and aliens.

Hank had known it would be a mistake to bring his father along in such a condition, but he'd been quite insistent about it. Nick Reynolds had learned about the unfolding crisis on New Eden the same way that billions of other human beings had, on the intergalactic news feed. The news had been reporting that Nicole Reynolds, the governor of the colony, was trapped and cutoff from the outside, along with the twenty-five thousand other colonists on New Eden, held hostage by an alien with a five-thousand year old grudge to settle. By the time Hank told Nick that he was leaving and might be away from Val for a while, his father had already determined the reason for his uncharacteristically cagey demeanor, and the incredibly short notice he'd given his family. Nick had confronted his son, who told him everything; Hank told his father that he was joining a fleet of League battle cruisers en route to meet with a Shataran delegation, to either diffuse the situation or rescue the colonists by force, if necessary. It wouldn't be easy, but the League was confident they would be able to breach the shields, though it would go much quicker with the help of Shataran scientists who were scheduled to rendezvous with the League ships just outside of the binary system. The League had already surrounded the planet, though they took great pains to keep their distance from the Shataran particle beam cannons.

Hank was determined to stay himself until something had been done to secure the safety of his daughter and every other colonist on the planet. But Nick was old and had become very sick, too sick to make the trip, though nothing Hank could do or say made any difference. He reached down and pulled the blanket up closer.

"How is he, any change?" His wife walked over and kissed him.

"You should have woke me, sweetheart; I'd have had breakfast with you."

"There was no need, Hailey. I wanted you both to get plenty of rest, and I'm supposed to meet with the Shataran scientists in an hour or so anyway. Don't worry, honey, I'll find a way through the Shataran shield, trust me. I just can't believe it's taking me so long." Hailey placed her hands around Hank's neck.

"Well, it wouldn't be much of a shield if it were that easy to break through now, would it?" she asked as she wrapped her arms around him. "One thing I know for certain, Hank Reynolds, is this; if there's anyone out here who can do it, it's *you*. Find a way past that shield, Hank, and find a way to save all those people on Mars; there must be a way. You're still the brightest man I've ever met."

It was one of the attributes he loved the most about his wife, her unfailing ability to find kernels of truth, hope, and pragmatism in even the darkest of times.

"I suppose you're right about that," he said, smiling back and kissing her.

"How's he doing?" she asked him, turning and looking down at Nick.

"He's been calling my mother's name a lot, Hailey. I'm afraid he's starting to slip away from me. If only he could take Meratac...it's virtually eliminated all forms of cancer over the past twenty-five years."

"I can't take it; I'm allergic to Meratac, son, you know that."

Hank turned and looked down at his father, who was now awake, his eyes still bright and alert despite the increasingly painful progression of pancreatic cancer.

"Yeah, I know; but I didn't know you were awake. Good morning, Pop, how are you feeling?"

"I'm still alive, son; I'm still breathing, and I'm still lucid enough to admire and appreciate my beautiful daughter-in law, so I guess I'm doing fine."

"Good morning, Dad," Hailey told him, leaning down to kiss him on his forehead.

"Good morning, Hailey."

"You were calling out for Mom in your sleep again, Dad."

Nick lay back down. "Ah, Kate; I sure miss your mother, boy. She was so beautiful, and so wonderful—" Nick smiled and put his hands under his head, memories of her flooding his mind.

"Yeah, I guess she was, Dad." Hank smiled back at his father, though behind the smile there was pain; it was a different kind of pain from his father's, but it *was* pain, and it hurt. He loved his father very much, and he knew that letting go, when the time came, would be difficult.

"Any word yet? Have they had any success breaking through the shield or jamming the signal?" Nick grimaced as he sat up in bed, holding up his hand to stop his son when Hank reached to help him. "Let me do what I can for myself now, Hank; only God knows how much longer I'll be able to."

"Sure, Dad."

Nick just smiled at Hank and nodded. "So what's going on at the colony, son? Any news?"

"No, nothing yet, Dad. I'm close to finding a way through that shield, I know I am. I expect the Shataran scientists will be able to help that process along very quickly; the shield's the least of our problems, however."

"You're worried about the remote detonator?"

Hank nodded. "Yeah, I am. I've explained the situation to everyone so they know how many lives hang in the balance. Once we find a way through the shield, we'll have to immediately jam all outbound communications from the entire planet."

"Is that even possible, Hank?" Hailey asked, looking doubtful.

"Well, maybe, honey…possibly…theoretically, at least. The truth is we have to try; there's just no way to trust that a madman like Motay won't destroy the Mars colony given the slightest provocation, and just consider them casualties of war. If we let him escape now, he'll escape with the detonator, and he'll be free to activate the explosives at any time. I know this is a risky plan, but it's what the Alliance and the League believe to be the best approach."

"What about you and your friend, Zing?" Nick asked him. "What do you think?"

Hank shook his head and threw his hands up in the air. "I don't know, Dad; I guess we agree with this plan in principle, though we both believe there must be a better way. All I want is to get Nicole out of there, and save the millions of human beings whose lives hang in the balance!" He took a deep breath and tried to calm himself. "I'm sorry; I guess the stress is getting to me. Zing and I've discussed this at length, and we both agree that we must stop Jokar Motay here and now, or we'll risk the lives of millions of human beings on Mars, the hundreds of millions of Machrys across the galaxy, and who knows how many of any other race of sentients who gets between the Shatarans and the Machrys along the way. So yeah, I guess this is it."

"What about the detonator?"

"One of the League ambassadors informed us that their government had success in the past jamming planetary communications during a field test, by deploying satellites in strategic locations around a world. They've graciously offered to place enough of these satellites in orbit around New

Eden that they should jam all outbound communications coming from the planet; they've been deploying them and will be at the meeting later this morning, where they are supposed to be providing an update."

"What about those particle beam cannons you told me about, Hank? I already have a daughter in great danger; I'd rather not risk losing my husband as well," Hailey added, her voice cracking slightly when her emotions got the better of her.

"The Shatarans' particle beam cannon technology is five-thousand year old technology, honey. The shields we've been using may not be enough to protect our ships, but the Shataran government has already given us the specs for a shield that's more than strong enough to protect us. Technicians have nearly completed building enough of the new shield generators to protect all of the ships involved in the assault."

"It sounds like the pieces are falling into place, son; great work!" his father said, adding a pat on the back for good measure.

"Yeah, well, let's just hope that everything works out the way it should," Hank replied with a serious look.

***

Nicole and Ignis watched the strange hooded figure enter the room, and Nicole was alarmed at what it meant for Jack. Who was it, and what new form of torture were they about to inflict on the man she had grown to love? She watched and listened as the hooded figure stopped at Jack's side and began pulling back the hood. Nicole was surprised to see a female Shataran standing over him. She began applying some type of cream to his wounds, and once finished, she pressed an end of a device she held in her hand against his carotid artery. Jack's face suddenly began showing more color, and his wounds immediately began to close, before disappearing altogether. Jack's eyelids began to flutter, then opened wide at the site of the Shataran female.

"Who are you and what have you done to me?" he asked, bewildered and apparently already very much recovered from his ordeal.

"My name is Aleena Talrussa, and I'm here to help you."

"Why would you do that?" Jack asked, deeply suspicious of the Shataran, who turned her head frequently to see who might be near.

"Jokar ordered me to come treat your wounds, to keep you alive, so he can get answers from you. But I've done more than what he wanted...I've nearly restored you to full health, because I'm going to help you get out of here." She pressed a button and the energy bonds disappeared. Jack sat up on the table.

"How and why are you helping me?"

"The castil, of course; it's a very powerful substance. That's why it's so valuable. As to why I'm going to help you It's simple; not everyone agrees with Jokar's plan to renew the Great Purge, and the extermination of the Machrys. We've been in stasis for over five-thousand years, Captain Lincoln, and the universe has changed; maybe it's time we changed too."

"How do I get out of here?"

She stopped and looked around for a moment. "Wait a moment." Aleena walked to the door, opened it, and looked around before closing it again. Jack jumped off the table and began walking to the door.

"I think it's clear at the moment, but you need to tell me where you want to go." At this Jack took his first, good look at her. With the long, flowing white hair, the soft lavender skin, and the golden eyes, she was quite beautiful. Despite having just met her and the rather suspicious circumstances, Jack found himself wanting to trust her. It made sense that not all of the Shatarans would agree to massacre an entire species, even if they had attacked their people first.

"I, um, I believe we need to head toward the hangar bay."

"Why the hangar bay, Captain? Surely you realize how heavily guarded it is. I don't know how I could possibly get you by so many guards unnoticed."

"We have to try," Jack responded. "There are many lives on the line, Aleena."

"What do you intend to do when we get there?" she asked. Something in him warned him not to say anything, but they had connected somehow, and she was so *beautiful*!

"We need to bring down the planetary shield in order for the Alliance to attack. We need to get to a ship that has an Entelli onboard. They should be able to hack into the Shataran systems that control the shield so we can deactivate it."

Jack was shocked to hear the sound of someone clapping their hands loudly just outside the door, which suddenly opened to reveal Jokar Motay standing in the doorway.

"Thank you very much, Captain Jack. I was unaware that these Entelli were so skilled as to be able to hack their way past a Shataran security system. I suppose they would have a five-thousand year advantage over us now, wouldn't they?" Jokar walked over to Aleena, embracing and kissing her passionately for quite some time.

"Aleena, my darling, you are so good at what you do!"

"It really wasn't difficult, Jokar. These humans seem particular sensitive to our empathic influence. I could have had him eating out of my hand had I wished it."

"Indeed, I noticed it myself early on with Nicole. Such influence could become rather helpful to our cause at some point, my dear, as we will need human allies during our renewed quest to exterminate the

Machrys."

Motay turned to face Lincoln once again. "So, Captain, you planned to lower the shields; is that where I can expect we'll find Nicole? Well then, let's not keep her waiting!" Jokar turned to one of the Shataran guards standing just outside the door. "Take him; we'll bring him to the hangar with us."

Nicole had been watching everything as it unfolded, shocked at what had just taken place. She was particularly disturbed to learn she had been under Jokar's influence before, mistakenly interpreting his empathic influence as feelings.

"You should deactivate the shields before they get here, Nicole. I've added a red button as well, which will deactivate their particle beam cannons. Once they've been deactivated, I'll send a power surge through both systems, damaging some of the internal components of each shield projector and particle beam cannon. You must act quickly, Nicole; they will be here soon."

"Okay." Nicole nodded before pressing the blue button to deactivate the shield, the red button to deactivate the particle beam cannons, and finally, the green button.

"Attention any Earth Space Alliance or League of Sentient Being ships in the vicinity of New Eden; can you hear me? Repeat, can you hear me? This is Governor Nicole Reynolds, governor of New Eden." Nicole repeated the sequence several times before tiring of it. She was running out of time and soon began questioning whether anyone had actually received her message. If there was no response soon, she would have to leave. Two minutes passed with no response. Nicole prepared to leave the ship when the communications system suddenly came alive.

"Nicole, is that you, honey?" She was hesitant to respond at first, suddenly realizing that the Shatarans could have intercepted her message.

"Nicole, are you still there, sweetheart? Please respond?"

"Dad, is that you? What are *you* doing here?"

"Yeas, baby, it's me. We're here to rescue you, but we haven't been able to break through the shields yet, and we've been trying to find a way to jam their remote detonator."

"There's no need to do anything, Dad. The shields and particle cannons are now down, and Jack Lincoln destroyed the remote detonator. They've captured Jack, though, and they're holding a number of children hostage on their ship so the colonists will harvest and process the castil for them. I've got to go, Dad, they'll be here any minute. I love you; please hurry!"

Nicole terminated the call and was preparing to leave when Ignis walked over to her.

268

"It's too late, Nicole," he told her. "They're here."

CHAPTER 43

They were down to two remaining ships, the one Nicole and Ignis were in and one other. She could see that they were heavily armed.

"Ignis, can they force their way in here?" Ignis's avatar, which was in the form of her great-grandfather, Henry Summers, froze for a moment with its eyes still open. It always felt creepy to her, how what appeared to be a human being could just turn on and off like that. Her mind wandered for a moment while she considered that the reason it seemed so real was because Ignis was indeed alive, a sentient, living computer, both organic and inorganic. It was both fascinating and...well, alien to her as well. Her attention snapped back to Ignis upon him once more becoming animated.

"I'm sorry for the delay, Nicole Reynolds. I have analyzed their weapons and regretfully, I must inform you that they are indeed capable of penetrating the shields. You see, the Shatarans were at war with the Machrys for quite some time, which necessitated the need for much stronger shields and heavier firepower. For thousands of years now, however, the galaxy has known mostly peace, so the need for the heavy shielding and firepower has been greatly reduced. Perhaps this needs to be revisited by the League, but that is a discussion for another time. They are carrying scaled down versions of the particle beam cannons."

"But I thought those weapons drew energy from micro-singularities!"

"That's true, Nicole, but they found a way to store some of that energy created by the micro-singularity, enough energy to enable the weapon to fire a few bursts with a level of power that, though of a much shorter duration, is still on the same scale of power as the cannons. In short, one burst from such a weapon would tear through the shield along with the hull of this ship. I'm sorry, I know it's not what you wanted to hear."

Nicole let out a heavy sigh of disappointment. "Okay, Ignis, thank you."

Nicole watched on the screen as the Shatarans approached the ship she was in. Ignis was providing audio as well as imaging of what was happening outside the ship. She could see and hear them as they approached the ship. She watched as Jokar pressed a button on a device strapped on his arm, which she soon learned was a communications device.

"Governor, we are being hailed."

Nicole let out another deep sigh. "All right, Ignis, this is it. Let's do this."

Ignis nodded and Jokar's image suddenly appeared.

"Ah, Nicole, it's so good to see you again, my dear."

"How did you find me?" she asked. She really didn't care at this point, but she needed to stall them for as long as she could.

"Why, your boyfriend, Jack Lincoln, told us everything."

Nicole knew she had to be careful; she couldn't let on that they'd successfully hacked into their systems.

"I don't believe you, Jokar," she lied. "Jack would never betray me!"

"Oh, but we can be quite persuasive, Governor Reynolds, as you'll soon find out for yourself. It seems your Alliance and the League have decided to not cooperate with us on our vendetta to rid the universe of the Machrys scourge. Now then, why don't you come on out so we don't have to destroy this ship, and you along with it, of course?"

She hesitated a moment before deciding she had to try to buy just a little more time.

"Give me some time to think it over, Jokar. Besides, you don't want to destroy the castil in here, do you?"

Motay smiled. "I'm afraid you are out of time, my dear. As for the castil, I suppose you're right; if you don't want to come out on your own, I guess we'll just have to come in to get you." Motay gestured to one of his men carrying the larger weapon, the one she assumed to be the mini-particle cannon.

"I'll give you three seconds to come out, Nicole; after that I'm afraid I might have to ruin that pretty little face of yours. One—"

Nicole struggled to come up with a way to stall Motay, to give the Alliance more time to launch a rescue mission.

"Two—"

Where are they? She closed her eyes and prepared herself for the inevitable.

"Three—"

She waited for a blast that never came. When she looked up she saw Motay was holding up a hand to the Shataran with the micro-cannon in hand. Another Shataran had approached him and was whispering something into his ear.

"What?" He shoved the other Shataran back so far that he landed on the ground. "Are you certain?" The Shataran on the ground nodded. Motay now looked up at her with such an intense look of visceral hatred that she nearly fell backwards.

"What have you done? You've disabled our shields and our cannons? Don't you realize what you've done, child? You've all but ended our chance to exterminate the Machrys, the same scourge that nearly murdered every man, woman, and child on New Eden! Why did you do it, Nicole? Why were you so intent on stopping us from destroying a race that was trying to destroy you?"

Nicole stood staring at him for a moment before answering him. "Because despite the obvious fact that what they did to your planet and mine was wrong, very wrong, what you did to them, and to us, was even worse. You nearly wiped out their entire species, which would have rendered any opportunity for redemption non-existent. You also tried to take away our children, and our freedom, and you threatened to destroy millions more than the Machrys ever did. You may have thought you were ridding the universe of monsters, Jokar, but the truth is you've become monsters yourselves, monsters far more terrifying, and dangerous than the Machrys."

"Sir, we have to go! They're closing in on our position rapidly. If we don't go now, we'll never make the ship in time!"

Jokar turned to leave. "Sir, what should we do with the prisoner?" the Shataran holding Lincoln asked.

Motay looked down for a moment before looking back at Nicole as he answered.

"Let him go, let them all go. There's no reason to take the children now. Good-bye, Nicole. Perhaps, in another time, in another place, we could have been true friends." Nicole considered replying, but before she'd had a chance to form a response the Shatarans had disappeared out one of the hangar doors.

"Ignis, quickly, open the hatch. Also, can you please help me with an exit? I need to hurry to Jack."

"Of course, Governor. Promise to come see me again?"

Nicole smiled. "I wouldn't have it any other way, Ignis."

A door appeared to her left. She reached out to shake his hand before turning and running for the door. She opened her eyes to find herself right where she'd started, in the captain's chair. A few seconds later, she leapt to her feet and ran toward the hatch before running down the ramp and jumping into Jack's outstretched arms. She wrapped hers around him so tightly she heard him gasp, and kissed him with such intense passion and feeling that it felt unreal, unlike any man she had ever kissed before. She'd realized the moment she witnessed him being tortured how deeply in love

273

she was with Jack Lincoln. Now that the immediate danger was past, all she could do was hope he loved her as much.

"Oh, Jack," she said once their lips finally parted. "I was so worried about you. I was so afraid that—I love you so much, Jack. I never knew how much until now—I never realized how much you meant to me. I can't imagine a life without you in it, Jack Lincoln!" she professed, terrified and fearing rejection now that she'd risked everything by telling him.

Jack only smiled. "Finally."

Nicole was confused by the response. "What does that mean?" she asked, searching his eyes nervously.

"I was afraid you'd never say those words to me, Nikki. The truth is, I've been in love with you from the moment we first met, and I've wanted you in my life every minute since; you're only now catching up."

Nicole smiled and wrapped her arms around him, and again she heard him gasp. She also kissed him again.

"Come on, Nikki, we've got to find out what's going on, and make sure those children got off their ship safely. It sounded as if they were going to take what castil they had and make a run for it."

"Okay," she said, smiling back at him once more before they too ran for the hangar door, totally uncertain about what they might find before them.

CHAPTER 44

Nicole followed Jack out the hangar door, and she was thrilled with what she saw. The sky was full of Alliance and League ships, mostly League cruisers and Alliance heavy troop transports. One of the heavy troop transport ships had already landed just outside the city, and one of the land transports from the ship was already headed in their direction. Her heart leapt when she saw her father, Hank Reynolds, riding in the front. In less than a minute the transport stopped near where they were standing, and Hank quickly exited the craft and ran to his daughter.

"Nikki, sweetheart, are you okay? I'm so glad to see you're safe—your mother and I were so worried!" Tears were streaming from both father and daughter as they embraced for the longest time. When they'd finished, Nikki looked up at her father.

"I'm okay…I'm okay. Dad, I'd like for you to meet someone, a man who's very special to me; his name is Jack Lincoln." She smiled warmly at Jack, who appeared momentarily stunned at meeting her father for the first time.

"Dr. Reynolds, she's told me a lot about you, sir."

Hank extended his hand and eyed Lincoln with suspicion. "Hmmm, I see."

"Dad, Jokar Motay let Jack go after he discovered you were coming. They're planning to get to their ship and make a run for it."

"They must have been on the transports we saw racing out of the city just as we were landing. We sent two transports after it already, but I'll get on the comm system to let them know. Can you tell me where their ship is located exactly?"

"Yes; it's approximately ten kilometers northeast of here, in that direction," she said, pointing out past the edge of town toward a distant mountain range. Hank immediately called in the information. Nicole made out that he was clearly surprised by something they said. "What did they say, Dad?" she asked him after the connection was terminated.

"The League already has a group of cruisers heading to that location.

I guess they were able to get a fix on the Shataran ship's location from space. Okay, let's get you two back to the command ship I've been staying on, where you'll be able to rest up a bit. Lord knows you've earned it."

"The command ship?" asked Jack.

"Yes, of course; both Alliance and League leadership will be wanting a debrief once they have the Shatarans in custody."

"No, Dad, not yet. We need to get to the crash site of the Shataran ship, to make sure the children are safe and to help with the Shatarans if we can."

"I don't think so, Nikki, not after everything you two have been through. Let the League and the Alliance handle it from here."

Nicole placed her hands on her father's shoulders. "Listen, Dad, I know I'll always be your little girl; I understand that, and I'm extremely proud to be your daughter. But I'm the governor of this colony; I've got to see this through. Our children were kidnapped just so the Shatarans could turn their parents into slaves. No matter what we do, we have to see them brought to justice. Besides, of everything I've done over the last six months, this is probably the *least* dangerous."

Hank looked at them and could see the same look of determination in each one's eyes.

"Captain?"

"Dr. Reynolds, I've just been tortured and nearly murdered by these Shatarans. They've taken our children and turned us into their slaves. The last thing I want to do is miss a single second of Jokar and his bunch being taken down and held responsible. There's nowhere else I'd rather be, sir."

"There's something else, Dad, something we need to make everyone aware of. The Shatarans, at least *these* Shatarans, have the ability to influence others; it's some sort of empathic ability. Jokar used it to win my trust—"

"And one of the Shataran females was easily able to persuade me to tell her our plan for stopping them."

"We don't know whether all Shatarans have this ability, but we do know that Jokar and at least some of his crew most certainly do."

"Okay then, we'll relay that information along on our way to the crash site."

While Hank picked up the comm link and started warning everyone about the Shatarans' unique gift, Nicole furrowed her brow. Underneath the bravado and her brave words, Nicole was well aware of the fear that still lurked deep down inside her. She knew enough about the Shatarans to appreciate how extremely dangerous they were, doubly so now that they were cornered. They'd only just escaped Jokar and his men with their lives, and even then only because he'd chosen to spare them once it was clear the League would soon be arriving in force. She would go to see him stopped, and she would relish the sight, but she knew that an alien who was as cunning and ferocious as Jokar would remain a very dangerous threat until it was all over.

***

The transport arrived at the site just before three others pulled up. One of the soldiers—Nicole assumed he was the one in charge—got out and came over to Hank.

"I'm sorry Mr. Ambassador; we lost them a few kilometers back in some thick woods."

"That's okay, Commander Ubuntu. We have to find the children and disable that ship immediately before they can get away. They've got quite a bit to answer for."

"Yes, sir."

Ubuntu divided the thirty men into two groups, one with twenty-five men to disable and seize control of the ship, and another five to retrieve the missing children. Nicole elected to go get the children, having given it the greater priority. The Alliance and the League would handle the Shatarans...the children were her responsibility. They'd nearly arrived at the ship when Nicole, standing atop a small hill, spotted something with her binoculars. She raised her arm and pressed the comm link on her wrist.

"I've found the children. It looks like the Shatarans let them go. They're about a half-kilometer from the ship, in a grove of trees. I can't see well enough to be sure, but it could be all of the missing children. There were a hundred and fourteen children taken. Please, let's take four of the transports, get a headcount, and begin transporting them back to the city. It's possible Jokar kept some on the ship as bargaining chips...I wouldn't put it past him."

"Yes, Governor," the senior ranking officer responded, before assigning a man to each of the four transports, the one Hank had arrived in and three others. They immediately made their way to the clearing, where the children had been deposited by the Shatarans. It looked as if they'd not moved from the spot where the Shatarans had left them. Most of them looked scared, some looked confused, and all of them wanted to go home to be with their parents.

While Nicole and the soldiers began taking a quick head count of the children, Jack and Hank walked toward the Shataran ship, along with the main body of Alliance troops, before stopping a half-kilometer from the ship. The first group of soldiers had been setting up high-energy plasma artillery shells, which they believed to be powerful enough to penetrate Motay's shields. They were nearly ready to begin the bombardment when the massive engines on the Shataran ship suddenly ignited, causing the

277

bottom of the ship to suddenly glow a bright blue. The sound of energy crackling could also be heard, even at the distance they were from the ship. Large boulders, sand, dirt, and even a number of trees began falling to the ground as the ship started to rise into the air. Hank got on his comm system.

"Commander Ubuntu, we cannot afford to let that ship escape. Do anything necessary, but bring it down!"

"You understand, sir, that we'd risk killing everyone on board?" Unbuntu asked.

"Yes, Commander, I understand—we'll have to take that chance," Hank replied, with a more solemn, somber tone.

Jack Lincoln walked over and stood in front of Hank. "You had no choice, sir," Jack said in a subdued tone. "They enslaved everyone on the colony and were prepared to roll right over us if necessary in order to get the Machrys. They're obsessed with wiping them out, Dr. Reynolds."

"I know, Jack. There was no doubt about their guilt then, nor is there now. We must try to keep in mind, however, that it was the *Machrys* who attacked the Shatarans first, starting the war. I know they tortured you, Captain, and I apologize if I seem insensitive, but Motay did save Nicole, you, and the others from certain death at the hands of the Machrys." He paused and sighed. "Oh, I know what it would mean to let them go, so don't worry…that's something we cannot allow. I guess it's just that I regret taking anyone's life, even Jokar's." Hank looked up at the Shataran ship, which continued rising.

"Fire at will, Commander." Dozens of artillery shells suddenly exploded out of their tubes and rocketed skyward to rain down on the ascending ship.

"It's a heavy burden I'll have to carry for the rest of my life, Captain, but I cannot allow this particular group of Shatarans to go free, not until they've stood trial to answer for their crimes, both old and new."

"Yes, sir, I—look, Dr. Reynolds, the shells are having no effect!" The shells had exploded upon reaching the ship's invisible shielding, but the explosions were merely being deflected outward. Hank immediately reached for his comm system.

"Zing, send them in, quickly; we haven't a moment to lose!"

"We saw it from here; they're already on their way, Dr. Reynolds. Wait just a moment and I'll patch you in so you can hear what's happening."

Zing was doing something that was not picked up by the holo-recorder. The Shataran ship was nearly far enough above the mountain range now that it could escape at nearly any angle. It was looking pretty bleak.

"Mr. Ambassador, they're escaping!"

"Jack, I don't think there's—"

Before he finished speaking a half-dozen ships appeared above and beside the prison ship, all of them silver and blue in color, and each of them very similar. Their positions all around the ship left Motay and his crew with nowhere to go. There was a long pause, until a voice was heard over the transport's communication system.

"Captain Jokar Motay and crew, I am Admiral Terillian with the Shataran Ninth Battle Fleet. You are ordered to set your ship down at its present location, open your hatch, and immediately exit down the ramp, where you will then be placed in custody. Failure to follow these instructions completely will result in the immediate destruction of your ship and everyone onboard. You will receive no further warnings."

"Thank you for offering us a chance to surrender, Admiral Terillian. It seems this is one offer I have no choice but to accept. But before you take us home to Shatara as prisoners, consider this; would it be so wrong to let us go? We are, after all, brothers. When the Machrys attacked Shatara's colonies and destroyed so many of our people, we were hailed as heroes, for it was I and my brothers who repelled the Machrys invaders. Did you know, Admiral, that we were decorated war heroes, hailed by everyone as the Protectors of Shatara?

"When the wretched Machrys attacked *this* planet, we repelled them once more, saving this population of humans from being slaughtered, the way my family was slaughtered. We saved the humans, and though we took some desperate measures to ensure their cooperation until we could leave this place, we had no desire to harm them!

"Let us go, Admiral, and we will continue where we left off millennia ago; we will hunt down and destroy the Machrys, so that they can never again do what they did to Shatara, and what they intended to do here. What say you, Admiral Terillian; will you let us go?"

There was another long pause, until the voice of the leader of the Shataran fleet was heard once more.

"I am a student of history, Captain Jokar Motay, and I can understand, from your point of view, why you might feel what you did was right. As a student of history, however, I am compelled to share with you some of what I have learned in my studies. It is true that in the beginning, you were indeed hailed as the Protectors of Shatara, for you saved many Shataran lives from being lost. Had you stopped there, you would indeed have gone down in history as a hero. But you didn't stop there, Captain Motay; instead you killed so many civilian Machrys, including Machrys children, that it was said to be far beyond counting. Public opinion on Shatara soon turned increasingly against you as the

Machrys body count grew exponentially. Shatarans soon began calling you Motay, the Butcher of Worlds. You cared nothing for what part the Machrys you killed might have played in the war, whether they were peace-loving or warmongers, whether they were young or whether they were old. It was said that you even destroyed nursery buildings full of Machrys infants. Your rage and your appetite for murdering the Machrys knew no bounds, because it had driven you to the edge of insanity. Do you want to know what the *greatest* tragedy of all was in regards to your 'Great Purge'? Yes, a single Machrys battle group had attacked several Shataran colonies unprovoked, but not at the behest of its government. A single military leader, General Igarteranok, had disobeyed orders when he led the attack against our people, in an attempt to take by force the technology that our people refused to share with them. In truth, an entire Machrys armada was soon dispatched to intercept Igarteranok's forces, only it was too late. By the time the armada neared the colonies under attack, the damage had already been done. Igarteranok and his lieutenants were executed for their crimes against us, but by then there was no turning back for many Shatarans who, like you, had lost so many loved ones that you were beyond listening to reason. Our people, led by you and others like you, were so distraught and overwhelmed with grief that they refused to listen to anything the Machrys said, believing everything they said to be lies. Only when the Machrys were nearly extinct did our people finally stop long enough to listen."

Admiral Terillian paused and a long silence ensued. Ships remained where they were, as if frozen in the sky. So long was the silence that Nicole began to wonder if they'd lost the signal. Eventually, however, what sounded like a shaken and very different Jokar finally replied.

"Why—why didn't anyone tell us the truth about what had happened?" Motay asked, obviously stunned by the revelations that had withstood five thousand years of scrutiny.

"From what we've found in the historical record, Jokar, they tried. Your despair and appetite for revenge must have deafened as well as blinded you."

"But—they attacked this world as well! Isn't that evidence of how barbaric and ruthless the Machrys are?"

"The Machrys had been to this planet even before the humans arrived. Unbeknownst to the League, a great plague has devastated the planet Machrys, so they'd been in search of a source for the castilian plant. The value now is even greater than it was in your day, and the planet Machrys lacks the wealth to purchase the amount of castil they need. They've been a solitary race ever since the Great Purge, distrustful of the other races. When the humans arrived, they tried to get them to leave with

280

verbal warnings, but the humans refused to leave, since their own world was nearly destroyed recently. The Machrys then decided to break through the shield protecting the city, and force the humans to leave. They had no intentions of destroying the colonists, they were only going to remove them from this world."

"Until we destroyed their ships." Motay responded in little more than a whisper.

"Yes," the admiral affirmed.

"I understand now, Admiral. Thank you for explaining this to me—to *all* of us. We will land, and accompany you as your prisoners back to Shatara, Admiral Terillian; we will offer no resistance."

Nicole noted how Jokar's voice had changed, how it no longer sounded so cocky and arrogant. Instead, he sounded more like a broken man, like someone who'd always imagined himself to be the hero of the story, only to suddenly discover that he had, instead, been the villain.

Motay's ship soon set down and a minute later, the hatch opened. Weapons began pouring out of the ship and onto the ground until both Shataran and Alliance-made weapons littered the ground around the ship. Within thirty minutes, all of the Shatarans had exited the ship, even Jokar Motay, who walked behind the rest, sullen and dejected. He cast a brief, pitiful glance at Jack and Hank before dropping his head. The renegade Shatarans were then shackled and loaded onto a Shataran transport before being taken to where the larger and newer Shataran ships had set down.

With the threat now over, Nicole and Jack, followed by her father Hank, walked back to the grove of trees, where dozens of children still stood under the waving branches of Edenian trees, waiting for their chance to go home.

CHAPTER 45

"Welcome, Admiral Skylok, on behalf of the people of New Eden and the Alliance."

"Thank you, Governor Reynolds, it is our pleasure to make your acquaintance," the visitor replied. Admiral Skylok was accompanied by two other Machrys, who followed them down the hallway and into the main conference room. Inside, they found various members of the League, the Alliance, and the Shataran Council, already seated around a large, oval table. Hank and Nicole Reynolds were there, as was Jack Lincoln and President Zing.

Nicole offered her guests something to drink, but they kindly refused. Everyone soon found a chair and took a seat at the table. Introductions were made, as they often were at such gatherings. Admiral Skylok, after turning to Nicole, was the first to speak.

"We would like to begin, Governor Reynolds, by offering our most sincere apology for the attack on your colony. It was an act of desperation by our people, one that set off a series of unfortunate events with unintended consequences, which could easily have resulted in a terrible outcome for us all. Please, we implore you, try to understand that our planet has been stricken by a terrible scourge, a disease that has left over a third of our people either dead or close to death. One of the scouting teams we sent out to find castilian plants found them here in great abundance; there was more here than we'd ever seen anywhere in the galaxy. You must understand, Governor, that our people...well, we're not a planet of tremendous wealth. It would have required great wealth to obtain the quantity of castil that we needed to heal our world and stop the plague. We never intended to attack your world; we only wanted to scare you into leaving voluntarily or failing that, remove your people from here. We would have committed a terrible wrong against your people, but please believe we never would have attacked with the intention of killing anyone, human or otherwise. It was a terrible lapse in judgment, and we assure you that it will never happen again, for *any* reason. Please, accept our most sincere of apologies." Skylok bowed his head to the ground in shame.

"General Skylok," Nicole began. "We also deeply regret the most unfortunate misunderstanding between our two peoples, and we are terribly sorry to hear about the great calamity that has claimed the lives of so many of your people. Now that we have a clearer understanding of your situation, we will certainly do everything we can to help you combat this epidemic of yours."

"We understand that the Shataran who attacked our ships, the one now in the custody of the Shataran government, was none other than Jokar Motay, the Butcher of Worlds. Is that correct?"

"It is," Nicole responded.

"How is this possible? It has been over five-thousand years!"

"That's true, Admiral. We found their ship crashed in the side of a mountain here on New Eden, where they were still in stasis until recently when, unfortunately, we woke them."

"And what will become of the Butcher of Worlds, and the other rogue Shatarans?"

"They are on their way to Shatara, where they will stand trial for their many crimes of genocide against your people so long ago, as well as for the crimes they committed recently against the people of New Eden. Needless to say, they will likely spend the rest of their lives imprisoned, unable to ever trouble you or your people again."

"We are curious about something, Governor; do you have an image of the Butcher of Worlds? We would know from his image if it is him, for we have studied the ancient battles many times."

"I have one here, Admiral," Hank offered. "He recently spoke with me during the crisis…hold on just a minute…."

After fiddling for a few seconds Motay's image suddenly appeared over the conference room table. Skylok jumped back slightly, jolted as if seeing an ancient fiend he'd only seen during his worst nightmares.

"Yes," he said, having regained his composure. "That's him—the butcher, Jokar Motay. We…." Skylok stopped in mid-sentence and stared intently at the image, his countenance much different this time. "*By the Eternal*, we cannot believe our eyes!" he blurted out, as if he'd been slapped in the face. "After all this time, is *that* where it went? Do you have any idea how important, how precious this is to our people?" All eyes fixated on Skylok and the other Machrys; all three were studying the image carefully. "Do our eyes deceive us?" he asked the other Machrys.

"No, Admiral, we believe we are quite correct," one of the Machrys said.

"It is the Scepter, Admiral Skylok, it has to be. It makes perfect sense that *he* would have taken it, though we're shocked that he's never destroyed it!"

"Pardon me, Admiral, but what are you talking about?" asked Nicole; it was the same question she knew was on every else's mind.

"It is the Scepter of the King, one of our most precious religious relics. It was lost during the Great Purge, and thought to be destroyed either by Motay or by one of his people. Please, tell us, is it still on his ship?"

"I would assume so, Admiral Skylok," Nicole replied. "The Shataran admiral told me he'd send someone back for the ship soon."

"Oh, how we long to lay our eyes on it, to hold it, and, most importantly, to take it back home to our people. May we take it with us?"

Nicole looked to Hank, who looked to Zing.

"The Scepter of the King figures prominently in ancient Machrys culture. It is among their most revered religious relics of all of Machrys history. No doubt it would mean a great deal to his people, especially during this trying time."

Nicole nodded at Zing and her father before turning to Jack.

"I'll take care of it, Governor," he said with a smile and a nod. Nicole offered an appreciative smile in return and watched as he left the conference room.

"I expect we'll have it for you by the time you're ready to leave, Admiral."

Skylok bowed his head low and held it for quite some time. "You have no idea how much this means to us, Governor Reynolds. Your gracious warmth and hospitality shames us for what we tried to do; again we ask for your forgiveness."

"And you have it, Admiral," she replied, leaning in towards him slightly. "There is, however, another matter we'd like to discuss with you, if we may."

"Yes, of course."

Nicole turned to face Zing. "President Zing?"

"Thank you Governor Reynolds. Admiral Skylok, I am the Valhari Ambassador to the League of Sentient Species, but I am also acting President of the League as well. I understand that the Machrys have been asked to join the League on many occasions, and frankly, given what I've learned since all of this began, I can understand why you have had reservations about joining. We have a proposal for you, Admiral, and for your people, one that we believe would prove beneficial to all involved. Would you like to hear more?"

"Indeed, Mr. Ambassador, please proceed."

"Very well. As you may know, Earth recently joined the League. It just so happens that the humans nearly lost their own home world recently, when a rogue planet entered their system and narrowly missed colliding with it. This colony was their first outside of their own system, and the only colony suitable for human life. This world is outside of Machrys space, yet your people are in dire need of castil. Our proposal is simple; New Eden will grow and cultivate the castilian plant and process it into castil. They will then commit to selling a portion of this castil to the League, who will in turn give it to the Machrys until your world has fully recovered from this plague. Our only stipulation is that your world join the League, and that your people make a wholehearted effort to remain an active member of the League following this crisis. That is our proposal, Admiral Skylok." Zing turned to Hank.

"What do you say, Admiral, interested?" Hank smiled at the Machrys, who smiled back.

"While we cannot provide an official response, of course, we feel quite certain our government will feel as we do—appreciative, and eager to finally join the League of Sentient Species. Our only regret, is that we haven't done so before now."

The door opened and Jack Lincoln walked in, carrying the Scepter of the King with him. He walked over to the Machrys admiral and carefully placed it in his hands. Everyone in the room watched in amazement as tears began streaming down the eyes of every Machrys in the room.

"This has proven to be a wonderful, miraculous day for the Machrys people. May this be the first day in a very long and enduring friendship."

CHAPTER 47

Nick was feeling tired, *really* tired, and he knew the reason wasn't only because of his advancing age. The doctors had told him that it would happen like this, that he would grow more and more tired, sleeping more and more until finally, one day, he just wouldn't wake up. Nick chuckled. One of the doctors had told him he should be thankful, since medications to treat the pain associated with cancer had come such a long way, allowing human beings to enjoy a much better quality of life before the end came than they once did. It was a shame that despite all of the research and the incredibly advanced technology at its disposal, humanity still lacked more than one cure for cancer. Many types of cancer had been successfully treated and eliminated with medicines other than Meratac, but it was still very much hit or miss. For Nick, of course, it had been a miss. He smiled and shook his head.

Nick was grateful for having lived to see his son achieve even greater things than he had, and to see his granddaughter achieve more than both of them. His thoughts turned back to Nicole; he still had no knowledge of what had become of his son and granddaughter. His son had left suddenly, telling him only that he'd been contacted by Nicole and had to move quickly. It sounded like she was in great danger, so he'd asked no questions of Hank, wanting him to get down to the surface of the planet as quickly as possible.

Hank had only been gone for a few hours when the space outside his temporary home in space was filled with a fleet of ships heading for the planet's surface. Struggling to see through the small window, he recognized some as Alliance ships, the rest were a mixture of shapes, colors, and designs, leading him to believe the rest were League ships.

He rose from his chair and made his way over to the bulkhead of the ship. He pressed a button and a panel lowered; pressing the same button a second time caused a small computer built into the paneling to send a signal to the alloy that formed the outer shell of the ship, causing it to become transparent. *It's so amazing, and so beautiful*! The golden atmosphere of the planet was unlike anything he ever could have imagined. In the distance he saw the binary stars, whose life-giving light made it possible to live on New Eden. Nick allowed his eyes to move freely, taking in all of the harsh, unforgiving beauty of space, and to wander from ship to ship among the many approaching the planet. He could see why Hank had enjoyed flying so much, and why Nicole had agreed to take a leadership role; it was a strange and exciting place.

His thoughts drifted back to Nicole, and this time his face grew sad. He loved his granddaughter dearly, in part because she had the same fire her grandmother had once had, only Nicole's was even fiercer than Kate's. She'd once been one of the brightest, happiest children he'd ever seen, as was her little brother, so full of life with nothing but a bright and amazing future ahead of her. The loss of her brother and the guilt she later felt for being unable to protect him had changed her, however, leaving her hard and bitter. It just wasn't right for any child to see what she'd witnessed at such an early age. She'd built an impenetrable wall around her ever since her brother's murder; she'd never allowed herself to love anyone quite the same way again, even after growing into an incredibly beautiful woman. She'd become a woman more comfortable in the office or at one of the many martial arts training halls, however, than she was in the company of an eligible bachelor. Nick knew she was even more radiant on the inside than she was on the outside, if only she would let down her defenses long enough to let someone in.

Nick's eyes were suddenly drawn to movement. In the distance a ship had just exited New Eden's atmosphere, a large ship by the looks of it, but it was still too far away to make out the design. He'd seen several ships whose configuration and design he didn't recognize leaving the planet's surface several minutes earlier, before heading out into deep space, but he'd not seen a League or Alliance ship since they entered New Eden's atmosphere. He continued to watch and was soon able to discern that indeed it was an Alliance ship; in fact, the large ship was an Alliance Command ship. It would be at least ten or fifteen minutes before he'd know if Hank had been on that ship or not, and he found himself growing angry that Hank had not contacted him from the surface to let him know what was going on. Should he contact someone? Was Hank okay? Was Nicole okay?

He found himself suddenly growing very impatient; after waiting for hours and hearing nothing, it was time to try contacting Hank to find out what was happening. He reached down to his belt and removed the comlink. Next he pressed a button, causing a virtual soft menu to appear. Nick selected the button for Hank's com and waited, and waited, and waited. Now Nick was worried. Had something happened? Why was

Hank not responding? Had something gone terribly wrong on the planet's surface?

His thoughts were interrupted by a series of tones that indicated there was someone at his door. Nick considered ignoring them; whoever was at the door could wait, Hank and Nicole came first. Realizing that it was probably Hailey at the locked door, however, checking up on him again, he reconsidered and started walking toward the door. He waved his hand over a panel and the door rose upward. He was startled, however, by a young woman with a radiant smile and a glow about her, a woman who seemed vaguely familiar, who suddenly wrapped her arms around him and squeezed so hard he had difficulty breathing.

"Whoa, easy, Nikki; he's been sick, remember?"

"Oh, yeah, sorry about that Grandpa. I'm just so happy to see you again!"

Nick's eyes widened. "Nikki? Nicole Reynolds, is that you?"

Nicole looked back at him with a puzzled expression before furrowing her brow. "Come on, Grandpa, it hasn't been that long, has it?"

"Oh, I think it's been a lot longer than you think, child," Nick answered, still shocked as the woman, who looked like his granddaughter—though she most certainly didn't act like her—motioned for someone still standing outside to come in.

"Hi, Dad."

Nick's eyes brightened when his son, Hank, stepped in from the hallway. "Hank! I guess things went well, hmm?"

"Oh yeah, you could say that," he answered with a grin.

Nikki stepped forward. "Grandpa, I'd like for you to meet someone; his name is Captain Jack Lincoln, a former Alliance scout now on assignment to New Eden! He's, umm—quite special to me."

Jack stepped forward out of the hallway where he'd been hidden from Nick's eyes and extended his hand, which the still-perplexed Nick Reynolds shook.

"It's a great honor to meet you, Dr. Reynolds. I've read all about you since I was a child; you're absolutely amazing, sir," the man said to him after shaking his hand. Nick didn't miss the way Nicole's hand soon found his as they stood side-by-side facing him. *So that's what happened to her; way to go, kid.*

"The honor is all mine, Captain Lincoln; and please believe me when I tell you I believe *you* must be amazing too, young man," Nick replied with a knowing smile. He then turned back to Nicole. "Okay then, Nikki, tell me everything that happened, and don't leave anything out!"

Nick noticed that Nicole and Jack did most of the talking, with Hank only filling in the missing pieces now and again. He caught a glimpse of his son's face a time or two during the recounting, and when Hank nodded and smiled once or twice it told Nick all he needed to know. Perhaps his death would come somewhat easier now knowing that Nikki had finally let down her wall long enough to find love, although strangely enough, it was on an alien planet light years from Earth. Nick smiled.

Nikki and Jack spent two full hours retelling the highlights of what had transpired, with Nick interrupting from time to time to ask a question here or there for clarification. When they finally finished, Nicole reached into a pocket in her coat and withdrew something.

"We've brought something for you, Grandpa."

Nicole presented a vial full of a green liquid and handed it to her ailing grandfather. He took it, held it in his hands, and smiled at her.

"Thank you Nikki, thank you so much. I'm just so thankful that you're alive!" He held the vial and reached out to hug her again. He waved for Hank to participate as well. "I was just so scared I'd lost you both; I prayed you know, for both of you, and now I see that the Lord's answered my prayers!" He held up the vial and stared at it for the longest time. Those around him could not understand the memories he cherished, the love he'd lost, the pain he'd experienced. Did he really want more of that? Did he want to go on without *her*?

"Go on, Dad, drink the castil; it can cure your cancer! It's incredible, I've seen what it can do."

He glanced up at an expectant Nicole, who was waiting expectantly to see how her grandfather would respond. The struggle within him intensified; his desire to stay with Hank and Nicole was strong, but was it strong enough? His continued hesitation troubled her, and he could see it was time to decide.

"What's the matter, Grandpa? It's okay, it's safe. Motay was torturing Jack until he was nearly dead. He took some castil and he's fully recovered…just look at him!" Nick began shaking his head, and extended the hand holding the vial toward her. "What—?"

"I can't accept it, Nikki; I'm very sorry." Nicole's eyes widened. He could see it would be difficult to explain his reason for refusing it. "Please, Nikki, Hank, everyone, come on in and sit down for a moment…we need to talk."

Hank, Nicole, and Jack followed an elderly Nick Reynolds into the living room, where they sat down. He moved slowly, and while he could tolerate the pain with the help of the medications, the disease was sapping more and more of his energy every day. While he didn't want to admit it to anyone, especially himself, he could feel life slipping away a little more each day. After everyone was seated and had refused his offer to get them something to drink, he was ready to begin when the door bells rang. Nick had some difficulty getting up, so Hank jumped out of his seat and motioned to Nick to remain seated.

"Don't worry, Dad, I got it." Hank opened the door to find his wife, Hailey Reynolds, standing there in shock.

"Hank, baby— you're back! Where's—?" She spotted Nicole seated in the living room. Her daughter jumped up and ran into her mother's arms.

"Hi, Mom!" Mother and daughter embraced, with the mother doing most of the crying.

Once everything had settled down and introductions were made, Nick began again.

"So where was I? Oh yes. Listen everyone, I'm an old man now, and while I've been slow to admit it, I'm dying."

Nicole interrupted him. "So take this, Grandpa. We need you to stay with us...we need your guidance, your counsel, your love!" Tears had already formed and were starting to pool and stream down her cheeks. Nick stood and reached over the table to wipe them away from her eyes.

"Nikki, honey, I've had a wonderful life; I met and fell in love with an extraordinary woman, your grandmother. We married and had an incredibly warm and intelligent son together. He, in turn, met an incredibly beautiful and intelligent woman, your mother, Hailey." He paused, staring at the castil. "Now, I know I could take that castil, and I'm sure it would somehow purge the cancer from my body. But I have to be honest with all of you...I find myself slipping away more and more every day, and I can imagine...no, I *feel* Kate waiting for me. I've done about all I wanted to do in this life," he said wistfully, "and praise God I have very few regrets."

"What are we going to do without you?" Nicole asked before turning towards her father. "Dad?"

Nick watched it play out, as his family began to understand the implications of what he'd said. Hank looked at Nicole, who was crying, then at Hailey, who by now had sat down close to Nicole and wrapped an arm around her. Lastly, Hank turned toward his father.

"Dad, are you certain about this? There are no ill effects from taking the castil, no serious side effects; it's a real wonder-drug."

Nick groaned inside. He was causing his family great distress and consternation, and that was just the opposite of what he'd intended. He felt his own eyes starting to water up, but he held the tears back, knowing if he gave into them, he would be taking the castil moments later.

"You know, Hank, how much I love the Lord, and that I have for a very long time, as did your mother. I'll be with *Him* soon, son, and I'll be with your mother. We all die eventually, even when taking castil. Now

291

don't misunderstand me, I think it's a fine, wonderful idea if all of you take the castil, and I respect your decision to do so. All I ask is that you do the same for me now, and respect *my decision*, okay?" Everyone nodded weakly, some still wiping away tears.

"Hey, Dad, why don't you tell us about how you, Mom, and Grandpa Summers saved the world by prevented a nuclear war?" Hank said, hoping to engage his father in something less dreary than his impending death.

"Gladly," he replied, grateful for the opportunity to change the subject. "Well, let me see, I had already caught wind of an impending attack against the United States, and everything pointed to the Chinese. My boss, General George Caprella, told me about a special project at S-4, a top secret military base at Papoose Lake, adjacent to the Area 51 base at Groom Lake, Nevada, and it was there where I met your mother...."

CHAPTER 48

It was one of those rare moments in life when so many random variables come together at the same time so perfectly, the outcome could not possibly be any better timed had it been scripted. The weather was fair, both stars bathed the event in a light warm sunlight, and a cool breeze kept everyone outside comfortable and relaxed.

Nicole Reynolds stood at the podium and looked out among the massive gathering of colonists and visitors. So many had notified her office that they'd be attending the funeral, which Dr. Nick Reynolds had asked to be held on New Eden, that she'd decided the only place convenient to the city large enough to hold the vast gathering would be a large open area in the center of town.

As the last few attendees were finding their way to their seats, she took a moment to survey the crowd. In the front row sat Jack, Hank, and Hailey. Behind them sat President Joseph Clark, his wife, Jennifer, and their two children. On the same row as Clark and his family sat a number of representatives from the Earth Space Alliance, including former staff members and colleagues who'd worked with Nick during his time as President of the Alliance.

A number of other attendees from her grandfather's past were there, including Sarah Caprella, the middle-aged granddaughter of General George Caprella, Nick's former boss and close friend. John Montana, the son of General James Montana, Hank's former boss and one of *his* mentors, was also in attendance, along with a number of former associates from Nick's old NSA and Cyber Command days. Surprisingly, an aging, former Chinese ambassador and an elderly, former Russian FSB officer, with whom Nick had worked during his time with Cyber Command, were also in attendance. A number of former scientists from the old S-4 base in Nevada had also attended out of respect for Nick's tremendous accomplishments while with Cyber Command and later, in association with the Frontier Program.

A rather unexpected guest had requested permission to attend as well;

Yuri Chervanko, the great-grandson of Nikolai Chervanko, the mass-murderer who'd also saved Nick's life once. Nicole had discussed it briefly with her father before deciding to extend an invitation to him as well.

President Zing from Val, Ambassador Lotan from Shatara, the Anteran Ambassador Itanus, and even Admiral Skylok, commander of the Machrys Attack Fleet, formed the core of the contingent of non-humans attending the funeral. What remained of the immense gathering, however, were her fellow citizens of New Eden. Nicole felt a tear stream down her face, touched at the number of lives her grandfather had touched.

"Good afternoon, everyone," she began. "I am Nicole Reynolds, governor of this colony, and granddaughter of Dr. Nick Reynolds—hero, former NSA and Cyber Command analyst, former President of the Earth Space Alliance, and more importantly, a wonderful husband, father, and grandfather. My father, Hank Reynolds, Earth's representative to the League of Sentient Species, and former President of the Earth Space Alliance, suggested I should say a few words about my grandfather, so here I am. Before I begin, however, I would like to share some wonderful, personal news—I'd like to announce publicly that I'm engaged to be married one month from today, to a wonderful man whom many of you know, Captain Jack Lincoln, an Alliance pilot and a hero. I'm so thankful that Grandpa had a chance to meet this man that I'm so in love with, just before his time came.

"Now I'd like to talk a little about Nick Reynolds. There have been few things that I've enjoyed more than the tremendous privilege of being Governor of New Eden…it truly is an honor. One thing I've enjoyed even more, however, was being Nick Reynolds's granddaughter. He was an incredible man, a man of unbelievable courage, compassion, and conviction. While working at Cyber Command, an organization for protecting the United States of America from computer-generated attacks, he was forced to handle a very difficult situation, a threat that could have escalated into global nuclear warfare, possibly even ending all life on Earth.

"Despite the enormous obstacles he faced, my grandfather was never one to back down. General George Caprella, his boss, sent him to a semi-secret military base called S-4 at Papoose Lake, near the infamous Area 51, where they first met Ignis, and where they worked to reverse engineer the ship Ignis had crashed, work that soon led to the creation of Earth's first interstellar spacecraft, Frontier, the ship test-piloted by my father, Hank Reynolds.

"While working at Area 51 he met my grandmother, Dr. Kate Summers. They worked together there trying to find an innovative solution to the threat the country faced, and they fell in love and married. Soon, they had a child together, a son they named Hank. Twenty-five years later they had a granddaughter—me. I can't tell you how thrilled my grandfather was when I took on this role as governor of Earth's first colony outside of our home star system, and he couldn't have been prouder.

"My grandfather, Nick Reynolds, was a courageous, amazing, and caring man. He...."

***

Once everyone who wanted to speak had the opportunity to do so, the reverend Kenneth Chow, pastor of one of the many new churches on New Eden, offered a brief sermon, which spoke to primarily the character of God, and the character of man, particularly to how each had impacted the life of Nick Reynolds. Pastor Chow highlighted some of the best and worst in the life of Nick Reynolds, including the role he'd played in the cyber warfare attack, as well as his invaluable leadership developing both the Alliance and the Frontier program. Most importantly, the minister addressed Nick's love for God and for his family. His spirit of self-sacrifice, and his ultimate desire to see God and to see his wife again, had helped prepare him for the end, but not before he'd helped shape the lives of so many.

By the time the sermon ended and the service finally concluded, the twin stars had dipped just below the horizon; the beautiful symbolism of the moment wasn't lost on Nicole Reynolds. Just as the final beautiful pink and orange rays of the suns crept over the edge of the horizon, the pall-bearers lowered the urn into the ground—Nicole smiled. With tears streaming down her face as she stood on the lighted platform, she raised her arm straight up in the air toward someone at the distant end of the field. Seconds later, fireworks began lighting up the now dark sky, and continued for fifteen minutes. It was the least she could do, in memory of a great man, a warm grandfather, and a bridge from a dangerous past to a fantastic future. Watching the excitement in the night sky, she suddenly felt as if the universe had somehow changed with his passing.

CHAPTER 49

Nicole looked around at all of the new buildings, and the many that were still in the process of going up. There was an endless stream of activity as new office buildings, new residential complexes, and new single family homes continued popping up all around the city, and beyond. The people of New Eden had been expanding beyond the security shield that surrounded the ever expanding city, but she no longer felt fearful about it. Nicole was confident that soon, the shield that had offered such security when they'd first arrived would prove to be unnecessary, and would probably not even be missed when it was deactivated.

New settlements were popping up all over New Eden as well, especially near the areas where the higher concentrations of the castilian plant had been found, with requests for new permits being submitted to her office almost every day. Locating the settlements and the processing plants closer to where the castilian plant itself was harvested had made good logistical sense and caused the process to flow much smoother. She'd recently seen forms come through for a business that was researching growing the plants themselves on large castilian farms. Castil was a major cash crop, and it was going to secure the financial future for New Eden for some time.

Nicole lay down on a blanket next to Jack in the middle of the new park they'd built in the open center of the city, near where her grandfather had been buried. They snuggled close together and looked up at the two moons named Castor and Pollux. The orbs hung in the sky like lanterns, lighting the landscape all around with a faint glow that reminded Nicole of twilight back on Earth. Tonight both satellites were out, and both were full moons. Castor and Pollux were much closer to New Eden than Luna was to Earth, and sometimes on a clear night like tonight, they were even able to make out some of the larger volcanoes on Pollux.

"They're beautiful, aren't they, Jack?" she asked.

"Yeah, I guess they are, Nikki, but they can't hold a candle to you." The look on his face conveyed far more than his words ever could. She looked away and smiled, her heart swelling with affection for the man next to her. Nicole looked up at the two moons again, and felt a warm glow course through her body.

"You know, Jack, my grandfather and grandmother were amazing together; they had a really beautiful relationship. He and my grandmother loved one another more than any couple I've ever seen. When she passed a few years ago...well, I believe a part of him died as well. Don't get me wrong, he loved all of us a great deal, but he missed Kate so much—"

"What they had must have been something really special."

"It was," she said, with a glimmer in her eye as she looked into his eyes. "I just hope that one day, *we* can find out what that's like," she said hopefully.

"Who knows?" he replied with a smile. "Maybe we already have."

Nicole looked into his eyes and smiled. The couple laid there, under the moonlight of Castor and Pollux, and for one brief moment Nicole considered how each and every moment of life is not something to get through...it is a gift to be cherished.

Epilogue

Nicole sat on the porch of their home, the screen-shielding providing her a view of the large, beautiful lake without having to worry about insects and the animal life that came with living so far from the bustle of the city. She watched as a beautiful bird with large feathers of pink, yellow, and red flew along the surface of the lake looking for a meal. High above her the twin stars Meta and Stratus bathed her face with their warmth.

On her lap she held her twin infants, John and Adriana, one on each leg. She sat back in her chair and smiled, reflecting on how far humanity had come in such a short time, and the amazing privilege her family had in being such an important part of it. Human beings had spread out across the galaxy. Already there were twenty-five cities on New Eden, with more being planned every day. The Earth Space Alliance, in coordination with the League of Sentient Species, had already identified two other planets in the habitable zone suitable for human colonization within the same sector of space, with two more identified in two other sectors. Bigger and faster ships were constantly being built, expanding humanity's reach even further. Within fifty years humanity had gone from sending probes to Earth's closest neighbor, Mars, to colonizing other worlds, traveling about the galaxy the way her grandparents had once traveled in automobiles back on Earth.

She imagined her grandparents, Nick and Kate Reynolds, working together on the Prometheus project to stop an ex-Soviet cyber-terrorist. She remembered the stories about how her parents, Hank and Hailey Reynolds, had struggled to keep the fledgling Alliance and Frontier programs alive. Then she thought about how she and Jack had struggled to save New Eden from the Machrys and then the Shatarans. What a remarkable family she had.

Little John cackled and Nicole looked down at the smiling child. She held her children, John and Adriana, close to her, wondering what life was going to be like for them, and she smiled.

It was truly an incredible time to be alive.

Take a look at these other great World Castle Publishing novels by Jeff W. Horton:
http://www.amazon.com/Jeff-W.-
Horton/e/B004NK5MJC/ref=ntt_athr_dp_pel_1

FRONTIERS- BOOK TWO IN THE CYBERSP@CE SERIES
Earth's first starship built on alien tech, is on its maiden voyage to Alpha
centauri. Someone wants him to fail, someone wants him dead.
Amazon: http://tinyurl.com/mnlg6fr

CYBERSP@CE- BOOK ONE IN THE CYBERSP@CE SERIES
A fast-paced, sci-fi story with international intrigue, action, & suspense
Amazon:http://www.amazon.com/dp/1938961579

THE WAY OF NACOR- BOOK ONE IN THE TALES OF EDEN SERIES
Four children are transported to a distant, alien planet.
Amazon: http://tinyurl.com/9w2tgpk

THE LAST PROPHET
What if someone told you that you were one of the last two prophets mentioned
in the book of Revelation?
Amazon: http://tinyurl.com/93fbuhg

THE DARK AGE-SURVIVORS OF THE PULSE
In the future, humanity once again survives by the sword, bow, and the arrow,
Amazon: http://tinyurl.com/3o3lty8

www.ingramcontent.com/pod-product-compliance
Lightning Source LLC
Chambersburg PA
CBHW020255200626
46816CB00001BA/309